Bridget Matawapit is an Indigenous activist, daughter of a Catholic deacon, and foster mother to Kyle, the son of an Ojibway father—the ex-fiancé she kicked to the curb after he chose alcohol over her love. With Adam out on parole and back in Thunder Bay, she is determined to stop him from obtaining custody of Kyle.

Adam Guimond is a recovering alcoholic and ex-gangbanger newly paroled. Through counseling, reconnecting with his Ojibway culture and twelve-step meetings while in prison, Adam now understands he's worthy of the love that frightened him enough to pick up the bottle he'd previously corked. He can't escape the damage he caused so many others, but he longs to rise like a true warrior in the pursuit of forgiveness and a second chance. There's nothing he isn't willing to do to win back his son—and Bridget.

When an old cell mate's daughter dies under mysterious circumstances in foster care, Adam begs Bridget to help him uncover the truth. Bound to the plight of the Indigenous children in care, Bridget agrees. But putting herself in contact with Adam threatens to resurrect her long-buried feelings for him, and even worse, she risks losing care of Kyle, by falling for a man who might destroy her faith in love completely this time.

Redeemed
Copyright © 2019 Maggie Blackbird
ISBN: 978-1-4874-2456-5
Cover art by Martine Jardin

Published by eXtasy Books Inc or
Devine Destinies, an imprint of eXtasy Books Inc

Look for us online at:
www.eXtasybooks.com or www.devinedestinies.com

Redeemed
Matawapit Family Book 2

By

Maggie Blackbird

DEDICATION

In memory of my precious niece, Katie May, and my godmother, Auntie Linda – two very special women who loved romance.

Thank you to the following people:

My husband and the Mals for your love and never-ending support. Kim Gosnell, MSW, for being a wonderful friend and sharing your expertise.
The eXtasy Books staff: Emma, my editor, Martine, my cover artist, Bri, my proofer, Angela, Art Director, and Jay, EIC.

CHAPTER ONE: I AIN'T NO NICE GUY

Lying was what Adam did best. He'd learned how to lie as a punk-ass kid. Believing the lie for the complete truth was key in confusing the cops, the Crown attorney, the judge—anyone trained to search his face, voice, or body language for signs of dishonesty. Only booze had tripped him up, nailed him good enough to send him down below because of his love for the bottle.

He wouldn't lie today. He hadn't lied during his parole hearing, either. Lying wasn't a part of his new life. Neither was whiskey.

From now on, fatherhood was what he'd do best.

Other parents sat in the waiting room at Children and Family Services. One paced the floor wearing yesterday's stubble. Another shifted in her seat, bleary-eyed, either from a hangover or crying. The tall guy with holes in his clothes crossed and uncrossed his legs. The girl, not much older than twenty, rocked back and forth, slurping coffee, while her legs twitched. A tweaker, probably.

The smell was the same in all government buildings. A lingering of something old and outdated, and the walls either a bland beige, faded white, or dull light gray. Off-white was the color of choice at Children and Family Services.

"Mr. Guimond?" The receptionist rose from behind the rounded counter against the wall. "Your caseworker's ready to see you. Second floor. The fourth office on your right." She used a pen to point in the direction of the elevator.

Adam stood. His feet remained rooted to the floor, and he

1

forced his legs to make the ten-yard trek to the elevator. Once he was enclosed inside the stuffy chute no bigger than the drunk tank he'd been tossed in after coming off a bender, he fumbled for the second-floor button.

There was no turning back. He was going up.

He could face a judge sentencing him, cops tossing him on the hood of a cruiser to handcuff him, scouting his range for the first time while being sized up by the toughest of toughs, or a beat-out from the Winnipeg Warriors to drop his colors. He could face anything but a caseworker who'd decide if and when he'd see his boy.

He checked his reflection in the mirror, smoothing his hair that kinked this way and waved that way. Damned wind was to blame after his walk to and from the bus stop. Since t-shirts, jeans, and running shoes wouldn't impress the caseworker, he'd borrowed a too-snug dress shirt and dress pants off a guy at the halfway house. The buttoned cuffs were silver bracelets locked around his wrists, and the starched collar a noose.

The doors opened. His breathing mirrored the rattle and hops when he'd been chased by the cops. The same for the hot pressure pounding at the back of his neck.

There were offices in both directions. Some doors were open, a couple of them closed. Voices carried out from the offices, workers either on the phone or meeting with a loser like himself.

He gave his left a try first and trudged down the hallway. The fourth door on the right was closed.

Show time. He'd done this lots—getting his shit together before his execution. He fisted and un-fisted his fingers while huffing and puffing three quick breaths of air.

He rapped his knuckles against the fake wood.

"One moment, Mr. Guimond," a woman said in a stern voice.

Adam's heartbeat slowed, and the ball of tension behind his neck vanished. A few more seconds. He leaned on the wall and folded his arms. At least he'd gotten the right door. He'd also made sure not to smoke outside. First impressions counted, whether at a parole hearing, before a judge, anything. Smelling like an old cigarette butt was the wrong impression, but the blood threading through his veins could use a dart right now.

"You may enter." The woman's supposed invitation came out as an order. She must have worked at the iron house or had a husband as a CO.

He opened the door to a hawk—a birdlike biddy in her sixties with gray hair pulled off her narrow face and twisted into a bun. Beady cold eyes looked him up and down with the scrutiny of a judge on the bench. Her nose, the shape of a beak, she held high in the air. She pointed her skinny finger at the chair positioned in front of the desk, square in the middle.

"You may sit." She lowered her hard gaze to a neat stack of papers and started writing.

Adam sat. The chair was positioned too close to the desk. Even when he opened his legs, his knees hit the cheap laminate. Maybe this was part of the caseworker's strategy to make clients uncomfortable.

"I'm Mrs. Dale. Your son's caseworker." She kept writing on the pad, her scrawny knuckles a bright red from how hard she gripped the pen.

There wasn't a smidgen of dust on the filing cabinet, desk, or bookshelf. One lone picture faced her. Pens kept in order of color sat in a tray. Even the essentials for an office were set square on the desk. There were no other files present but one manila folder which also sat square beside the paper she wrote on. The off-white vertical blinds were adjusted to keep the sunlight off her but allow the two blooming plants on a shelf to take in a tan.

With all this silence, she must want him to speak first. He swallowed a helping of saliva to keep his voice strong and calm. "I'm Adam Guimond. Kyle's father."

"I already know who you are and why you are here, Mr. Guimond." The Hawk kept writing. "I have been responsible for your file since your incarceration."

Double great. This old biddy had it out for him. Adam kept his arms unfolded. He stared at her rolled bun. He wouldn't look anywhere else or shift in his chair.

After five more minutes, and Adam refusing to twitch, the Hawk raised her head. She laid aside the pen vertical to the pad of paper, which she rested her skinny fingers on. "Why are you requesting approval to see your son?"

Adam hadn't expected this question. He continued to stare at her narrowed eyes tucked behind matching glasses. Again, he made sure to keep his voice even. "He's my son."

"I know he's your son, a son you lost to care, because you not only abused alcohol, but also committed a serious crime while under the influence. Tell me, why are you requesting approval to see your son?"

She'd made a damned good point. He'd cut the old biddy some slack. The twelve steps of his recovery program, the Seven Grandfathers teachings of the Ojibway, and the anger management course he'd followed while in the iron house had prepared him for this moment.

"Saved up enough money working on day parole. Gonna use the coin to rent a small apartment. Got a plan."

"What plan would that be?"

With her shitload of questions, her unchanging cold stare that was a block of ice, The Hawk was in the wrong line of work. Adam should recommend she become a detective instead of a caseworker.

"Good place for my kid."

"Mr. Guimond, you are going to have to be specific and find your tongue to elaborate. We are discussing the welfare of your child." Her voice remained the same stern tone.

She was good. Really good. Better than the too-many cops who'd hauled Adam into an interrogation room for questioning.

"You got the info on me. Came up with a plan in the pen." He squeezed his toes, a great way to destress when under scrutinizing eyes and effectively hide the flicker of anxiety twitching along his spine.

"A plan?"

"Yeah. Got my grade twelve. Went to twelve-step meetings. Was part of the aboriginal healing program. Took my anger management class and passed. It was my plan. To change. Become a true dad to my son."

"This is why you relocated from Winnipeg to Thunder Bay — again?"

"My boy lives here. I wanna live here."

"Why else do you wish to reside here? As I said, you had better be more specific and talk." She tightened her jaw and lifted her brow.

Adam kept the smile itching to stretch his lips tucked deep inside him. She'd broke first. Confidence swelled in his chest. Maybe, just maybe, he stood a chance at getting his son back. "After my last rubbie bit, I dropped my colors — "

"This is not the federal corrections institution, Mr. Guimond. Proper English. Not street code." Her voice rose an octave.

He'd broken her again. So he set his hands on his thighs and leaned in a smidgen. Crowding her space was imperative to force her to lean back. He kept his stare rigid and spoke in the same low monologue. "During my second last incarceration, the mother of my kid told me she was pregnant. I wanted a better life for my son. Stopped drinking and

5

left the gang. Went to rehab. My back was against the wall. No protection anymore. Other gangs wanted a piece of me still. Moved here to start a better life. Didn't wanna get in any more trouble."

The Hawk failed to recoil into her chair. She remained a statue in her seat. "But you did when you first lived here with your son . . ."

"I shouldn't have moved back to . . ." Nope, he'd better not say *the 'Peg.* " . . . Winnipeg after things fell apart here. That was a big mistake."

"Then why did you move back to Winnipeg, again, if you knew trouble awaited?" The Hawk's tone shifted to her natural sternness.

Adam kept returning her stare. "It was a mistake. Told you already. Things fell apart here."

"You mean your ex-fiancée, who's been responsible for your son for almost four years now, ended your engagement and you couldn't handle the rejection." The Hawk's mask of plaster cracked into a half-smile of part sneer and part triumph.

So this was her game, huh? She did want Adam to fail. Authority. They were all the same. Good thing he'd come in here with the right kind of attitude and game plan. "My ex-fiancée had every right to do what she did. I started drinking again. She gave me the boot."

"What about your drinking now?" Mrs. Dale redonned her mask of plaster.

"Kept sober while doing my time. Attended twelve-step meetings at the jail in Winnipeg while I was on day parole. A guy from the outside came in and chaired them. I'm still sober. First thing I did when I got into town was check where all the meetings are. Attending one tonight."

"And when your parole term is finished?"

"I don't plan on going back to drinking. I'm done with

that."

Mrs. Dale clucked her tongue and crooked her narrowed brow in a *we'll-wait-and-see* manner.

She didn't have to wait and see. He'd tell her right now. "My old boss lined me up a job here. Chain restaurant. He called his buddy here at the Thunder Bay chain."

"When do you start?"

"He's gonna call me. Once I find out, I'll let you know what my hours are."

Mrs. Dale sat back in her chair.

Confident, much? She could take her confidence and shove it. She'd lose. Nothing was stopping Adam from getting his boy back.

"I see men and women like you every single day in my office, Mr. Guimond. I also visit the homes of people like you to remove your children whom you are not providing adequate care for. Do you know how many times people such as yourself regain custody of your children, and then lose them again?"

"I thought the purpose here was to care for the kids until we . . ." He couldn't say *get our shit together*. " . . . until we've taken care of biz, made our lives better?"

"I will recommend to my supervisor one hour per week, supervised visits in the family room." Mrs. Dale sat up in her chair and began writing again.

One hour? One measly hour to see his boy after he hadn't seen Kyle in almost four years? "Why?" The word flew from Adam's mouth.

He squeezed his toes. Careless. Fucking careless. Dammit, she'd broken him. Now she knew his weakness. How to get under his skin. He'd failed.

"Mr. Guimond . . ." The Hawk's half-sneer returned. Even her cold eyes glimmered. "I am considering the welfare of your child. Not your welfare. Your son has not seen you in almost four years. He recently celebrated his seventh birthday. This means he was extremely young when you were institutionalized. He has only known the care of his foster mother. Don't you think reacquainting yourselves should be the priority so he can make the emotional adjustments he will require to have you back in his life? Or do you not care? Is this about what you want, instead of what your child needs?"

Adam's gut burned. She was right. This meeting wasn't about who played a better game of chess. Kyle's feelings came first. "Whatever you recommend," he managed to grunt out.

If he had one measly hour to give to his boy, he'd make their time the best hour possible.

I'm coming, kiddo. Daddy's here. He's made a lot of mistakes. A lot of bad mistakes that you're paying for, when you shouldn't be. I won't let you down this time. That's a promise.

He ran the tip of his tongue along the roof of his mouth. But from the day he'd kicked and clawed his way from the womb, whenever he challenged authority, he'd lost.

Bridget slammed the door shut and stormed to the building. She smacked the button on her key set to lock the truck. Nobody had to tell her what this meeting was about. Nobody had to tell her Adam had raced back to Thunder Bay once the son of a bitch had finished his day parole. Nobody had to tell her he'd overlooked informing anyone about his intentions. Adam only thought about Adam.

She stomped into Children and Family Services and huffed to the front desk. "I have an appointment to see Mrs. Dale. She's my caseworker."

"One moment." The receptionist picked up the phone. "Ms. Matawapit's here . . . Okay . . . Thank you . . . I'll send her right up."

The receptionist set down the phone. "Go on up. She's waiting."

"Thank you." Bridget stamped to the elevator and got in. She used her knuckle to punch the button for the second floor.

Adam was going to try to gain full custody of Kyle, after she'd looked after the boy for almost four years, after she'd refused to allow Adam to take Kyle to Winnipeg, after agreeing not to call Children and Family Services on him when the bastard had fallen off the wagon. After all she'd done for the loser.

The elevator doors opened. Bridget trounced to Mrs. Dale's office and rapped on the door.

"Enter, Ms. Matawapit."

Bridget opened the door and flounced to the chair in front of the desk.

"I am grateful you could come on your lunch hour." Mrs. Dale shuffled some papers. "What I have to say merits a face-to-face meeting. How is Kyle? Did he enjoy his birthday party?"

The angry, raw heat faded. Mrs. Dale was a straight-to-the-point woman who never engaged in small talk. And like any proud mother, Bridget loved talking about her child. "I held his party at Sleeping Giant Park. The kids had a lot of fun. They swam and hiked. I even arranged to have his favorite hero show up—Laser from the Z Men."

"Wonderful." Mrs. Dale tapped her pen against the desk. "I met with Kyle's father yesterday for a full assessment. Mr. Guimond has relocated here. My supervisor and I agreed to one hour, once a week supervised visits for Kyle and his father."

The blood flowing through Bridget's veins slowed. "I see . . . Does . . . does this mean, uh, does this mean—" She dug her nails into the arm of the chair.

"Understand, Kyle hasn't seen his father in almost four years." Mrs. Dale's normal sharper-than-her-pointed-nose voice warmed to a reassuring tone. Even her hard gaze softened, liquifying her cold gray eyes to melted clay.

"This doesn't mean he'll gain full custody. He may never gain full custody. Transitions, especially those of Adam Guimond's case, take a long time. A very long time." The melted clay of Mrs. Dale's eyes re-hardened to their natural concrete. Her thin upper lip twitched.

All Bridget had to do was stay silent and let Mrs. Dale sabotage Adam's chances at regaining custody of Kyle. Was this what the woman was insinuating?

But Bridget was Catholic. Her parents, the church, and God expected her to handle the most important facet of her life with faith—a faith as shaky as her trembling knees and clacking teeth after what she'd endured at Adam's recklessness.

CHAPTER TWO: DO YOU BELIEVE?

Today was the day. Kyle's first visit with his dad. Bridget settled her hand against her heaving chest to keep from jabbing the mascara wand into her eye.

Deep breaths. Stay calm. She could do this. *Straighten. Stand tall.* She capped the mascara tube and twisted it shut.

"Mom?" Kyle's softer-than-cotton voice slid into the bedroom.

Bridget turned from the full-length mirror.

All without Bridget nagging him to dress, Kyle had slipped on his backpack, laced his shoes, scrubbed his round face to a shine, and his gleaming white teeth said he'd brushed and flossed.

He held one of the chocolate bars he'd received as a gift during his birthday party. "Please?"

Pain smothered Bridget's chest. The *no* word sucked more than a vacuum cleaner during such a crucial time for Kyle. Today, he deserved a treat. "You're going to see your dad. You have to stay clean."

Kyle bowed his head. "Do we have to go?" His question was smaller than his apprehensive whisper.

"You know we have to." *And I wish we didn't.* "I explained everything to you last night." *Even though your father doesn't deserve an explanation.* "You said you were okay with seeing him." *But I'm not.*

"Uh-huh." Kyle kept his head bowed.

"What is it?"

When Kyle lifted his head, fear suffocated his dark eyes.

"Am I going to have to live with him? Will you stop being my mom?"

How could Bridget reassure Kyle when her own hope had curled into a defeated ball? Time to don her Mom hat of bravery. "I told you last night, Mrs. Dale's supervising your dad. She'll decide what'll happen. Decisions won't be made for a long time. We'd better get going. We can't be late."

Bridget snatched her purse off the bed. "I told you. I'm going to work very hard to keep us together."

Kyle flashed a toothy, crooked grin. "I know, Mom. You can do anything. You're a Z Man!" He jumped and landed on spread feet while pointing.

Bridget's shriveled hope continued to shrink. If only that were true.

"Maybe . . ." He licked his plump lips. "Maybe we can go see Grandpa and Grandma this weekend."

"I think we should." Dad's faith was unshakable. Perhaps Bridget could steal some from her father to plump up hers that was the size of a pea. "Remember, I'll be in the room. You're not doing this alone."

"I know, Mom." Kyle twirled off into the main part of their condo.

Bridget smoothed her shirt and the pleats to her pants. She followed him to the foyer. "It's already five to nine. Our appointment's at nine-thirty. Let's go."

Kyle flung open the door and darted into the hallway.

"Wait. Don't run ahead." Kyle knew the rules. He must stay close. She fumbled with the deadbolt.

"Are we stopping for a double-double at Reggie's Donuts?" Kyle dashed to the elevator. "I got dibs on the down button." He pushed it, grinning.

"Yes." She slung her purse strap over her shoulder while skimming down the hall, knees jittering.

"Can I get a doughnut?"

The elevator door opened. "Anything but chocolate."

"Why not?"

Bridget shepherded him into the elevator. "Because you have to stay clean."

"Clean." Kyle sneered. "I hate clean." Using his little finger, the one he always wrapped around Bridget's before she kissed him goodnight, he pressed the lobby button.

"I know you do." Bridget tweaked his wide nose. Touching him expelled some of the anxiety climbing up her spine. "For me . . . please stay clean. Mrs. Dale's going to watch everything."

Kyle's fingers browsed the elevator buttons. He stopped at the big red one.

"Don't you dare. We can't be late." The high-pitched order flew from Bridget's mouth before she could take back the words.

"Mom?" Kyle's eyes popped to the shape of dinner plates.

"It's okay, honey. I'm sorry. I didn't mean to yell." Bridget rubbed the back of his neck.

The door opened. They scooted to their parking spot outside of the condominium. Once Bridget made sure Kyle was buckled in, she started the truck and backed out.

"At seven-thirty this morning, the OPP underwater recovery unit pulled a body from the McIntyre River near Isabel and Simpson Street," the radio announcer said. "Police refused to comment if the body was Sheena Keesha, a sixteen-year-old Indigenous girl from Big Rock First Nation, which is four hundred and fifty kilometers north of the city. Keesha, as previously reported, went missing six days ago while in protective child care. Friends confirmed she was last seen outside of The Gator Bar on Brodie Street and Victoria Avenue. This marks the fourth Indigenous youth to go missing this year."

Bridget switched off the stereo. Each time she heard this

kind of horrible news, fear dug into her flesh like burly palms gripping her throat.

Adam shifted in the plastic chair. He pulled at his shirt collar. For the third time, he smoothed his forearms. A better impression called for cuffed sleeves, but a running furnace was colder than the room for supervised visits.

Toys were piled in the corner. A round kiddie table and kiddie chairs were available for the children to sit at. Adam stood. His thirsty throat demanded a cola from the vending machine in the corner, but he needed the last of his change to catch a bus back to the halfway house. As for the toonie he kept in his other pocket, he'd saved the two-dollar coin for Kyle in case the boy wanted a treat.

The door opened. The Hawk marched into the room, carrying a clipboard.

"Good morning, Mr. Guimond. I see you are here bright and early." Her grim, thin mouth failed to flicker with a hint of a smile.

What'd she expect him to do? Show up an hour late? He hadn't seen Kyle in almost four years. "Is there any coffee?"

"This is a supervised visit, not a correctional institution taxpayers fund from their hard-earned wages so inmates can partake in beverages at our expense. Next time, if you desire coffee, please bring one."

Winnipeg's Portage and Main in the dead of winter was warmer than this frosty old biddy. "Got it." Adam meandered to the window and leaned against the sill, placing his hands on either side of him.

Mrs. Dale sat on one of the plastic chairs. She crossed her thin legs at the ankles and scribbled on her clipboard.

Sweat formed at the nape of Adam's neck. Any second, Kyle and Bridget would come through the door.

Bridget ushered Kyle down the hall, passing the line of offices, straight to the visitation room. He clutched his doughnut bag, and she strangled the handle of her travel mug. Holding hands, she kept squeezing her son's fingers.

They stopped at the door where Adam waited on the other side.

For Kyle's sake, Bridget must expunge the tingles juddering through her limbs. "It's going to be okay. I'll be there. Mrs. Dale'll be there. You won't be alone."

"O-okay." Kyle's lower lip quivered. "I'm ready, Mommy."

Not good. On his sixth birthday, he'd proudly announced he was too old to call her by that name. This was worse than Bridget had expected. She rubbed the spot between his shoulder blades. "Let's go. Remember, God's with . . . He's with us."

"He is, isn't He, Mommy?" Color returned to Kyle's brown skin.

"Always, He is. I'm going to open the door." Bridget kept her voice hushed.

Kyle's small muscles beneath Bridget's palm tightened.

She turned the handle. Keeping her cool was imperative, although the accusing words of *asshole, liar,* and *jerk,* inched up her throat.

When Bridget opened the door, Adam was leaning against the windowsill, and the bitter words kept blinking in her brain. She gripped and re-gripped Kyle's hand.

A short-sleeved white dress shirt hugged Adam's strong upper chest and broad shoulders. He'd tucked the hem into the slim waist of his beige dress pants. His shoulder-length pitch-black hair, minus the familiar beige cowboy hat, was combed off his square face, but stray strands brushed his straight black brows.

The saliva thickened in Bridget's throat at the sight of his long, wide nose, strong jawline, and the plush mouth he used to brush at her earlobe.

His black eyes held hers, his gaze as impenetrable as it had been in the past, unmoving, refusing to let her inside.

Bridget recoiled. Her heart, ready to melt all over the floor, hardened to stone. She lifted her chin.

Adam's nod was slow, a careful tilt of his head.

Bridget looked to Kyle and pointed at the chair next to Mrs. Dale. "I'll be right there."

"Okay . . . Mom." Kyle continued to grip her hand.

She wiggled her fingers free. "Go on." She made sure her gentle order came out soft and drawn-out.

He inched forward, clutching his small Reggie's Donuts bag.

"Hey." Adam shifted to his haunches. His pants cuddled his muscular thighs.

Mouth wet and lungs shrinking, Bridget shimmied to Mrs. Dale and sat on the edge of the plastic chair. She dug her nails into her purse and her muscles contracted — this could be the longest hour of her life.

Adam's throat wouldn't stop constricting. A hard ball formed at the base of his neck.

This visit was about his son. If he looked at Bridget again in the sleeveless blouse baring her sleek arms that she used to wrap around his shoulders, or the tight pants draping her slim thighs she'd spread wide for him, or the sexy high-heeled sandals giving him a peek at her red-painted toenails she'd caressed across his calf, or her red-painted nails she'd scratched across his back, it'd be all over for him.

He'd close his mind to her thick, long, black hair, the delicate bone structure of her face, shining midnight eyes, and sensual lips.

Kyle kept quivering, gaping at Adam. His son's buzz cut must have been Bridget's idea. Before his incarceration, Adam hadn't allowed scissors to touch his only child's black hair. Now was the time to put his anger management classes to use. If he'd been on the outside, Kyle's hair would be halfway down his back by now.

Using the voice of the past, the one reserved for his boy that was a good three octaves higher and sweeter than maple syrup, Adam offered what he hoped was a dazzling smile and said, "Hey. You had a birthday, didn't you?"

Kyle nodded.

"What'cha got there?" Adam pointed at the bag.

"A doughnut. Mommy ... Mommy let me get one." Kyle's tiny voice shook, barely a whisper.

"For our next visit, I'll bring cookies. I make a mean chocolate chip cookie."

"I ... I ..." The little guy kept trembling as if Adam was some monster from a bad kiddie cartoon.

Adam fished the toonie from his pants pocket. He must act quickly, or tears would erupt from his boy, straight in front of the note-taking Hawk, who'd probably slam the brakes on Adam's visits. "Want a pop? We can get whatever you like."

Lower lip trembling, Kyle sadly shook his head. He shifted, stealing a peek at Bridget.

"You wanna sit over here? There's some coloring books." Adam pointed at the round table and tiny chairs.

"N-no." Kyle stared at his running shoes with the words Z Men emblazoned on the sides.

Defeat dragged Adam's shoulders downwards. He forced his sunken chest outwards. *Help me, Creator. Help me and my boy reconnect.*

He sat on the floor cross-legged, having done this tons of

times when Kyle had been small. Under his breath, Adam hummed the Ojibway morning song.

Kyle squinted.

A light glowed inside of Adam.

"That's neat." Kyle's soft words echoed against Adam's ears.

He kept singing and held out his hands for the big test.

Kyle shifted and sat cross-legged, too. His small hands shook, but he wrapped his fingers around Adam's. Their first contact in almost four years. The warmth of Kyle's hands, the boy's smooth palms, and the trust he'd shown by holding hands almost melted Adam's scarred heart.

He sang the last words of the song and squeezed Kyle's fingers.

"Do you go to powwows? Do you wear feathers?"

Hope beat against Adam's ribcage. They did stand a chance of becoming father and son.

"You did. I brought you with me. I put 'em right here." Adam tapped the back of Kyle's head where he used to attach the roach of porcupine hairs and the two feathers fastened to the spreader.

"I . . . I did? Wow. Can I wear it again?" Anticipation clung to Kyle's question.

"You'll need a new one. The old one's too small." Adam had better find a woman at the Kitchi-Gaming Friendship Center to make a northern traditional dance outfit for Kyle. As for money, he'd dig into his precious savings, what he'd stashed away for his new life with Kyle, for new regalia.

From the corner of his eye, he stole a peek at Bridget's tight ruby-red lips. Her frigid glare was as hard as any man's on the range in the pen.

"I hear you want to be an altar server."

Kyle's buzzed head bobbed. His long, white teeth gleamed. "I start grade two when summer's done. Mom said when I do . . . um . . . the bread of Christ thing, I can help Father Arnold at church. It's a really important job." He came off his butt, leaning forward. "Uncle Emery said when he was my age he did it. He . . . he's not gonna be a priest anymore. I have a new uncle now. Uncle Darryl. Uncle Emery got married. He married Uncle Darryl."

"Your mom told me in her last letter."

"Mom said you finished the big school."

"Big school?"

"Where the big kids go."

"Oh, high school." Adam had better take a refresher on *kid speak.* "Yep. Dad finished high school when he was away."

"Where'd you go?" Kyle tilted his head and puckered his lips. "Why'd you go away?"

Adam inched his hand forward and stroked Kyle's fuzzy head of prickly hair. When the boy didn't draw back, Adam's breathing seemed to simmer like the relaxing shower he had last night.

"We'll talk about it another time. I want you to understand I didn't want to leave or go away that long."

"Then why'd you go?" Kyle's large eyes drooped at the corners.

"I had to. Sometimes we gotta do things we don't wanna. But I'm back now. I'm not going anywhere."

The sharp intake of breath belonged to Bridget. Adam looked over his shoulder at his ex-fiancée's rigid jaw and eyes colder and harder than onyx.

She didn't believe him? She believed he'd return to his old ways? He not only wanted Kyle back, he wanted Bridget back. They were the reason Adam had kept his head low in the pen.

As the counselor had said, Adam deserved happiness like anyone else. This time he wouldn't run in fear from what

Creator offered. And Creator was offering Adam a second chance—his son and a new life with Bridget.

Chapter Three: On Parole

The pristine Catholic neighborhood on a tree-lined cul-de-sac and her brother's grand two-story brick house shingled with cedar shakes, stately windows, two-door entrance, and a full basement was a metaphor of his life, mocking Bridget.

She could've have had this life, too, if she'd used her brain instead of relying on her vagina to do the thinking.

Kyle skipped up the stone walkway to the home bookended by matching houses and manicured lawns. The light-blue sky and the puffy white clouds had drawn out the children who rode bikes, bounced balls, and skate-boarded along the big cement circle at the end of the street.

Bridget rang the doorbell and entered the two-story foyer with its majestic staircase winding up to the second floor. Kyle scrambled to the family room, doing what he always did, searching for his cousins, while she trounced to Jude's study, where he'd be buried in his perennial mound of work.

When she entered her brother's sanctuary, sunlight streamed in from the French doors leading out to the patio and the glass fence surrounding the pool.

Jude sat behind his mahogany desk and glanced up.

"You're on summer vacation. Even principals are allowed time off." Bridget plopped into the plush arm chair facing the desk.

"There's coffee." Jude kept typing on his laptop. He used his left hand to indicate the carafe and plate of muffins on the side table.

"You were expecting me?" Bridget retrieved the goodies. She poured a cup and refilled Jude's mug.

"Yep. The drunken jailbird sprung the coop. I figured you'd need to talk." Jude clasped his hands behind his head in the high-back leather chair. "How's Kyle?"

Forget discussing Kyle's first visit, or how seeing Adam had created a perfect storm of anger, confusion, and wistfulness to blaze through Bridget's insides like a tsunami.

"Good," she said in the same sweet voice as artificial as the sweetener she'd plopped into her mug.

"Nice answer. Good. Isn't that what everyone says? How're you really doing?" The smirk Jude bared was the same know-it-all grin he'd shoved at her from the time they'd been toddlers.

Bridget lifted the cup. She made the same ghoulish face of crossed eyes, wrinkled nose, and exaggerated sneer in response to Jude's big-brother asshattery.

He sat forward in the chair, chuckling. "Ooh. I see someone pushed your temper button."

"It's not funny." Bridget aimed her chin at him.

"Oh-ho, now I'm getting *the chin*. I did push a button." Jude's smile faded, and he folded his hands on the desk, the same as Dad always did. He was too much like Dad, from his thick, black hair, Roman nose, and firm mouth, to his eyes blacker than a moonless night up at the reserve, and dark-brown skin dusted with red undertones. No doubt he'd yank one of Dad's famous lectures from his pants pocket.

"If you need help with a lawyer—"

"I don't need help." She sipped the steaming brew. Instead of the coffee uncoiling the knots chafing Bridget's shoulders, the tsunami invaded her stomach.

"Nobody does it on their own. Lookit Emery. He had a lot of help when he decided to leave seminary." Jude flexed his index finger just like Dad.

Bridget bristled at the pointed finger, but the mention of Emery's name at least conquered the tsunami. She should put aside her invading pride and visit her little brother this weekend, even if it meant enduring Dad's unwelcome advice.

"Before she left, Char dropped some good news. There's talk of nominating you for president-elect for the diocese."

Oh my goodness. This couldn't be true. Bridget had been a part of the Catholic Women's Association from the age of sixteen. "I-I don't know what to say."

"Start by saying yes."

"Of course I'll say yes. You know how much this means to me."

"You're more than qualified. You covered all the bases at the parish level—convenorships, treasurer, secretary, president. You're now on the diocesan council. The women believe in you."

True, but much to Bridget's embarrassment, the parish women had piled on a boatload of sympathy, understanding, and worst of all, pity, after she'd sent Adam packing. Then there was the humiliation of his arrest and incarceration.

"Judging by your red face, I'd say your mind's elsewhere. How long's his parole?"

"Three years."

"Oh yeah, I forgot the judge tossed eight hundred books, the bench, the jurors chairs . . ." If Jude shook his head any harder in disdain, he'd morph into a bobblehead.

"What I don't understand is why they let him out so early. What he did to that guy—he shoulda served two-thirds of his sentence, no matter what," Jude continued on in Dad's condescending, authoritative tone.

Neither did Bridget understand. Model prisoner was

what the parole board had said. She'd written a letter, stating Adam faithfully wrote Kyle, constantly enquired about his son, sent small presents when Adam's canteen was plump enough to afford so. "Maybe it had to do with his uncle's murder."

"You said a rival gang killed the uncle in prison?"

Bridget shuddered. "The Syndicate Skins. It happened during Adam's first week of his sentence. Maybe he didn't want to die in prison? His uncle was in for murder. I think Adam might have seen his own future. His uncle was killed in the shower. Someone stabbed him."

Jude pressed his fist against his mouth. His cheeks puffed. "You never answered my other question. How'd the visit go?"

"Oh, Adam put on his usual charade." Bridget waved her hand.

"The concerned father?" Jude's black brows lowered and pinched together.

"Did he ever." Bridget's gut still flamed at Adam's behavior, as if he really cared about Kyle.

"You want me to pay him a visit?" Jude cracked his knuckles, grinning.

"I think I'm a little old for you to fight my battles."

"Thirty-six isn't old. Neither is thirty-seven."

"Please don't bother him. You're the one always saying to leave everything in the Lord's hands."

"And the Lord helps those who help themselves."

Now that she sat in the nosey family hot seat, Bridget sympathized with what Emery had endured when he'd contemplated leaving seminary.

Yes, Adam deserved everyone's wrath, but facing Dad's meddling and obstinate accusations was enough to sour the coffee in Bridget's stomach.

Still, she'd take Kyle to Ottertail Lake to visit his grandparents. Her family was all he had left now. Adam would return to his old ways. She'd give him three months — tops.

Adam flopped on the twin bed he'd been using for the past week. The mattress creaked and groaned under his weight. The room was a metaphor of his life — old, used furniture better served at the local dump, dull, gray walls in need of a new paint job, linoleum peeling and cracked. He might as well be in his old cell.

He rubbed his temples where a light throb had erupted. He couldn't get down on himself. He wouldn't get down on himself. For once he'd take responsibility for how his life had turned out, instead of blaming his mother, his father, his sisters, his uncles, his aunts, the government . . .

Being the youngest of the family, he'd prove change was possible. Just because someone was born into a hopeless situation didn't make them hopeless.

Someone rapped on the door. "Guimond, phone call."

Adam sat up. Who the heck was calling him here? He rose. His family didn't give a shit what happened to him. He thrust open the door and clomped down the hallway, passing the closed doors of other boarders at the halfway house.

Only one person would contact him. It was that time when phone calls to friends and family happened at the iron house. The big clock at the end of the hallway confirmed his suspicion. Stony Creek was an hour behind.

Dougie, one of the supervisors, plopped in the chair in the sitting area.

Adam had no choice but to take the call. If anyone was listening or traced the conversation, he could expect to wear another set of silver bracelets. He lifted the receiver. "'Sup?"

"Listen to the news. She's doing her four-day walk. Find out what happened."

Before Adam replied, the line went dead. He set down the phone. Four-day walk. Cutter's daughter. The news.

Adam reached for the remote from the coffee table and flipped to Northwestern Ontario News. For a half an hour he sat on the sofa. Finally, the camera panned in on the McIntyre River. Light from the rising sun crept across the sky. The Ontario Provincial Police's dive team moved about the shoreline. Some stood at the waiting ambulance. A city police officer pushed back the small crowd of reporters.

"This morning at seven-thirty, the OPP underwater recovery unit pulled a body from the McIntyre River near Isabel and Simpson Street," the newswoman said. "Police refused to comment if the body was Sheena Keesha, a sixteen-year-old Indigenous girl from Big Rock First Nation, which is four hundred and fifty kilometers north of the city. Keesha, as previously reported, went missing six days ago while in protective child care. Friends confirmed she was last seen outside of The Gator Bar on Brodie Street and Victoria Avenue. This marks the fourth Indigenous youth to go missing this year."

Cutter was right. The police wouldn't do anything about Sheena's disappearance. She was just another lowlife Indian, drunk or drugged up, getting what she deserved for hooking herself outside of a bar for cash.

This was why Adam had spent his time in the pen studying up on the most important people of the *Anishinaabe Nation* — women and children whom he'd failed.

The men sitting in a cell, or on a bar stool drunk, or tweaking at a flop house had failed those they'd once held precious. As warriors, their role was to protect, feed, shelter, and clothe the women and children. But as men, they'd forgotten how to be fathers, husbands, hunters, and most important, spiritual — the direct path to Creator and what made a man a man.

There were twelve of them for supper. They sat at the big dining table, passing around the bowl of mashed potatoes, platter of meat loaf, and plates of fresh tomatoes and bread. After a week of this food, Adam might as well be back in the pen. Bland. Tasteless. Seasonless. But food was food.

He shoveled a big helping of meatloaf into his mouth. From across the table, the eighteen-year-old punk watched. There were only two whites here. The punk was one of them. He'd come in the other day fresh from rehab. The rest of the men were 'Nish, good ol' slang for *Anishinaabe*.

Nobody talked at supper. Nobody talked at breakfast. Nobody talked during chores. Stupid people ran their mouths. Smart people kept their traps shut.

Tonight, Adam would hit a twelve-step meeting. Ninety meetings in ninety days was the rule of thumb, but Wednesday evenings were his men's sharing circles at the Kitchi-Gaming Friendship Center. The last Thursday of each month was the sweat lodge ceremony.

He still hadn't found an elder to confide in, but he needed one to help him continue the learnings of his culture. He already had his *Anishinaabe* name from an elder who'd visited the pen. *Wabun-Inini* — Man of Dawn.

Quite appropriate. He'd been given the name because of his rebirth. Dawn brought a new day. Promises. Hope and faith, the elder had said.

"Heard you're going to a meeting tonight." The punk, Logan, plopped on the couch.

Adam rubbed his full stomach and checked the clock on the wall of the lounge. Six-thirty. The meeting started in an hour. Perfect timing, because he'd have a half an hour to return before his nine o'clock curfew. "Yep."

"S'okay if I go with?"

Adam couldn't say no. Part of the program was giving away what he had, and what he possessed was sobriety. Even so, looking out for someone and sharing his experience was still new to him.

"Yeah." There, he'd agreed, when he normally would have told the punk to *fuck off.*

Logan was straight out of rehab for heroin abuse. Eighteen and a junkie. Adam wasn't supposed to judge, but a guy had better luck stopping traffic on the Trans Canada than getting off the crap. Too many of his friends had died sticking needles into their veins or chasing the dragon.

"Got no ink?" Logan studied the bare parts of Adam's skin. "Thought you would, 'cause I heard you were an—"

The silencing look Adam sent the punk shut down Logan fast.

He held up his hands in retreat. "It's cool. It's cool. Hey, check out mine." Logan bared his forearm. "I'm gonna get more. My bud did this one. He can do one for you."

"Nope."

"Why not? Everyone gets inked." Curiosity filled Logan's blue eyes.

"Yeah. *Everyone.* Pass."

"Oh? You think it's too mainstream now?" Logan half-smiled.

"Yep."

"Figured you weren't the sort of guy who did mainstream. Go your own path, y'know? People follow you. You don't follow them." Logan balled up a piece of paper in his hand. "I ... err ... uh ... I don't wanna go to slippery places. Y'know? We gotta talk."

"About what?"

"My uh ... girlfriend. She kept ... I gotta do it. Gotta do it."

"Never mind your girlfriend." Adam kept his arms and

legs crossed and stared at the TV screen. "This is about you."

"She's dead."

"Dead?" Adam turned to Logan's stiller-than-glass eyes.

"She . . . she went missing when I was in 'hab. I told her to chill before I went in. Said I'd come and get her when I got out. She wouldn't listen. She . . . they pulled her from the river. I know it's her. I know it's her."

Cutter's daughter was Logan's girlfriend?

The punk's skinny body trembled. His long, blond hair cut into a seventies-like feather hung in front of his thin face.

"I dunno if she was still using. She told me when I last saw her that she wasn't. But being at the bar . . . the news said that's where she was last seen. It's my fault. All my fault." Tears rolled from Logan's big eyes, and he swiped at them. "I'm no pussy."

Adam hadn't said as much. "Keep on." He made sure his command was soft—well, as soft as his deep voice allowed.

"I gotta find out what happened. The cops don't care. Nobody cares. It's what Sheena said. But I care even if her fam don't. Her ol' man, he's in the pen. He don't care. Her mom's six feet below. Drank herself to death."

Adam shuddered. If he hadn't straightened out, this could be Kyle as a teenager, shit-talking his parents.

"The counselors at 'hab told me to stay away from slippery places. How am I s'posed to find out what happened if I don't go to those . . . places?"

The same for Adam. Both he and Logan were from the streets, though. "Were you in the system?"

"Yeah." Logan sniffled. "'Aid helped me get into treatment. They got this program that helps me until I'm twenty-one. Some transition thing. I'm . . . I'm gonna get my high school. A lady from the university teaches at the Kitchi-Gaming Friendship Center at night."

"You Métis?"

"Yeah. Through my dad. He's Métis. Whatever that is."

Many kids had no clue about their heritage. Neither had Adam before he'd begun hanging out at a The Red Sky Friendship Center in Winnipeg, determined to find out what the heck Ojibway was and meant. He'd never even set foot on his home reserve, an hour and a half northeast of Winnipeg. He'd been born and raised in the city. The streets of the North End were all he'd known, growing up in North Point Douglas.

"What should I do? I gotta go there. Gotta check The Gator."

The punk wasn't old enough to get in the bars. Not that The Gator was famous for checking ID. Still, Adam had promised Cutter he'd find out what had happened to Sheena. If Kyle had gone missing, Cutter would do the same for Adam.

But if his parole officer found out . . . they'd ship him back to the clink.

Chapter Four: Heart of Stone

Bridget set the groceries on the counter. Kyle dashed straight for the TV to watch his favorite cartoon, a ritual they'd performed every evening for almost four years. She cooked while Kyle cheered for the Z Men.

Nobody was taking this ritual away from her. She seized the cordless phone and called up the emergency number contacts.

"Good evening, Joseph Howarth Society."

"This is Bridget Matawapit. I am the caregiver for Kyle Guimond. Might I speak to his father, Adam Guimond."

"Sure thing. Give me one second."

A few moments later, Adam's deep "Hello?" came through the receiver.

Bridget squeezed the tomato she held. "It's me."

"Bridget . . ." Adam's normally low pitch was an octave higher. "How you doing?"

The soft concern in his voice almost melted the film of ice around Bridget's heart. But he'd humiliated her. He'd lied to her. He'd chosen alcohol over her. "I need to speak to you about something." She made sure the hardness smothering her chest filled her words.

"What about?"

"It's about . . . Kyle." She moved from the island to the refrigerator. "I know you promised to bake him cookies for your next visit. I'd appreciate it if you'd not make him any more promises."

His sharp intake of breath carried over the receiver.

"That's all I have to say. I'll let you—"

"Wait a minute, *kwe*."

She bristled at the Ojibway word meaning woman—what Adam had always addressed Bridget by. At first, she'd found the endearment insulting, like an outlaw biker referring to his woman as the ol' lady. When Adam had explained the word's true meaning—life-giver, powerful and full of respect for those who carried light and love in their wombs, the heart of the *Anishinaabe* nation—she'd melted at the romantic gesture.

Now he thought to use the same word to melt her resolve? He could try again—and keep trying.

"What is it?" She fired a zap of impatience into her question.

"Why?"

For such a commanding, strong timbre, Adam's velvet plea skittered across Bridget's skin. She dropped the tomato on the counter by the oven. Tingles lightened her head. She scuttled across the floor to the sink. "Why what?"

"Why're you acting this way?" His voice remained low and gentle, still skittering across her skin.

Bridget palmed her mouth to stop the string of curses ready to jump off her tongue. To smother the red heat baking her skin, she zeroed in on Kyle from the vantage point in the kitchen, who sat in front of the TV, staring blankly at the screen.

"I don't think I need to explain myself. You've made promises in the past that you didn't meet. It really hurt Kyle."

The long pause on the other end sizzled in Bridget's ear. Adam's eyes, jawline, and lips had probably transmuted to stone. What rolled around in his mind during these long moments of silence? They'd always pierced Bridget's rear end like a fishhook. He'd probably folded his arms, too.

Bridget didn't have all night to wait for a reply. "I gotta go. We'll see you next week." Before Adam could say anything further, she switched off the cordless phone.

Adam continued to grip the receiver. Man, if not for the recovery meeting starting in a half hour, he'd give Bridget a taste of his temper. Anger management class told him to assess what he'd contributed in the past or present to escalate their dispute. The twelve steps told him to concentrate on his reaction to Bridget's behavior and not take inventory of her flaws, because this was his life and his program to work.

Taking responsibility for his own actions sucked bullshit. He slammed down the phone.

"We gonna book?" Logan stood in the entranceway of the lounge.

"Yeah." The heat burning behind Adam's eyes should have dried up his natural tear production.

Never mind his rage. Logan needed help. If agitated, the program had taught Adam to turn his thoughts to aiding others. Shit, he'd rather wallow in anger. Swaddle himself in a blanket of hate. Bathe in a tub of resentment. But he couldn't, or he'd be picking up the bottle again. Those days were done.

"Let's go." Adam tucked the cigarettes and lighter into his shirt pocket.

Once he went to his meeting, he'd be in a better mind to confront Bridget about the phone call and what had provoked her temper. Maybe this was the perfect opportunity to complete his ninth step? He still hadn't made amends to Bridget. When he returned to the halfway house, he'd call.

The thick heat of August stuck to Adam's skin. He pulled at his t-shirt, tearing away the cotton fabric damp from sweat. At the start of the meeting, the air conditioner had broken down, leaving everyone drowning in perspiration.

Outside the brick building, there was a light breeze, not cool enough to dispel the heat.

He puffed on the cigarette, doing what everyone did after a meeting—talking, smoking, and visiting. Six of them were present. Two old guys who'd probably been sober longer than Bill W., and two guys around his age who'd been attending meetings for a couple of years.

"Good to have you back." Hank spoke in a voice grittier than the curl of smoke wafting down Adam's throat.

Adam nodded. They'd remembered him from when he'd previously faithfully attended meetings—before he'd gone back out drinking and fucked up his life. "Here to stay this time."

"That's the attitude." Jimmy, the other old-timer, patted Adam's shoulder. "You gone and done ninety meetings in ninety days before, you'll do it again."

"That's what I'm doing." Logan scratched at his face. "Hey . . . um, I know we're not s'posed to go to slippery places. Uh, what if you have no choice?"

"No choice?" Hank rubbed his chin.

"Yeah. I gotta try get some info. It's really important."

"Information at a bar?"

"Uh-huh." Logan wet his lips. "I gotta—"

"We got a bus to catch." Why Adam had bothered to intervene was beyond him. It wasn't his business Logan wanted to go to slippery places. But as a member of the program, Adam had a responsibility to help other members.

"Yeah. Uh-huh. 'Kay. Catch you guys later," Logan said.

After bidding everyone goodnight, Adam steered them away from the front entrance of the Kitchi-Gaming Friendship Center to the sidewalk.

"You didn't let me finish talking." Logan's voice was

whinier than a bottle of the most expensive grapes.

"Y'know the slogans of the program. Getting ahead of yourself. Nobody has proof the girl pulled from the river's Sheena."

"I feel it here." Logan banged his fist against his chest. "I know it's her."

"Patience." Adam puffed on the cigarette and kept walking.

"But what if it is?"

"What if it isn't?"

"That's why I gotta go to The Gator. People'll know. They can pass me info —"

"You're not long enough in the program to go there. You go there, you'll end up using."

Logan's sharp intake of breath scattered on the breeze. "You telling me what I can and can't do?"

"I'm telling you from experience." Damned punk-ass kid. Dragging Bridget into this mess wasn't a good idea, but Adam had no choice. Although she hated his guts, his ex-fiancée was the only person who could help them, otherwise Logan would do something stupid.

"Lemme make a call. I know someone who can check it out."

"Who?"

"It don't matter."

Was Adam being selfish by asking Bridget for help? The children at risk and in foster care were near and dear to her heart. She volunteered a lot of her time enlightening the public about the tragedy.

What if she accused him of using the children to get close to her? No, Bridget wasn't stuck on herself. As far as she was concerned, her love had died for him when he'd started boozing and fucked up their engagement.

Aww hell, he might as well admit he wanted an excuse to

call. Wanted to hear her voice again. Waiting a full week for his next supervised visit was seven days too long. Bridget was the only connection to his son.

What were they doing right now? Maybe curled up on the sofa watching a movie? It was quarter to nine. Kyle was probably in bed. As for Bridget, what did she do while the boy slept?

Adam halted at the bus stop. When he got back to the halfway house, he'd call.

After almost four years, Bridget should have gotten used to the quiet nights while Kyle slept. Alone, in the living room, glass of wine on the end table, a good book in her lap, the TV on low, she should savor these moments after a busy day.

Before Adam had screwed up not only his life but that of those who loved him, they'd cuddled on the couch and watched a movie. Afterwards, they'd retire to her bedroom.

The landline rang. She reached over and grabbed the cordless. "Hello."

"Hey. How are you?"

Bridget stiffened. They'd already spoken earlier this evening. If Adam thought to barge into her life just because she was fostering his son, he could think again. "I'm winding down for the evening. It's late."

"It's only nine-thirty."

"I have responsibilities." *Unlike you.* "You know I get up at five-thirty."

"Yeah . . . responsibilities. You told me a hundred times when we were engaged." He muttered the words.

Bridget clenched the stem of the wine glass. "What do you want?"

"You watch the news?"

"Yes."

"They pulled a body from the McIntyre."

"I heard about it."

"My old cell mate thinks it's his daughter."

Old cell mate? Adam wasn't supposed to contact convicts or ex-convicts during parole. This man would never change if he was already breaking the rules. "And why are you telling me this?"

"I owe him."

"You owe him what?"

The light sound of the TV hummed in Bridget's hot ear. Adam was thinking instead of speaking. He was probably calling her ten different expletives in his thoughts.

"I owe him my early release." His words crunched like footsteps beneath bitter, broken glass.

"What does this have to do with me?" She had better things to do, like watch time erode her olive-colored walls.

"There's a kid here. Just got out of 'hab. His girlfriend was Sheena Keesha."

The wine trembled in Bridget's hand, and she set aside the glass. For goodness sake. "How old is he?"

"Eighteen."

Bridget would have to pry more information from Adam. Why couldn't he elaborate like everyone else on planet earth? "Sheena was sixteen, the radio said. He was seeing a minor?"

"Had his birthday a few months ago."

"They began dating when he was a minor?"

"Yeah."

"Was he also in the foster care system?"

"Yeah."

"And Sheena couldn't go to rehab unless her caregiver consented?"

"Yeah."

"The caregiver didn't consent?"

"Nope."

"Do you know why?"

"Dunno. Lemme get the kid. Hang on."

"Wait . . ." Yes, Bridget was concerned about Sheena Keesha, but the police had never confirmed whose body had been pulled from the river.

"Hi . . . It's me. Logan. You wanted to talk?" The boy's introduction bubbled with excitement.

Bridget sank into the couch. This was all Mom and Dad's fault for raising her to help others. "Hello. I'm Bridget."

"Adam said you have some questions for me. He said I could trust you."

"You can. What we talk about will stay between us." Bridget used her most compassionate voice. "Tell me about yourself."

"Uh . . . yeah, sure. What'd you wanna know?"

"For starters, how did you end up in care?"

"My parents are wastes of space. Y'know? Been in care, like, forever. I left when I turned the big one-eight."

"Are you aboriginal?"

"Métis. My dad is. My mom's white."

"Sheena Keesha is your girlfriend?"

"Yeah. We've been hanging for a couple of years. We met in high school."

"And Sheena went missing while you were in rehab?"

"Yeah. I told her to wait for me. I told her I'd figure everything out, y'know?"

"Figure out what, exactly?"

"Get clean. Get a job. Get a place for us to have the baby."

"The baby?" A boulder formed in Bridget's stomach, and her lungs teetered on collapsing. She managed to choke out, "Sheena's pregnant?"

"Yeah. It's why she told me to go to rehab. She wanted to stop using, too."

"Was she still involved in drugs when you last talked to her?"

"Not sure. We had it all worked out. I was gonna get her clean once I got clean. Y'know, in 'hab I'd get all the answers to get us off . . . stuff. Make us better. She said I'd be able to get her clean then."

The two were so young and naïve. They had no idea of the odds stacked against them. "Thank you for sharing, Logan. What you said will stay with me. Could I speak to Adam?"

"Uh-huh. Hang on."

"Hey."

"Hello." Bridget rubbed her brow. "You have to let Logan know we can't do anything until the police release the news."

"We could do something while we're waiting."

"What's that?"

"Check The Gator."

Bridget sputtered. "You can't go there. It's against the condition of your parole."

"Neither can Logan."

Did Adam mean Bridget was supposed to patronize the most notorious bar in the city? He was out of his mind. "I'm responsible for your son. If the caseworker finds out I went to a place like The Gator, this could put my care in jeopardy."

"It's just a bar."

"It's more than a bar. It's where drug dealers go. It's where criminals gather. It's a dangerous place. You have to think of Kyle."

"The program says to put everything in Creator's hands."

The familiar heat crept beneath Bridget's skin—how dare he spout his twelve-step rhetoric. "How long have you been sober?"

"First week in the iron house. After they shanked my uncle in the shower."

Bridget's blood froze. Adam had never elaborated before when answering a question. She and Jude had guessed correctly about the uncle's death impacting Adam's decision to walk a straight path if he'd stayed sober in prison and while on day parole in Winnipeg.

"You want me to go to this bar and ask around about Sheena?"

"You'll be fine. Tell the bouncer Adam sent you. Ed'll make sure nobody gives you lip."

"What am I supposed to say?" Bridget shifted on the couch, squirming.

"Ed'll point you to who's in the know. He'll handle it."

"Have you contacted this Ed already?"

"Nope. He'll know. We served time in the iron house before. He's clean now."

Clean? And bouncing at the most notorious bar in the city?

"I'll be nearby, *kwe*. I wouldn't send you into a dangerous place without my protection."

Bridget leaned against the back of the sofa. No, Adam wouldn't. He was a lot of things, but he'd always looked after women properly. "It's late. I need to think about this. Can I call you once I have an answer?"

"Yeah. Don't think too long, *kwe*. Later."

The line went dead.

CHAPTER FIVE: LOST WOMAN BLUES

Bridget set the other suitcase at the door. They were ready for the weekend at Mom and Dad's. Kyle deserved to see his grandparents. Her days of working weekends to hide from problems had stopped when she'd become a foster mother.

"I'm ready. I'm ready." Kyle tore down the hall, the backpack bouncing against his back.

His big smile, missing front tooth he'd lost the other night, and dancing dark eyes reaffirmed Bridget had made the right decision to get away for the weekend, even if she'd spend two days dodging Dad's questions.

Bridget had asked Jude to make the trip, but he'd begged off, stating Charlene was too busy. Lately, Charlene was always busy, which was strange, because church activities ceased during the summer months. Perhaps her job as a nurse practitioner had become demanding, although she worked for a private clinic that operated from Monday to Friday, nine-to-five.

Kyle would have enjoyed playing with his cousins for the weekend. The children loved swimming out in front of the house.

When Bridget returned to Thunder Bay, she'd have her decision for Adam.

Bridget held Kyle's hand and helped him off the plane. They'd taken the caravan, a comfy nine-seater not as stable as the thirty-seven-passenger beacon. She didn't mind, because the caravan offered a better view of the reserve with its lush beaches, spruce-covered forest, steep cliffs, and the rolling, grassy district.

Mom and Dad stood in front of the airport's big window. Finger-digging tension gripped Bridget's shoulders.

Kyle snatched his hand free and dashed for the door.

Sand swirled around Bridget. She waved away the blanket of dust generated from the plane's touchdown on the gravel runway. She'd better get used to the constant haze of grit, since none of the roads at the reserve were paved.

When she opened the door, Mom hurried forward. *Not the mandatory hug.* After enduring Adam's return, obligatory hugs and kisses didn't sit well in Bridget's pit-filled stomach. She needed a moment to paste on a cheery smile so her parents wouldn't fire a million questions.

She stepped behind Kyle, a shameful, cowardly move, and he barreled to his grandmother for a kiss, giving Bridget a moment to breathe and pep-talk herself into enjoying a weekend at the reserve.

"How was your trip?" Mom asked in her dainty voice. She shifted to her haunches and hugged a squealing Kyle.

"I loved it, Grandma! I talked to the pilots. They told me all about the plane. I'm gonna be one. I'm gonna drive planes."

"That's my boy. You keep talking to them." Mom continued to embrace a still-squealing Kyle. "Uncle Emery and Uncle Darryl are joining us for dinner."

Bridget could use some alone time with her little brother, a man too wise, compassionate, and patient for his twenty-seven years. "Awesome. I haven't talked to him since last week."

She hadn't talked to any of her family except for Jude.

Kyle dashed off to get a hug from his grandpa.

Bridget cringed at the forthcoming questions.

"How're you holding up? I got your text." Mom motioned at the attendants unloading the luggage.

"I'm fine."

"What about Kyle? How was his visit?"

"We can talk about that later." Bridget pulled up the suitcase's handle.

Mom retrieved the carry-all.

Dad herded a prancing and dancing Kyle to the truck.

Once they stored the luggage in the bed of the vehicle, and with Kyle buckled in the back beside Bridget, and Mom and Dad riding up front, they headed away from the airport, straight for the main part of the reserve.

Box-shaped houses lined the road. Much had changed since Bridget had first started coming up to the reserve. The airport was one of them. In the past, she'd traveled on the float plane. Mom and Dad's house now had indoor plumbing. No more trips to the outhouse to use the bathroom.

Kyle stretched upward and peered out his window at two dogs trotting along the side of the road.

Bridget patted his leg. Even the dogs were free up here, something not found in the city. On the reserve, Kyle could skip down to the church to visit Father Bennie, or join the other children to play in the ditches or on the road.

If not for her job and Adam's visitations, living at the reserve proved tempting. The conveniences found in the city weren't available, and if they were, Bridget would almost have to take out a bank loan, but being in the community was cozier than being snuggled in a blanket beside the woodstove at Mom and Dad's house during the dead of winter.

"Look! Look!" Kyle thrust his finger at the deer leaping from the ditch. "Uncle Emery said he'd teach me how to hunt."

Dad's booming laugh filled the truck. "In time. In time."

"They're so pretty. I don't know if I want to hunt them." Kyle set his finger against his lip.

The deer disappeared into the bush.

"That's a decision you can make when you're older." Bridget rubbed his prickly hair.

"I wanna go on Uncle's trap line this year. Where does the line go? Is it made of rope?"

Bridget stifled her laugh. She could imagine this line her son had visualized. "Sweetie, a line is an area where your uncle sets his traps. He walks and decides where he'll place them."

"They're going to scout the line in the fall." Dad gazed in the rearview mirror. "The old one they previously used."

"Nobody's using it?"

"Not that I know of. You know how tradition runs. The line belongs to the Keejik family."

Yes, trap lines were inherited on the reserve. Bridget's stomach grumbled at the thought of Mom's homemade rabbit stew.

She glanced back out the window. Coming here was supposed to lift her spirits, but the dull ache continued to steep in her heart.

"Do you think he'll change?" Mom stood at the kitchen counter, cutting the dinner vegetables.

Bridget spanked another patty into the shape of a hamburger. No surprise there that Mom didn't even use Adam's name. "I don't know."

"How does Kyle feel?"

"He's happy. Also scared." Which was the truth.

"Scared?"

Bridget had better throw up the stop sign before Mom and Dad poked any further into her business. "He's seven. During his formative years he's only known me. He doesn't want to live anywhere else. It's only natural."

"Did you tell your caseworker this?"

"Yes."

"Does she also know what happened during your engagement?"

"Yes. I had to give her my life story to become Kyle's foster parent. Remember?"

"Did you contact a lawyer?"

"No."

Mom heaved a heavy breath.

Great. Bridget was pissing off her mother with Adam-esque brusque answers.

"You should consider a lawyer. He's my grandchild. If this is all an act for the benefit of the social worker so Adam can obtain full custody, we'll lose Kyle. Adam's the only biological parent Kyle has left." Mom placed the vegetables into the steamer where water bubbled on the stove.

Although Mom spoke the truth, since Kyle's mother had died from an overdose and his biological grandparents preferred alcohol over children, Bridget didn't need a lecture about lawyers and whoever else to involve themselves in her personal life.

"Did you hear me?"

"Huh?" Bridget dug in the bowl for more ground beef.

"I said we should ask Father Arnold to speak on our behalf. He is Saint Patrick's pastor."

"It's something to consider." Three cheers that Bridget had answered nicely, even though the defensive armor she'd worn from her teenaged years—whenever Dad offered suggestions or barged in on Bridget's personal problems—remained wrapped tight around her body.

"Your father's concerned. I'm concerned." Mom reached into one of the many cupboards Dad had refinished to a country blue. She retrieved a bowl. "Kyle's as much a part of this family as Noah and Rebekah."

Maybe Bridget was being selfish by keeping her problems under wraps. Kyle adored Jude's children. Noah's being the same age meant they attended the same school where Jude served as principal. The BFFs golfed, swam, and played on the same soccer and hockey teams.

"It's not fair to Noah and Rebekah, either. Kyle's been a big part of their lives ever since you met Adam." Mom shut the cupboard door.

Bridget set the last patty on the plate. She'd speak to Emery.

There was so much splashing going on, a whale might as well have flopped in the lake. The culprits responsible for the ruckus were Kyle, and Emery's husband, Darryl. The two were tossing a beach ball back and forth in the water.

Bridget relaxed in the lawn chair beside her brother. The dock in front of their parents' house was the best place to unwind. At seven o'clock, the sun remained well above the tree line.

Inside, Mom and Dad cleaned up the dirty dinner dishes, having shooed everyone outdoors fifteen minutes earlier. More like Dad wanted Bridget and Emery to talk, because Dad had suggested Darryl accompany Kyle for his evening swim. Dad couldn't fool Bridget. The planets had aligned in his favor.

"It's normal to feel anger. Adam caused you a lot of grief." Emery sipped his iced tea. His legs were stretched out and crossed at the ankles.

"Would you have reacted the same way?" Right. Little brother wasn't capable of anger.

"I'm not you and you're not me. You reacted as you'd react."

Emery's logic and understanding, combined with his soft-spoken voice, reaffirmed he'd make a wonderful and compassionate individual or community counselor.

"And how did you expect me to react?"

Pink spread across Emery's fair skin.

"That bad?" Her brother's embarrassment produced a giggle.

"As I said, you're you, not me." A dash of humor salted Emery's light tone.

"I'd say I was pretty tolerant." The imp in Bridget fluttered to the surface. "I only gave Adam one stink eye at his visitation. Okay, maybe two."

"Two? That's pretty good. You didn't slap him into next week?"

Bridget stifled a snort. She let her gaze roam to Kyle and Darryl still tossing around the beach ball. "I wanted to. Believe me."

"How else did you feel?"

"Don't go there." Her brother could put away his counseling hat. "He's the father of the child I'm fostering. Nothing more."

Emery shifted in his lawn chair.

Tension seeped across Bridget's forehead.

"You know, I spent a lot of time denying my true feelings . . ."

If this was Jude, Bridget would've slipped on the gloves, because his debates produced ten rounds in the ring that left her staggering from his sharp words thumping her chin. As for Emery, for such a tall man, little brother was too gentle and nice. Bridget would feel like a bully if she gave him attitude, so she swallowed the snark.

"Mind you, I wasn't angry at Darryl. And he didn't do something to betray me. But when I took the time to really listen to what he had to say, we reached an understanding. I concentrated so much on my own beliefs that I failed to open my mind to other possibilities — possibilities that maybe he was right."

"And your point is . . ."

"I don't know Adam that well, so I can only assume. From what you told me, he had a tough life. Maybe he feared happiness? People who don't experience happiness and love while they're growing up can be scared of the positive feelings they produce, especially if they've only known negativity.

"Abusive situations are out of their control." Emery looked out to the water. "When they leave that kind of environment, they're conditioned to believe they're not worthy of anything positive. They even fear positive relationships because a loving environment elicits new emotions they've yet to experience, and they're unsure how to process those emotions."

Emery faced her.

Too bad he had on sunglasses, leaving Bridget unable to read his bright green eyes.

"Remember, not having control over their environment led them to control their emotions. When one is flooded with new emotions they can't control, their first response is to destroy or flee, because this is what they did while being abused. They hid under beds and in closets. They learned not to cry. They learned to remain silent. They controlled their feelings as a way to survive in their environment."

Emery did have his Bachelor of Social Work. In seminary, he'd taken pastoral counseling, too. People were his job, what he'd made a career of. Although he'd been in London at Saint Michael's Seminary when Bridget had met Adam, her brother could assess anyone based on their background.

"So you're going to take his side?" Bridget cringed. She sounded ten years old, pouting that her friends had chosen the enemy's word over hers.

"There're no sides to take." Emery sipped his iced tea. "Only a situation involving three people. You don't want to lose Kyle. As a father, Adam wants to rebuild his relationship and become a full-time dad again. Kyle wants you in his life because you're his mother."

"Oh, I get it. We're supposed to become one big happy family after what he did." The bitterness in Bridget's sarcastic words matched the sour taste in her mouth.

"I didn't say that."

"Then what did you mean?"

"I'm saying if you try to force your hand, you may not get the result you desire."

CHAPTER SIX: WEARING YOUR HEART ON YOUR SLEEVE

A dam sat in the folding chair, a chair meant for people of average height and build, and even they shifted and moved to try to get comfy.

Each twelve-step meeting room was the same. Outdated furniture from the seventies. Outdated paint on the wall. Outdated cheap-tiled floor. The upstairs lounge at the United Church wasn't any different, smelling of fresh-brewed coffee.

Logan sat beside Adam. The chairs formed a circle around two coffee tables and a round table. One thing about alcoholism and drug addiction—the disease didn't discriminate. Every race, religion, education, occupation, and social class was welcome to sample its dark depths, from the nurse sitting adjacent to Adam who'd been charged with drunk driving to the lawyer whose wife and children had left him. Then there was the chief from one of the northern reserves with a former penchant for crack-cocaine, who was in the city on business, and a prior two-bottles-a-day-wine-drinking homemaker.

A couple of young *Anishinaabe-kweg* sat on the blue sofa. They whispered and giggled while stealing peeks at Adam and Logan. The girls must be new, so they didn't understand these were meetings of recovery, not for checking out the opposite sex.

Adam glanced away. The only woman for him was Bridget, but she was gone for the weekend. Starting his job on Monday would keep him busy during the days.

The chairperson finished the announcements. Now that they'd completed a reading from the big blue book and everyone had refilled their coffees, they'd discuss the story they'd read.

"Adam, would you like to start?" The chairperson was a well-groomed *Anishinaabe-kwe* in her forties. She had kind brown eyes. A dash of softness speckled her clear, firm voice.

"Sure." Adam set his coffee on his knee. "I'm Adam and I'm an alcoholic."

Everyone offered the usual, "Hi, Adam."

"Good reading." He squeezed his toes. "I like the part where he learned acceptance is the answer. Sometimes we got no choice but to accept. If we don't, it makes life a helluva lot more tough."

He ran his tongue against the roof of his mouth. "I can't control how people feel or how they react." Like Bridget, the biggest example. "All I can do is accept their answer. It doesn't mean I gotta give up. It means I gotta be a little patient."

Patience was a must with Kyle and Bridget. "Respect their boundaries. Work within their boundaries. That's it. All I got to say."

Bridget stood in the laundry room, sorting through the clothes she had to wash now that they had returned from Ottertail Lake.

Tomorrow, she'd drop off Kyle at Jude's house, where he stayed during the day from Monday to Friday while she worked.

Adam's request continued to invade Bridget's thoughts. A

teenage girl might have been murdered. Too many youths from the northern reserves stayed in Thunder Bay to attend school if their communities didn't have adequate education facilities. And six had died so far.

She sat on the Indigenous Women's Alliance board of directors for this reason. Since Kyle was asleep, she'd call the halfway house.

After she started the laundry, she plopped on the sofa and picked up the cordless phone. With a glass of red courage in hand, she speed-dialed the halfway house.

"Good evening. Joseph Howarth Society."

"This is Bridget Matawapit. I'm the caregiver for Adam Guimond's child. Might I speak to him?"

"One second."

Bridget sipped at her wine. The alcohol warmed her blood.

"'Sup, *kwe*?"

Against her hardened resolve, Bridget's skin tingled at Adam's deep, rough voice he always softened for her benefit, and Kyle's. "I made my decision."

He grunted.

Bridget banged the off button on the TV remote. What did he have to be annoyed about? "I'll help you and Logan."

"How was your weekend?" He kept the same soft tone, his words a rowboat dabbling across the water of a pond.

"Uh . . ." Saliva coated Bridget's mouth. "It, uh, it went good. Very good."

"Yeah? Kyle have a good time?" His voice remained bright—well, as bright as his perennial threatening bark could manage.

"He always has a great time at his . . ." She shouldn't say grandparents'. Adam might protest to Mrs. Dale that Kyle was becoming too integrated into the family. He also might demand another foster home.

"He always has a great time at the rez. We, um, flew in Saturday morning. Kyle went swimming with his new uncle. We barbecued. Visited. Went to church."

"You get in this evening?"

Bridget pressed the wine glass against her chest. "A couple of hours ago. I'm . . . doing laundry."

"I got mine done. Start work tomorrow." He sounded as proud as Kyle when he'd dashed to the door at Jude's to show Bridget a project he'd completed at school.

"At Benny's?" Tilting the rim to her mouth, Bridget managed a gulp. Mrs. Dale had mentioned Adam's boss from Winnipeg had referred him since Benny's was a chain restaurant.

"Yep. Short order cook. Morning shift."

"The morning? Will you be able to make your scheduled visit on Thursday?" Confidence was failing to come out in her words. Failing ever since Adam had decided to have a conversation like a normal person.

"I gotta talk to The Hawk. Tell her we have to reschedule the visits."

"The who?"

"The warden. Mrs. Dale."

"Oh . . ." The tight ball pressing against Bridget's ribcage vanished, and something resembling floating bubbles climbed up her throat. The laugh sprang from her mouth. She'd forgotten how Adam nicknamed people based on their dispositions or physical appearance. "I guess she tends to have some bird-like features."

"Yep. A hawk. Looks like one. Acts like one."

Bridget suppressed the giggle and managed to say, "Will we be considering evening visits?"

"Tuesdays and Wednesdays are good. My days off."

"I'm sure she'll contact me once she talks to you about rearranging your visitation schedule." She set her feet on the coffee table and let the wine glass lounge on the armrest.

"Wednesday night would be a good time to hit The Gator."

"Have they released any information on the body they pulled from the river?"

"Yep. Family was notified. Cutter called yesterday during his phone time. It was Sheena."

Bridget's heart resembled a grape shrinking to a raisin. "I'm sorry."

"So am I."

There was a long silence eerier than a haunted house. If the creepy quietness continued, Bridget expected to hear a door creaking and a nasty hot breath on her ear. She moved her feet off the coffee table and sat cross-legged. "Adam?"

"You gonna make arrangements for Kyle then? Wednesday night?" His voice grew hushed.

"Yes. Yes. I'll talk to Jude. During the summer break, he watches Kyle during the day."

"Sounds good. Get me around seven-thirty. I gotta be back here at nine. Curfew time."

"Okay. I'll see you Wednesday night, if not, before then when you visit Kyle."

"Gotcha. Later."

Bridget switched off the phone. She gulped back the remainder of the wine.

Going to The Gator should scare her under the bed, not having a conversation like two normal people with Adam.

Bridget held Kyle's hand and led him down the hallway to the same door they'd opened during their last visit at the Children and Family Services building. Instead of Thursday morning, they were meeting on Wednesday during her lunch hour. Once she got clearance from the board of directors, she'd rework the visitation to late Wednesday afternoons.

When they opened the door, Adam stood on one side of the room, and Mrs. Dale sat on the chair she'd previously used, the one by the pop cooler.

Bridget's gaze whipped back to Adam. It'd been almost a week since she'd last seen him. He still had his cream-colored cowboy hat, the one with the curling brim that made the waves of his hair kink in every direction. A tank top hugged his dark skin. A jean shirt caressed his broad shoulders.

Adam nodded. His dark eyes brightened at Kyle.

"Go ahead. I'll be right there." Bridget managed to eke out the words while pointing at the chair beside Mrs. Dale.

Kyle inched toward his father. His lips spread into a big smile, flashing his missing tooth.

"Hey." Adam shifted to his haunches. "How ya doing?"

"Awesome." Kyle ducked his head and blushed.

Bridget sat. Kyle's bashfulness was a good sign. She choked the handle of her travel mug. Maybe too good of a sign. If Emery was present, who'd previously visited convicted felons in prison during his discernment at seminary, he'd tell Bridget that Adam deserved this chance.

She gave her head a good shake, anything to get rid of Emery's nagging voice.

"Thank you, Dad." Kyle clutched a bag. "May I have this one?" He held up a monster cookie, his favorite.

"You can have 'em all. I made them for you." Adam led them to the small table.

"Really? Let's color this one." Kyle pointed at the Z Men coloring book.

"We sure can." Adam set his big hand on the back of Kyle's chair.

Against her will, Bridget's skin warmed. Kyle used his imagination wonderfully, and she prohibited him from becoming absorbed in TV, computers, or other technological devices. Jude felt the same way and limited his children's time in front of the too-many screens available to youngsters.

For Kyle's sake, she should buy a house. Not only would he benefit, this might help her chances at keeping him permanently. With a home, he'd have a backyard to play in.

The real estate market was expensive, but Bridget could broker a sweet deal on the condo to acquire a sizeable down payment for a house. She'd paid off the truck early, leaving her a bi-weekly mortgage payment and the usual bills.

Children and Family Services provided an allowance for Kyle's care. She did dig into her own wallet for his golf classes. Then there was soccer. Kyle's first year of hockey had kept him amused this past winter.

As the director of the Aboriginal Student Center at the university, Bridget made an excellent salary that afforded her many extras. Even with Kyle's extracurricular activities, a house was doable.

Mrs. Dale continued to take notes, peeking over her clipboard at Adam and Kyle. "How are you today, Ms. Matawapit?"

"I'm good. How about you?"

"Busy. There aren't enough hours in the day." Mrs. Dale ticked off a box on the sheet of paper.

Bridget snuck a peek. The woman whom Adam referred to as The Hawk had checked off *still uncomfortable* regarding Kyle's progress with his dad. Bridget glanced up at Kyle coloring away and grinning at Adam, both quietly laughing. Adam held a red crayon Kyle had picked out, and he helped color the picture.

She shifted, clicking her nails against the bottom of the chair.

"I went swimming . . . I went for a ride on Uncle Darryl's

four-wheeler . . . I helped Grandpa polish the important cups after church . . . I got to watch the stars come up . . ." Kyle kept coloring. "I always get to watch the stars come up. I never see them here. They're really bright and pretty at Grandma and Grandpa's house. There weren't any dancing lights this time."

"Dancing lights?" Adam also kept coloring.

"Yeah. The green dancing lights in the sky when it's dark."

"He means the aurora borealis," Bridget piped in.

"Yeah, that's the big name Mom calls it." Kyle giggled and gazed up at Adam.

Through his dark lashes, Adam peeked at Bridget. More than peeked. His tender look caressed the bare skin of her arms.

"I didn't mean to interrupt." Bridget fumbled to call up the notes section on her cell phone. "I have to write a few things out I need to get after work."

"I don't mind." Adam's tender gaze kept stroking the gooseflesh peppering Bridget's skin. "You can join us if you want."

Bridget almost dropped the phone. "I'm fine. I need to make a list." Dammit, she hadn't meant to snap.

Mrs. Dale's bemused expression bordered on laughing at Adam.

What was the caseworker finding amusing? Adam had a right to try. Kyle was his child. The words Bridget had furiously typed on the phone blurred. Where was her brain? Adam didn't deserve sympathy. He was a big boy and could defend himself.

"A wise decision." Mrs. Dale wrote on her clipboard. "Men who've been in the system a long time never change."

"Thank you for your observation, but remember, you're Kyle's caseworker. I'm quite capable of handling my own personal life." Bridget made sure iced coated her words.

Mrs. Dale's prim mouth moved into a half-moon. Her beady eyes remained gray cement. "I quite agree. If I didn't, you wouldn't be Kyle's caregiver, would you?"

Was that supposed to be a threat? If the old witch thought to stick her nose in the inappropriate place, she was pulling out the gloves on the wrong person. "Adam asked if I'd care for Kyle. Your supervisor agreed."

"Yes, she did, based on my recommendation after I interviewed you in my office and assessed your home." A warning lingered on Mrs. Dale's words. "You have an excellent job. A condominium. A splendid mode of transportation. You're . . . well, you're not like . . . you do well for yourself . . ." She sniffed.

What had Mrs. Dale meant? There was a ton of racism lingering in the non-aboriginal population of Northwestern Ontario. Bridget had run into those who'd divided the Indigenous people into the good tax-paying Indians who fit neatly into Western Society, and the drunken, drug-addicted, homeless bad Indians who were a drain on the taxpayers. She was nobody's good little Indian.

As for tonight, Bridget had promised Adam she'd go to The Gator. If Mrs. Dale found out, she'd probably class Bridget as another drunken Indian who relied on the handouts of society. The hard-assed woman might even terminate Bridget as a caregiver for Kyle.

She must talk to Adam after. Going to The Gator might prove too risky.

After dropping off Kyle at Jude's for an overnighter, Bridget pulled up in the no-parking zone in front of the brown-brick, three-story building. Seven-thirty. The bar scene didn't liven up until after ten o'clock. They couldn't go that late because of Adam's parole curfew.

To fit in at the bar, she'd kept her dress simple. Jeans, a t-shirt, and sandals. Only a hint of eyeliner, mascara, and lip gloss. Her hair was bound in a long braid.

Adam emerged from the double-glass doors in his customary jeans, t-shirt, running shoes, and cowboy hat. With his hard onyx eyes, firm jawline, and the stony set to his lips, he'd fit right in at The Gator. He swaggered down the walkway and stopped at the truck.

With the windows lowered, his low whistle carried inside.

"Nice ride."

"Thanks."

Adam opened the door. His muscular form consumed the over-sized bucket seat, so much he removed his hat and set it on his lap. His waves of hair kinked. He adjusted the chair all the way back. "Yep. Nice." He glanced behind him. "A guy could stretch out there, too. You always dug trucks."

"We're in Northwestern Ontario. Trucks are a necessity."

"Not too many women drive 'em in the 'Peg. Hell, you don't see many trucks at all. Lots of SUVs instead."

"I'm not any other woman." Bridget slid the floor shifter into gear.

"That you sure ain't." There was a huskiness to Adam's compliment.

Warmth crawled along Bridget's skin. She guided them away from the curb.

"This an Annihilator edition? Sure is sporty."

"Yes." Pride blossomed in Bridget. She loved her ride — bucket leather seats, ten-speed transmission, four-wheel drive, and a top-of-the-line stereo. There was even a moonroof and sliding back window Kyle preferred over air conditioning.

"Where's the boy?"

"At Jude's. We won't be done until after nine. I thought it

was best he stayed overnight so he can go to bed on time."

"Oh?"

Bridget stopped at the light. When she turned her head, the breath jumped from her throat at the sight of Adam's dark eyes that first glittered with distress and then eagerness.

CHAPTER SEVEN: SYMPATHY FOR THE DEVIL

They drove south on Brodie Street. The Gator was at the corner of Brodie and Victoria. Adam kept his visor down because of the sunlight penetrating the interior of the truck.

He shouldn't have interfered with Kyle's evening. His son came first. But having Kyle staying at Jude's for the night produced a rush of adrenaline that chugged through his veins.

He squeezed his toes to keep himself in check.

"About The Gator . . ." Bridget pressed her lips together. She tapped one long nail on the steering wheel.

"How'd you do that?" He pointed. Rather sexy.

Bridget lifted her hand. "Do what?"

"Get that gradient look. The red's darker at your cuticle and goes lighter to the tip."

"Ask my manicurist. She's the magician, not me."

"They look great."

Pink crept onto Bridget's cheeks.

Adam's lungs expanded against his chest. He shifted to face her, what he'd always done in the past because this beautiful woman deserved a man's undivided attention. Aww shit, this wasn't going to work. Even in a full-size cab, he couldn't maneuver into a good position, but if he angled his knee in Bridget's direction and set his hand on the console between them, she'd get the hint that what she had to say was important to him.

"I'm worried if Mrs. Dale finds out I've been there, she might cause problems. She doesn't seem to think much of *Anishinaabeg*."

"She doesn't." Adam fingered the brim of his hat. "Look, I don't want you doing anything you're not comfortable doing."

Didn't Bridget understand her feelings meant everything to him? If she wasn't comfortable, then he wasn't comfortable.

The pink brightened to red on Bridget striking cheekbones. "I know how the police are. They don't put much effort into the deaths of our people. I do want to help. She was only sixteen and deserves the truth revealed about her death."

"Maybe it'll help if you know what her ol' man means to me. What you say we do coffee? We can always go another night if you decide you wanna."

"Coffee?"

"A harmless cup of coffee." She'd better not think he was out to score. Damned straight he'd give anything to have Bridget beneath him again, her slim thighs spread, sleek arms draping his shoulders, drawing him against her tits, but if anything happened, she'd make the call, not him.

"Okay. Coffee." Bridget nodded. "A harmless cup of coffee."

Adam pulled at the scooped neckline of his t-shirt where sweat was beginning to form.

The truck rolled in to the Reggie's Donuts on Frederica Street, since Bridget had spied Mrs. Dale many times patronizing the establishment on Arthur at this hour. If the caseworker saw Bridget and Adam together, trouble would erupt. At least Adam hadn't asked why they'd driven so far south.

She guided the Annihilator into one of the parking spots. Tension skittered across her shoulders.

They vacated the vehicle. As they walked to the restaurant, Bridget snuck peeks at Adam's confident swagger, his *get out of my way* strut. She'd never forget when he'd first walked into the big hall at the job fair, filling the room with his overabundance of testosterone that seemed to seep from his hard muscles.

Adam pulled on the handle and opened the door.

Legs moving in short jerks, Bridget ducked inside. Gosh, he still performed every task like a gentleman. She couldn't believe he'd been raised by an abusive father. Raised was a joke. Adam's older sisters had cared for him since his mother had been too busy bar-hopping. Maybe being the only boy in the family and the youngest had something to do with his view of women.

"How're your sisters?" Bridget fought for long strides, even as she jerked to the counter where a young girl stood.

Adam shrugged. He stared at the menu board. "Same ol'. Same ol'."

Since he most likely didn't have any money, Bridget withdrew her wallet. "I got this."

Folding his arms until his biceps bulged, Adam grunted and hardened his gaze at the juice cooler.

Irritation crept under Bridget' skin. If he hadn't leapt off the wagon into a vat of alcohol, he'd have money, so he could stuff his male ego back into his jeans pocket.

Once Bridget paid for their coffees, she directed them to the table by the window, far from the only other couple in the restaurant. She took the chair facing the street. Instead of sitting opposite her, Adam dropped in the adjacent chair.

Finger-like caresses teased Bridget's thighs, threatening to invade a spot very much off-limits. She gripped the coffee mug. Adam studied her the way he used to, his gaze tracing her skin, stroking her arm, feathering her taut hand.

"You—you wanted to tell me about your friend." She snatched her braid and twisted the uncoiled ends around her fingers.

"Always did that whenever you were nervous." Adam used his chin to motion at the braid. "Played with your hair."

In her most business-like voice, she choked out, "Your friend?"

"Cutter." Adam's big hands smothered the mug he cupped.

"He was at Stony?" Bridget spoke right away before her brain ran off at his hands overpowering everything and anything, and the way they'd once . . . She coughed.

"Yep." Adam sipped the coffee. "Was my recovery sponsor."

"When's he getting out?" Her heart shifted to a slower gear, and she high-fived herself at being back in control.

Adam's eyes moved up and to the right. He frowned. "Hard to say."

"What's he in for?"

"Murder."

The saliva drained from Bridget's throat. She fought to spill the words from her mouth. "A murderer was your sponsor?"

"He's a good man." Adam sipped more coffee. "He'd already served ten years before I got sent down below."

"Ten years? That's a long time." What kind of prison allowed a murderer to sponsor someone?

"It is. Just 'cause someone's gotta live out their life in the iron house doesn't mean they gotta do it the way everyone expects them to."

"He found religion?" Emery had mentioned many prisoners turned to God while incarcerated.

"Nope. He found himself."

"Himself?"

"Yeah."

"And?"

"Did his own version of a vision quest. Gave him direction. He's big in the Aboriginal Healing Program. Sweat lodge. Twelve-step recovery."

"He worked with an elder?" Emery had said elders could conduct the programs for Indigenous men.

"Yep. Still works with the old guy. Introduced me to him."

"What happened? How did . . . Cutter . . . end up in there?"

The look Adam directed at Bridget said only innocent ten-year-olds were dumb enough to ask such a question.

"It's only a question." She drew back her shoulders.

"You don't ask a man why he's doing time." Adam withdrew his cigarettes from his shirt pocket.

Bridget stood to do what she used to do—head outside so Adam could have his cigarette.

They carried their mugs, nodding at the girl behind the counter who'd probably witnessed many people going outside to have a quick smoke before coming back inside.

Bridget should buy Adam one of those e-cigarettes. There were many shops around the city that sold them. "Did you ever try an e-cigarette?"

"You mean a vape?" Adam held open the door.

"Oh? That's what it's called?" When Bridget stepped outside, the warm air caressed her skin, and the smell of fresh doughnuts vanished.

"Yeah. Nobody says e-cigarette. They say vape."

"Vape?"

"'Cause of the vapor it produces. Y'know—*I'm going out-*

side to vape." Adam meandered toward the stand where a person could deposit their leftover cigarette butts.

"Vape is used as a verb and a noun?"

"What?"

"Never mind. I heard they come in all kinds of flavors."

"Too expensive." Adam slid the smoke between his lips and tilted his head to set the tip in the lighter he'd flicked.

Vaping couldn't be any more expensive than smoking. From what Bridget heard, the taxes on cigarettes were enormous in Canada, even when someone purchased tax-free smokes at the reserve outside the city.

"You never found out why Cutter" — how strange to call a man by his prison name — "was in Stony?"

"I told you. Murder."

"What happened?"

"*Kwe . . .*" His dark eyes narrowed. He puffed on the cigarette. The smoke curled upward. "You're still full of a million questions."

"I think I have a right to know." When Bridget folded her arms beneath her breasts, Adam's gaze followed. Nor did his eyes shift elsewhere. Heat blanketed her underwear. She widened her stance, anything to cool off. But having her legs open meant . . . She set her feet together.

"Okay. For you." Adam sucked on the smoke, his hard stare killing the traffic. "He went down for second degree. His lawyer tried to argue self-defense, but the Crown wasn't buying."

"Second degree is murder not premeditated."

"Gang-related." Adam puffed again on the smoke. "They marked him."

Bridget gasped.

"He was laying low at his ol' lady's. According to her, she said they threatened her into giving him up. They came. He shot and killed one. The other got away."

"Why did they mark him?"

"Long story." He licked his lips. "I did it, *kwe*. Got my diploma."

"I know. You said so in one of your letters." She'd let him change the subject.

"In time, gonna visit your center."

"Anything in particular you're considering?"

"Won't be for another year. Wanna see how this job pans out. Worked in the kitchen in the iron house. Learned lots."

"You were always an excellent cook." The memory of Adam grinning away in the kitchen, his booming laugh carrying through the condo while he whipped up another specialty, floated across Bridget's eyes. "How's your job going?"

"Supervisor's a good guy. Other kitchen staff are good. No dicks . . . yet."

"If there were . . . dicks?" Bridget shivered at the way Adam's jaw had always molded to steel whenever someone had upset him.

"That's where the program comes in." Adam kept puffing on the cigarette.

The anger simmering beneath Adam's skin failed to appear, such as when his upper lip used to curl, or when he'd run his thumb across the tips of his fingers, contemplating whether to hit someone.

The thickness pushing against Bridget's chest vanished. "Was Sheena his only child?"

Adam flicked away the cigarette butt. "Nope. He has four boys and another girl. Three are back at his rez. The other two are in the 'Peg."

"What about Cutter's exes?"

"One's living with someone else. Not sure of the others. Sheena's mother's dead. Cirrhosis. Died while Cutter was doing his time."

"Is that when Sheena went into care?"

"Yep."

"What does Cutter want you to do exactly?"

"Find out what happened to Sheena."

Would Cutter go after Sheena's caregivers? Men in prison still had contact with their gangs from the inside, and many of the gang members were also behind bars. "What's he going to do *if* he learns the truth?"

"Never asked."

"Maybe you should. What if he hurts someone?"

"*Kwe*, that's his business. Not mine."

"I can't help someone who might hurt others. It doesn't matter if Sheena's foster parents acted negligently. There's a system in place to handle irresponsible caregivers."

"He lives by the Seven Grandfathers Teachings. He lives by the twelve steps. He's not gonna hurt anyone. If he did, it'd go against everything he believes in."

"You have to remember I never met him. I don't know what kind of person he is."

"I can guarantee you he's not gonna send out a war party."

"I know you wouldn't, but I don't know him."

"You trust my word, don't you?"

Trust? He dared to ask about trust after betraying her? But for this situation, Bridget could trust him. Adam wouldn't lie about the safety of another human being. At least she hoped not.

"You still don't believe me, huh?" His dark eyes crinkled.

"The parole board believed you, didn't they, otherwise they'd never have granted day parole and full parole."

"I don't care what they think. I care what you think." He continued to study her.

Bridget hugged herself. What was she doing here? She had Kyle to think about. She had a job to think about. She had her own reputation to think about. The diocesan council wouldn't approve of her helping a felon, even if he was her former fiancé.

"What did Cutter do for you exactly?"

"Let's get our coffees to go."

"Okay." A drive might do them both good. In the truck, they had a full console and a floor shifter between them. Out here, only air separated them.

A left turn was required to remain on Fort William Road, but Bridget kept going straight since the road changed to Water Street, although there wasn't a view of the water because of the railroad tracks. For a clear view of the bay and the Sleeping Giant, she kept driving until reaching Pearl Street that took them to a nice park. There were docks here, even a small peninsula they could walk and sit at a picnic table.

Kyle loved these drives. He'd gape at the massive rock formation resembling a man resting on his back. Too bad they couldn't drive to Sleeping Giant Park, her favorite place to take Kyle on the weekends, but Adam had a curfew.

Bridget guided the truck into the sparse lot and parked. She grabbed her tea. They walked the paved path, the wind blowing off the bay. She drew the fresh scent of Lake Superior into her lungs.

Adam led them to a bench. While Bridget sat on the seat, he stepped up and plopped on top of the backrest.

Seagulls fluttered high above them.

Adam withdrew a cigarette. He stared out at the water.

Bridget lowered her gaze to Adam's running shoes. His toes moved beneath the material. She shifted her attention to his face, as unreadable as a book written in Vulcan.

"I didn't wanna die in there." Adam lit the cigarette. "Met Cutter in the kitchen. He helped me."

"Your uncle was in there."

Adam directed his hard eyes at the bay.

For over a minute only the seagulls talked, the wrong species. If this was going to result in playing twenty questions, forget it. Bridget stood. "Let's go. I have stuff to do still."

"Sit down, *kwe*."

"No. I'm not wasting any more of my evening prying something from your mouth. If you want to talk, then talk. Otherwise, let's go." She wrenched the keys from her purse.

Just as Bridget was about to huff away, he said, "I couldn't sober up for my kid. I couldn't stay sober for you."

She stopped and turned.

Adam stared straight ahead. His toes kept moving beneath his running shoes. "I learned I had to do it for me." Smoke curled from his mouth. "When Angela told me she was pregnant, I . . . my . . . my first thought was—*I can't let my kid grow up the way I did.*"

Bridget sank back on the bench.

"We saw the addictions counselor at the Friendship Center." He took another drag off the cigarette that didn't tremble in his thick fingers, but his toes kept twitching, stretching the material of his shoes.

"He got us into treatment. Angela went to one place, and I went to another. Thought it worked for me. Thought I was ready to live a sober life. It's why I split when she went back out there. Split with Kyle."

He took a few more puffs off the cigarette, still staring at the enormous lake. "I was meant to be here. Not Winnipeg. There's something about this place." He pointed to the Sleeping Giant. "I felt it when I first got off the bus. Smelled cleaner. Looked cleaner. Even the people were cleaner. It wasn't Point Douglas."

A few moments passed while he continued to stare out at the massive rock formation. "I walked the river lots growing up, but it wasn't the same as walking the bay here." He flicked away the last of the cigarette. "There's freedom here. In Point Douglas, you're suffocating. The traffic doesn't stop. The trains don't stop. The noise doesn't stop. Thunder Bay . . . it doesn't feel like a city. More like a big town."

Funny, everyone said the same thing about the beautiful place Bridget had lived her whole life.

"It's easy to navigate. You just gotta look for the mountain to know where you are." He pointed.

Bridget followed his finger toward the steep, flat mafic sill, crowned with spruce trees around its middle, rising to fourteen hundred feet over the city, nested in the south at the reserve.

"The mountain and the giant seem to guard this place."

"Maybe they do."

He turned, his dark gaze seeming to cup her face. "You know my uncle got shanked inside. First week I was there. I saw my own death. Saw what would happen if I kept doing what I was doing. When I met Cutter . . ."

He looked back out to the water. The material of his running shoes continued to shift. "I didn't wanna end up offing anyone, *kwe*. I didn't wanna get that bad. After . . . after what I did to that guy in the bar, I knew I was going as low as everyone else in there."

Bridget clasped her knees together.

"I got a kid to think about."

She pressed her knees even harder together. The conviction in Adam's voice said he had a good chance at succeeding. He was determined — determined to win.

Chapter Eight: Please Don't Touch

Adam clasped his hands together. "I get it, y'know? I got a lot of strikes against me. I deserve those strikes. I'm not asking for a free pass. I know trust's earned."

He'd better not be asking Bridget to trust him again.

"The Hawk sees a lot of guys like me who fucked up. I know it's gonna be a tough road."

The confession about Mrs. Dale's far-from-the-truth report during Adam's last visit poked at Bridget's conscience.

"I've been saving money. Saving for first and last months' rent for a bachelor pad. It won't be much. I'm hoping The Hawk'll eventually let Kyle come over unsupervised."

"I see . . ." There went Bridget's new life she'd built.

Trust the Lord, Emery had said. Bullshit. If Bridget didn't take control, she'd lose Kyle. She weaved slightly in her seat. No court would side in her favor unless she proved Adam as an unfit parent. And smearing another's reputation . . . her deception might win her Kyle, but at a horrible cost.

"*Kwe?*" Adam's soft voice glided over Bridget's skin.

Nail-driving-like spikes dug into her flesh. "Thanks for telling me about Cutter. We should go. It's already quarter-after-eight."

"I don't gotta be back till nine." His dark eyes held hope, and so did his gentle tone.

"I have things to do before I turn in."

"What kind of things?"

Bridget raised her chin. "Things."

"*Kwe*, the lobes of your ears are pink. They always turn

72

pink when you're not being upfront."

"My ears turn pink?" Someone should have told Bridget about this quirk. Jude had probably refrained from saying anything so he'd have one up on her. Damned brothers.

"Yep. They do. And don't say it's your earrings." Adam's husky chuckle tickled Bridget's skin. "They're pretty. Where'd you get 'em?"

She fingered the porcupine quill earrings with red, rose, and pink beads. "A young woman made them for me. She's a regular at the center."

"Where you work?"

"Yes. She designs and makes her own jewelry. She's been on the powwow trail all summer, making a killing at her booth. She's starting her second year for her BA at the end of August."

"The rez here already hold its powwow?"

"July the first."

"You and Kyle go?"

"No. We were busy."

Adam frowned.

Tough. Mom and Dad had flown in. They'd all gone camping, Jude's family included, at Sleeping Giant Park. "Now that you're here, maybe you can take Kyle next year."

"I will." Brightness returned to Adam's eyes. "Already thinking about getting him some new regalia. There's a woman at the Friendship Center who does that stuff."

"So does the girl who made my earrings." Bridget again fingered the one on the right of her lobe.

"She does?" Adam's lips came together, eyes still shining. "Maybe you can ask her if she'll make one for Kyle."

"I can . . ." Bridget clutched her purse against her chest. "I can do that."

"Great. It'd mean a lot to him. He seems to enjoy when I show him his culture."

"Yes, he does." Bridget wet her lips. "What was it like in there?" The question popped out before she could think or wonder why she'd asked.

Adam scrunched his eyebrows. "The pen?"

She nodded.

He withdrew the cigarettes and lit one. He puffed on the filter while pocketing his lighter. "Same ol' bullshit," he muttered as smoke escaped from between his lips and drifted over his crinkled eyes.

"What *bullshit*?"

"Keep your head low. Try stay outta trouble. Watch your back." He shrugged.

"Try?" There couldn't have been trouble if he'd been released on parole.

"Yep." The cigarette made a suction-popping sound from how hard he must have sucked on the filter. "There's always trouble going down." He held the butt between his index finger and thumb.

"How'd you stay out of trouble?" She set her purse on the bench.

"Told you already. Stuck to guys in the recovery program. Kept my mouth shut."

Bridget couldn't resist pointing out the obvious. "Uh . . . you never say much."

Adam took another drag. "I'm talking now, ain't I?"

"True." The heat in his gaze seemed to touch Bridget's cheek. She rubbed the purse strap.

"I don't got nothing to hide. 'Kay?"

"You were hiding something last time?"

"Nope. But I know my not speaking pissed you off."

"There's no reason to bring up the past. I told you I'd help and that's what I'm doing."

"Yeah, you agreed to help . . ." His gaze roamed around her face.

Bridget recoiled and glanced away.

"Y'know, *kwe*, we're doing a lot of dancing."

"Dancing?"

"Lookit me."

She forced herself to raise her head.

His dark eyes smoldered. He leaned forward. His hand stretched out, and he ran his strong fingers along her braid.

Sensuous heat and angry lightning erupted under Bridget's skin. "Don't you dare." The words hissed from her mouth.

"What're you afraid of, *kwe*?"

"Quit calling me that." The order snapped from deep inside Bridget's constricting chest. "You have no right calling me by that name. Not after what you did." She stood and yanked her purse off the bench.

He tilted his head up, his jawline tightening. "I know what I did, *kwe*. You remind me all the time."

"I do no such thing." How dare Adam turn this around as her fault.

"Yeah, you do. It's in your eyes. They hang me like a noose. It's in your lips. They condemn me like a villain. It's in your voice. You slap me with your tone."

"What'd you expect after what you did?" she huffed out. "You were charged with aggravated assault. The judge had every right to throw the book at you."

"I know what I did, *kwe*." Adam's voice remained flat. "I live with it every day. I don't take the easy way out and blame it on the booze."

"You were skidding around four months. I can only imagine what else you did." And no, she wasn't jealous.

"I drank. I drank some more. I did something really bad to another human being. Got arrested. Sat in remand until my trial. I won't say he deserved it. I won't say anything. I did it. I went to prison for it."

"And did you *only* drink?" She silently cuffed her rear end for continuing to poke at the damned same question.

Adam's thick lips tugged at the corner. "If you mean was I out screwing around? Nope. You're the only woman for me, *kwe*."

Delight exploded through Bridget's veins. Then she clamped a lock on her heart. Only a moron bought his answer. He'd been drunk for four months in Winnipeg. He must have picked up some woman in a bar.

"I was hurting bad." His voice sagged. "You think I was happy when you told me to fuck off? You killed me, *woman*."

The sharp tone of his last statement was pure insult, an affront to the feminine strength that had dragged Bridget up from the depths of Hell where Adam had stuck her. "If you want to continue speaking, tell *Dirty Harry* to leave. I only deal with *Mr. Darcy*."

Adam stood and set his enormous hands on his hips. "Mr. Who —? Look, I'll tell *Dirty Harry* to take a hike if you call off *Sarah Conner*. I'm not the *Terminator* sent back in time to harm you."

At his full height, Adam towered over Bridget, made her five-nine stance shrink to a doll. He'd reduced her to a doll, helpless in the possession of his hands, made to dance, talk, or walk under his orders.

Heat built in her lungs. She was too independent to draw back and scuttle away. No man provoked fear in her. The worst part was, she didn't fear Adam's physical presence, she feared the thick, steamy aroma of testosterone he forever used to challenge her, weaken her, seduce her. The masculine aroma dripped from the pits of his arms, his thick chest, and the bulge of his biceps.

"Out of my thirty-eight years, I fucked up thirty-seven of 'em. I ain't fucking up again."

"Thirty-seven?" His scent kept assaulting Bridget's knees, swirling around her, until she wobbled.

"Yeah. Thirty-seven. I can't count the year the three of us were a family. Me. You. Kyle."

Bridget's resolve continued to crumble. Adam kept dusting her femininity with his husky declarations, fierce scent, and sensual stare.

She pivoted on her heel and bolted for the truck. She'd dump him off at the halfway house and go home. If he wanted to tease and torment her during their drive, he could, but she'd don her mask of hate-fueled resentment created by him.

She pushed the button on the keys, and the locked doors opened.

The crunch of Adam's shoes carried on the cement. He was walking his determined strut without Bridget having to look—legs slamming one in front of the other, hands fisted, chin jutted, and eyes mean slits.

She slid into the truck. The passenger door opened, and Adam got in. His big presence saturated the cab.

This drive would be the longest ten minutes of Bridget's life.

When the truck pulled up at the halfway house, Adam's disgust threatened to spill over. No woman could slam on the brakes like Bridget. He threw off his seat belt. "I didn't mean to make you pissed."

"I'm not pissed." She stared straight ahead.

Adam cracked open the door. She was going to let him go? Damn her. Promising himself to use patience was a stupid idea. The woman was stubborn enough to wait out the next coming of Jesus.

The twelve-step program, the anger management classes,

his one-on-one counseling all screamed at him to leave his desires in the hands of his higher power. Yeah right. Creator had forgotten He'd shaped and breathed life into a woman a pack of mules couldn't push.

Welp, he could be stubborn, too. Adam shut the door.

Bridget almost jumped in her seat. "What're you doing? I told you I have things to do."

"Cut it. It's only eight-thirty. You're going home to pout." Adam folded his arms and sat back.

"P-p-pout?"

Any second his beloved *kwe's* internal volcano should erupt. Time for the countdown. *Ten, nine, eight, seven, six, five . . .*

"Listen here. Don't you dare assume anything about me. Got it?" Bridget swiveled to face him, steam almost exploding from her flared nostrils and flaming-red ears.

"Got it." Keeping his cool was easier than expected. Maybe because Bridget's temper had never unsettled Adam. Her spunk was the lighter to his wood. Any kind of wood. A certain kind of wood in his pants.

He shifted as much as he could in the seat. And these were big, comfy seats. He met Bridget's glittering eyes.

"*Kwe,* you've been pissed since you first looked at me. Let loose. I'm serious. Tell me what you really think of me." If cussing him out cleared the fog thickening between them, Adam could hack a slap or two.

Bridget's red lips flattened. "I have nothing to say because we have nothing between us but Kyle. That's it."

Adam's own temper grumbled at the back of his neck. His skin burned. This woman's words always cut a man's balls in half. No con in the pen knocked the wind from him like Bridget Maria Matawapit. He had one up on her, though. She'd never taken an anger management class or earned praises from the instructor.

This might secure him a smack or something else, but at

least he'd know the score. "*Kwe*, did I ever tell you how beautiful you are when you're pissed?"

The flash in Bridget's eyes died. The flatness of her lips faded. The fiery red shade coating her ears ebbed. Her mouth formed into a delicate O. Fire flickered behind her dark irises.

Adam's heart rattled. He lifted his hand and ran his index finger across her narrow jawline.

The smoothness of her skin softened the rough edge of his fingertip. When Bridget's gaze continued to hold his, she locked Adam in a moment he'd dreamed about behind bars with nothing but his beloved *kwe*'s picture to keep him company.

The tight bones of Bridget's jawline diminished beneath his touch. She kept staring. Adam's heart kept rattling. He leaned in and brushed his lips against hers. As soon as his mouth met Bridget's, her yielding lips released an ache in his chest. An ache he'd carried for almost four years. He moved his mouth into a light pucker. Bridget's kiss matched his sweet movements, and his heart swelled.

Her scent invaded him. The familiar feminine fragrance teased his muscles, stroked his skin, caressed his flesh. Her deep breaths fluttered against his ears. Their mouths moved in the same slow rhythm, a waltz of sensual heat full of longing and wanting.

His tongue yearned to taste her, claim her as his own again. He forced himself to draw back a breath from her. "*Kwe*," he whispered.

A puff of air from her lips skimmed Adam's skin. Bridget's smooth lids fluttered, along with her rich, thick lashes.

"I gotta go." Her voice was as drowsy as her eyes. Then her dreamy stare hardened. "I gotta go." This time her declaration matched the tension sharpening her jawline.

She shifted and stared straight ahead, delicate hands

braced on the steering wheel.

Adam had given Bridget something to think about, and that was what he'd intended to do from the start. That was enough for him. "Goodnight, *kwe*."

Bridget kept staring straight ahead.

He slipped from the truck. With the passenger door barely closed, she drove off.

Adam slid the cigarettes from his shirt pocket and stuck one between his lips. He dug around in his pocket and withdrew the lighter.

Her delicate scent and the lushness of her lips continued to pound through his veins. He'd set out to unearth whether she still possessed feelings for him, and she did.

Sleep wouldn't come easy tonight. Nope. Not at all. Her kiss had given him too much hope.

Maybe he should consider finding his own digs sooner rather than later. No, he couldn't. He was following the twelve steps. If he had a sponsor, the man would tell him to keep his dick under control.

Patience.

Chapter Nine: Nothing Up My Sleeve

"Hey, what's up?" Jude clicked his fingers against the glass table in the foyer. He wore his *don't-bullshit-me* look with his sweatpants and t-shirt.

Bridget should have spent her time cultivating a tribe of tight-knit girlfriends instead of spending her life volunteering for causes she believed in and devoting every other second to shimmying up the career ladder. The only place she had to run to was her big brother. She slammed the door shut.

"Where's Char?"

"At a meeting ... I think." Jude meandered toward the kitchen. "C'mon, I need a beer."

"No alcohol for me. I'm driving." Bridget followed him down the hall. Her heels clicked against the hardwood floors. "What meeting?"

"Work ... maybe. I can't remember." Jude swung open the fridge door and pointed. "There you go. A six-pack of your favorite alcohol-free wild mango coolers we buy for spoiled lil' ol' you."

"Thanks." Bridget cupped the cooler.

She plopped on the stool at the eating bar attached to the island. The waterfall granite counter top cooled her arms where heat still prickled from Adam's kiss.

"Well?" Jude twisted off the beer cap. "What brings you here this late? You told me you had a meeting. What's with all these meetings? Summer isn't over yet. Last time I checked the calendar, it was still August. I'm starting to think you and Char are up to something."

"I have no clue what Char's up to." Bridget took a long drink off the cooler and washed away the warmth in her throat and Adam's scent on her lips.

"Neither do I." Jude snatched a dishcloth from the vegetable sink built into the island and wiped down the already clean counter.

"Did you ask Char?"

He shook his head. "Never mind her. It's late. Where'd you really go?"

"Is Kyle in bed?"

"Already tucked away for the night. Where'd you really go?" Jude stopped scrubbing.

Bridget took another drink. She set the bottle on the counter. "For coffee."

"Adam?"

"How'd you guess?" She shifted on the stool.

"Why?" Jude's investigative dark eyes capable of penetrating a person's deepest and darkest secrets replicated Dad's x-ray vision whenever he'd caught Bridget in one of her teenage lies.

"He needs my help." There was no point in lying. This was Jude.

"Come off it." His lips pinched. "Help? What—does he need a Bonnie to his Clyde to rob a bank now?"

"No. Not a bank. The Beer Store."

"Too true. As if he'd pay for his booze like everyone else does." If Jude's tone got any drier, he'd turn the rain forest into a desert.

"You have every right to hate him. Everyone does. Try to remember he's Kyle's father."

"Father? How much time has he spent with Kyle?" Jude

held up his fingers. "Let's see. Three years? Tops?"

"Three and a half."

"Yeah, and for year seven he sees him an hour a week. He's not Kyle's father. Just the sperm donor."

"He's making an effort." If Bridget slumped any more in the chair, she'd be sitting on the floor soon. "If his new job works out, he's going to rent a bachelor apartment. It's where he was putting his money when he was on day parole in Winnipeg."

"Did he ask you for money?" Suspicion clouded Jude's gaze.

"No. He asked for help. He owes a debt of gratitude to a man in Stony who sponsored Adam while he was incarcerated."

"He wants you to help a con?" Jude's eyes widened.

Bridget scraped her heel against the foothold on the stool. "Emery spent a lot of time with convicts as part of his field work."

"He sure did . . ." Jude positioned his hands on the counter and leaned in. "But he wasn't letting them con him."

Annoyance gathered under Bridget's skin. "I'm not being conned. The body they pulled from the McIntyre River is this man's daughter. Okay?"

"The police only found a body. Nobody knows who it is." Jude raised his finger like Dad did when laying down the law.

Bridget straightened in the chair and also leaned in. "The authorities called the man at Stony. He's Sheena Keesha's father. She was in care when she died."

"Maybe if this man thought of his daughter first, instead of doing who-knows-what to land him in prison, she'd be alive." Jude drew in his cheeks.

If Bridget mentioned Cutter was in for murder, big brother would end up in Stony for murdering her ex-fiancé. "Adam owes this man a great debt. The man simply asked him to find out what happened to his daughter."

"Adam isn't supposed to be patronizing bars or any other places where alcohol's served." Jude tapped his finger against the counter. "He can't be two feet near an ex-con. How's he supposed to find out anything? He sure as shit won't learn what really happened by talking to honest, hard-working people."

"That's why he asked me to help. He doesn't want to jeopardize his parole or his chances at . . ." Bridget gulped. " . . . jeopardize his chance at getting Kyle back."

Jude's firm jaw slackened. His mouth fell open. Then he pressed his lips together, shaking his head. "You're kidding me. He doesn't deserve Kyle back. Not after what he did. You've been . . . we've been . . . everyone but Adam's been caring for his son while he's been playing *New Jack City*."

A wave of helplessness washed over Bridget. "I can't say no. You know damn well what the police are like. It doesn't matter if they're local, provincial, or federal. Look what happened to that girl in Winnipeg. She was murdered and thrown into the river, and a jury still let the man walk. You know as well as I do there's no justice for aboriginal people."

A flame flickered in her chest. "The Catholic Women's Association can do all the walks they want, our own people can call for three hundred and sixty-five days to wear red in honor of the murdered and missing Indigenous women, but whether we like it or not, the general public doesn't care. The only coverage we get is from our own television channel. How many people watch the Indigenous Peoples Network, besides Indigenous people?"

"Girl, you should have been a lawyer." Jude flopped on the stool, and his sagging shoulders followed. "With you as his attorney, Adam never would've gone to prison."

At least Jude was no longer upset. Bridget couldn't help

the snicker in her throat. She giggled.

Jude also snickered.

"You know what the children in care mean to me." Pleading bled into her words. "A sixteen-year-old girl, who was pregnant, and in foster care, could have been murdered."

"And what happens if you find out the truth?" Jude reached for his beer. A half-smile replaced his x-ray stare.

"I don't know. Adam only wants me to follow some leads at The Gator."

Her answer wiped the smile from Jude's face. "The Gator? No way." Dad's infamous gesture reappeared in Jude's finger-pointing. "Every week someone's getting shot or stabbed. The police should have built their headquarters next door."

"Adam has it covered. He has a friend who works there." The words kept spilling from Bridget's mouth in rapid succession. "This friend is a bouncer. He'll take care of me."

"What about the diocesan council? You have a chance at president-elect." Jude threw out one hand, palm up. "How will they feel if they hear you're hanging around The Gator? Your dream's to become the president of the Catholic Women's Association at the national level. It's been your dream ever since Auntie bought you your membership."

"I doubt they'll rescind the nomination because I'm going to a bar to find information."

"Will they know this?"

"No." Bridget winced. "Adam wants us to be quiet about it."

"There you go." Jude again threw up his hand. "There'll be rumors running around you're hanging at The Gator and some outlaw biker's ol' lady."

"I have to do this. I promised him I would." There was no getting through to Jude, dammit.

"You don't owe him anything. Not after what he did to

you and Kyle."

Why was Bridget even debating about Adam? Her family would never forgive him for his reckless and irresponsible behavior. And if they wouldn't, why should she? Was The Gator for Sheena Keesha's sake or Adam's?

"I can always back out if it gets dangerous. I'm going to check it out at least."

"You're gonna do what you're gonna do no matter what I say." Jude's flaring nostrils reeked of disgust. "Dad should've done more than ground you when we were growing up. Maybe if he would've taken a strap to your backside, you'd listen for once."

Bridget squealed. "How can you say that?"

Jude glared at the fridge. He then directed his narrowed eyes at her. "Is it really over between you two? Is this why you're helping him?"

His accusation sent judders of shock through Bridget's limbs. "No!"

"I don't want to see another Emery and Darryl situation." Big brother mode was in Jude's lecturing tone and stare. "Darryl caused a lot of problems for Mom, Dad, and the church. If Darryl hadn't met the family halfway, it would've been pretty hard for me to approve of him when Emery married the guy behind our backs."

Bridget rubbed her brow. Only she'd understood Emery's feelings for Darryl and how torn her brother had been over loving a man, something Emery had considered forbidden, which was why he'd contemplated the priesthood in the first place. At least everything had worked out for him.

She wasn't like Emery, though, who'd always conformed to what Mom and Dad wanted. Or what Jude wanted. Or what Catechism demanded. She had her own set of beliefs, many that clashed with the Church's doctrine. "Maybe I should reconsider running for president-elect."

"Wh-what?"

"I knew about Emery and Darryl's affair long before anyone else did. I caught them when they were teenagers. I didn't say anything because I didn't think what they were doing was wrong."

"You didn't tell anyone at all?"

"No. It was Emery's business. Who was I to interfere? He was tormented enough. Tormented enough to enroll at seminary."

"I told him I understood. We had a long chat when I was up visiting Mom and Dad last month. Dad called me." The tension lining Jude's eyes and mouth softened. "He told me to talk sense into Emery. Normally, I would've, but at times I agree, Mom and Dad have to pack up and leave nineteen seventy and relocate to the twenty-first century."

"It's nice to know you have a liberal mind." Bridget should have remembered Jude always understood. He wasn't a true hard-ass like Dad. Close, though, but not quite.

"It's not about being liberal. It's about being realistic. They're times I have to keep my mouth shut. I'm a principal for the Catholic District School Board. I'd get my ass canned if I told them I support gay marriage."

"So if you can support gay marriage, how do you feel about ex-convicts?"

"Aww, geez." Jude took a drink of beer. He set the bottle down and rested his palms on the counter. "I don't like when people use excuses to justify what they did. Lookit Darryl. He's an intergenerational survivor of the residential schools. He never attended one, but his parents and aunt did. He didn't use their deaths as an excuse to become a criminal or an alcoholic."

What Jude said was true. When Emery had chosen religion over love during their teenaged years, Darryl had been hell-bent on revenge.

"Maybe he didn't abuse drugs or alcohol, but he did have it out for the Catholic Church."

"The same goes for Dad," Jude said in his know-it-all tone. "The thing is, he reconciled his differences with the church. If anyone should've held a grudge, Dad's your man. He went to one of those schools."

"Dad suffered from alcoholism before he met Mom."

"Dad also put a plug in the jug after he started attending church."

Jude was always on the other side of the lawn. He'd never understand her viewpoint. "I'm trying to say everyone suffers in different ways, and they use different coping mechanisms to survive what they've endured. For Darryl, it was revenge. For Dad, it was, um, using non-native women and beating on their men."

"Are you trying to tell me Adam's problems are intergenerational?"

"I don't know if they are or aren't. All I know is he was physically abused when he was growing up and constantly neglected. His sisters raised him while someone should've been raising them. Those girls were wild from what he told me."

Bridget threw her hands against her temples. If she understood Adam's motivations for turning to alcohol, anger shouldn't continue to claw up her spine at the mere thought of him.

"If you feel that way, then by all means, invite Adam to Healing the Spirit." Jude buttered his words with a thick layer of sarcasm.

"He's on parole. He'd have to get special permission from his PO. He also started a new job. I don't think the manager would let him."

"Healing the Spirit is up his alley. Or should I say his prison range? The workshop's about reconciliation between residential school survivors and the following generations affected by them. Maybe he'll have some kind of break-through and never land in prison again after attending it." Jude continued to butter his words with sarcasm.

"His PO's supposed to support Adam's transition into society. I'm sure this man could persuade Adam's employer to let him take a week's leave."

Jude had made a good point. Mom and Dad had fought hard to host the workshop the diocese had developed for First Nations and Christian communities suffering from Indian Residential School syndrome. The contribution Mom and Dad had asked on behalf of the parish to host Healing the Spirit was what had set off Darryl's plan of revenge against the local church in the first place.

Bridget had booked a week's vacation to assist Mom and the parish's Catholic Women's Association with cooking, cleaning, serving meals for the participants, and readying the church basement for the workshop.

She'd ask Adam to consider attending. Maybe he'd have a breakthrough and never again pick up the bottle.

Kissing Bridget continued to roll through Adam's thoughts. Her moist flesh. Her soft lips. Her breath steaming the depression above his mouth.

He flopped on his bed. The mattress creaked and groaned.

Someone knocked on the door.

Adam checked the clock. Nine-thirty. The visitor had to be Logan. He did go to a meeting this evening.

"Enter."

Logan scurried into the room. "How'd it go? Did she find out anything?"

"Didn't go. Went for coffee. Told her why I need her

help."

"Y'mean she's not gonna do it?" Logan's face fell.

"She'll help. She always helps, even when she's pissed."

"Is she your girlfriend?" Logan plopped in the chair by the window.

Girlfriend? What a question to ask. "Nope."

"Ex-girlfriend?"

Adam sighed and sat up. "She's a friend."

Logan snickered. "You don't seem like the kind of guy who has babes as friends."

"Later, kid. I gotta shower."

"Shower? This late?" Logan bolted from the chair and blocked the door. "There's something else I gotta ask you."

"What's that." Adam grabbed his cigarettes off the dresser.

"They talked about sponsorship at the meeting tonight. They said the best way to pick a sponsor is, duh, a no-brainer—someone with more sobriety than you and who works the program. They also said this person should have what you want. Y'know. I was wondering . . ." Pleading reflected in Logan's blue eyes.

Adam gripped his lighter.

"I was wondering if you'd be my sponsor."

Logan's request was a pointed shotgun fired at Adam's chest, spraying him with a cartridge of pellets. "Me?" *I'm a fucking ex-con.*

"Yeah. I want you."

"They're other guys who—"

"Nope. It's gotta be you."

They were living in the same digs and someone had to watch this kid's back. "You got a Big Book?" Adam motioned at his blue copy of the twelve-step program on the dresser.

"Yeah. They gave us one in 'hab."

"What steps you already take?"

"Only up to three. They said we have to do the rest with our sponsor."

"I got rules."

"Rules?" Logan squinted.

"Yup. No using. Meetings every night. Mornings—daily meditations. Read your Big Book before going to sleep. Got it?"

"Yeah, yeah, yeah. I got it." Logan shook his head a good eight times.

"Let's go smoke." For some strange reason, anxiety inched up Adam's spine. He wasn't sure why. But it was the same dreadful feeling that had seeped through his veins and buzzed in his head whenever something bad was about to happen as an enforcer for the Winnipeg Warriors. The last time he'd felt this way, he'd gotten jumped at a drug pad he'd been checking and had received a bullet in his thigh.

CHAPTER TEN: I WON'T PAY YOUR PRICE

All week Adam had stopped himself from picking up the phone and calling Bridget. After what he'd pulled, she needed space, and hopefully the space leaned toward the positive instead of the negative.

He kept himself glued to the windowsill in the visitation room where the old crab sat in her usual chair, taking notes. With the amount of writing The Hawk did, she must be penning his biography, a real nasty one, probably called Fucked-Up Failed Felons.

The door opened. Kyle bounded into the room, grinning. Behind him, Bridget meandered in, nodding, and plopped in the chair beside Mrs. Dale.

At least she hadn't yanked a tomahawk from her purse and cracked open Adam's skull.

Kyle sprinted forward. Adam scrambled to his haunches. He opened his arms, and his boy landed straight on Adam's chest. The scent of Kyle's clean soap and innocent warmth smothered Adam like a comfortable blanket.

"You're getting bigger, ya little rug rat."

"Uncle Emery said the same thing. I always make him catch me." Kyle flashed his missing front tooth. "What're we doing today? Can we go outside?"

"No can do. Mrs. Dale says we have to stay here."

"But why?" Kyle turned to Mrs. Dale who watched them over her narrow glasses. "Can we go outside? Please?"

Mrs. Dale's upturned lips bordered on cracking her ice-like face. "We have rules to follow, as you do at home and school. My supervisor expects visits to happen here."

"Will you ever let us go to the park together?" A tinge of whining floated on Kyle's question.

"That will be up to your father. His progress depends upon it."

Great. The old bat was going to make Adam play the heavy.

Kyle frowned. "What does she mean?"

"She takes notes." Adam pointed at the clipboard. "The more she takes when she sees us together, she'll be able to tell her supervisor our visits are going great."

"Mom, do you have to take notes, too?"

Bridget blushed. "No. I'm asked to come to the visits so you're comfortable."

"Will you always bring me?"

"Yes."

"Will you always sit here?"

Bridget shifted in the chair. "We'll talk about it later. Okay?"

The Hawk had said in time Bridget would be asked to leave the room for Adam and Kyle to bond personally under the old hard-ass's supervision. Obviously, Bridget hadn't bothered to tell Kyle this because she'd expected Adam to fail.

"Why later, Mom?"

"Because you're visiting your dad right now."

Kyle stared at Adam. "What're we going to do?"

"First, we're gonna eat these." Adam reached behind him where he'd left the package on the square table. "Look what I made for you."

Eyes dancing, Kyle peeked inside the white box. "What are they?" He licked his lips.

"Nanaimo bars."

"Oh boy. Mom . . . please, please, please can I have one?"

"You may eat only one. We're going to have supper soon."

Better get this show on the road. His visits lasted one hour. From what he understood, Bridget was done work for the day. She must have arranged with the board of directors to have the last hour off from her fancy office on Wednesdays.

Clutching his box of Nanaimo bars, Kyle strolled between Bridget and Adam. Mrs. Dale brought up the rear. At four-thirty on the second floor, no telephone conversations, clients complaining, or the usual voices invading the sterile white hallway came from the many offices.

They reached the elevator. Much to Bridget's surprise, Adam accompanied them. Normally, he disappeared into Mrs. Dale's spotless office after visits.

Kyle twirled. He pushed the down button.

"Have a good evening." Mrs. Dale vanished behind her office door.

Adam pressed his big hand on the wall. "You have time to think it over?"

"Think what over?" Kyle gazed up at his dad.

The elevator doors opened, and they piled inside.

While Kyle went through his usual routine in an elevator, Adam leaned against the wall, staring at Bridget.

"Yes, I did. It'll have to be next week. I have a lot to do."

"When next week?"

"I thought Friday, since it'll be busy then."

"Friday it is."

The doors opened.

Nobody sat on the gray chairs or stood at the main counter where the receptionist greeted clients as Bridget ushered

Kyle through the reception area. They headed outside.

"What's keeping you busy?"

Bridget withdrew her keys and steered Kyle to the parking lot. "We're nearing the end of August. Classes are starting. Students are making full use of the center."

"Maybe I'll be one of those students one day."

"You're going to school, Dad?" Kyle exclaimed. "With me?"

Adam chuckled. "Nah. I already took grade two. I'm talking about the university."

"Are you going to be a professor?"

"Not a professor. Maybe an entrepreneur."

"What's that?" Kyle rested his index finger on his lip.

Bridget stopped at the truck and opened the back door.

"Someone who owns their own business." Adam plopped Kyle in the backseat. He reached over and drew the seat belt across the boy's chest and lap.

There was no point in Bridget telling Adam that Kyle could get in the truck and buckle his own seat belt. He probably welcomed any opportunity to help his son.

"I'll see you next Wednesday. Okay?" Adam's palm grazed Kyle's stubble of hair.

"Okay, Dad."

Adam shut the door. He followed Bridget around the truck.

"And what're you up to tonight?" Bridget kicked herself for asking. As if she needed to engage in small-talk.

"Meeting. Always a meeting." Adam opened the door. He motioned for her to get in.

They were not behaving like a family. Adam was only being polite. And Bridget would keep telling herself this over and over.

"What about you?"

"The usual. Laundry. Dinner. Bath for Kyle."

"Yeah?" His dark eyes crinkled.

She slid inside the truck. "What time's your meeting done?"

"I get back before nine."

"Have a good meeting, then."

"Always do."

"Mom, aren't we going to give Dad a ride?" Kyle called from the backseat.

Bridget's throat seemed to shut closed. If she didn't invite Adam, she'd disappoint Kyle. "Do you need a ride?"

"Sure. Would save me on bus fare." Adam rounded the truck.

He sure hadn't hesitated. Bridget trembled while Adam opened the door and got in. His masculine scent invaded the interior, skimming Bridget's skin.

Squirming, she glanced at the screen image on the dashboard and backed from the parking spot.

Adam drew the seat belt strap across his strong chest and flat stomach.

Huffing out a breath, Bridget guided the truck to the street.

"Can Dad stay for supper, Mom?"

Bridget gaped at Adam who simply grinned.

"I don't think Mrs. Dale would approve. Remember, she supervises you and your dad's visits for a reason. She must be present at all times."

"She's not here now, Mom."

"She isn't, is she?" Panic thumped at the back of Bridget's neck. "Will we get into trouble?" She slammed on the brake at the stop sign.

"Dunno." Adam shrugged. "Only if she finds out. I'm not saying anything. Are you?"

"No. No. No. Why would I?"

"Can we ask Mrs. Dale if Dad can come over for supper?"

"I'd have to call, and she's already done work for the evening. He can't come tonight."

"Aww . . ." From the sound of the disappointment in Kyle's voice, his lower lip protruded.

"We have rules to follow. Mrs. Dale explained this earlier. We can't disobey the rules." Bridget used her firmest tone. She guided them onto the next street.

Kyle's downturned lower lip appeared in the rearview mirror.

Adam craned his neck. "It's okay, bud. There's always next time."

"Really? For sure?" Delight gushed from Kyle's mouth.

How dare Adam finagle an invite by giving Kyle false hope. When Bridget called Adam tonight, he'd get an earful.

"Easy, *kwe*," Adam said under his breath.

"Don't call me that anymore." Bridget also kept her furious voice low. "We're going to talk when you return from your meeting."

"I didn't—"

"You did, too."

"No, I didn't. I was only trying to—"

"You're forgetting I'm his foster mother. You asked me to care for him after you screwed up and went to prison, which I'm trying to do, if you'd let me."

"What the . . ." Adam grunted. "I'm his father. I'm trying to get my kid back."

She glared straight ahead. Everything always had to be about Adam. Nothing had changed.

"Oh man." He almost crushed his cowboy hat in his big hand. "What'd I do now?"

"I said we'll talk later." End of conversation.

Going to a meeting had been the smart thing to do. Whatever Bridget was pissed about, she'd give Adam a list of complaints in a matter of seconds. He should be able to keep his temper in check.

He sat in the lounge at the halfway house, waiting for the phone to ring. At least everyone was in their rooms. They didn't need to hear him and his ex-fiancée tossing angry words back and forth. Hell, there was always some poor sucker holding the phone to his ear, looking like he ate a mouthful of dirt while his wife, girlfriend, ex-wife, or ex-something blasted him over the wire.

Too bad none of them could afford cell phones. At least they'd have some privacy by retreating to their rooms while getting bitched out. But guys fresh from the iron houses or rehab didn't have a dime to fork over. Cell service in the Canadian Shield wasn't cheap.

Maybe Adam could afford one now that he was working. Bad idea. Every dollar must go to his new digs, such as first and last months' rent, damage deposit, groceries since he'd have to buy the essentials of salt, pepper, ketchup, and whatnot.

The phone rang. He picked up. "Joseph Howarth Society."

"Oh, I didn't realize you were allowed to answer." Bridget's voice was naturally tight, as Adam had expected.

"Whoever's around answers. Was waiting for you."

"I'll get to the point. You gave Kyle a false impression when you said you'd come over for dinner the next time. There was no first time. And there'll be no next time. Your supervised visits are happening for a reason."

The grit in her voice raked Adam's skin. "Listen to me, *kwe*. He asked if I'd come for dinner. What was I supposed to say to my own son? Yeah, *my* son. My flesh and blood. Tell him never?"

"Your son, who you abandoned and neglected, when you

didn't think of him—"

"I did my time. I paid my debt. How long you gonna hold this over my head?" This woman's mouth never stopped running. Adam stood, fisting and un-fisting his free hand.

"And what happens the next time you get drunk and beat someone? Now that you know I won't let you drag Kyle into your drunkenness, will you sneak him out of the city and leave him at one of your sisters' places? You told me yourself the messes they made of their lives."

Oh man, Bridget sure knew how to deal low blows. And she'd never forgive him, much less forget the biggest mistake of his life. Anger management. Adam couldn't say things he'd regret. The twelve steps. He was responsible for his reaction to her actions.

"Yeah, my family's fucked up. I hear it from you all the time. Yours ain't so perfect, either."

"No, my family's not, but we'd never do what you did. Have I gone out drinking while watching your son? Have I gone into a bar and beat on a man?"

"You don't know all the details. He deserved it." Adam squeezed his eyes shut. He wasn't supposed to blame others for his behavior.

Bridget gasped.

"Never mind. I shouldn't have said that." Adam flopped in the chair. "Man, you really know what buttons to push. I did my time. I paid for my crime. All I want is a second chance to raise my son."

"Jude's right." The anger left her voice, and Bridget's tone dropped a few decibels.

"What's that?"

"He said you'd benefit from Healing the Spirit."

"Healing the what?" Cripes, this woman could switch gears. Now what was going through her brain?

"Healing the Spirit. It's a workshop my parents are hosting at the reserve. It's been in development for a few months now. It's for survivors of the Indian Residential Schools and their children and grandchildren."

Adam rubbed his chin. They'd spoken about the Indian Residential Schools many times during the healing workshops for aboriginal men in the iron house. His grandparents had been forced to go to those schools. The same for his parents. During sharing circles, older inmates had spoken about the horrors they'd endured at the schools.

"It's legit?"

"Yes. Healing the Spirit was developed by a chief, an apostolic sister, and a bishop to address the legacy the schools left on First Nations people and Christian communities. My parents hosted the first workshop about five years ago. It was a huge success, so successful, the people asked for another one."

"When is it?"

"After the Labor Day weekend. I'll be gone a full week. A day to set up and a day to clean up."

"You're . . . you're . . . you're . . . going?" Adam did his best not to sputter.

"Of course. I volunteered for the last one. Cooking. Cleaning. Wherever they need me."

"What about Kyle?" She couldn't leave Adam for a week.

"I already made arrangements. Jude's watching him."

"Jude's not going?"

"No. School'll have started. He'll be at work, and Kyle will be in class."

Adam clenched his teeth. "I'm his father. You could've told me."

"Why? Jude'll take Kyle to his Wednesday afternoon visit."

"Classes are starting at the university. Won't the center need you? You're the executive director." Somehow, he must convince Bridget to stay.

"I already cleared my holidays with the board of directors. I have a great staff. They'll be fine."

Was this Bridget's sly way to convince Adam to attend Healing the Spirit? If so, she'd done a good job. His parole officer would approve. The ornery cuss was supposed to help Adam rehabilitate. "Fine. I'll talk to my PO. He'll talk to my supervisor. If they approve, I'll go."

Bridget's sharp intake of breath almost deafened Adam. "What're you talking about?"

"I'm gonna attend that healing workshop. Shit, I might as well. I've attended every other healing workshop the prison offered."

"I wasn't inviting—"

"You recommended it. Not me." The woman could take some damned responsibility for once, instead of blaming him for everything. "I'll talk to you later. I'm over my limit on the phone."

A lie, but big deal. Adam had to hang up before he lost his temper. "I'll talk to you tomorrow." He set down the receiver.

CHAPTER ELEVEN: I'M YOUR MAN

Bridget paced the living room. The clock read nine-thirty, which meant eight-thirty in Ottertail Lake. Mom and Dad would freak when they saw Adam's name on the workshop participant list. She snatched the cordless phone and speed-dialed Emery's number.

"Hello."

Thank goodness he'd answered. "It's me."

"How're you doing?"

Instead of giving Jude's *what's up* Bridget received whenever she called him, Emery, of course, took the time to ask, so Bridget might as well blurt it out. "Adam's coming to Healing the Spirit. I know you and Darryl offered to billet participants."

"Really? That's great. Can he afford the flight?"

"His PO will figure something out. Since it's a healing workshop designed for people affected by the residential schools, Adam's family qualifies big time."

"I think it's a great idea. How do you feel about it?"

Her brother's soothing voice kneaded away the tight knots grinding against the bones of Bridget's shoulders. "Jude suggested it. I'm pretty sure he was being sarcastic, though."

Emery's soft chuckle carried through the receiver. "That sounds like Jude. You suggested it to Adam?"

"I guess I did. We were . . . um, having a heated discussion."

"Let me guess. You told him he should attend the workshop because he needs it more than the people who've already signed up. And you said so in a, well, a less than diplomatic way."

Bridget toyed with one of the angel figurines on the end table. "Yes."

"I don't understand what the problem is, then. He can stay here. We have a spare room. Darryl's already signed up. Adam can ride with him."

"You're still going to train as a facilitator?"

"Yes." He paused for about five seconds.

Uh-oh, little brother was thinking.

"Are you happy he's coming?"

Are you out of your mind? "What Adam does isn't my business."

"He's Kyle's father," Emery gently reminded her.

The desperation twitching Bridget's muscles tumbled from her mouth. "He's trying to get close to us, and I don't like it."

"There's always a *why* to everything we feel. What is your *why*?" Stupid Emery kept speaking in his calm, reassuring voice. Didn't anything rile baby brother?

Bridget huffed to the kitchen. "I worked hard building a life for me. For Kyle. For the two of us. Adam wasn't supposed to be released this early. The judge threw the book at him. He should have served two-thirds of his time."

"The parole board believed it's best he serves the rest of his time outside, otherwise they wouldn't have granted him day parole, and then full parole." Emery and his damned common sense. "I'd say they felt he'd changed for the better. Considering his record, starting all the way from his juvenile years, this time he's making a difference. He made a difference before he met you. He sobered up. He left Winnipeg and moved to Thunder Bay to start a new life. What did you see in him why you agreed to a date? To marriage?"

Why oh why did he ask such hard questions? Bridget leaned against the counter and bit her lower lip. She couldn't share about Adam's swagger, his sexy grin, his deep voice, and the way he'd looked directly at her whether she was speaking or silent had not only curled her toes, but had curled her hair, even the hair between her legs.

As for what was within Adam, he tried, he really did. He was kind. Considerate. Thoughtful. Giving. A true gentleman. He possessed the qualities from the warriors of long ago.

"I assume you answered my question." Emery softly chuckled. "Try to remember why you gave him a chance. True, he messed up. He really messed up. But consider who our Lord chose for disciples. Men like Adam. In the Gospel of Luke, our Lord was crucified between two criminals. One understood his sins and accepted his punishment. He asked Jesus to remember him. Jesus obliged."

Bridget hugged herself.

"Adam understands what he did was wrong. He accepted his penance. He's forgiven by God. Although God forgave him, have we, the people he was locked away from as unfit for society, also forgiven him?"

"You would use the Bible against me." Bridget slammed the cutting board on the island.

"I'm not using the Bible against you. I'm sharing with you what we've learned as Christians and why we attend Mass."

"Fine, I can work on forgiving him, but it doesn't mean I'm going to give up Kyle or . . ." She stabbed the steak knife into the cutting board. They'd acted like a family when she'd driven Adam back to the halfway house. Kyle was eagerly accepting his dad in his life.

"How does Kyle feel?"

"He's . . . he's happy to see his, uh, dad. He, um, can't wait for their visits. He's starting to complain that a week is too long." The rest of the words rushed from her mouth.

"Have you told your caseworker this?"

No. She's writing awful things about Adam, and I'm not saying anything in his defense.

"Have you?"

"No." She winced.

"I think you should." Emery spoke as if he were present, his gentle gaze prodding Bridget to do the right thing.

"Then it's mission accomplished for Adam. He'll have Kyle back." The cold, gritty taste of bitterness crept into Bridget's mouth.

"I know it's tough. We all love him. None of us want to lose him. But we have to remember Adam's his father."

"Sure. When it's convenient for him." The bitterness on her tongue flooded her reply. "When it isn't, everyone else has to take care of his son while he does his thing."

"I don't think landing in prison is what he wanted." Emery's voice remained relaxing cotton.

"So you want me to give up Kyle?"

"I didn't say that. I said Adam is Kyle's father. If the roles were reversed, wouldn't you want a second chance?"

"How many chances do you give someone? You know the saying. Fool me once, shame on you. Fool me twice, shame on me."

"I understand he didn't live up to his responsibilities the first time. This is where second chances happen. He's asking for one. Do you think he deserves one?"

Bridget grumbled. Her brother and his logic. Why couldn't Emery react with emotion like everyone else? Because his faith was too strong. He always sought answers from God first. As should she.

"Fine. Maybe he does." Her voice shrank while she shrank against the kitchen counter. "I know I'm only the foster mother. I know God only asked me to care for Kyle as a . . . caregiver, but this doesn't mean I'm going to be happy

Maggie Blackbird

to hand him over if the caseworker gives Adam a flying-colors grade."

"You're not *only the foster mother*. Kyle sees you as his mother. God has a plan. Maybe you should trust Him to slowly reveal His plan."

"And what plan would that be?"

"I don't know. I'm not God."

Bridget should have expected such an answer. "Fine. I'll do my best to let God take care of this." *Not! So not!*

Bridget held the hymnal, singing the last song after Father Arnold had given the concluding rites, dismissing the congregation with his blessing. Kyle stood beside her, holding tight to the pew in front of them where Jude, Charlene, Noah, and Rebekah stood.

The overhead fans spinning round and round kept the packed church from becoming too hot.

When the pipe organ stopped playing, Bridget shut the hymnal.

"Can we go now? Can we go now?" Kyle shuffled in the pew.

"Yes."

"Here he is." Jude gestured, his dimples appearing.

A tall man with blond hair, ice-water blue eyes, and broad shoulders sashayed up the aisle, moving against the people leaving their pews and heading for the narthex.

Bridget dug her nails into the leather of her purse. What on earth was Jude doing?

"This is Stephen Baker. He's visiting his mother for the week. Stephen, this is my wife, Charlene. My kids, Rebekah and Noah. My sister, Bridget. And her foster son, Kyle." Using his hand, Jude made a sweeping motion. "Everyone, I met Stephen at the principals' workshop that was held on Thursday and Friday. Stephen's the big pooh-bah of Sacred

106

Heart in Kenora."

Mrs. Baker approached, a recent member of the parish's Catholic Women's Association after relocating to Thunder Bay at the start of spring, who always smelled of rich perfume. "Good morning. Forgive my tardiness. I was chatting with a couple of ladies. I see everyone met my son."

"Good morning, Mrs. Baker. I was about to tell everyone I asked Stephen if he'd join us for brunch, and suggested he ask you to join us." Deception didn't lurk in Jude's smile, so maybe he wasn't attempting to play matchmaker.

"Yes. Yes. Stephen told me." Mrs. Baker tittered. "It's a pleasure. Always a pleasure. Everyone in Thunder Bay is as kind and friendly as they are in Kenora."

"Did you reserve enough seats?" Bridget made sure to send her brother a full-out stink eye.

Jude's upper lip tugged at the corner, but he refrained from smirking. "Stephen's a fan of the Benny's chain. He asked if we could eat there instead of The Bistro. Since he's our guest, I said yes."

Okay, there wasn't a need for Bridget to panic. Thunder Bay had two Benny's. "Which one?"

"The one on Arthur."

Bridget's mouth dried. She couldn't blame Jude for causing an uncomfortable situation because the dumb-ass had no idea Adam worked at Benny's.

This was Emery's fault and his talk about fate.

Life couldn't get any worse, and why should Bridget care that Adam would see her at the restaurant? Who she joined for brunch wasn't any of his business. Still, her hands trembled from sitting beside Stephen to her left and Kyle to her right.

Since it was eleven o'clock, everyone who attended one of the many churches in the neighborhood filled the tables and booths, all decked out in their Sunday finest.

The waitress had already taken their orders. Bridget added a dash of cream and two sweeteners to her coffee. At least they were seated by the window and could watch the traffic humming up and down Arthur Street.

"You're not a fan of sugar?" Stephen's white teeth appeared as he smiled a cozy smile, the kind a man bestowed on a woman during a date.

"No. I try watch whatever I eat. I'm not one of those health freaks." Bridget stirred the coffee, thankful to keep her hands busy. "But I'm careful about what goes into my mouth."

"Mom says too much sugar wrecks my teeth." Kyle lifted his glass of milk. "She said this is good for me because it makes my teeth stronger."

"It sure does." Stephen's eyes twinkled. "What you're doing is quite honorable."

"Excuse me?" All Bridget had done was stir coffee.

"Being a foster mother."

"Oh." She laughed. "There's nothing honorable about it. I love caring for him." She ran her hand along Kyle's prickly, short hair.

"Almost four years, Mom says." Kyle raised his fingers. "That's how long we've been together."

"Really? I bet you love it, hey?" Stephen asked.

"Yep. Dad's back. I see him on Wednesdays at the place where children go if they don't have a mom and dad. A lady watches us. She takes notes. Mom's there, too."

Bridget's face burned hot.

"Oh?" Stephen's mink brow arched. "I bet you enjoy that, don't you?" His blue eyes warmed again.

"I do. Me and Mom gave Dad a ride after our last visit. It was fun. Mom's going to ask Mrs. Dale if Dad can have supper with us. There are rules we have to follow, Mom said.

Mrs. Dale always has to be there when we see Dad."

"Honey, I don't think this is an appropriate conversation at the dinner table." For the second time Bridget smoothed Kyle's hair. "Remember, we're supposed to talk about fun stuff. Tell Mr. Baker what grade you'll start right away."

"Two." Kyle again held up his fingers. "I get to help Father Arnold serve Mass. My Uncle Emery did. He said it's very important."

"Your uncle's right. It's very important." Stephen lifted his mug to his slim lips. "I bet you're looking forward to making your First Communion."

"I am. Mom said the teacher will teach us about it."

"He's very friendly." Warmth and a hint of curiosity lurked in Stephen's voice.

Bridget squirmed closer against the back of her chair and toward Kyle.

"Jude told me you're the director of the Indigenous Students Center at the university."

"Yes. I worked my way up. I started out as the Indigenous Advisor after I earned my degree. When the original director moved back east, I applied for the position, and they hired me." Bridget gathered the napkin into her palm. "That was six years ago."

"You climbed the career ladder pretty young, then."

"I'm not that young. I'm thirty-six."

"A woman who reveals her age." Stephen grinned.

"I'm one of those women who isn't scared to tell anyone my age or weight." Bridget sipped her coffee. "Both are numbers. Nothing more."

"That's a great outlook. I don't mean to be bold, but not seeing a ring on your finger surprises me."

The coffee sat funny in Bridget's stomach. She faced Stephen. "My life's too busy. There's work. I also volunteer for the Kitchi-Gaming Friendship Center and the Indigenous

Women's Alliance. I can't forget the Catholic Women's Association. I not only serve on our CWA's parish council, I'm also on the diocesan council. And then there's number one here, who comes first, above everything and anything."

She rested her arm on the back of Kyle's chair.

"Where do you find the time?"

"I'm not sure." She rubbed the back of Kyle's chair.

Stephen's lips tugged at the corners. "Do you allow yourself free time to socialize?"

The next few months might be Bridget's last with Kyle if Adam had a say. "No. I don't. Kyle's number one for now."

Eyes slightly narrowed, Stephen tilted his head. He could try read someone else's mind. Bridget wouldn't give him any more information. It was time to talk about why Stephen was single.

From the kitchen, Adam pushed on the exit swinging door and wandered into the hallway. People stood in the lobby area, waiting for a table. He had ten minutes before the overflowing grill demanded his attention again.

The window offered a clear view of the parking lot. His stomach jumped when he spotted Bridget's sporty black truck parked in front of him. If she was here, Kyle must be here. They'd probably come from church.

He eased down the hallway, not too close but close enough to get a view of the seating area. Through the clutter and crowd, her long black hair shone under the sunlight streaming in through the big window. Jude's family was there, and an old woman. A blond-haired man sat beside Bridget.

Adam's throat constricted. He stumbled backward and banged against the wall. The employee door was directly in front of him, and he pushed it open. When he stormed outside, wind ruffled his hair but did nothing to cool the hot anger pricking his skin. Even when he lit the cigarette and sucked on the filter, the nicotine failed to expel the continuous waves of heat flooding his face.

He cast aside the butt and stomped back inside. Workers continued to race from the kitchen with orders for guests. Adam threaded his way through the staff and trounced into the employee lounge where a payphone was kept.

Through black spots in front of his eyes, he managed to yank a quarter from his pocket and shove the coin into the slot. He wrenched the receiver from the phone and punched in Bridget's number.

If she didn't answer, goddamned right he was going out there to confront her.

Chapter Twelve: Listen to Your Heart

The cell phone in Bridget's purse rang. Voice mail could take the call. Never did she rudely interrupt a meal by talking on the phone. She cut into her pancakes. The cell rang again. Mom, Dad, and Emery knew of Bridget and Jude's after-church ritual. This must be an emergency.

She snatched the phone from her purse. A strange number flashed on the screen.

Jude peered.

Bridget mouthed *I don't know* and pressed the answer button. "Hello."

"What the hell's going on? Where the fuck do you get off bringing my son along on your dates?" Adam's snarling voice was a vicious grizzly bear, mouth foaming and fierce eyes ready to rip apart a man with its ferocious claws.

The blood seemed to clot in Bridget's veins. Then a rumble erupted in the pit of her stomach, straining to twist into an explosion. Lightning thundered through her limbs, sending her blood racing.

Conversations stopped. A spoon clattered against the table. All eyes drilled on Bridget.

"Mommy?" Kyle's warm finger poked at her forearm.

Swallowing, Bridget managed to say in her most polite voice, "I'm sorry. I can't speak right now. I'm in the middle of brunch. We'll talk later," and hung up.

Her intestines curled into violent knots, squeezing the

pancakes she'd swallowed earlier.

"You okay?" Across the table, Jude's jaw and fingers twitched, ready to ransack the restaurant, looking for whoever had upset his sister.

Bridget forced a nod. "I'm fine."

To hell with Adam. If he wanted to humiliate her with his false assumptions, swear at her, threaten her, she'd say *yes* if Stephen proposed a date.

Adam flopped on the bed. What a long day. At least he'd been smart enough to go to a recovery meeting after his shift had finished.

There went three months of anger management and the third step of his recovery program. He rubbed his temples. A meeting always told a man he'd behaved like a dick.

He checked the alarm clock he'd bought at a secondhand store on the nightstand. Five minutes to nine. Each time the red number shifted, the dull throb at the base of his neck grew. He clutched his hands together. When the clock flashed nine-thirty, the throb morphed to a ball of painful tension that not even a couple of ibuprofen could extinguish.

Bridget wasn't calling. What if she was on another date? Who was watching Kyle? Or was the man from the restaurant, Mr. Toothpaste Smile, at Bridget's?

Adam hauled himself off the bed. Screw it. He was calling. If this pissed off Bridget, big deal. He'd handled her temper in the past, and he'd do so again.

He stomped down the hall, straight to the lounge and yanked up the phone. Her landline rang and rang until voice mail greeted him. The temper he'd kicked himself about earlier grew like a wort. He punched in the numbers to her cell phone, and another voice mail greeting ran down his ear drum.

Panic swallowed his temper. His heartbeat quickened. He sputtered into the phone, "*Kwe*, I had no right swearing at you. You got every right to be pissed. But we gotta talk. You owe me an explanation. I'm gonna keep calling and filling up your voice mail until you talk to me. You're the foster mother of my son. What if I need to speak to him? It goes against the rules. You can't ignore me."

He hung up.

The phone rang. He yanked up the receiver. "*Kwe?*"

"How dare you." Her accusing words bordered on screeching.

He sat forward. "Yep. I got a lot of nerve. Who is he?"

"None of your business."

"It's my business if he's sitting at a table in a restaurant with my son. I got every right to know."

"Fine." Sand didn't possess the amount of grit that Bridget's voice did. "He's a friend of my brother's. They met at a workshop designed for principals of the Catholic School Boards in various districts. We know Stephen's mother through church. He's visiting her before the school year begins. Naturally, Jude invited Stephen to join us for brunch. We usually eat at The Bistro, but Stephen suggested Benny's. Is there anything else you need to know? Let's see. I switched dish soap brands. I'm now using Sunshine Soap."

Adam stifled his snort. "What was wrong with the other brand?"

"It failed to fulfill its promise."

Ouch. She sure knew how to bite someone. "Yeah? What exactly did it fail to do?"

"It promised longer lasting suds. At first it did the job but then it stopped. I was washing dishes in nothing but hot water."

"Stopped, hey? Maybe you should give it another chance? Maybe the brand is better now. New and improved. Isn't that what those companies are always promoting? Finding ways to improve the stuff?"

"Why should I bother when I found a new brand that does a better job?"

"Does it really, *kwe*?" His voice softened. "It may work now, but it ain't Super Suds. You said Super Suds didn't dry your hands. Left them feeling really nice. Had a great smell. Pots and pans came out super-clean. Even shone."

There was about a five second pause that left Adam flexing and un-flexing his fingers.

"Why should I shell out money on a brand that stopped working for me?"

"It doesn't cost much. Take a chance."

"I won't give Super Suds another chance. It failed me . . . big time."

"Then I'll buy you another. I betcha you're gonna remember all that it did for you." He squeezed the receiver he clutched.

"Maybe I'm trying to forget all that it did for me." The sand in Bridget's voice vanished. Her pitch echoed the lost teenage girls on the streets of Winnipeg, trying to find a safe place to hide, anything better than the homes they'd fled from.

Adam set his elbow on his knee and cupped his forehead with his palm. He'd done this to Bridget—hurt her badly, took her trust and stomped her faith into the mud.

"*Kwe*, I know I made promises in the past, fucked them up bad, too. I don't expect you to believe me if I make new promises—"

"I thought we were talking about Super Suds?" Dejection tinged Bridget's answer.

"Never mind the dish soap." Times like these, when Bridget's shoulders sagged in defeat and her lower lip dragged downwards, she wasn't his spunky *kwe* wearing the boxing

115

gloves, ready to trounce him. Her misery was his misery. Her grief, his grief.

"*Kwe . . .*" Adam swallowed. He walked on hot coals now. Hell, he'd rather take on four Syndicate Skins than tangle with Bridget. "Do me a favor and keep an open mind."

"An open mind about what?" A hint of Bridget's shoulders back, chin raised, and eyes harder than rocks soaked the question she'd asked.

Her old fire reawakening dissolved the worry flecking the back of Adam's neck. "An open mind about . . . anything."

"Anything?" Flames erupted in her abrupt answer. "Anything is all you have to say?"

Adam gulped. Sweat slithered along his brow and down his back. He squeezed his toes. The words sitting at the base of his throat, he forced through his clattering teeth. "Me. Us."

The dreaded silence washed over the lounge. Adam rose. He held the phone in one hand and the receiver in the other.

"No." Bridget's response was flatter than the pancakes the new kid had made this morning for table twelve.

Something resembling a needle invaded Adam's chest. She couldn't mean *no*. He searched to even his breathing. "I'm not asking right now. I'm saying keep an open mind for later."

"Later? Seriously?" Her voice rose an octave.

"Well, you let me kiss you." Adam flopped back in the chair.

"*That* was a mistake." The sharpness in her tone said she was readying to yank on the gloves. "How dare you—"

"Can you put a lid on it and hear me out?" This damned conversation had gotten out of hand. The things Adam did for this woman. "I fucked up. I fucked up bad. Really bad. I let you down. I let my son down. I let myself down. I'm working on me. I'm working on my son. Now I'm trying to work on you."

"Why?"

Oh boy, not only was Bridget wielding an axe at his pride, now she had his balls in sight. "Why'd you think?"

"Never mind. I gotta go."

"Dammit. 'Cause I love you, woman." Adam slammed his palm against his temple. He'd gone and done the unthinkable. His head fell back against the top of the chair.

Bridget clutched the bottle of Sunshine Soap. She leaned against the kitchen counter. Her chest vibrated from fear. Something like a wad of cotton filled her mouth. He still loved her. "I'll . . . I'll call you. I-I need t-time to think."

"At least you didn't hang up." Resignation coated Adam's reply. "I guess I should count myself lucky."

"Bye." She fumbled to press the *off* button. His number still flashing on the screen was a tidal wave of panic crashing down her spine. She tossed the phone on the counter and bolted for the bedroom.

A flood of memories appeared. She squeezed her eyes shut and pressed her fists on her temples.

The first time in her bed—his strong hands powerful enough to choke a man to death had melted to feathers when he'd caressed her thigh, slid his palm along her hip, and settled his fingers a breeze away from the nest of hair trailing to regions he'd yet to touch. And she'd touched him. Stroked the strong muscles of his shoulders, explored the hard flesh of his stomach, kissed the powerful balls of his biceps.

His words. *I love you, kwe.*

Words, only mere words.

The whiskey on his breath when she'd surprised him with takeout that night. He'd stood there, unflinching, telling lie after lie. But she'd known the truth. Her gazed had dropped to his feet covered by socks, and his toes had fisted. Toes she'd witnessed curling and uncurling while in bed two weeks earlier as he'd cupped her face and declared his love, stating they should marry.

Bridget stumbled to the other side of her queen-size bed. She rested her hand on the nightstand, a hidden spot for her vibrator. Lonely nights spent sliding a plastic object inside her, cupping her own breast, but longing for . . .

No! There'd be no second chances.

When Adam got off the bus after finishing his shift at work, Logan, who must've been waiting and watching, came down the street.

"'Sup?"

"I got a job." Logan jogged over. "I'm working at Burger World."

Way to go for both of them—cooking, while Mr. Toothpaste Smile was the principal for a Catholic school. At least during the meeting with his PO on the lunch hour, Adam had gotten permission to attend Healing the Spirit. The PO was going to write up a letter for Adam's boss to review so he'd grant time off.

"We going to a meeting tonight?"

"Yep." Adam lit a cigarette.

"Did you hear anything from your friend about The Gator?"

"Friday."

"It's taking too long." Logan's voice was as whining as Kyle's when he didn't get his way. "We should go there."

"Can't. You don't got enough sobriety time and you ain't old enough. And I can't violate my parole."

"Nobody'll find out." Logan's voice shifted to pleading.

"We're just gonna go there and check it out, see if anybody knows anything. I can't do this anymore." He kicked a rock. "I gotta find out what happened to her. It's driving me nuts, man. I can't sleep. Can't eat."

"Easy." Adam rested his palm on Logan's shoulder. The kid was holding up pretty good considering he'd lost his girlfriend and unborn baby. Life was fragile for Logan right now, and he might end up using after losing the woman he'd loved and the child he'd never know.

Adam should talk to Bridget again. To hell if she had lined up another date.

They headed inside the halfway house. Adam meandered into the lounge. He'd shower after supper.

Logan continued to stare, eyes glassy.

Adam rubbed his face. Maybe it wouldn't hurt to hit a pool hall and other places where teenagers into drugs hung out. First, he'd call Bridget.

Chapter Thirteen: All Gone to Hell

Just as Bridget opened the door to the condo, the landline rang. After sitting on her cell phone all day, waiting for the dreaded call, it'd arrived while balancing a bag of groceries, her purse, and a child squirming to dart inside.

"Change your clothes first."

"'Kay." Kyle scrambled down the hall.

Bridget scooted into the kitchen and set the groceries and her purse on the island. The number for the halfway house flashed on the screen. Her chest expanded, threatening to push through her skin.

She squared her shoulders and pressed the answer button. "Hello."

"Hey, it's me. Look, I threw you a curve ball last night, but this isn't about that. It's about the kid."

The heaving in Bridget's chest shifted to a slow breath up and a slow breath down. *Praise the Lord.* "What kid?" She removed the lettuce from the soft bag.

"Logan."

"How is he?"

"Not good. He's getting impatient. He doesn't wanna wait until Friday."

"We have no choice. I understand he deserves answers, but I have a busy schedule. I asked until this Friday." She shoved the produce into the fridge bins.

"Look, I was eighteen once. You were eighteen once. Nobody's patient at eighteen. Especially a kid who had a shitty life. All he had was Sheena and the baby. It's why he went to rehab."

"I know. I know." Frustration crept up Bridget's spine as she kept shoving groceries into cupboards. "I don't want him to wait either, but I have other responsibilities."

"Like a date?" Jealousy smothered Adam's quick-spoken question.

"No, not a date." Presumptuous man. Bridget held the bag of rice in the crook of her arm. "I do belong to the Catholic Women's Association and the Indigenous Women's Alliance. I have a board meeting on Thursday. And we're meeting about Sheena."

"You are?" Adam's demanding tone became hope-filled.

"Yes. It's an emergency meeting. They don't want another girl falling through the cracks. We also have grave concerns about another child in care dying." She shoved the rice into the turntable cupboard.

"Thanks, *kwe*." The gratitude in his words shimmered with velvet.

"You're ... welcome." Bridget clicked her nails against the counter, groceries put away.

"You think about what I told you?" The way he spoke, husky, she could see him wetting his lips and his dark eyes pinching ever so slightly, scrutinizing her.

She leaned against the kitchen island and rested her forearm over her stomach that tweaked. "I'm still trying to digest what you told me."

"Y'know, a friend in the program told me we feel something right away when someone tells us something. What we think on is what action we're gonna take about what we've been told."

When he'd confessed his love, elation and fear had consumed Bridget. "You're right."

"What'd you first feel?"

"I ... I can't say right now. I need time to think. Think

about what action I'm going to take in response to what I was told." Thank goodness she didn't stutter, because her knees sure did.

"Guess you shoulda been the social worker instead of your brother. That sounds like something I'd hear from a counselor."

What did he expect—for her to jump into his arms after what he'd done? "I need time to think."

"It's fear. I bet one of the feelings you felt was fear."

She ground her teeth. "I didn't give you permission to peek at my brain."

"I'm not. It's normal to feel what you're feeling. Everyone feels it."

They were getting too close. If Bridget lowered the massive wall a smidgen, he'd drink again. Wind up in prison again. Hurt Kyle again. Hurt her again.

"*Kwe?*"

"No." The word flew from Bridget's mouth.

"No what?"

"No, I won't give you another chance. Before, you had good intentions. This time, you still have good intentions. But nothing's changed."

"What'd you `mean nothing's changed? Everything's changed." Gone was the sweet velvet tone. He'd morphed back into demanding damn Adam.

Bridget sharpened her own tone. "I can't see what's different this time. I can't see what would stop you from pulling the same crap on me."

"You don't believe me?" He sputtered.

"Adam, what's changed this time?"

"I told you what's changed. I saw myself going the same way as my uncle. In the program, we're told if we don't sober up, there're only three places we go—prison, the psych ward, or six feet under. I've been to prison. I ain't going to the looney bin where my sister is. And I sure ain't going where my uncle is."

Shocked smothered Bridget's skin in goosebumps. "Your sister's in a psych ward?"

"Yeah. Tried to kill herself about three months ago."

"Which sister?"

"Candace."

"How's she doing?"

"The same."

If Bridget didn't slam on the brakes, she'd end up helping the royal family of dysfunction. "I have myself to think about. I'm thirty-six. I'm not getting younger. Maybe I want a family of my own? Maybe I want a home of my own?"

"I can give you that." Silk draped Adam's low rumble.

Bridget's nose twitched. "How? You're a cook at Benny's."

"Yeah. I am." Hurt and anger lurked in his voice. "It's an honest living. I'm not doing B and E's. I'm not pulling armed robberies. I'm not dealing drugs. I'm not stealing cars."

"No, you're not. But you're not right for me."

"I s'pose Bible Boy is, huh?" The hurt vanished. Only anger remained, brittle, like crunching broken glass.

"Who?"

"That principal church guy."

Bridget sucked in a big breath. "I have to go. I'll see you on Wednesday for Kyle's visitation."

"Fine," Adam huffed out.

Bridget switched off the phone. There'd be no regrets. Then she should tell that to her heart beginning to curl up and whither.

The phone rang again. Bridget snatched the cell, but the number on the display wasn't the halfway house. She sagged against the kitchen island. "Hello."

A man cleared his throat. "Bridget?"

123

She remained sagging against the island. "Yes."

"I hope you don't mind that I asked Jude for your number."

"It's okay," she managed to politely say.

"Great." Stephen breathed a sigh. "How's Kyle? I didn't want to call earlier. I assumed you needed to unwind when you got home."

"Thanks for your thoughtfulness. As I told you before, my schedule's quite hectic. I devote my free time to my foster son." She reached into the fridge to retrieve the marinating pork chops she'd broil for supper.

"Do you have a heavy schedule this week?" A flicker of hope filled his voice.

Bridget tossed the pork chops on the island. Thursday evening was the meeting about Sheena Keesha. Then there was Kyle's soccer practice on Tuesday evening. Friday, she'd go to The Gator. "Three nights are busy."

"Which nights are those?"

"Tuesday, Thursday, and Friday." She removed the lid from the container that held the pork chops.

"Oh. I see." He paused for a moment. "What about Wednesday evening?"

Bridget cringed. Wednesday was when she met Adam for Kyle's visitation. "Uh, Wednesday's fine. It's what I call our takeout night. We're busy after work."

"Perhaps I could bring you both out for pizza?"

"It's a wonderful offer, but I don't allow Kyle to accompany me on dates." Shit, she hadn't meant to sound so darn firm.

"Ah, highly understandable." Stephen lightly laughed. "Would you have time then? I know it's last minute. Normally, I'd ask you out for next week, but I'll be back in Kenora then. School year. You must know staff returns a week early."

"Of course I do. Jude and I split a sitter for the kids when he returns to school. She's quite reliable. I could ask her if she's available Wednesday night." Bridget made a face at the pork chops. Why wasn't she blowing Stephen off with excuses?

"When can you let me know?"

"I'll call her tomorrow at work. Then I'll call you back. What's your number?"

He gave it to her. Bridget tapped the digits into her contact list. "Okay. I'll get back to you as soon as I can."

"Thank you. Jude mentioned you enjoy The Bistro. I'll make reservations for then."

"Sure. Bye."

"Bye."

She switched off the phone. Jude deserved a smack across the face for giving out her number. Stephen lived in Kenora, though. He had a great career working with the Catholic School Board. It was one harmless date and one harmless night.

After almost four years, she deserved to go out and enjoy a no-strings evening.

A casual dinner might free her mind from Adam and what he'd professed. Maybe this was what the Lord had ordered for her.

Adam stared at the phone. Red heat infiltrated his chest. Bridget didn't believe he'd changed. What the hell else was he supposed to do to prove he wasn't going to drink again? He'd better calm down. The old-timers would tell him *one day at a time.*

Logan slouched in the entryway. "'Sup?"

"Nothing." Adam stood. "Having my cig before supper."

"Are we going to The Gator before Friday?"

"Nope. Cool your heels, kid." Adam lumbered to the door.

Logan trotted beside him along the walkway. "What're we gonna do? Friday's too late."

"It's not too late. We might even have extra help. Bridget's committee or whatever they call themselves are meeting this week."

"Meeting? Who's meeting? About what?"

Adam leaned on the lamppost and lit his cigarette. "Some women's group Bridget belongs to. Said they're gonna do something about your girlfriend."

Logan's eyes brightened. "Really? When? Who? Where?"

"The Indigenous Women's Alliance. They meet about native issues. You must've heard of them. They started all that stuff about the missing and murdered native women. They're also raising shit about kids being lost in foster care."

"Sheena went to a couple of their workshops."

"Did they help?" Dumb question since Sheena was dead.

"I dunno." Logan shrugged. "Maybe we should go to the meeting?"

After what Bridget had done, ten miles near her was too close for Adam. "I guess we can. She said they're meeting on Thursday night."

"Cool. Maybe it'll help us decide what we'll do Friday night."

"Guess so." All Adam had left was Kyle. There wouldn't be a full family reunion, but he and his son didn't need anyone else.

Too bad Logan was here, because the lamppost sure could use a beating.

Bridget stood in front of the mirror at the dressing table. For a woman who'd made a firm decision to an ex-fiancé and was about to embark on a harmless date with a great Christian man, a switched off lamp illuminated a deeper glow than her skin, and an overcast night dazzled brighter than her eyes. She enjoyed dressing up, but selecting an outfit to wear for tomorrow evening at The Bistro sounded about as exciting as doing a load of laundry.

Instead of her feet padding to the walk-in closet, they dragged against the carpet, dragged so much Bridget should have gotten rug burn. She sorted through her enormous shoe collection and many blouses.

Mom was right about Bridget and Adam's relationship moving too fast last time. Within a year they'd become engaged, ready to start a life together.

She sank to the carpet and opened the bottom drawer to retrieve a shawl to drape over her shoulders for later in the night during the date. The various colors and fabrics failed to make Bridget's chest glimmer. She dug all the way to the back. Maybe she'd get rid of some of these, since she didn't wear them too often.

Bridget's fingers skimmed flannel. The dull thud beneath her ribcage balled into a tight knot. She yanked, and the red-and-black shirt popped out. Her pulse points accelerated to the vroom of the truck's engine when she stomped on the gas.

She gathered the long-sleeved shirt against her breast and rubbed her face along the soft fabric. Adam's masculine scent no longer invaded the material. He'd worn the shirt when they'd spent their last night together—before she'd unearthed the truth about his lies.

"You lie so much, you don't know what's real and what's fiction," she'd screamed in his face. "You wiggle your toes when you're nervous. I saw you do it when you told me . . . told me . . . was that a lie, too?"

She'd snatched Kyle from the makeshift bed at the bachelor apartment Adam had been renting, while the bastard had stood beside the kitchenette counter, too drunk to say anything else.

While Kyle cried, she'd packed up the boy's belongings, threatening to call Children and Family Services if Adam dared to stop her, but he hadn't. She'd run past him, her stomach curling from the stench of whiskey, and fled out the door with Kyle screaming for his daddy.

Bridget crumbled the shirt she held and leaned her head on the clothing rack stand in the walk-in closet. She'd toss the garment in the trash bin where she'd thrown her love for Adam four years ago.

CHAPTER FOURTEEN: DON'T LET 'EM GRIND YOU DOWN

When Bridget thrust open the door to the visitation room, the scent of sage kneaded away the tension pushing on her shoulders. In the past, Adam had always burned one of the four soothing sacred medicines before praying.

Mrs. Dale sat in the chair by the pop cooler while Adam sat cross-legged on the floor by the window. A hand drum rested against his bulging bicep. His strong fingers gripped a drumstick. Smoke rose from an abalone bowl.

"Wow." Kyle tore across the floor. He screeched to a stop in front of Adam. "Cool. What're you doing?"

"Praying." Adam kept his deep voice to a whisper. "You're learning in school how to pray to the Christian god. I'm going to teach you how to pray to Creator, like we used to do."

"Okay. Okay." Kyle plopped in front of the bowl. "I think I remember this." He pointed.

From a rectangular cedar box, Adam removed an eagle feather, the base wrapped in white and brown leather with decorative aquamarine and white beads. "Do you recall when I'd do this to you?"

He moved the feather over the bowl, fanning Kyle with the strong-smelling smoke.

"Um . . . I think so." Kyle used his hands to guide the smoke over his head and face.

Adam placed the eagle feather back in the box. He picked up his hand drum and drumstick. "Our prayer to Creator."

Mrs. Dale harrumphed under her breath.

Bridget stiffened. Adam's prayer was allowed, so was the sage burning in the bowl. Did the woman disapprove of the ceremony or Adam? Probably both.

A flicker of guilt bubbled in Bridget's chest. She'd also been disapproving. Last night she'd rejected Adam's profession of love. No. She wouldn't let the guilt go a smidgen further. Her reasoning was correct. In time his uncle's death would fade from Adam's memory and he'd be up to his old tricks.

When Kyle joined Adam in singing, Bridget's heart leapt. Her foster son didn't know the words, but trying to pray to Creator while seated cross-legged on the floor with his father took Bridget to the past. She'd witnessed those precious moments before, when the two had stayed the night at her condo.

He let me baptize Kyle when Adam thought he'd be in prison for a long, long time, because he wanted his son to have some form of a spiritual connection.

Emery would refer to her stance as unfair.

At seven o' clock, she'd leave on her date.

Adam sat at the table while Kyle colored, having finished their prayer forty-five minutes ago. He and his son needed more time together. According to The Hawk, Adam had two additional months to endure of a measly hour a week. Then the old bat and her supervisor would review his progress.

With the way the cranky bird studied him from her chair, he'd get a bad report. If Bridget refused to believe he'd changed, Mrs. Dale sure wouldn't.

"I wish you could babysit me." Kyle gazed up from his coloring.

"Babysit?" Oh yeah, Bridget had some meetings this week.

"Uh-huh." Kyle used his blue crayon to fill in the sky on the picture. "Mom's going out for dinner."

"Dinner?" Suspicion hunkered in Adam's gut.

"Her and a friend."

"A friend?" Adam glanced up to Bridget texting on her phone.

"Mr. Baker. The principal. He was at church. He also came to lunch."

Hot jealousy invaded Adam's chest, legs ready to stomp over to Bridget and order her to stay put. She belonged to him, not the Bible thumper.

Just as fast, deflation swathed Adam. Bridget had made herself more than clear last night how she felt. Big deal. So what? He didn't need her anyway. Not if she passed up his love for someone she considered a better man. If she couldn't see how hard he was trying, screw her.

Even though his old temper itched to kick over the table, stomp from the room, and head for The Gator, a place where losers like himself belonged, and tip back some hard whiskey, he stayed put. He wouldn't blow his sobriety for anything. He wasn't going back to prison, because if he drank, a cell waited for him.

Trembling, he placed his hand over Kyle's. His child glanced up, a big-eyed stare and his mouth open.

Adam squeezed Kyle's fingers. Little fingers. Warm fingers. Helpless fingers that needed him, like Adam had needed his parents but hadn't received a shred of love from them. His love for Kyle was bigger than a whiskey bottle. Bigger than what he felt for Bridget. Bigger than anything he'd ever experienced.

They only had each other.

"Dad?" Kyle's dark eyes glittered.

His boy shifted off the chair. While still holding hands, his son nested between Adam's legs. Kyle set his head on Adam's shoulder. "Can you ask Mrs. Dale if we can see more of each other?"

After almost four years, Adam wrapped his arm around Kyle's waist and gathered the boy against his chest. The fresh scent of soap and cheery smell of cookies smothered Adam. His son's tiny body, his soft skin, and prickly hair melted Adam's limbs. He kissed the top of Kyle's head. Warm. Fuzzy.

"Please, Dad?" Kyle buried his face in Adam's chest.

"I can ask, but I don't make the rules." Adam couldn't say he wished for them to spend every waking moment together. His words had power, the kind of power to give false hope to his son. He wouldn't disappoint Kyle. Adam had disappointed the boy enough.

"Then ask. Please?" Still snuggled against Adam's chest, Kyle turned his face. He pointed. "Mrs. Dale, please. Please can I see my dad more?"

Adam followed Kyle's pleading stare. Not a hint of compassion lurked in the old bat's frozen eyes. He peeked at a red-faced and open-mouthed Bridget.

"I don't make the rules, Kyle," Mrs. Dale said in her squawking, hawk-like voice.

"But-but you can talk to this important person. Your . . . um, your supervisor?"

"Yes, I can, but I have a process to follow. It means I have to wait until a certain date to speak about more time for you and your father." No sympathy reflected in Mrs. Dale's dissecting look.

Leave it to the old biddy to not have an ounce of sympathy for a kid. Adam stifled his snort.

"It's okay," he whispered. "Remember, we prayed to Creator together. Creator will help us." He must have faith Creator heard his begging and pleading in the song.

Kyle nodded. "He's God, right?"

"One and the same."

"Then why is there church and drums?"

"I'll tell you another time. We only got five more minutes."

"I know." Disappointed flickered in Kyle's little words.

"Hey." Using his finger, Adam coaxed Kyle's fallen chin upward. "I want you to remember something. I'm always thinking about you. Always. When we ain't together, keep telling yourself, *Dad's thinking of me.*"

Kyle's solemn gaze brightened. "I will. I'm gonna think about you all the time. Then we'll always be thinking of each other."

"That's as close as being together." Adam ran his finger along Kyle's plump cheek.

They might not have won the war, but they'd won a small battle. The Hawk might have succeeded in keeping them apart, but she couldn't take away their love or thoughts of each other.

Neither could Bridget. If she believed Adam was going to roll over and let her take his son so she could ride off into her dumb sunset on Prince Bible Boy's arm, she was wrong. Wrong. Wrong. Wrong.

Bridget ran her hands along the front of her sleeveless blouse.

Kyle played on the queen-size bed, making his two Z Men action figures fight. "When will you be home?"

"No later than nine. You'll be sleeping by then."

"I don't like Mrs. Dale."

Neither did Bridget, but she couldn't allow Kyle to speak rudely of another. "Because she won't let you see your dad more often?"

"Yep."

"Honey, she's only doing her job." Bridget set aside the brush and turned from the full-length mirror. "Mrs. Dale doesn't make the rules. She follows them, just as we follow rules, like at school, at work, while I drive. I don't think that's a good reason to dislike someone."

"I know," Kyle said, using his pouting voice.

"We should respect someone who follows the rules. Too many people break them."

"Did Dad break the rules why he went away?"

"Yes. He broke some rules." Bridget sat on the edge of the bed they shared when Kyle crawled in during storms that blew in off Lake Superior.

"Is he going to break more rules?"

"That's for your dad to answer. Remember, you can ask as many questions as you want while you're visiting him."

"I will."

"Ginny's waiting. Let's go see her."

Kyle dragged himself off the bed. Bridget followed him out to the living room, where the babysitter sat on the sofa.

The intercom buzzed.

Bridget froze. She could do this. She deserved a night out with adult company.

"He's here. He's here." Kyle darted to the intercom beside the door. He pressed the button. "Hello?"

"Hello, Kyle. It's Stephen. May I come up?"

"Sure. Mom's waiting. My babysitter's here. You can meet her. Her name's Ginny. She's really nice."

During the two minutes it took Stephen to reach their floor, Bridget retrieved her purse, gave additional numbers and orders to Ginny, and scooted beside Kyle who held the door knob.

Stephen knocked.

Bridget nodded.

Kyle opened the door. "You're lucky Mom's here. I can only answer the intercom if she's standing here."

"I'd say your mom's right." Stephen held out a small bag from Bucky's Burgers. "I hope this is okay. I stopped and picked up Kyle some fries on my way here. I thought he'd like the snack."

"My favorite. Bucky's fries. Thank you." Kyle beamed and took the bag.

"He can have a snack." Bridget turned to Ginny. "No popcorn," she mouthed, since Kyle had something to eat while watching Z Men.

"Shall we . . ." Stephen motioned at the open door. "We don't want to be late."

"I'll see you in the morning." Bridget bent down and kissed the top of Kyle's head.

A tear slid from her heart. In the past, Kyle had always accompanied her and Adam everywhere. "You have to listen to everything Ginny tells you to do. Remember those rules we talked about?"

"Uh-huh."

"Okay. I'll be in to kiss you goodnight when I get home, but you have to stay asleep."

"You promised to be home by nine." Kyle hugged Bridget, his face settling against her stomach.

"I always keep my promises. You know this." She again kissed the top of his head and returned his snuggling hug. "Be good. Ginny'll text if she needs me."

Stephen held open the door. "Goodnight, Kyle. Enjoy your fries."

"I will. Thank you, Mr. Baker."

"You're welcome, Kyle."

Bridget followed Stephen out the door. A chill seeped across her skin.

"Everything okay?" Stephen guided them to the elevator.

"I'm fine. It's weird, that's all. I've left him with Ginny many times when I have meetings in the evenings, but this is the first time I've left him for a . . . dinner."

Adam got off the bus. Another evening, another recovery meeting, one he really needed after breaking his son's heart this afternoon. He trudged down the sidewalk. Warm air gathered around his skin.

Logan lit a cigarette. "You're always quiet, but man, you're totally quiet tonight."

My ex-fiancée left my child with a babysitter so she could go on a date. How am I supposed to feel?

"Tired," Adam muttered.

"Huh? You didn't work, dude. Why're you tired?"

The itching continued, an itch to say *fuck it* and head for the liquor store. Adam kept walking to the church where the meeting was held. He was supposed to accept the things he could not change and change the things that he could. Accepting Bridget's cold response after he'd handed her his balls, which she'd crushed, sucked shit.

He could well imagine how her date was going. Ol' Bible Boy probably had some smooth lines. Or did this Mr. Baker wear a halo? No kissing on the first date? No hand holding? Treat a lady like a lady?

The bastard had better show Bridget the ultimate respect, even if she didn't deserve it with the way Adam felt right now.

He sure had, although on their first date he'd almost had to sit on his lips to stop his mouth from stealing a kiss. Hell, taking Bridget out had been his first ever official date. Every other broad he'd met at the bar or a party, half-drunk off his ass and his woman of the night also in the same shape as him.

Bridget had set Adam at ease when they'd gone for a picnic at Sleeping Giant Park, Kyle in tow. They'd swum at Mary Louise Lake. Built a sandcastle for Kyle, who'd toddled and fell right over the darned thing. Adam chuckled. He'd eaten homemade sandwiches, drank chilled lemonade, and enjoyed a lemon meringue pie Bridget had bought at a bakery.

Would she do the same thing for Bible Boy? At least she hadn't taken Kyle along for the dinner date. She was smart enough to keep his son separate from the all-important principal. Teachers made good money in Ontario. A hell of a lot more than what he earned cooking up specials at Benny's Restaurant.

"Did you even hear me?" Logan stepped over the low chain fence in front of the church's lawn.

"What?"

"When are we gonna work on the twelve steps?" Logan shook back his hair and stopped. He stared at the brick building through hollowed eyes. "I can't do this. I can't. I can't do this anymore."

"Do what?" Now what had crawled up the kid's ass?

"What's the point? She's dead." What color Logan had on his pale skin drained away.

Nothing was tougher than someone as young as the punk to sober up. "Let's go. Getting drunk isn't gonna bring her back."

"Neither is staying sober." Logan hung his head.

"C'mon. You asked me to sponsor you. I'm ordering you into the meeting."

"Why?" Logan sniffed. "You're not even listening."

No, Adam hadn't been. He'd been too busy feeling sorry for himself, caught in self-pity, dangerous ground for a recovering alcoholic.

"I'm listening now. C'mon." He'd failed too many people.

He wouldn't fail Logan. Adam slipped his arm around the kid. He patted Logan's shoulder. "Let's go."

Adam guided them into the church. He'd passed his first big test. So had Logan. They could do this. Agreeing to join the kid in a drunken binge wouldn't accomplish anything for either of them. Right now, they only had each other.

Although Bridget had eaten at the Bistro for years, on Stephen's arm she gazed at the familiar restaurant through new eyes. Like the stone fireplace she'd never taken an interest in before, probably because the magnificent piece complemented the raised panel wainscoting stained to a rich brown. Each decorative wasn't meant to draw a person's eye but to create a rich, warm ambience, like the off-white walls. The same for the golden lighting cast from the chandeliers, and the dark wood tables and matching cushioned chairs.

The maître d' led them up three stairs to the second dining area overlooking Lake Superior.

Once they were seated and the waiter had provided their menus, Bridget gripped hers. Adam shouldn't invade her thoughts, but he did. He'd be at a twelve-step meeting right now.

"Would you like any wine?" Stephen asked.

"If you don't mind, I'll pass. I enjoy an occasional glass now and then. An iced tea might be better."

"Not at all. I'll enjoy an iced tea, too. Maybe you could also recommend some entrees."

A light air of joy filled Bridget's chest. "We dine here quite a bit. Sunday. Always Sundays. Birthdays. Anniversaries."

"Your family strikes me as rather close." Stephen lifted his water and sipped.

"We are. Even though my parents returned to the reserve

when I was sixteen, and Jude and I stayed here to finish our schooling, we remained close with them and our younger brother, Emery."

The maître d' seated a table of four adjacent from them.

"Jude mentioned staying at a relative's place." Stephen leaned in.

"We did. My mom's older sister and her husband." Bridget raised her voice a smidgen, since the foursome at the next table talked rather loud. "Aunt Patti. She and Uncle Robert bought a condo in Port Arthur after their kids and Jude and I finished university. They attend a different parish. My cousins, they're three, live across Canada."

"Oh? Do they ever go to this reserve? Jude mentioned it's called Ottertail Lake."

"No. My cousins aren't aboriginal. They're Irish Catholic like Mom's side of the family." Her peripheral vision caught the waiter dashing to the other table.

"I should have guessed. Bridget is a fine Irish Catholic name."

"Saint Bridget . . ." She giggled. "But please don't liken me to a saint. My parents wouldn't agree. So I'm not sure why they named us after saints."

"I think your parents made a smart decision. Jude's a great guy." Stephen folded his hands on the white tablecloth. "He mentioned your other brother, Emery, was studying to become a priest up until almost a month ago."

"He was. Emery's a very spiritual man." Bridget sat back in the comfortable chair.

"Here we are." Stephen grinned at the waiter striding to their table. He cupped his chin in his palm, eyes feathering Bridget. "Perhaps I'll let you recommend my entree for me."

"I'd be glad to." She twisted the napkin around her fingers.

Stephen kept grinning, his fingers skimming the glass of

water like a man traced a woman's skin.

Chapter Fifteen: Desperate for You

Adam set the coffee cup on the end table beside him. He should have drunk a pop instead. The sun shone in this room during the day, and come evening, the stuffy meeting room morphed into a furnace. Having listened to a man share his story, Logan was next to speak.

Logan did what he always did. Coughed into his fist. Wiped his nose. Cleared his throat. Rubbed his running shoes against the floor. He sat forward. "I didn't get wasted. Didn't get high. I really wanted to, but I didn't."

Everyone clapped.

"I . . . I came here." Logan sniffed. He folded and unfolded his arms. "I . . . I told my sponsor I don't see the point in staying clean, y'know? My girlfriend's dead. Our baby's dead. What's the point? I got no fam. Living in a stupid halfway house. Dumb-ass job asking a bunch of jerks if they wanna super-size their orders."

"You got this program and you got us," an old-timer sitting in the wooden rocking chair said, waving his finger. "You keep coming back. Keep going to meetings."

"Guess so." Logan glared at the coffee table. "That's it. Pass."

Adam kept his hand put before he cuffed the side of Logan's head. "I'm Adam and I'm an alcoholic."

Everyone murmured their hellos.

"When I was eighteen, I kept asking myself the same thing—why bother? Maybe I should've bothered? If I would've, I'd be living a different life." He stared straight ahead at the one-quarter-filled coffee pot on the counter leading into the small kitchen.

"I'm thirty-eight and starting over. Gotta accept responsibility that I put myself here. Nobody forced booze down my throat. Nobody forced me to commit crimes." He moved his tongue back and forth along the roof of his closed mouth.

"I've been reading lots. Making good use of the time sitting alone in my room at the halfway house." He curled and uncurled his toes. "Ninety percent of crimes are committed when someone's drunk. And yeah, I did a lot of bad shit when I was sober, too. Thing is, my drinking and drugging led me to dark places. If I didn't drink the way I did, if I didn't use blow the way I did, I wouldn't have gotten involved in a street gang.

"Easy money. Easy life. Easy women. I wasn't willing to work for anything. I felt after the way I grew up, I deserved free shit. Life owed me something." He kept squeezing his toes. "Life doesn't work that way. Some of us have it tougher than others. It's still no excuse for doing what I did just 'cause life handed me a raw deal growing up.

"We make ourselves believe our life is normal. But if it was normal, why do we want what we see as normal around us?" His hands remained on his thighs, heat from his palms dampening his jeans slightly. "So I knew better. Knew what I was doing was wrong. When my son was born, and I looked into his eyes, held him, I vowed I wasn't gonna live that way anymore, and I wasn't gonna put him through the same bullshit."

His stomach tightened. "I screwed up. I won't say I relapsed almost four years ago. I *chose* to start drinking again. One drink wasn't enough. Fourteen was too much. And I landed back in prison, a place I swore I'd never go back to."

Again, he clamped his lips closed and ran his tongue over the roof of his mouth. "I got a second chance. Life ain't going my way. Nope, not at all. Hell, it sucks. But I'm sober. I'm working. I got a place to bunk. I'm giving back by sponsoring someone. I'm doing my best to count my blessings, even when I'm getting a kick to the teeth right now.

"All I can do is leave everything in my higher power's hands. Trust it'll work out how it's s'posed to work out."

My ex-fiancée's on a fucking date while I'm sitting in a recovery meeting baring my soul and feeling sorry for myself.

Adam set his hand on the back of Logan's chair. "This may not be the happiest moment of my life, but it sure beats a prison cell. It sure beats a hangover. It sure beats waking up on the street. It sure beats bumming money for booze or cigarettes. That's all I got to say."

"Thanks, Adam," the other people in the room said.

"You're right," Logan muttered.

"Help me close the meeting," the chairperson called out.

Once they said the final prayer, Adam and Logan filed out of the meeting room.

"You're right," Logan said, this time his voice a pitch higher.

They started down the cement stairs.

"Right about what?"

"It beats being in jail or other shit like that." Logan hopped the last step. "I wanna do this. I really wanna do this. I . . . I . . . what am I gonna do when you get your own pad?"

"Don't think so far ahead. One day at a time. Remember?" Maybe the two of them could get a place. It'd do Logan good. The kid needed a father. Uncle. Big Brother. Something other than what he had now.

"You gonna let me visit you?" Logan opened the double door.

"Kid, you're welcome to stop over whenever you wanna. Who knows? Maybe things'll work out differently. Maybe if you stay clean, keep going to meetings, you'll get outta that halfway house sooner than you think."

Logan's blue eyes brightened. "What'd you mean? Y'mean me and you?"

Why not? "We'll see. See how you do. If I get a roommate, he's gotta be committed to sobriety."

"I am committed. I made it, didn't I? I went tonight. I told them how I felt."

"You did. Honesty's what gets us through bullshit." Adam lit a cigarette.

Eight-thirty. Bridget wouldn't get home probably until around nine.

Stephen cut into his steak. His manicured hands guided his knife and fork. Starched cuffs. Gold cuff links. A matching gold clip keeping his speckled blue tie from falling into his dinner. His smell wasn't overpowering either. A light, spicy fragrance. He'd gelled back the waves of his golden hair.

As Bridget stared at him, decked out in devastatingly good looks, her heart didn't soar. Not even a blip of her pulse.

"After working in Winnipeg, I decided it was time to come home to my original school district. I never imagined I'd be overseeing the high school I used to attend." Stephen smiled at the waiter who refilled their water glasses.

"Your mother said she moved here to be closer to her sister. I think it's wonderful. She mentioned your aunt has rheumatoid arthritis."

"Very bad." Stephen never broke his warm gaze while reaching for his newly filled water. "Unfortunately, our grandmother had a very bad case of it, too. The disease crippled her before she turned sixty. My aunt found herself in the same mess. When my uncle died, Mother made the decision to move here to help my aunt. She's in too much pain to engage in social activities. So the senior center is the best place for her. They provide fantastic care. Mother still felt my aunt shouldn't be alone. She bought a condo in the same area as the senior center."

"Yes, your mom's the new outreach worker for Saint Patrick's. She coordinates the weekly Masses held at the senior center." Bridget forced another bite of chicken parmesan between her teeth.

"Seems we share a lot in common." Stephen's pink lips shifted into a cozy smile. "I knew we would, since Jude and I shared many common entries during the workshop. You and I were raised the same way. We possess the same outlook on life. We have the same beliefs. We were even too devoted to our careers to think of . . . well . . . families of our own."

"I do have a family. Kyle." The waiter refilled the water glasses at the table of the boisterous foursome at the next table who hadn't stopped laughing since their arrival.

"How did you go about sponsoring a foster child? Was it always a dream?" Stephen helped himself to some rice on his plate.

"I've always been concerned about the Indigenous children in care." The chicken sat funny in Bridget's stomach. "When his father contacted me to care for Kyle, I said yes."

"His father's . . ."

Bridget used her fork to move the chicken around on her plate. "His father was previously incarcerated. He asked me to care for Kyle during his incarceration."

"I see. How long was he incarcerated for?"

"Three years."

The man at the next table had his arm draped on the back of the woman's chair, while the other couple leaned in, laughing about something.

Bridget yanked her gaze from the foursome. "Once a

week, Kyle visits his father under supervised care."

"Children and Family Services are transitioning Kyle over to his father?"

"That's the plan." Bridget twirled the long noodles around her fork.

"Forgive me." Stephen's ice-blue-colored eyes swung to a clear, warm summer sky. "I didn't mean to pry."

Bridget tapped her water glass. "It's okay. We're on a date. On dates, people get to know each other. That's done by asking questions."

"I don't want my questions to make you uncomfortable. Okay?" Stephen's manicured hand snaked across the table, and his fingers touched the tips of Bridget's nails.

Tension crept along her shoulders.

"I didn't mean to . . ." Stephen drew away his hand.

"It's okay." Bridget grabbed the knife while still holding the fork. A rash of heat warmed her hairline.

"I want you to know I've never taken advantage of . . . err, I mean I have the utmost respect for women." Sincerity reflected in Stephen's eyes.

The knots in Bridget's stomach uncurled. She set aside her cutlery. "Of course you do. My brother . . ." She couldn't help the smile forcing her lips upward. "My brother never forgets he's the oldest or one day he'll be the patriarch of our family."

"He takes good care of you and Emery?" Stephen said, voice teasing.

"Hmm . . . more like meddling." A light glow filled Bridget's chest. She shifted in the chair to cross her legs and rest her elbow on the table to lean in.

"Something tells me you're more than capable of taking good care of yourself." Stephen rested his chin on his knuckles.

"It's been a sore spot at times." A chuckle bubbled in

Bridget's throat. "I guess I can be a little bit too independent."

"I'm one of those men who admires strong women." There was a hint of wolfishness in the closed-mouth smile Stephen cast by the arch of his brow and the scrunch of his eyes.

"Thank you." And she meant it.

Eyes still twinkling, Stephen set his napkin on his empty plate. "Are you up for dessert?"

"Yes, I am." Bridget's stomach rumbled at the thought of cheesecake. "The desserts here are yummy. Call over the cart."

"I admire a woman with a healthy appetite." Stephen signaled the waiter.

The waiter scooted over. "All finished?"

"Yes. Can you please bring over the dessert cart?"

"Right away."

Stephen leaned in, tilting his head in a *you-have-all-of-my-attention* gesture. "What do you recommend?"

"They make the best cheesecake. I do think I should only have half a slice. As much as I enjoy eating, I also have to make sure I stay within my limits."

"Then do you care to share a piece?"

"I'd like that."

The waiter pushed over the dessert cart.

"Which delectable treat tantalizes your taste buds?" he asked

"The turtle cheesecake. It's delicious."

"Then the turtle it is," Stephen said to the waiter.

Once they had their after-dinner dessert on a plate in front of them, Bridget cut into the cheesecake. Stephen followed, his warm gaze still trained on her. At the same time, they both slid the bite into their mouths. Fuzz peppered Bridget's skin. The same kind of fuzz she experienced with

Kyle, or her brothers, even a friend while sharing something together.

The Lord had brought a wonderful man into her life. Maybe God wanted her to feel comfortable instead of excited. Satisfied instead of feverish. Mellow instead of jumpy.

"I appreciate you bringing Kyle French fries. I know he does, too." Bridget cut off another piece of cheesecake.

"I thought it was the least I could do. I sensed he wanted to come out for dinner."

"He did. So much is up in the air, though."

"I understand. I hope it works out to your satisfaction."

"I guess it's not about my satisfaction." Glumness enveloped Bridget. "It's about what's best for him."

Stephen pulled up in front of Bridget's condominium building.

She clutched her purse, fingering the delicate leather fringes secured to the zipper of the outer compartment.

"That's nice." He motioned at the satchel.

"Thank you. I'm . . . a bit of a collector." Bridget chuckled, proud that her laugh was genuine.

"A connoisseur of ladies' handbags?" He arched his mink brow.

"Perhaps. I guess it's true about our shoes and purse collections." She wet her lips. "Earrings, too."

"Anything else to add?" Teasing lingered in Stephen's smooth voice.

"Lots." She gripped the door handle. "I'd better go. I promised Kyle I'd be home at nine."

"You have a curfew?"

"He's a little bit bossy."

"You know . . ." He stared at the steering wheel. "I'm flying out Friday. I have much to do on the weekend before I return to work on Monday. I understand you have a lot of responsibilities . . ."

He shook his head, tittering. His fingers grazed his temples. "I'm making a mess of this."

Bridget's bones stiffened.

"I'd like to see you again." His gaze shifted to her, his weak smile gone and eyebrows drawn.

"Stephen, I had —"

"Please. Give me one minute. Okay?" Stephen moved in his seat so he faced her. "I'm five hours away. We're both busy. I get it. But this is the technological age. There're many options to communicate. My mother and aunt live here. I plan on visiting again. She even loaned me her car for tonight.

"I promise I have no skeletons hiding in my closet." He even drew back his jacket to show his inner pockets. "See? Nothing."

A giggle demanded release from Bridget's chest.

"It's not often a man . . ." He licked his lips. "I think we both have certain expectations from people. I'm thirty-seven and not getting any younger."

"No, we're not." Her voice quieted along with her hammering chest.

"Being a Christian man, I prefer to date women who share the same devotion to Christ as I do."

"I understand."

"Mother says you're devoted to Saint Patrick's."

"Yes. I've been a member of the CWA since I was sixteen. My aunt bought me my membership. I'm also devoted to Indigenous causes. I have a meeting tomorrow night regarding children in care."

"Awful business." Stephen pressed his lips together. "I read about that young girl who was found in the river. Terrible."

"Children in care is one of the biggest roads to the murdered and missing Indigenous women in Canada. There're more children in care than during the residential school era."

"Why is that?"

"I sit on the board. We obtained a grant to hire a coordinator and volunteers to conduct a study for northwestern Ontario. It's the catchment area for the Indigenous Women Alliance."

"You're a foster mother. Do you mind if I asked what happened to Kyle's parents?"

Bridget rubbed the fringes on the purse. "It's complicated. His mother died. And as I mentioned, his father was incarcerated."

"I'm sorry to hear about his mother. And I'm sorry his father chose crime over Kyle's well-being."

Yes, Adam had, but why did hearing what he'd done rolling off of Stephen's tongue prick the back of Bridget's neck like a mosquito bite? "As I said, it's complicated. Please understand colonization had a heavy impact on the native population. I'm referring to a cycle that goes back well over two centuries."

"Perhaps you could enlighten me over lunch tomorrow? You sound well-versed in the subject."

The subject? The *Anishinaabe* people were more than a subject. They were living, breathing human beings. But here was Bridget's chance to educate another willing individual about the concerns of the Indigenous population. "I take lunch at noon."

"Then noon it is. I'll let you pick the place." Stephen didn't smile. Genuine concern flecked his gaze. "I'd really like to hear more. I have a lot of aboriginal children in my school. I taught many in Winnipeg, too."

"I'll see you tomorrow, then." Bridget cracked open the door. "Goodnight. And thank you for dinner. I had a wonderful evening."

"I did, too." Stephen didn't lean in for a goodnight kiss but remained in his seat.

Bridget slipped out of the car. She scurried to the main door, chest finally light after being squeezed shut tight for the past fifteen minutes.

Chapter Sixteen: Out to Lunch

Bridget reached for her purse. Lunchtime. She'd slept well last night, content Stephen hadn't pushed for what she wasn't willing to acknowledge yet.

"Oh, boss lady. Someone's out here waiting for you." Tania's voice singsonged over the intercom on Bridget's office phone.

Hah, as if she'd be lucky to have Tania assume Stephen was a colleague and nothing more. Bridget pressed the button. "I'll be right out."

When she entered the reception area, Stephen sat at one of the tables where students liked to gather and study. She was proud of the center and its wood-paneled walls to create an atmosphere of an old library with brown leather armchairs, a matching sofa, and hardwood floors. A thick, multi-colored rug added a beautiful pop of yellow, red, teal blue, and orange sunniness to warm the room. The same for the paintings done by local Indigenous artists.

Stephen stood. "I'm double parked. I guess we'd better get going."

"I'll be back after my lunch hour." Bridget made sure to flash Tania a *don't ask* look. "Later."

"Oh, for sure. Have a great time." Tania's giggles followed them out the door and to the car.

Once they got in, Bridget gave Stephen directions to the restaurant.

"Your assistant's a friendly woman."

"I suppose she asked a million questions before she

buzzed me."

"She simply asked if I had an appointment. I told her I was present to take you to lunch. She . . . laughed." Stephen also laughed.

If not Tania, it was Maude or Chloe attempting to set up Bridget on dates. Staff. "They're simply glad I'm getting out and doing something more sociable, instead of volunteering my life away."

"When did you begin sitting on the Indigenous Women's Alliance board?"

"Since my university days. I was elected to the board when I was twenty-nine."

"If you're still on the board, this means you're doing a wonderful job."

"I hope I am. The children in care mean a lot to me."

"Is this why you decided to foster a child?" Stephen stared straight ahead.

"There are . . . many reasons. Anyway, we're meeting tonight."

"You mentioned that to me last night." Stephen turned into the parking lot of Canada's Finest. "I hope it goes well."

"I do, too." Bridget unbuckled the seat belt.

With Stephen by her side, they entered the restaurant where a hostess led them to a booth in an area full of ample lighting and many customers.

"It's the lunch hour. It'll be busy." Bridget opened her menu.

"Have you dined here before?"

"Yes. Many times. Staff or colleagues from the university."

"It must be nice to get away for the lunch hour. Us? It's the teachers' lounge at the school."

"Jude says the same thing." Bridget set aside her menu.

Again, Stephen was dressed impeccably. Collared, short-sleeved dress shirt. Khakis. Gold watch. Golden waves slicked to the side. A fine stubble of facial hair. A few women had cast him lingering looks when they'd taken their seats.

Bridget should count herself lucky, but her eyes probably hadn't sparkled like the women's had when Stephen had strolled through the restaurant to their booth.

"You mentioned the problems go back almost two centuries." Stephen folded his hands on the table and leaned in, close enough for Bridget to catch a whiff of his cologne, a fresh citrus aroma.

The waitress came and took their orders and set down their drinks.

Bridget picked up the iced tea and sipped. "It was more than the residential schools. The Indigenous population was always being displaced."

"Three men who attended the residential schools spoke at our school. It was most enlightening." Stephen continued to lean in. He set his chin on his knuckles, gazing at her. "Maybe even discomforting."

"Discomforting? Because of their experiences?"

"Because of what . . . well, my own people did to them. My ancestors. Our government. Two of the survivors were devout Catholics. The other was traditional. Very nice men. They attended the residential schools at different times. One was in his early sixties. Another around eighty. The other mid-seventies."

"They weren't present to make you feel bad. They were present to educate people about *all* of Canada's history." Bridget moved her hand on the table up a good foot into the air. "For a long time, nobody mentioned what the Indigenous people had endured. Or, nobody believed what our government was capable of doing to another race of human beings."

"You have an eloquent way of speaking. You're capable of much compassion for everyone."

"I was one of the fortunate ones. I understand how blessed I am. I grew up in Thunder Bay. My parents shielded me from what Dad had faced as a child. My father led a hard life because of the residential school. I'm thankful he found Mom and was able to overcome what had previously haunted him.

"Before those schools became operational, everyone knows the aboriginal people were rounded up and put on reserves. They were even displaced from their original reserves when natural resources were found in communities. Silver. Farmland. Timber. Anything that could benefit the growing population in Canada at the time. The government wanted to build a country. They sacrificed the Indigenous people to get what they wanted. A lot of reserves were flooded to build hydro-electric dams. They dumped waste into the rivers, contaminating—"

"That . . ." Stephen cleared his throat. "That happened to one of the First Nations in our area. Mercury poisoning. It's still having a devastating impact on the health of the people after all these years."

"So when you ask me about the children in care and why Kyle's father wound up in prison, I can tell you although his dad never lived on a reserve or went to a residential school, he grew up in an environment that did. And Kyle's grandparents suffered just as my dad did."

"Are they still alive?"

"Yes."

"Do they acknowledge their son? Their grandson?"

Bridget shook her head. Sad to admit. "They're too deep in alcohol. I don't judge them. I understand why they are the way they are. It's why my brother, Emery, wanted to become a priest. He wanted to help people like Kyle's father and grandparents."

"You said the father gets to visit Kyle. How are the visits going, if you don't mind me asking?"

"They're going well." They were going too well. "In time, I imagine Kyle will be transitioned full-time into his father's care." *And there's not a damned thing I can do about it unless I fight dirty and go against my principles.*

"I'm sorry." Stephen's condolence was soft and remorseful.

"Don't be." Bridget forced a smile. "Listen to me. Feeling sorry for myself. As I said, it's what's best for the child."

"I know, but it still hurts, doesn't it? You devoted — is it four years? — to Kyle."

Yes, he's been my life ever since I met Adam. "Before I leave . . . his life, I'll remain a part of it. Visits. Until I eventually let him go for good." Her stomach soured. "As I said, it'll be a transitional process where my visits will become farther and farther in-between, so Kyle can begin a new life."

Part of the maddening weight that had sat on Bridget's chest lifted. Finally, she'd told someone who stood on neutral ground. "Thank you."

"What are you thanking me for?" Stephen quirked an eyebrow.

"For simply listening. I haven't been able to speak to anyone about what I'm facing. I can't talk to my family. They love Kyle as much as I do. They don't want to lose him either. My parents consider him their grandchild. My brothers think of Kyle as their nephew. I'm not the only one who's going to hurt when Kyle's slowly transitioned out of our lives."

"I want to lend an ear." Stephen's hand snaked across the table.

Bridget froze. When his fingers wrapped hers, she clutched the smooth, firm softness of his hand. Comforting. His finger-squeezing patched a couple of holes in her heart.

He was a good friend.

"You're a great listener." She returned his gentle embrace.

His gaze burned hot. The noise in the restaurant vanished. Just Stephen was present, his fresh citrus scent, his caring eyes, the delicate touch of his hand.

"Here you go." The waitress set down their meals.

They released their fingers.

After such an intense moment, Bridget's heart still refused to pound. Her breathing still refused to jump. Maybe the Lord had sent Stephen to help her work through the thoughts and questions spinning around.

She poured dressing over the salad. The roast beef sandwich on whole wheat bread looked delicious. As for Stephen, he'd ordered the hot hamburger sandwich.

"I'd like to meet your brother Emery. He sounds like an interesting man."

"Emery's a very spiritual man. He's an old soul in a young body." Bridget lifted the fork and speared a pea pod. "I'll see him when I fly up for Healing the Spirit next week."

"Jude mentioned the workshop. He was disappointed he couldn't help."

"He helped at the previous one. Mom and Dad hosted the first one five years ago. It was a huge success. Two participants even converted to Catholicism." Bridget munched on a tomato. "It sparked some controversy, especially when my parents proposed a financial donation from the reserve to run the workshop scheduled for next week."

"Oh?" Stephen's groomed hands held his fork and knife—hands used to reassure, hands to comfort. Not big, strong hands sliding over a woman's shoulders, coaxing her to give in to the touch such a potent presence generated.

"Unfortunately, a group of traditionalists believe the workshop shouldn't happen."

"Traditionalists are those who practice their culture,

right?"

"Yes. Funny." Bridget cracked a grin. "Emery's spouse was one of those against the workshop. If not for Darryl aiding a few people, whom I consider very passionate about their traditional beliefs, he and my brother might not have reconciled."

"Emery's spouse was on the opposing side?" Stephen blinked more than a car's hazard signals.

"Yes. Darryl was adamant about the workshop not happening. He joined forces with a man who is very vocal about his stance on religion."

"This man is against religion? Or was?"

"He still is. Although everyone in the community, traditionalists and Catholics, ironed out their differences, this man and his family won't budge. I hope they're not holding protest signs outside of the workshop next week."

"Can anyone attend?"

"Yes." Bridget nibbled at her inner cheek. "Kyle's father, as far as I know, is going. At least when we last spoke, he told me he wanted to make arrangements to attend."

"It sounds like Kyle's father is making great progress."

Adam's progress was too good. Maybe too good to be true. Was this all an act? The little voice kept whispering *no*.

What a way for Adam to spend his lunch hour once a week. Visiting his parole officer in an office that always smelled of food. Today, pastrami on rye.

The bald man on the other side of the desk chewing on a bite of sandwich held a lot of power, determining whether Adam stayed on the outside or got tossed back on the inside.

"Well, I gotta say, if you stick to what you're doing, you might have a chance." Harold tossed aside the pen and sat back in the chair that creaked and groaned whenever he shifted. He reached for his can of cream soda. "As for this Healing the Spirit stuff, I talked to your supervisor this morning. He said he's fine. Said you're doing great and if this helps you, why not?"

Adam exhaled a spell of relief. At least two people were for him, not against him.

"He's a little concerned over you losing five days' wage. So am I." Harold slurped a drink.

"I'm not. If it means it'll help me and my boy, I'm for losing five days' pay. I don't like it, but I don't have any holiday time to use."

"It'll set you back getting your own place. How do you feel about that?" Harold rubbed his furry brow. Even with the air conditioning cranked, his big face shone, and perspiration stains coated his armpits. If he wasn't a parole officer, he'd fit right in on the range with his beady eyes, constant uneven stubble, big gut squeezed into a shirt a size too small, and hair sprouting from his nostrils and ears.

"There's a program that'll assist you for your flight." Harold sat forward. The chair groaned again. "Lemme see where I put that stuff."

He riffled through a few folders and papers, unsettling his sandwich in the process. "Son of a bitch. Where'd I put it?" He searched more papers and withdrew a mustard-stained sheet. "Here it is. Sign it. I'll send it in for approval."

Adam's chest brightened inside. He wouldn't have to dig into his precious savings for his flight. "Sure." He leaned in and signed the paper.

Everything else but Bridget was working in his favor. After she'd smacked his face good, he continued to debate whether he had a future with her, or if even wanted to get in the ring and fight Bible Boy for her hand.

Bridget sat in the passenger seat. Traffic hummed in the opposite direction. People meandered up and down the sidewalks. They were closing in on the university.

Stephen stared straight ahead. "I had a great time."

"Me, too." She fingered the purse's leather strap.

"I imagine you'll be busy for a while"

"Very busy. I'll be leaving for Ottertail Lake, getting Kyle settled at Jude's, and making sure he's ready to start school."

"I planned on flying in for the Thanksgiving weekend. It's a good month away, but perhaps we could go out for dinner on that Saturday night since I'll be arriving Friday evening after work."

Dinner sounded nice. She'd have a month to devote to Kyle after her hectic week in September. "Sure. I'd like that."

Stephen guided the car to the spot in front of the center. "I fly out tomorrow evening. I have personal business to attend to before I return to work on Monday. I know you have a meeting tonight and I also understand you don't like to commit too many evenings away from Kyle."

Bridget held her breath. Was he asking for another date? They'd already been out twice this week. Still, she could understand his dilemma because time was a luxury he didn't have since he lived in Kenora.

"I wondered . . ." He tapped the keychain dangling from the ignition. "I wondered if I flew in during the middle of September, if we could go out on a Saturday?"

Her stomach tightened. He was serious if he wanted to see her again before Thanksgiving weekend. "Oh . . ."

"I know it's unexpected." Stephen's laugh was slightly strained. For once, worry crept into his ice-blue eyes. "We both have our own separate lives in separate towns. We live five hours apart. I understand Kyle's care is important and this is a crucial time for you."

Bridget squirmed. "I enjoyed your company and I'm

thankful my brother introduced us. I admit you're easy to speak to. As easy as Emery, and he's the kind of man strangers will give their deepest, darkest secrets to."

"And do you have deep, dark secrets?" Again, Stephen's laugh was strained.

"Nothing too deep or too dark." Bridget's face warmed with a tinge of bashfulness.

Stephen must have seen a blush or something, because he leaned forward, resting his palm on the steering wheel. His fresh aroma caressed Bridget's skin.

"Why don't you text me around the middle of September. No pressure." He held her hand.

Trembling, Bridget forced a nod.

"And I'll see you on the October long weekend, anyway." His lips brushed the back of Bridget's hand.

He was such a nice man. Elation should ring through Bridget's limbs, but life was such a mess right now. She was a mess. "Okay. October."

"I'll text you when you return from Ottertail Lake. A couple of days after. I know you'll be busy unpacking and seeing to Kyle. I don't want you feeling I'm invading your personal space or responsibilities."

"Thank you."

"No. Thank you." His hand still held hers.

Chapter Seventeen: Born to Lose

"She's ... um ... she was my girlfriend." Logan stood, hands in pockets.

Adam remained seated in one of the many plush leather chairs against the wall. The board of directors sat in the chairs surrounding the cherrywood table. The Indigenous Women's Alliance sure knew how to spiff up a board room, from the matching cherrywood buffet to the thick carpeting. They even had native arts and crafts decorating the walls.

The chairperson, Priscilla, had finished ranting about children in care and whether justice would be served for Sheena Keesha. She peeked over the rims of her glasses. "Please. Sit." She motioned at one of the seats at the table.

Logan plopped in the chair beside Bridget.

"You're Adam's friend," Logan said.

"Yes, I am." Warmth toasted Bridget's dark eyes.

Logan twiddled his thumbs. He glared. "Me and Adam're trying to figure out what happened. You're s'posed to help us and you keep blowing us off. What's the deal?"

Bridget gasped.

Adam rubbed his brow. This was *kwe's* fight, not his. She had to answer to the kid, not him.

"It wasn't my intention to defer my assistance to a later date, but as you can see, I have other obligations to meet first. I hope you understand helping you is important to me." Sincerity reflected in Bridget's dark eyes.

"How'd you agree to help?" Priscilla asked. "We do have a protocol —"

"I agreed to make enquiries at the last place Sheena was seen." Pink spread across Bridget's cheeks.

"The Gator's a dangerous place. We should pressure the police and Children and Family Services for answers." Priscilla sat back and focused her no-nonsense look at Logan. "Are you also in care?"

"Nope. Left when I turned eighteen a few months ago."

"Where're you residing now?"

"Joseph Howarth halfway house. I got sent there after I got out of rehab."

"As a board, we should direct our efforts toward those responsible for Sheena's care and safety. How many more children have to die before something's done about it?" Priscilla's face reddened. "Bridget, you mentioned helping Logan. I think what we should do is develop a special committee to draft our concerns to the police and Children and Family Services. Once this is done, the board will review the committee's draft and formalize it at the next meeting. From there, we can begin an action plan on how we'll approach the police and Children and Family Services."

Adam threw back his head. More fucking red tape. The old-timers would tell him to be part of the solution instead of silently complaining. "I'll volunteer to sit on this committee." He raised his hand.

"Excuse me?" Priscilla's dark eyebrows knitted.

"You heard me."

"As a courtesy, we allow the Indigenous public to sit in on our meetings, unless we are in-camera. I'm pleased you've shown an interest in what we do. However, I never got your name." She tapped her pen on a pad of paper.

"Adam Guimond. I'm looking out for him." He used his chin to motion at Logan.

"I see . . ." Priscilla's gaze darted around the table.

"I'll volunteer for the committee. If the board approves,

I'll begin requesting assistance from our membership for people who are interested in being a part of it." Bridget spoke in her clear, professional tone, the take-charge one that had first captured Adam from the start.

"I already said I'd be on it." He stared at Bridget.

Her hair was secured off of her face with a beaded barrette. A tan coated her toned arms. As beautiful as she was, Adam would do what he could for Logan, even if it meant working with a woman who'd chosen another man over him.

Bridget carried her briefcase, the meeting having adjourned fifteen minutes earlier. She left the building through the main doors. Adam and Logan stood on the sidewalk at the bus stop sign, both smoking. Logan's lips moved, but his voice never carried to where Bridget walked.

She should offer them a ride. The look in Logan's eyes, his accusations earlier . . . her stomach still rolled from how she'd let him down, all because of her fear and selfishness.

"Do you need a ride?" Bridget called out.

Adam shook his head.

"Awesome. Saves me money." Logan trotted over.

Adam dragged his feet as if he'd been sentenced to life in prison.

"I'm over here." She pointed to the back of the building where staff parked.

They followed her along the sidewalk. When they reached the truck, Logan exclaimed, "Nice ride. Pretty bitchin'. I'd expect a guy to drive this. Not a . . ."

He sheepishly grinned.

"I get that all the time." Bridget pressed the button on her keys to unlock the doors.

Logan moved to open the back door.

"Go ahead and sit in the front, kid," Adam muttered.

"Right on." Logan jumped in the passenger seat.

Bridget's body temperature climbed. Adam's cold countenance was ten times worse when he behaved this way. No, she didn't expect him to be overly friendly after she'd turned away his declaration of love, but he could at least be civil.

She huffed around the truck and got in.

During their drive to the halfway house, Logan babbled about Sheena while Adam sat in stony silence. Every time Bridget snuck a peek in the rearview mirror, Adam continued to stare out the tinted window. The tension matched a thick fog malicious enough to stop traffic on the street if it had seeped out from the truck.

She pulled over in front of the brick building.

"Thanks for the ride." Logan grinned. "You're okay in my book."

Yes, in your book, but not Adam's. "You're welcome. And thank you."

"We're not on for The Gator tomorrow night, then?" Logan cracked open the door.

"As a committee we'll ensure a proper investigation's done for Sheena." Bridget should reassure Logan. He'd been through so much. She reached over and patted his hand.

Adam vacated the truck.

"Sounds cool." Logan's smile brightened to the intensity of the sun. "Thanks. I mean it." He hopped out. "See ya then."

They wandered up the walkway.

A weight filled Bridget. Fine. They'd work together on the committee and only the committee. If Adam wanted to hate her for protecting herself, he could damn well go ahead. It wasn't her fault she'd made a wise decision any other intelligent woman would have made.

She drove off. The only man she needed was Kyle. But

once Adam obtained full custody, he'd probably bolt for Winnipeg. She'd never hear from Kyle, never see him for the rest of her waking days.

Bridget punched the steering wheel. Why was God doing this to her? Why bring Adam back into her life?

Adam sat in the visitation room. He'd brought a board game and a new treat for his boy. This visit had to be extra special since he'd fly out for Ottertail Lake on Sunday night. If Bridget was volunteering for Healing the Spirit, she'd probably catch an earlier flight to the reserve.

He'd filled out the application form and had gotten Harold to fax it off. Emery had contacted Adam at the halfway house, saying he'd get him at the airport. During his engagement to Bridget, Adam hadn't met her younger brother, who'd been in London at the time, preparing to become a priest.

From what he'd heard about Darryl, the guy sounded pretty cool, a hardcore traditionalist who served on band council and worked as the self-governance coordinator.

The couple knew of Adam's past and had still agreed to house him. This meant they didn't judge ex-cons. Too bad Bridget didn't feel the same way.

The door opened. The Hawk strode into the room, clipboard in hand. "Good afternoon, Mr. Guimond."

"Afternoon."

"I understand you'll be away next week." She sat in the chair and crossed her bird legs at the ankles.

"Yep. It's why I wanted to meet before my boy gets here."

"What is there to meet about?" She pursed her skinnier-than-her-legs lips. "You made a decision to cancel your weekly visitation."

Damn bitch. Did she have to make his decision sound like

166

he had chosen booze over Kyle? "I wanted to give you information on the workshop I'm taking. This is why I won't be here next week."

Adam reached inside his jeans pocket and withdrew the crumpled paper. He stood and sauntered over to the gray-haired biddy whose bun was tighter than her attitude.

Using the tips of her fingers, The Hawk snatched the corner of the paper, as if making sure not to touch his criminal red hand. "Give me a moment."

Her cold eyes shifted back and forth, reading about Healing the Spirit. After a couple of minutes of making Adam stand in front of her, she looked up. "A reconciliation of Christian and First Nations communities?"

"Yep." He folded his arms and stared down at her.

"Please, sit." She motioned at the chair beside her, the one Bridget always occupied.

Stupid old biddy. She probably didn't like him having the advantage of glaring down at her.

"And how is this workshop supposed to help you become a responsible father, which you neglected to do the first time you attempted to care for your son?"

Was she serious? Adam stamped down the growl ready to erupt from his hot throat. "It's about the Indian Residential Schools and the ... uh ..." How could he explain himself? He wasn't a smooth speaker. That'd been Bad Bob's department, the man with the golden tongue who'd served as the Winnipeg Warriors' prime negotiator.

"The schools had more than an effect on the kids who went. It also had a bad effect on their kids."

"And your parents attended these schools?"

"Yep. And my grandparents. Their parents, too. Get it?"

"How does this pertain to you?"

"The schools weren't good. Everybody knows this. My parents and grandparents left the school not knowing how to parent. Only knew abuse. Sure didn't help them raise my parents right. And my parents weren't the greatest parents either. You see what I mean? Dominoes."

"Mr. Guimond, do you know how many times I hear this excuse?" The Hawk's voice sharpened to the severity of her beak.

"I ain't giving excuses. I messed up bad. What I'm trying to do is make a better life for myself. I think this workshop will help. It's about . . ." He'd better try to quote the paper. "It's about discovering your inner spirit and engaging the Creator so you can learn to forgive the people who hurt you. Who hurt your race."

"I see." The old bat's dead eyes said she didn't buy what Adam was selling. "Well, if you feel this'll help you, by all means, go to your workshop. I hope you'll explain yourself better to your son than you did to me."

"That's what I plan on doing." He stood and tromped back over to where he'd set his belongings.

The door opened. Kyle dashed inside, big eyes brighter than the sun and his big grin larger than a crescent moon. "Dad! Dad!"

Adam gulped. Maybe he'd made a mistake? Not seeing Kyle next week was a prison shank plunged into his gut. "Hey."

He squatted and opened his arms. Kyle melted against Adam's chest, and he wrapped his boy in a bear hug. His child's warmth, his innocent scent, his light breaths on Adam's ear, talk about capable of making the toughest convict grow a lump in his throat.

"How you been?" he whispered.

"Awesome, Dad. I love Wednesdays."

Hearing those words sweetened Adam's heart to a big tablespoon of sugar. Each visit, his boy was trusting Adam and giving him much-needed love. "So do I. So do I." He patted Kyle's back.

"What're we gonna do?" Kyle beamed.

"I brought this." Adam picked up the board game. "Checkers."

"Checkers?" Kyle peered at the box. "What's that?"

"Something I played as a kid. C'mon, I'll show you how to play."

"Okay." Kyle pranced to the small table where he always sat.

Adam grabbed a bigger chair. If he sat on one of those tiny things, he'd go down fast. Just as he sat, he finally looked at Bridget outfitted in a leg-baring yellow mini-skirt, fuck-me beige sandals with the straps secured around her slim ankles, and sleek arms bared in a white-collared sleeveless blouse. Did she get all sexed up for the Bible thumper, too?

Adam sat. His boy was here, and only he deserved Adam's attention. "It's easy to play. All you gotta do is ste— Err, win all the checkers." A much better word. If he'd said *steal* aloud, The Hawk would have x'd another strike against him.

They played for a half an hour. Kyle's giggles bathed the room in warmth that kneaded away the steel blades in Adam's shoulders since having two women picking him apart was never a picnic.

Now came the moment Adam had dreaded. He cleared his throat while Kyle munched on the cinnamon apple bars Adam had baked. "Y'know how hard I'm trying so we can go out for the afternoon without anyone tagging along."

"Yep." Kyle kept munching, staring up at Adam like he was one of those Z Men his boy worshiped, taking on criminals for the good of society.

I ain't no hero, not at all, but one day I'll be deserving of being called one. "I'm working hard. Going to special meetings every night that are s'posed to make me a better person and father."

"You already are." Kyle grinned and poked Adam's knee.

His son always touched Adam now. He grasped Kyle's fingers. "There's a special workshop starting on Monday at your mom's reserve."

"Yeah. Mom's going. She's leaving on Sunday. I'm staying at Uncle Jude's." Kyle grinned. "Uncle's gonna bring me next week to see you."

There wasn't any saliva in Adam's mouth, and saying what he had to say was tough enough without a good helping of spit. "The workshop's really special."

"Yeah, it is. Uncle Emery's gonna learn how to be a healer of spirits. Grandpa already is and helps the speakers. Uncle Darryl's gonna be a part of the workshop. It's gonna make him happy, Mom said."

"It'll make your Uncle Darryl very happy. It's why I wanna go. I wanna be happy, too."

"You're already happy."

"Yep, seeing you every Wednesday is what makes me super-happy." Adam patted Kyle's knee. "Your Uncle Emery and Uncle Darryl said I could stay at their place for the workshop."

"But you don't need to go." Kyle's lower lip protruded. "You're already happy."

"I know . . ." Adam gulped. "But I'll be a better father and super-happy if I go."

Hate thundered in Kyle's condemning stare, and he wrenched himself from Adam's embrace. "You're going away again. You're leaving."

The accusation in his big, innocent eyes cut across Adam's stomach. Any second his innards should spill onto the floor. "No. No. I'm not leaving."

Adam held up his fingers so Kyle could count them. "I'll be back on Friday evening."

"You're going away again." Kyle shook his head, the hate

continuing to brew like a reckless thunder storm gathering momentum to twist into a threatening tornado. "Going away. Going away for four more years."

"No. No. Not four years." Adam reached out to draw Kyle back into his embrace.

"Go away!" Kyle scampered backward. "Go away! Mom'll never leave me! She loves me! You don't! You're going away! Get lost!"

"Kyle!" Bridget stood.

Everything happened in a millisecond. Kyle darted for Bridget, Adam's heart fell to the floor and burst, and The Hawk sucked in what fat she had on her cheeks while her thin lips twisted into an *I knew it* satisfied look.

CHAPTER EIGHTEEN: GOD WAS NEVER ON YOUR SIDE

Bridget paced the kitchen. Kyle had cried all the way to the car. Cried all the way to Pizza World. Cried all the way home. Cried all the way to his bedroom. He'd thrown himself on the lower bunk, a place he loathed because it was too dark below, and had cried himself to sleep while she'd rubbed his back and kissed the top of his head.

He'd never eaten one slice of his favorite treat or sipped any cola, another of his number one delights.

If Bridget kept her trap shut or encouraged Kyle's outburst, she'd win custody. Mrs. Dale was already on Bridget's side. Damn the conscience that told her to do the right thing. God did not want her to turn Kyle against his father.

Life wasn't fair. She always did the right thing and got nowhere. Alone. With nothing but a career again if she lost Kyle.

Bridget hustled from the kitchen to the living room and dropped on the sofa. The suede upholstery and feather-filled cushions always swathed her in comfort. Not tonight. The throw pillow's velvet smoothness she hugged might as well be a rock. Nothing would expunge the tightness in her chest until she talked to Kyle and reassured Adam, who'd been left behind in the visitation room, devastation carved into his sunken eyes, downturned lips, and dejected jawline.

She glanced at the crystal clock perched on the glass square side table. Seven. Kyle still had to bathe. She'd talk to him and defend a man who didn't deserve defending.

"Sweetie, it's seven-thirty. Time for your bath." Bridget stood in the doorway of Kyle's room. She could do this. She'd prayed the Rosary, asking for strength.

"No." Disappointment filled his tiny voice.

"Remember what I said about rules we have to follow, even when we don't want to follow them? C'mon." She kept her tone light, coaxing.

Kyle rose from the lower bunk. He hugged himself.

She rubbed the back of his head. "It won't take long, honey. A quick bath before you sleep."

They padded to the main bathroom where Bridget had already filled the jetted tub and had added a generous helping of Mr. Suds, another treat Kyle was only allowed on Saturday nights. She'd even added his favorite toys to the water.

"C'mon. Time to undress before it gets cold."

"Fine." Kyle yanked off his clothes and threw them in the corner.

Even though her son was hurting, Bridget couldn't allow such behavior. "That's not where they go. Hamper." She pointed.

"Fine." He snatched his belongings, tossed them into the bin, and slammed shut the lid. "There. Happy?"

"No. I'm not happy. Why would I be? How can I be happy when you're upset?" She sat on the bathing stool and motioned at the tub.

Kyle climbed in. "I'm not going anymore."

"Going where?" She dipped the bowl into the water. "Cover your eyes. Mom's wetting your hair."

He did as told while she emptied the bowl over his prickly hair. "I'm not visiting him again. He's not my dad."

Here was Bridget's cue to talk up an unworthy Adam. "We have rules to follow. Children and Family Services expect us to visit every Wednesday at three-thirty."

"He broke the rule." Kyle scowled. "He won't be there next Wednesday. He's going to the workshop. He's going away. He's not coming back."

"He's coming back." Bridget set aside the bowl and squirted some shampoo into her palm. She massaged Kyle's scalp. "He'll be there for the next visit."

"I don't wanna go. You can't make me go." Kyle kept his arms folded and lower lip turned down in a big pout.

"If you don't go, I'll be in trouble." Bridget dipped the bowl back into the water and rinsed off his hair.

"No, you won't. We'll go. We'll go live at Grandpa and Grandma's."

"That's called running away. You know God doesn't want us to do that. He wants us to trust Him." Then why did the urge to flee to the safety of her parents like an eight-year-old tempt Bridget? The days of Daddy making everything right were long done.

She was thirty-six. A grown woman. Her parents' faith had sustained her as a child, and when she'd received Confirmation by the bishop in grade eight, Mom and Dad had told her she was old enough to begin seeking her own faith by enrolling her in the Catholic Youth Group that Jude participated in.

"Understand, this was a very hard decision for your dad. He counts the clock every day, and then he checks off each day on the calendar, waiting to see you. It broke his heart to . . ." Bridget choked back the disgust in her throat. Adam had never made sacrifices for her. Ever.

"It broke his heart to choose the workshop over visiting you. But he understood attending Healing the Spirit was the best thing for him, and you. He's doing this for you. Not only him. He's going to miss you very much next week."

"No, he won't. He didn't miss me . . . miss me when he

went to the big house."

"I told you. He broke a rule. He had to go to the big house to make up for breaking the rule. He's back now. He wants to be a part of your life again. I . . ."

Lord, spit it out for me.

"I want you to be a part of his life, too. Your dad's a . . ." *Say it.* "A good man who's trying very hard. If I didn't think he was worthy of being your dad, we wouldn't go to these visits. I'd fight the people in charge by telling them you shouldn't visit your dad."

The tight line straightening Kyle's mouth slackened. "You'd fight them for me, even if it went against the rules?"

"Yes." Bridget lathered the washcloth and held it out since she was teaching Kyle to bathe himself. "Okay, it's ready. Show Mom how you wash up."

Beaming, he took the cloth. "And we'll talk every night?"

"I already told you, at six-thirty, once you're done supper and before it's time for bed, we'll talk on Uncle Jude's computer."

"Will Dad talk to me?" His big eyes glittered, full of hope.

Video chatting might be considered visiting. "I don't know, honey. I think your dad would have to get permission from Mrs. Dale. I can ask him to speak to her. Uncle Emery has a laptop your dad can use."

"Really?" Kyle clapped.

"You know you'll have to apologize to your dad. He was awfully hurt today."

"I know." Kyle lowered his head. "I didn't mean to say that. I thought he was going away again."

Something resembling white-hot lightning flashed through Bridget's chest. Boy, after what she'd done, Adam had better not screw up. If he hurt Kyle again, there'd be no more chances. She'd been *this close* to calling this boy her very own today.

Adam heaved himself to his room. He should have skipped tonight's meeting since he hadn't listened to one word from the reading or the comments from the other members.

When feeling like this, he was supposed to help another alcoholic. Fuck it. Why bother? His own son hated him. Bridget would probably have to drag Kyle to the next visit. And at the visit, he'd have to endure Kyle's forced presence full of loathing. The Hawk was probably at her nest right now, squawking and singing at his failure.

He'd lost. Bridget had gotten her way. She'd get to keep Kyle.

Adam fingered his Big Book. Maybe he'd meander down to Logan's room and they'd read a story together.

Someone banged on the door. "Guimond. Phone."

Raw fury erupted in Adam's veins, his blood thundering. Only one person called at this hour. He ripped open the door and stomped down the hall. If Bridget dared to tell him Kyle wanted no part of Adam anymore, he'd let her have it.

He snatched up the phone in the lounge. "Yep."

"Hello. It's Bridget."

Ice didn't coat her voice. She sounded . . . weary. "What's up?"

"I spoke to Kyle. He's fine and understands why you're attending the workshop. He's making a . . . he's going to surprise you with a present during your next visit. Art's his favorite subject. I imagine he'll be working hard on something while he's at Jude's."

The floor pretty much fell out from beneath Adam. What the hell? Bridget had gone to bat for him? She hadn't used Kyle's outburst to turn Adam's own son against him? This was why he'd fallen madly in love with her. This was why he'd wanted to marry her. This was why she had the power to bring him to his knees. Never before had he met a woman who'd cast aside her own desires for those she loved, or those she didn't love.

Adam didn't deserve Bridget's compassionate, generous spirit. "Thank you." *I'm not supposed to love you anymore. I'm supposed to hate you for choosing Bible Boy over me. But I still love you. I'll never stop loving you.*

"You don't need to thank me. You're Kyle's father. I'm his caregiver. It's my responsibility to help you build a healthy relationship with him." Pain lingered in her words.

She was hurting big time. She didn't want to lose Kyle any more than Adam did. As bad as he felt, he couldn't turn his son over to Bridget. The boy came from him. He'd helped create Kyle. "You're one in a million."

"You should speak to Mrs. Dale. Kyle's hoping you two can video chat. I told him Emery has a laptop you could use, but I'm not sure if video chatting is considered ... well, visiting."

"I'll ask The Hawk." He'd phone the old bird tomorrow. Then she'd see he was sincere. He did want more than a weekly measly hour.

"Okay. I'll talk to you later. Bye."

"Wait." The word hurled from Adam's mouth. He gripped the phone. His heartbeat quickened.

"What is it?"

I miss you, kwe. *I wish you'd give me a second chance. I wanna move on. I wanna forget you, us, but I can't.* "Uh ... I ... thanks."

"You're welcome. Bye."

"Bridget?"

"Yes?"

"Why?"

"Why what?"

Adam cleared his throat. Damn, this was hard to ask. "Why'd you do it?"

"Do what?"

"Y'know. Why'd you help me?"

"Because you're his father, and although I didn't give you a second chance, Kyle deserves to if you're truly sincere this time." The weariness in Bridget's tone changed to her familiar snapping.

Adam choked down his sputter. Boy, she really hated him. She'd never forgive him. Ever. "I am sincere."

"Then I'll see you at the workshop. I simply wanted you to know your son and I had a long talk. Goodnight."

This time she hung up. The dial tone, snottier than Bridget's attitude, buzzed in Adam's ear. He slammed down the phone.

Bridget set the cordless phone on the glass table. She lurched to the balcony's railing. This was Mom and Dad's fault. because from birth they'd filled her conscience with church doctrine. And the same for the Catholic school she'd attended. The same went for her former teachers. Also Father Arnold.

Would the Catholic Church keep her company after Kyle left? Hell no. She'd be alone, cleaning Kyle's bedroom after he disappeared with his dad, all because the pinch of guilt and her own strict morals had told her to do the right thing and defend Adam.

So much for revenge. So much for making Adam pay. The only one paying was Bridget.

She slumped in the wicker chair and hugged herself. A lump built in her throat. Tears stung her eyes. The ache in her heart swelled.

Adam set the last of his shirts into the duffel bag.

Logan sat in the chair beside the dresser.

"When I get back, you'd better have gone to all your meetings." Adam zipped the duffel bag.

"I will. I will."

"Readings. Every night. Go for coffee with the old-timers. They'll keep you busy until I get back. Sponsor's orders." Adam thrust his finger.

"Chill, man. You don't gotta go all parent on me." Logan grinned, but his crooked smile didn't match the sadness in his blue eyes.

"You'll be all right. My cab's probably here. Gotta get. I don't wanna miss my plane." There was nothing to worry about. The kid would be okay on his own for a few days. Adam headed for the door.

"Dude?"

"Yeah?" He turned.

Logan stood. He pulled at the hem of his shirt. His gaze traveled about. He licked his lips. "I wanna give you major props. Nobody's done this for me before. Y'know? Nobody. You're . . . I can't believe the old bitch is giving you grief about your kid. Anybody would want you for a dad. Serious, man."

His begging, bright-blue eyes, glassy and full of need said, *I wish you were my dad.*

"Hey . . ." Adam meandered over. He shifted the duffel bag. He held out his hand.

Logan laid his palm in Adam's. They tightened their fingers to a firm grip. Adam yanked the kid against him. He'd never hugged a grown man before, but patting Logan's skinny back left a warm feeling as comforting as a gentle breeze in the pit of Adam's stomach.

"You're gonna be fine. I'll be back Friday night."

"I know, dude." Logan's words were muffled. "I know. Be good. Stay frosty."

"I will. The same for you, man." Adam patted Logan's

back again. "I gotta bounce. I'll see you on Friday. We'll do chow somewhere. My treat. I'll be hungry."

"Okay." Logan continued to cling to Adam.

For some reason, Adam loathed leaving Logan behind, just as he loathed having to miss seeing Kyle on Wednesday. The old-timers at the recovery meetings would tell Adam to put his trust in his higher power. They'd tell him everything would work out the way Creator had planned everything to work out.

Chapter Nineteen: Brave New World

Bridget hung her shirts on the hangers. The bedroom at Mom and Dad's used to belong to Emery, before he'd moved out after graduating high school and relocated to Thunder Bay to attend university.

Everyone used this room now, the only one available. If Jude visited, her brother and sister-in-law shared the double bed while the kids slept in sleeping bags on the living room floor.

As for Kyle, he and Bridget bunked together. She'd better unpack her laptop right away so she could talk to him this evening.

Mom poked her head in the bedroom. "We'll go to the church soon. Your dad and Roy want to set up the tables."

"Are we keeping the stuff here or bringing it to the church?" Bridget hung the last shirt. She'd spend Saturday afternoon grocery shopping for the workshop. Food was extremely expensive in the north. To keep costs down, she'd purchased the supplies at the big outlets in the city and stowed them on the plane.

"The church. Roy and George are hauling everything over from the airport right now." Mom sat on the edge of the bed. Her painted pink nails skimmed her slim arm. "I thought you'd speak more about your date. How's Stephen?"

"I'm assuming he's returned to Kenora. School starts tomorrow."

Gooseflesh spread across Mom's arm she continued to knead. This meant she wanted to talk. She'd probably seen Adam's name on the registry sheet. "You know I have the utmost faith in you to make the right decisions."

"I know." Bridget emptied her toiletry bag on the dresser.

"Adam's parole officer must have had some concerns about him attending the workshop." Mom's light tone was stiffer than Dad's clerical collar.

"I don't know. They must have talked. He told Kyle he wouldn't see him this Wednesday."

"How did Kyle take it?"

Horribly. "Fine."

"Adam's staying at Emery and Darryl's."

"I know."

Mom sighed. "You used to share everything with me. After you met Adam . . ."

Maybe Bridget had kept quiet because Mom and Dad had silently disapproved of her whirlwind romance that had led to an engagement in one year to an ex-convict.

Her parents were right. She'd been a total fool. Was she one of those women who believed in reforming hard cases? No. Adam had reformed himself. They'd met when he'd had a year and a half of sobriety under his belt.

"Bridget?"

She set the can of mousse on the dresser. Mom wasn't going to let their conversation end until she had answers. Bridget might as well give up the goods because Mom truly cared. "He's trying his best to gain full custody of Kyle."

"Is he ready?"

"I don't know." Bridget set the barrettes and other clips to tie back her hair next to the mousse. "He seems to be doing good. As far as I know, he attends his support meetings every night. He's mentioned going to sweats. I don't think he has a sponsor."

"He should have one."

"He only moved back over a month ago. It takes time for people in the program to find a good sponsor. I think he's sponsoring someone."

"Oh?"

"He's a young man out of treatment. His name's Logan. His girlfriend is the girl in care who was pulled from the river."

"Heavens." Mom palmed her mouth.

"Logan's struggling. Adam's helping him."

"Is this a good time for him to leave this young man alone?"

"I don't know Logan that well. IWA's setting up a committee to look into Sheena Keesha's death. From what I understand, she didn't have anyone. Her mother's dead. Her father's in prison."

"You'll be on the committee?"

"Yes. And Adam. He volunteered."

Mom folded her arms. She then unfolded them. Then she refolded them.

"Spit it out." Bridget zipped the empty toiletry case.

"We're supposed to leave everything in the Lord's hands, but I wonder sometimes. I wonder if he's trying to get close to you . . . to . . . reconcile."

"I think it's up to me to say no."

"Have you?" Mom's slim throat moved as if she'd swallowed. "It's not my business. I know." She dropped her head of golden curls flecked with gray.

"Did Dad ask you to talk to me?" Mom wasn't this nosey or pushy. Doggedness was Dad's department.

"You know how your father is. He's concerned. He'll always show concern for his children, no matter how old you are."

Dad had shown more than concern when Emery and Darryl had reconnected. Her father had put poor Emery through hell. Dad would never meddle in Bridget's life after they'd butted heads too many times. He was a shrewd one because he always sent Mom to do his dirty work.

"Tell Dad I'm fine. I didn't bring Adam here. He brought himself."

"That's what concerns your father. He's worried about Kyle and if Adam can sincerely care for him."

"His visits are still supervised. I imagine they'll be supervised for a long time. And it's not Kyle he's concerned about. It's me. Admit it."

"Honey . . ." Mom wrung her hands. "We're both concerned. It happened so fast last time."

"Nothing's happening this time. I told Adam no."

"He asked?" Mom's intense green eyes only Emery had inherited bulged.

"Yes. I said no." Bridget faced the mirror.

Mom's reflection, full of concern, stared back. "What about Stephen. How'd your date go?"

"Great. Stephen's a nice man. Easy to talk to."

"Will you see him again?"

"Not until Thanksgiving weekend. He's flying in to see his mom. We're going to go out Saturday night."

"You won't see him at all during September?" Disappointment lurked in Mom's question.

"I told him how busy I am. He said he'd text me to see if I have time to get together around the middle of the month. We'll see." Bridget pushed her hair over her shoulder. "I'll be a week up here. The first fall meeting for the CWA is the following Thursday after I get back. I have a couple of work meetings scheduled. My priority's Kyle. I don't like leaving him too often."

"I understand. Motherhood's a great responsibility, and you're doing a fine job. Try to remember you also need a personal life."

"I do. It's why I went out for dinner. But I don't want to get involved again. Not right now. If this ends up being my last year . . ." Bridget's throat burned. "If it's Kyle's last year, our last year together, I want to spend it with him."

Mom's mouth sank. "Have you spoken to a lawyer?"

"Is it right?" Bridget swiveled on her heel. "Is it right to fight Adam for custody? He's Kyle's father."

"Why the change of heart? When we last spoke, you were adamant about keeping Kyle."

"Maybe the Lord's getting under my skin. Maybe He's telling me I have to do the right thing . . . for Kyle. He loves Adam. They're getting along great. Adam's going to ask Mrs. Dale if he can video chat this week since he won't see Kyle on Wednesday."

"And what if Adam returns to his former ways? Honey, we're talking about a man who led a hard life. Crime and alcohol are all he knows. I understand he tried to change at one time, but he couldn't. He served time in a federal prison. It doesn't get any worse than that."

"He also spent six months on day parole and worked. He's on full parole and still working."

"He did all that before." Mom stood. She closed the gap between them. Their fingers brushed. "I worry about Kyle. Adam's indecision could hurt him, hurt him enough he might not recover this time."

A blade raked Bridget's chest. Mom was right. Adam had crushed Kyle under his boot heel when he'd chosen to attend the workshop. The boy's heart was fragile. If Adam screwed up again, Kyle's heart might remain broken forever.

Adam hadn't experienced a gravel runway before. Hell, he'd never been on a plane before. The flight had provided a peaceful view of the endless sea of forest, rock cuts, and lakes while he was being jostled and bounced about during his four hundred and eighty kilometer jaunt from Thunder Bay.

They were close to the Manitoba border, central standard time, according to the pilot, the time zone Adam had been accustomed to until he'd moved to Thunder Bay.

He squinted through the cloud of sand, maybe having spied a small building known as Ottertail Lake's airport. The pilot had mentioned the reserve was one of five that had invested in their own air service to provide passage and delivery to over twenty-five First Nations communities up this way.

There were only two accessible routes to get here—fly or drive an ice road during the winter.

The plane started a slow turn. Adam continued to peer out the window. The pilot had mentioned he'd flown the workshop trainers to the reserve this morning. Adam guessed he was the only out-of-town participant.

Ten minutes later, the small plane parked in front of the airport, and the disembark door opened. Adam rose, crouching so his head wouldn't hit the ceiling as he moved to the back to get off the plane. A man about six-feet, or maybe taller, stood at the airport window, watching. This must be Emery, Bridget's brother.

While heading to the entrance, Adam slipped on his cowboy hat he hadn't worn during the flight because he was too damned tall. He waved away the dust and opened the door.

The man came forward, hand outstretched. Warmth flooded his bright-green eyes. "Adam, it's great to finally meet you. I'm Emery."

"Good meeting you." Adam loathed shaking hands, too damn proper, but he responded to Emery's polite gesture.

"Let me get your luggage. Darryl can't be here. He had to

go into the office, but he'll be at the house later. I hope you don't mind that I brought company. Our dog always has to be with one of us."

"Not a problem. I like dogs."

Another man of *Anishinaabe* heritage plunked down Adam's duffel bag.

"This isn't like most airports." Emery's soft chuckle matched his voice, the kind of tone capable of lulling a guy to sleep during a bout of insomnia. "No waiting for your luggage to appear on the baggage carousel."

"It's my first flight. Wouldn't know about that stuff." Adam slung the duffel bag strap over his shoulder. "Don't need much, either."

"You should see what my sister packs." Emery's face twisted to horror. "Oh geez. Please excuse me. I didn't mean—"

"No problem. I was engaged to her. Know all about her. She's got shoes and purses to match every outfit."

"Don't forget her earrings and barrettes." The horror on Emery's face faded to a comforting smile. He strode to the exit door.

"Yeah, she's got a lot of those, too." Her girly femininity was a nice touch to her extreme independence. Adam followed along outside to more gravel and a big truck as flashy as Bridget's Annihilator. "Nice ride."

A black-and-white dog poked its head out the window.

"Darryl bought this when he lived in Winnipeg." Emery got in. He slipped on black sunglasses. "That's Bandit. She rules the house and the truck."

Adam opened the back door and patted the dog, who yipped. He set his duffel bag on the floor. Bandit demanded another pat, so Adam obliged. Her fur was soft and clean. Warm. At one point he'd considered getting Kyle a dog or even a cat if they'd found a new place that had allowed pets, because he'd wanted normalcy for his son, a normal most children experienced. Pets. Sports. Good grades.

"One thing I'm learning about this area. People like their trucks." Adam got in the front.

"You have to have them, living up this way." The engine hummed to life. Emery guided them away from the airport.

"In the 'Peg, it's SUVs. You see trucks, but not too many. It's the parking. Spaces are tight. Guess it's easier for people to find a spot."

"It's the same in Southern Ontario. I had an all-wheel drive car." Emery took them down a road full of box-shaped houses and overgrown ditches. Some of the lawns needed a good mowing.

Maybe Adam's own home reserve looked this way.

Bandit continued to stick her head out the window, barking.

"You like it up here?" Children played on the side of the road. A few old people sat outside on their front steps.

"Love it. My parents moved back when I was eight. It's my strongest memory. I can recall when we lived in Thunder Bay, but this place sticks to my brain. It's always been and always will be home." Emery stared straight ahead.

Adam had never called a place home before. He'd never felt at home anywhere until he'd met Bridget. After Kyle had been born, Adam had meandered from rented room to rented room, trying to find a safe place for his son to grow up. Thunder Bay had been his answer. Sure, he'd managed a small bachelor apartment for Kyle downtown within their welfare allotment. It hadn't been easy raising a baby and attending recovery meetings.

Work? Not a chance. Adam hadn't known any babysitters, let alone any he could trust. That'd all changed after Bridget had whirled into his life. She'd recommended Jude's sitter, who'd gladly taken Kyle in while also watching Noah and Rebekah.

How could Adam have blown such a big chance at a new life? Stupid. Fucking stupid. He rubbed his temple. They looked to be in the main part of the reserve. A big office building. A restaurant. Some other buildings.

"We have our own radio station." Emery pointed at a small blue shack.

"Pretty cool. Didn't think reserves had much of anything."

"Some communities are more progressive than others. We have lots of businesses up this way. A motel. A tourist camp. Different services like health care, education, a recreation center. Even a golf course. Now, it's hardly a masterpiece . . ." Emery chuckled. "But it's playable."

"You golf?"

"Yes. I'm teaching my husband. He's learning but has a way to go. His golf swing is more like a baseball swing. A big hook that never sees the fairway."

Adam had no idea about golf. He'd always likened the sport to rich people and fancy country clubs.

They left behind the main part and took another dirt road where the area was hillier with rock cuts and lots of trees. "This is nice."

"It's more bush this way. We're going to Long River. It's where we live."

"You work?"

Emery shook his head. "The only job opening was for a new teacher. I couldn't apply. I don't have the qualifications."

"I thought you had a degree."

"Bachelor of Social Work. Wrong field."

"So what you do then?"

"Lots of volunteering. I work with the youth of the community. I help at the church. Once I start my master's in January, my schedule will be swamped."

"Master's?"

"Yes. My MSW."

What the heck was an MSW? Adam wouldn't ask.

The winding road was a long stretch of about ten clicks.

Emery turned the truck onto another gravel road. "Almost there. I'm sure you want to unpack and rest. I'm making fish for supper."

"Sounds good. Been awhile when I last had fish. Walleye?"

"Yes. I caught lots over the summer that I keep in the freezer."

What was it about Bridget's brother that brought out the conversation in Adam? He wasn't much for strangers. Maybe it was Emery's voice. Or his sincerity. He seemed to want to know Adam. "Sounds good. I don't eat fish often. Hell. Maybe twice."

Emery guided them down a road full of small log homes. "This is the older part of the community. The first homes were built this way."

"Nice."

"Sturdy, too. Our house dates back to Darryl's great-grandparents. It used to have a dirt floor. I think his grandparents added the wood floor. Real hardwood. Darryl redid them last year."

"Peaceful." Towering spruce trees stood sentry behind the row of houses. The smell of the river sure wasn't like the one bordering his old range in the 'Peg. Fresh. Clean. Not full of waste and other crap.

Adam chuckled under his breath at the *range* word. Funny, he still had prison thinking going through his brain now and then.

"What is it?"

"Not much. Thinking of my old nabe as a range."

Emery entered the driveway of a small log home facing the river. "Range. Ah. What you refer to as cell blocks."

"You know?" Adam hadn't expected a man who'd contemplated the priesthood to recognize iron house slang.

"Yes. We were educated in the jargon used by inmates as part of our teachings at seminary. For my fieldwork, I accompanied the chaplain on his visits."

"You really wanted to work with the down and out, huh?" Adam cracked open the passenger door.

Bandit hopped out from the window.

"I don't see anyone as down and out. I see people as people, some needing more help than others." Emery also vacated the truck.

"Is that why you wanna get more education?" Adam slung the duffel bag strap over his shoulder.

"I always wanted to complete my master's in social work." Emery strode to the house.

Grass encroached on the gravel path. Nothing could stop nature. It was nice to have a break from pavement and tiny pebbles beneath Adam's running shoes.

He'd made the right decision. Staying with Emery and Darryl could be a life-changing week for Adam.

CHAPTER TWENTY: MARCHING OFF TO WAR

Adam gazed around at the Treaty Grounds. So this was what they looked like. Grass everywhere, cut and kept neat. A big arbor for powwows with grandstands for spectators to watch. On the north side, there was a raised booth where the MC spoke to the participants. A couple of other buildings were probably washrooms and changing rooms for people to change into their traditional regalia. Even the smell of spruce was abundant here.

Bandit barked and trotted along the grass, sniffing here and there.

"They built this place a few years ago to celebrate the centennial of the Treaty the reserve signed with the government." Darryl meandered to the grandstands, hands stuffed in his pockets.

The breeze rustled the leaves on the birch trees that circled the area all the way to the lake. A few birds flew overhead. The water lapping against the rocks carried to where Adam stood. "Now I know why you like to visit the rez's new digs. It's nice out here. Right next to the lake."

"I find nature's the best place to speak to *Gitche Manidoo*," Darryl replied in a silvery voice. He folded his arms across the light paunch of his stomach. His long black hair was tied off his round face. "I'll be coming out here lots during the workshop. Reflect. Pray."

"Cool. It'd hit the spot if I could find one of my own."

Somewhere to sit and hash out in his head what he had learned at the workshop each day.

"Hey, I know the perfect spot for you. C'mon." Darryl stocked to the truck. "You're gonna love it. It's right where the church is."

"The church?" Adam followed.

Bridget removed the big pot from the stove top. Thank goodness the parish basement was cool. Members of the Catholic Women's Association filled the kitchen, the ladies preparing food for tomorrow's commencement of Healing the Spirit.

Having already cut everything that would go into the potato salad, all Bridget had to do was drain the pot and then add the contents to the big bowl beside her on the counter.

Mom fanned herself while stirring another big pot, this one full of beans. "Once I drain these, we're done. I'll bake them tomorrow so they're fresh."

"Not how you imagined you'd spend your vacation, hmm?" Jenny, a good friend of Mom's, poked Bridget's side.

"I don't mind using my vacation time to help." Steam whooshed up from the sink where Bridget had emptied half the potatoes into a big colander.

Video chatting with Kyle before coming to the church had been smart idea. When Bridget got home, her aching body would seek a relaxing, comforting bed. Then she'd be up at six to begin making pancakes and sausages for the workshop participants.

"Let me get that, sweetheart. You haven't stopped since we got here." The offer came from Rosanne, a nice older lady and one of the eucharistic ministers for the church.

"Thanks. I could use a small break." Bridget poured two iced teas. She wandered from the kitchen to the main part of the church hall where the men set up tables, assembled a small stage for the trainers to speak from, and readied other necessities for the workshop.

Dad stood in the middle of everything, speaking to the two trainers.

A laptop and LCD projector claimed Emery's attention. He double-checked the equipment.

"Here." Bridget held out an iced tea. Although the basement was cool, the off-beige colors and numerous pictures of past parishioners and priests lining one wall offered a blanket of comfort she forever experienced whenever here.

"Thanks." Emery took the cup and sat. He motioned at the other chair.

"Is that your laptop?" Bridget also sat.

"No. It belongs to the trainers." Emery glanced around. "They're here . . . somewhere."

"Talking to Dad." Bridget motioned. "Where's Bandit?"

"At home. Dad picked me up in case Darryl wanted to take Adam for a tour of the reserve in the truck."

Bridget wouldn't rub her cup, or shift in her chair, or pick at her clothes. She and Adam were here by chance. He wanted to help himself. She wanted to help the participants.

"You didn't hear me, did you?" Emery's question sounded more like a statement.

"What did you say?"

Amusement lingered in her brother's gaze. "Hmm, I was in the same quagmire two months ago."

Did he imply she had deep feelings for Adam and that she'd end up marrying him as Emery had done with Darryl? "What exactly are you saying?"

"You froze my iced tea." Emery held up the cup. His smile wasn't smug but bemusement-filled.

"Are you saying my answer was cold?"

"No. Your tone was." Emery stood. "C'mon, let's go cool

off at the lake."

Bridget followed him to the back of the church where the other set of stairs was located. This door faced the water at the main entrance of the church.

"Do a lot of people use it?" Bridget opened the door. She pointed at the chair lift installed over three years ago, which had, according to Mom and Dad, eaten every cent of the parish's budget in order to accommodate the disabled parishioners.

"It's pretty popular." Emery wandered outside. "A lot of the regulars are getting older."

"Is the pastoral council worried about nobody replacing them?" The outside stairs were built to accommodate the elderly since each step was wider and shallower than a normal staircase. A landing provided a resting spot for those using walkers or canes.

"They're worried. I'm not." Emery meandered to the lake edge where a few big trees grazed.

The peaceful spot was a place where Bridget had enjoyed sitting as a teenager, especially on the big branch that hung over the lake. "Why aren't you worried?"

"People will always need God. And God is here, waiting." Emery shifted to his haunches, staring out at the lake. "At the beginning of July, when you told me about Darryl joining forces with the Kabatay family to stop the workshop from happening, I came back here believing my call from God was to help the church and the laity."

Bridget might as well humor her brother. He deserved to have his say. Unlike Dad and Jude, Emery didn't push his beliefs on others. He was merely trying to help.

"I believed I was responsible for Darryl's hatred of the church. You always knew the truth about us. I kept denying how I felt." He rubbed the side of the cup, words slower and voice hushed. "I knew God wanted this workshop to happen. At the time, I believed it was for the people who wanted to seek healing from the residential schools."

He faced her. Thoughtfulness filled his gaze. "God has a plan for everyone attending this workshop. I was also included in His plan. He created Darryl for me. I turned away from a wonderful gift our Lord had given me, all because I believed I was doing the right thing by denying who I was by seeking the priesthood.

"I was wrong." He frowned. "God desired for Darryl and me to resolve our differences, and we did. The Lord has a plan for everyone, if we are willing to trust Him."

The million-dollar question sat on the tip of Bridget's tongue. "So you think there's more to Adam moving to Thunder Bay than having full custody of Kyle again."

"Darryl gave me great advice on our vision quest." Emery again rubbed the side of his cup. "He told me what matters is the truth I discover, not anyone else's truth."

"I'm not going into the bush to sit in a swarm of mosquitoes for a whole weekend like you and Darryl did." A vision quest might have helped Emery and Darryl reconnect, but Bridget's case was hopeless.

"I'm not suggesting you do." Emery's chuckle cut the mounting tension circulating in Bridget's limbs. Even his crinkling green eyes melted her wall of defense. "Besides, the humidity would ruin your hairdo."

"Oh, puh-leeze, stop it." She teasingly poked Emery's knee.

"There is a place up there to reflect." He used his thumb to motion at the stairs. Gone was his smile. In its place was his gentle, prodding gaze.

"There's nothing to discern." Bridget yanked at some grass. "This is different. Darryl didn't make promises he couldn't keep. Darryl isn't an alcoholic. Darryl didn't turn his back on a fiancée and a child to run off and . . . wallow in self-pity. Darryl didn't end up in prison . . . again."

"I'm not suggesting you and Adam reconcile. I'm simply asking you to keep an open mind to what our Lord has planned for you."

"I know His plan already. Adam's doing great. In time, he'll gain full custody of Kyle. God used me as a servant— what He always does—so I could mother Kyle while the Big Guy waited on Adam to get his shit together."

The story of Bridget's life. Sacrifice for others. Helping others. The women were right. She'd used a week's vacation time to cook and clean. "I promised myself I'd look out for me for round two." So much for that.

"Are you?"

"No. Kyle comes first." Bridget's muscles ached from sitting on her haunches. She plopped on the grass and crossed her legs. "Don't say anything to anyone."

"I won't."

"I shouldn't have asked." She sighed. "As if you'd reveal someone's secret."

They both shared a quiet smile.

"Adam and Kyle's last visit went horrible." She puffed out a breath and told Emery everything—her talk to Kyle and call to Adam. "Now am I sucker or what?" She drained the last of the iced tea.

"You're not a sucker. You did what you thought was right. And it was the right decision for everyone, including you."

"Then why does it hurt?" The dull ache in Bridget's chest continued to throb.

"Why wouldn't it hurt? You consider Kyle your son. You've known him since you met Adam." Emery's soothing tone seemed to brush Bridget's hair in reassurance in the same way she always lulled Kyle's anxiety. "Doing the right thing doesn't mean it won't hurt."

"I'm not in the mood for your logic." Bridget didn't mean to snap, but for once, couldn't someone see things from her point of view?

"I'm not trying to be logical. I'm being understanding—at least I hoped I was. I didn't mean to upset you . . ."

Guilt niggled in Bridget's stomach. "I'm sorry. I didn't mean to—"

"Don't apologize. Adam put you in a tough position. What you're feeling is normal. I wish I had some words of wisdom or could magically take away your pain, but I can't. I'm sorry. I really am. I don't want you to lose Kyle either." He wet his lips. "What I'm trying to say is have faith. It's why I suggested you should go upstairs and visit Christ. Dad set out the consecrated host for this reason. He wants God's Son available to those who need Him during the workshop."

"When did they set it out?"

"After Mass this morning."

"Will they continue with the daily Mass schedules?"

"Yes. The Catholic participants wish to attend Mass before the workshop starts. Darryl and Basil are going to run a morning prayer downstairs for the traditional participants. It's always best to start with prayer before addressing the day."

Tires rolling over gravel carried to where they sat. Bridget shifted her focus to Darryl's truck pulling up. Someone was in the passenger seat. Adam.

"What're they doing here?" A flicker of panic sat at the base of Bridget's spine.

"It's a workshop. He'll be here all week." Emery's voice remained calm.

"I know he will, but I didn't expect him tonight. I thought he'd—"

"I told you Darryl's probably giving Adam a tour of the

reserve. The church is part of the reserve."

"He'll see the church all week." Great, she'd snapped again.

The truck doors slammed shut. Bandit scampered to where they sat.

"He's probably going to show Adam our old trail. It's a great place to sit and pray."

"Oh, your old trail. Darryl took Kyle there when we were last here." Bridget petted the dog as Bandit yipped and sniffed. Maybe Adam did have a legitimate reason for coming to the church.

"Hey, how's it going?" Darryl called out.

Adam swaggered across the grass. His strong thighs bulged against his jeans, and a beige t-shirt hugged his thick muscles. Black waves of hair edged out from his cowboy hat.

"I wanted to show Adam a great spot to get away and meditate." Darryl pointed at the thick bush about five hundred meters away. "There's a path there. It leads to a set of rocks where you can sit at the water and be alone."

"I'll check it out." Adam stared at the trail.

"You didn't bring the drum?" Emery asked Darryl.

"Yeah. Got it in the box. Help me bring it inside. Basil wants it set up in the middle." Darryl meandered to the truck.

Emery followed.

Had those two disappeared purposely?

Bridget rose. She ought to smack her brother and brother-in-law. "I should get inside. The women probably need me."

"Whatever you need to do." Adam's brow flickered, and his jaw hardened.

"Bridget, can you do me a favor and show Adam where the trail is?" Darryl called out.

Tension crawled along Bridget's shoulders. If Emery had asked, she'd have a reason to be suspicious, but Darryl was busy unloading the sacred drum from his truck.

"You don't gotta get all pissy, *kwe*." Adam snorted. "I may not have any experience in the bush, but I think I can find a simple trail."

"Don't call me that. C'mon." She huffed across the grass. "It's over here."

Bridget approached the bush where a stand of poplar trees stood proud. She didn't have to push against the underbrush because Darryl, she assumed, had kept the old trail clear. "It's this way."

"Guess I should have brought my compass. I wouldn't have thought of using the opening in the . . . all this stuff."

"It's underbrush."

"Thanks for telling the homeboy what it is." Sarcasm dripped on Adam's reply. "I only know how to navigate through the hood."

If he didn't shut his mouth, Bridget would lead him to where the poison ivy was. She pushed at the stray brush along the path.

"What's the matter, *kwe*? Should I ask what you're thinking?" His stomping feet could have chased away a moose.

"Do you know what poison ivy is?" She used her sweetest voice.

"Yeah. Heard of it. What? Is that what you got planned? Gonna toss me in the stuff so I miss the workshop and you don't gotta look at my ugly mug for the rest of the week?"

When she tried not to peek over her shoulder, but inched her head very casually to a branch on her left, Bridget's peripheral vision caught his square jaw, thick lips, hard black eyes, and smooth brown skin. And he wasn't staring at the trail. He was looking . . .

Bridget picked up her pace and scooted to the opening. She stopped at the rocks where a peaceful setting of the lake was supposed to put someone at ease. Instead, the air was sucked from her lungs.

CHAPTER TWENTY-ONE: LOVE ME FOREVER

Bridget was just about to pick at her braid. She stopped her shaking hand in midair and forced her traitorous limb to settle on her quivering knee.

The cruel, straight line of Adam's lips tugged at the corners. Even his cold eyes unfrosted to black silk. "It's nice out here." A loon bobbed in the small waves he pointed at. "Darryl told me to give this spot a try."

Bridget shifted on the rock and sat taller. "Emery and Darryl discovered this place when they were kids. They cleared it and came here after Mass."

"Darryl went to church?" Adam plopped down on the opposite rock. "Thought he was traditional."

"He attended for Emery's sake, I believe. They were extremely close."

"Yeah, kinda thought so. They're gay."

"What do you mean?" The question snapped from Bridget.

"Easy, *kwe*. I'm only saying what I see. I don't go no problem with your brother and his ol' man. I'm bunking at their crib, ain't I?"

"I didn't mean to jump down your throat." She smoothed her pants. "I get very defensive when it comes to Emery."

"If you wanna jump down my throat, go ahead. At least you're jumping on something . . . on me." Adam's low rumbling laugh could have shaken the rocks.

His double meaning hushed the annoyance in Bridget's chest. A giggle edged up her throat. When she swallowed, the laughter refused to go down and escaped from her mouth.

"At least I got you laughing, instead of killing me with your eyes." Adam's lips remained a smidgen turned up.

Bridget ran her fingers along the exposed part of her calves.

"Those are nice. You always got interesting clothes." He pointed at Bridget's flower-patterned, wide-leg crops.

"I ignored the Labor Day rule."

"The what?" Adam squinted.

"You're not supposed to wear summer clothes after Labor Day. But it's still hot out."

"Wear whatever you want. They look good on you. Hell, anything looks good on you."

The compliment scooted up Bridget's legs, caressing her skin.

"Don't worry about it. I'm feeling the same way." His smile vanished, and his gaze hardened to his familiar almost-a-scowl.

Bridget rubbed her bare arms. She should have worn more than a tank top. The flat, open-toed sandals exposed her feet. Goodness, *she* was exposed. Heart ready to bust through her ribs. An ocean of water in her throat.

"How's your boyfriend?"

The fever vanished. The pricks and shivers disappeared. "Who?"

"Bible Boy."

"He's not my boyfriend. I already have a man in my life."

Adam's black brow flickered. "Oh? Who?"

"Kyle."

"Yeah? Then why'd you go out for dinner with him?" Adam didn't scowl. His voice wasn't accusing, either.

A slight breeze rustling through the trees was the only sound present.

"I simply wanted to go out for dinner. It's been a long time."

"I coulda took you out for dinner. I can't afford a fancy restaurant, but I can take you somewhere decent."

The dreaded fever reappeared, and Bridget glanced away.

"*Kwe*, look at me." His command was gentle enough to smooth Bridget's hair the way he used to run his strong fingers through each strand, coaxing her to relax and trust him.

Bridget placed her trembling hands on her knees.

His eyes softened at the corners. "I'm gonna kiss you." Each word Adam spoke was husky, as if he'd cupped her face with his big hands.

The air in Bridget's lungs collapsed for a moment. She gripped the rock.

Adam leaned in. The familiar aroma of the water swirled around Bridget. His eyes were half closed, lips slightly parted. The slickness of his dark-brown skin and thickness of his black lashes was a temptation that tugged at Bridget's limbs. She tried to recoil, but her body refused to listen to her brain.

His hand cupped her chin. Reassurance filled his sleepy eyes. He guided her lips to his.

Helplessness engulfed Bridget's shaking body, tangling her in its stiff web.

He was bearing down, his masculine scent invading her space. When his lips swept against her mouth, she edged in, slightly. His moist flesh moving in rhythm with hers tangled Bridget in a layer of velvet. For a big, strong man, his kiss was tender.

Adam eased his tongue between Bridget's lips. His saliva melted along her tongue, his scent tasty and balmy with a hint of tobacco. A moan skittered up her throat. The kiss wrapped Bridget in a ball of confusion, coaxing her to surrender to the desire massaging the ache inside her panties.

She stroked his cheekbone, and he groaned.

When Adam's strong arms encircled Bridget's waist, she was guided off the rock and settled on his brawny thighs.

"Adam," she whispered.

"Easy." His voice mirrored a lullaby, enticing Bridget to let the fevered heat guide her back into the kiss.

She accepted Adam's gentle assault on her mouth. His palm rubbed the small of her back. His other hand brushed her outer thigh, his strokes mirroring his past reassuring caresses.

Bridget ran her nails along his shoulders. Adam's grunt of pleasure said he still enjoyed when she lightly scratched him, or dug hard into his flesh, bold enough to break the skin stretching across his muscles.

His tongue became an invading force, robbing Bridget of her breath, demanding she succumb to his assault. She melted to his forceful attack of claiming licks.

Adam's palm stroking her outer thigh inched to her buttock. Bridget tensed but kept sampling the silk of his mouth. The heat of his skin rested beneath her ass, hot enough to penetrate the cotton pants and sear his imprint through the satin panties.

She curled her fingers around his thick waves and pushed off the cowboy hat. His other hand skimmed Bridget's bare arm. For a moment, her heart seemed to shrivel and hide because this meant he planned on working his way to her breast.

His hand was below Bridget's ribcage, easing upward. His demanding kiss didn't allow her a second of air that her aching lungs needed.

When Adam's finger skimmed Bridget's nipple, his flesh singed the fabric to tease and taunt the tip straining for his touch. The print of his finger was a hushed breath of air, a light exploration he must have savored by the moan that came from him and reverberated inside Bridget's mouth.

His hard cock pushed against her thigh. Excitement throbbed between Bridget's legs, a quivering anticipation that coiled from her clit to her closing throat.

She tugged at his t-shirt and drew the garment from the waist of Adam's jeans. This earned her breast hard caresses and a light nipple pinch. His tongue plunged deeper, searching. She glided her fingers across his smooth flesh, tracing the muscles of his chest that heaved from his heavy breaths.

Adam yanked Bridget's shirt free from the waistband of the pants. Panic vibrated in her aching lungs.

He must have sensed her stiffen, or noticed she'd stopped exploring his hard pecs. His tongue slipped from Bridget's mouth. Her lids flickered. A mixture of excitement and concern prowled in his eyes. His thumb kneaded her cheek.

"*Kwe?*"

The pain she experienced almost four years ago drifted away on the breeze. Her hands needed to explore his taut muscles again. Her lips yearned to kiss his sleek skin again. Her pussy ached to feel him deep inside her again. "Nothing. I'm fine."

When Adam's tongue encircled hers, steam scorched Bridget's flesh. His grunts and groans danced along her ears. His mighty arms wrapped her waist. She was hauled against his massive chest.

His tongue kept bathing hers with deep licks. He stood. Bridget squealed and latched her legs around Adam's waist. Grass rustled under his shoes. A twig here and a branch there skimmed Bridget's arms. They were on the trail, safe from prying eyes if anyone happened to be fishing in the bay.

Mom and Dad would wonder of Bridget's whereabouts. She'd deal with them later. The constant pulsations creating thick tension about her clit never ceased. Only Adam could relieve the unbearable anticipation.

He maneuvered them to the trail of grass, Adam on the bottom and Bridget on top. A gentleman as always. Her insides melted at his gallantry so she wouldn't endure the discomfort of foliage, sticks, or rocks.

"Adam . . ." she whispered.

He ran his hand along her ponytail. "I wish it was a bed, *kwe*, but neither of us have a place here."

"No, we don't." Bridget wormed her hand to his jeans where his erection nestled between her legs.

"I got it. Lemme take care of this." Passion made his low rumble a crackling whisper, a tone she'd delighted hearing in the past.

Bridget shifted from his crotch and sat on Adam's thighs. When he jerked down his zipper to reveal his hard excitement, the breath racing up Bridget's windpipe juddered.

His thick cock was an invitation to kiss and caress. She ran her nail along the length. He shuddered, gasping.

Adam loosened Bridget's pants. She kicked off her sandals. While wiggling from her crops and underwear, she groaned at his wide-eyed stare taking in her bare skin. She began to sink to her haunches, but he shook his head.

"Lemme look at you." He licked his lips, hot elation burning behind his eyes.

He might as well have slid his finger between Bridget's pussy lips and rubbed her clit.

"I'm taking you for a ride, *kwe*." Grit sanded his husky whisper.

She'd be on the ground? Bridget's confusion must have shown because a big grin spread across Adam's powerful features. He melted their bodies together and stood.

Oh God, they'd done this before. He'd remember how much she'd loved giving him full control.

"Next time, we're getting a room at the hotel," Adam murmured. His tongue invaded her mouth.

The tip of his cock brushed Bridget's hole. Her breasts were crushed against his chest. Although the slick head feathered her opening, she couldn't slide on Adam's cock. He gripped her ass, each cheek blanketed by his warm palms.

The anticipation surging through Bridget's veins was enough to lighten her head. She secured her arms around Adam's shoulders as he eased himself inside her.

"Oh, *kwe.*" Adam gasped. For a moment he held her to the cacophony of robins chirping and lapping waves.

He was in her. They were one. His massive length stretched her flesh, commanding her insides to open to his cock.

"Cripe, you got a nice pussy." He groaned.

All Bridget could do was lay her head on Adam's big shoulder and enjoy the teasing sensations that his erection produced. His palms clasped her ass, his fingers massaging her skin. His tongue bathed her neck with hot saliva. His masculine essence saturated her skin, the scent as ripe as his hard length.

He glided, smooth and easy.

"Oh, Adam." She sighed. He was a supple dream, swathing her in the finest silk. Each pump was ripples of pleasure. The sweat from his chest showered her breasts with his potent aroma. What she wouldn't give to remove her bra and feel his macho dampness on her skin. Adam was right. They must rent a hotel room.

His suckles on Bridget's neck slithered to the lobe of her ear. She wiggled to rock in rhythm with Adam's languid pumps but couldn't fuck his cock. Helpless. He always drew her into a spell with his magical touch and thick length.

His groans became grunts. He slammed his erection into

her pussy. The head of his cock, pure velvet, coated Bridget's flesh with its rich, satin-like strength.

He worked her buttocks up and down, forcing her to succumb to his invasion.

"That's it, *kwe.*" He panted. "Your cunt's all mine. It's always been mine."

Her clit throbbed from his brash, dirty declaration.

"Oh man, I wanna lick your pussy so bad." He groaned again, his moan steamy enough to heat Bridget's hair.

The bubbling hotness climbed to an unbearable temperature. Bridget was close to shattering. The exhilaration from his quick ruts sent spasms along her spine. She tried to slam down on his erection and steal everything he had, but under Adam's fierce grip, she could only pant and moan.

When he stiffened, so did Bridget. She arched her back as the heady fervor throbbed deep inside her. The explosion of delight came fast.

She couldn't cry out, so she buried her face in his shoulder, biting down. The brilliant vibrations rolled along her thighs and shimmied through her blood.

His cries of pleasure were buried in her hair.

CHAPTER TWENTY-TWO: BACK ON THE CHAIN

Adam's heart thumped beneath Bridget's ear, the side of her face nestled against his strong chest. *Ba-bump. Ba-bump. Ba-bump.* He was as content as she, his hand resting on the small of her back and his lips brushing the top of her head.

The trampling of grass, of twigs snapping, of brush fluttering froze Bridget's blood. She scrambled off Adam, who swiveled around and shifted to a standing position to hide her naked lower body.

Bandit appeared, wagging her tail. She barked.

"You gave me a scare," Bridget hissed under her breath.

Bandit barked again.

Car tires and engines rumbling carried down the path, sounds Bridget hadn't heard earlier because she'd been too intent on Adam.

"Everyone must be leaving. Emery and Darryl are probably looking for us." Bridget's words hiccupped. Goodness, where had she put her brain? She'd had sex on a trail while everyone was at the church, setting up for Healing the Spirit.

"I think they sent in the dog for a reason." Adam held out his shorts. "Here. Use this."

Heat crawled on Bridget's cheeks. "Thank you." She gingerly took the boxer-briefs.

"No prob. Won't be the first time I went commando." Adam snickered.

Bridget's skin prickled at the memory. They'd ignored their underwear when going for a picnic that evening. Of all the risqué activities she'd engaged in while under his thumb. But she'd wanted to participate in something racy with Adam. He'd always had a way of making her forget about the rules that she religiously followed because of her upbringing.

She wiped herself down. Maybe this was why Randy Mandamin, a local boy from the rez she'd dated, had been so appealing during her teen years. He'd coaxed Bridget to fly free, which of course had gotten her into trouble, and even grounded a few times, although she'd been on the verge of graduating high school.

Adam returned, having fetched his hat while Bridget had dressed.

"Here . . ." Face still hot, she held out the underwear.

Adam's gaze slithered up and down. He grabbed the shorts. "We gotta talk, *kwe* . . ."

She edged backward. "It's going to be a busy week . . ."

"Not at night." Adam tilted his head, peering. "C'mon. Let's go."

He stalked down the path. Bridget followed. Bandit trailed behind.

They emerged from the trail to an empty parking lot, except for Darryl's truck. Emery must have persuaded Mom and Dad to go home.

"Hey," Darryl called out. "Everyone left. We told them you went over to the rectory." He flashed a big, crooked grin.

"The rectory?" Bridget sputtered.

"Yeah. We told them you went to introduce Adam to Father Bennie. We said you were probably visiting so we'd give you a ride home." Darryl kept grinning.

Emery didn't face them. He stared at the truck. "The

church is still open." His soft voice was barely a whisper. He got into the vehicle.

Shit, Emery had figured out the score. Mortified, Bridget scurried inside the basement, Adam on her trail. They both needed to wash away the scent of sex, which was why Emery hadn't locked the back door. How embarrassing. Once finished in the women's washroom, Bridget darted back outside, ensuring to lock the door behind her.

Adam was already outside, waiting by the truck. Darryl chattered to Emery, who kept his head down. Bandit bounded into the back of the vehicle. Bridget slunk in and sat in the middle. When Adam took his place behind Emery's seat, the truck heaved.

The engine roared to life.

Bridget's thigh brushed Adam's. She squirmed at his underwear peeking out from his jeans pocket. Emery and Darryl had probably engaged in the unmentionable at the same spot, and that was why Darryl kept grinning while Emery remained silent.

Just as Bridget opened the door to the house, Mom poked her head out from the kitchen.

"I was readying the coffee for the morning. Your dad's . . . tired. He went to bed to finish his Hours." Mom inched down the hall. "I made tea. Do you want to talk?"

Double great. Mom and Dad knew Bridget had been with Adam. There was no other reason why Dad would turn in at nine o'clock. He'd probably told Mom to speak to Bridget like a bad little girl for daring to disappear.

"Sure. Tea's fine." Bridget took the shortcut to the dining room through the living room. She plopped in a chair.

Mom had already returned to the kitchen, readying a tray. "Your father and I appreciate you spending the week here to help out at the workshop." She set the tray on the dining room table covered with a white, lace cloth.

Bridget fingered the matching lace napkin.

"Emery and Darryl mentioned you brought Adam over to the rectory." Mom's lips, painted a soft shade of pink, formed into a straight line.

"I thought it'd be nice for Adam to meet the priest in case he has questions." Bridget took the dainty china cup Mom offered.

"Your dad went to the rectory to retrieve you so we could go home. You weren't there." Mom sat. The worry lines around her green eyes briefly showed her age.

Triple great. Emery hadn't told Bridget that Dad had sent out a war party. Her brother should have given some kind of advance warning. "We went for a walk after we visited."

"Men like your dad have a lot of scars." Mom added honey to the dainty cup. "They need a lot of understanding and patience."

This was strange. Mom hadn't complained about Dad before. What was going on?

"Your dad suffered, truly suffered because of the Indian Residential school. Scars may heal over, but they remain."

"Is Dad okay?" How selfish of Bridget to have assumed the conversation was about Adam. Maybe Healing the Spirit was bringing forth horrible memories for Dad.

"He's fine. I'm simply saying at times he's not easy to live with." Mom raised the cup to her lips, hand trembling.

"Are you okay?" Bridget clutched Mom's free hand.

Mom fixed her worried gaze on Bridget. "Adam has a lot of scars because of the Indian Residential schools. Didn't his grandparents and parents attend them?"

Bridget nodded.

"Some manage to move past the trauma. Others . . . can't."

"What're you saying?" Suspicion inched up Bridget's

spine.

"Adam tried to unsuccessfully overcome the obstacles placed in his path. Now, he's again trying. He may take many tries before he reaches his goal. Nobody attains peace on the first try. Your father struggles to this day with what happened to him."

Oh my God, Dad still suffered? "What happened?"

"He reverts back to his old behavior. Becomes angry. Becomes too reflective. Becomes . . . resentful. Don't think your dad's magically cured. God saved him, but if your father doesn't stay focused on the Lord's will, and strays, he regresses to his former conduct."

"Adam's attending twelve-step meetings. He's here, isn't he?"

"I realize this, but it's not easy." Mom's eyes were as reflective as glass. "Are you prepared to accommodate Adam's moods for the rest of your life?"

Bridget snatched away her hand. "What're you talking about?"

"I understand his appeal." Mom wet her lips. "In some ways, he's like your father. He's bold. He's determined. He's . . . well, we called them *the wrong kind of boys* back in my day."

"Adam's not a boy."

"No, he's not, but I recall how you were drawn to Randy Mandamin when you'd visit. There are *bad* boys, and then there are *dangerous* men."

"You think Adam's dangerous?"

"Honey, he was in prison. And not once, either. He was also in jail, youth detention centers. Don't you think that's dangerous enough?"

The Adam of the past was dangerous, but not the Adam that Bridget had met at the career fair. "He's not dangerous to me."

"He's dangerous to society. It's why the judge sent him to prison." Mom sat back in the chair. "I don't like doing this to you. You're thirty-six. I trust your judgement. I do. You've done well for yourself. Extremely well."

"It's Dad, isn't it? He asked you to talk to me." Bridget should have known Dad was behind this lecture.

"Maybe your father asked me to speak to you because he knows Adam better than all of us. Your father understands Adam's roots and why he is the way he is. Your father may not have gone to prison—he only served time overnight in jail on public intoxication—but he's had experience with many Adams, because your dad was also much like Adam."

"Dad changed," Bridget quickly said.

"He changed to a point. Don't think he did a one-eighty. He still carries a lot of pain from his past. I told you—when your dad starts thinking of himself, instead of God's will for him, he becomes quite unbearable."

Bridget gasped.

"Maybe I shielded you kids too much from your dad's shortcomings." Mom shook her head, fingertips grazing her temples and gaze on the teacup.

"Emery got more than his share of it in July, and he survived. Darryl may not have gone to prison, but he suffers intergenerational trauma from the residential schools."

"Yes, he does. It's why he's attending the workshop."

"And that's the same reason Adam is." Bridget palmed the teacup. "Maybe this is part of God's plan? Adam's staying at Darryl's. Maybe sharing with Darryl will help Adam?"

"I believe it's a good thing. Don't think I'm against Adam as a person. I'm not." Mom reached for her own teacup. "I'm simply telling you if Adam returned to his old ways before, he might do so again. Any kind of trauma could set him off. He may have been sober for almost four years, but he was behind bars. He couldn't waltz down to the liquor store when he was inside a cell. For the other half a year, he was on day parole and returned to the local jail every night."

"Mom, if Adam really wanted to drink, he could've bought booze in prison. Those places are full of drugs and alcohol. More so in there than on the outside."

"Oh, Bridget . . ." Mom rubbed her brow.

She was probably thinking what she'd said to Bridget while growing up—*I might as well speak to the garbage can, because you always have to stick your fingers into the flame even though you know the fire's hot and you'll burn yourself.*

"I'm not Emery who obeys everything you two ask of him. I'm not Jude, living the perfect Catholic life. But I can accept responsibility for my actions. I always have, haven't I?"

"Yes." Mom's reply was as weak as her limp wrist. "I just wish . . . I wish you'd understand your decisions don't only impact you. They impact the people who love you."

A niggle of guilt appeared at the base of Bridget's neck. "I know what I'm doing. I haven't agreed to reconcile, so don't assume I have."

"Then where did you really go this evening?"

Mom would never believe Bridget had sex on the trail. Oh, her mother probably assumed she'd let Adam sneak a kiss, or even a smidgen more than kissing.

"We went down the trail and sat at the lake. Adam's already tried to reconcile, but I told him no. Okay?"

"Did you?" A hint of delight warmed Mom's eyes.

"Yes. Then Stephen and I went on a date." Bridget gazed out the sliding doors, beyond the screened-in deck and out to the bay where she enjoyed swimming.

"Please remember, as much as we respect what Adam's doing, we're aware it could take him many tries before he remains sober for good." Mom's voice rose an octave higher from her pleading.

Bridget slumped in the chair. Wasn't this what she'd told herself countless times, and why she'd refuted Adam's declaration of love? She had the same big fear—he'd hurt her again. As for giving in . . . she couldn't keep lying. A part of her heart held hope. Hope that he could change—that he *would* change and succeed this time.

Adam sat out on the deck. One thing about Indian Reserves, there was lots of nature and plenty of room to stretch out. Not like in the city where a guy had to walk a *get-out-of-my-way* gait, or in prison where he'd never turned his back and watched everyone from behind his head.

The waves lapping against the rocks produced a great outdoor soundtrack. Certain bugs sang a song. What kind of bugs they were, he wasn't sure. Maybe crickets? He'd expected a shitload of mosquitoes to attack him, being this deep in the forest, but maybe they were only bad during July and August.

The door opened. Darryl meandered outside, carrying two cans of colas. "Thought you might be thirsty."

"Yep. Hit the spot." Adam took the offered drink. He swilled back a helping of the pop that burned slightly down his throat. "You mentioned you lived in the 'Peg. Where about?"

"Osborne." Darryl grinned. "Where else?"

Adam should have guessed the guy would bunk down in the happening gay neighborhood.

"The high-rises. Middle one."

"Oh, those buildings." Adam nodded, aware of the three tall apartment complexes looming over the Village. "Nice crib?"

"It did the job and gave me a home. It was where I wanted to be, and close enough to downtown to get to work. You were in Point Douglas, hey?"

"My whole life." Adam gulped down another slurp. He set the can on his knee. Normally, he avoided his favorite mixer, having always added three shots of rye to his shot of cola.

"Hey, I didn't mean to embarrass you and Bridget earlier." Darryl cleared his throat. "You two reminded me of . . . what Em and I used to do."

"Yeah?" Adam couldn't help the snicker climbing up his throat. "I didn't care. But I don't like upsetting Bridget. She's a lady and—"

"No worries. I don't judge anybody. I did too much of that already." Darryl stroked his neck and grimaced.

"That why you're attending the workshop?" This was a no-brainer that Darryl had come outside to apologize, or maybe talk, why Emery and the dog remained inside. Either was fine for Adam.

"You betcha. I made myself a promise I'd keep an open mind."

"We say that in our meetings all the time. Keep an open mind."

"I'm glad you're gonna."

Adam shrugged. "Not sure how it'll help, but it don't hurt to try."

"Y'know, sometimes we think something hasn't affected us, even when it has. I understand your parents and grand-parents attended the residential schools."

"Sure did." Adam snatched his cigarettes off the table. He lit one. Nothing beat smoke curling down his windpipe and into his lungs. There was something relaxing about the ritual.

"Those schools stripped kids of a home life. None of them came out understanding how a family functioned or the role of parenting."

"Nope. Sure didn't." Adam tried not to laugh at the invisible political hat Darryl slipped on.

"They also carried lots of scars from the abuse they'd endured." Darryl set his drink on the table.

"Y'know, I don't blame anyone for how I turned out. I had choices."

"Did you really?"

Adam grunted. What was Darryl on about?

"Sometimes we accept situations as normal, when they're not. I don't mean to pry, but it's apparent you don't want your son growing up in the same environment you did."

Darryl's words were sincere, even caring. Adam took a drag off the smoke. Stories were important to hear, Cutter had always said. Everyone had a story. Darryl probably wanted to share his. Maybe what he had to say would help Adam. Ignoring assistance and thinking he was tough enough to handle everything on his own was what had landed Adam in prison.

"Okay. I'm listening. Fire away." Keeping an open mind was imperative. If Adam didn't, he'd be back to his old way of thinking, and he wasn't returning to that place—ever. His job was to listen and learn, as the old-timers said in the twelve-step meetings.

Chapter Twenty-three: Keep Us on the Road

"I had it out for a lot of people and places — the church and government being the biggies." Darryl sipped his cola. The bugs continued to sing and buzz.

Adam sat forward in the chair.

"I thought they were to blame for how my life had turned out. In some ways they were. My parents went to the residential school, and it screwed them up big-time. It also screwed up my aunt. She died in July." Darryl angled his leg and rested his foot on his knee. He moved his running shoe in a circular movement.

"Sorry to hear that, man." Adam only heard people bare their souls in sharing circles and twelve-step meetings, not on a deck overlooking the river.

"Thanks, but don't be sorry. You barely know me." Darryl flicked at the tab on the pop can, gaze pinned downwards.

"Still am. Heard your aunt raised you."

"She did. I was four when my parents died." Darryl kept rolling his foot in a circle. "They were drunk, as always, and went for supplies. They took my older brother and sister with them. They all died."

Adam ran his tongue along the roof of his mouth. Not good.

"All I had was Emery." Darryl's voice dropped a couple of octaves. He looked out to the river. "We had big-ass differing beliefs at the time. I blamed the church for what happened. I also blamed it for losing my parents." He lifted the can and took a drink. "Being forced to stay at the school until they turned sixteen destroyed them. My aunt attended the same school. It drove her to drink and destroyed her, too."

He wet his lips. His gaze focused beyond Adam's shoulder. "The biggie was losing Emery. He was completely loyal to a place I hated, and he chose *that* place over me." Darryl's tone sharpened slightly. "When the church proposed the Healing the Spirit workshop, I was against it. At the time, I believed everyone should practice traditionalism—I felt it was a betrayal to our ancestors if anyone chose Catholicism over our original way of life, especially after what the church and government had done to us."

He gulped back more cola. His foot kept twirling round and round. "What clinched it for me was a chance to get even. The church took from me, so I'd take from it. There's a man on band council who I agreed to help. His name's Clayton Kabatay."

Darryl rubbed his mouth. "I thought I had a big chip on my shoulder. Mine's nothing compared to his. As a matter of fact, I expect him and his family to show up tomorrow morning, protesting the workshop."

"Protesting?" Adam couldn't involve himself in reserve politics, not after deciding to walk a straight line. Getting caught in a brawl if shit got ugly would land him back in prison.

"It's okay. You'll be fine." Darryl shifted forward in the chair, reassurance in his tone. "If Clayton and his family are outside the church tomorrow, ignore them. We'll use the back door to get to the basement. It faces the road and is under the car port."

"Yeah. Saw that door last night."

"The last time they protested, they were on the lawn beside the church."

"I thought everyone was cool with the workshop now?" From what Adam had been told, he'd assumed as much.

"Not the Kabatay family." Darryl shook his head. "They got a real hard-on for the Matawapits. They believe Emery's dad betrayed his own people by becoming a deacon for the church and marrying a non-native woman, who raised the kids Catholic."

Since Adam had never lived at his home reserve, people fighting over what they should worship seemed crazy. On the streets, nobody cared. It was all about staying alive and finding a place to crash. "Sounds like they should worry about themselves instead of what others are doing." Adam stuck another cigarette between his lips.

"Try seeing it from this perspective." Darryl's small, hooded eyes crinkled. "You were a gangbanger. I bet your gang spent a lot of time keeping an eye on other gangs. And making sure they didn't sneak into your territory to move in on your, err, ah, customers."

"Yep."

"Is that what you did?"

A hint of discomfort stretched across Adam's back. He'd never spoken about being an enforcer for the Winnipeg Warriors. "Let's say I made sure nobody muscled in on our biz or our turf."

Darryl kept staring at Adam. "I see. Sorry, man. Didn't mean to make you uncomfortable."

"You didn't. Not used to talking about this kind of stuff."

"You never talked to anyone about it?"

"Nope. Goes against the code, y'know? You never rat out anyone." Adam shrugged. Why was he protecting those guys, anyway? When he'd taken his two minutes out, the boys hadn't blinked at beating his sorry ass. And they sure hadn't given a shit when his old enemies had gone after him.

He squeezed his toes. "Hooked up with 'em when I was twelve. A runner at first. Mule. That sort of stuff." He puffed on the cigarette. "Didn't join until I was seventeen. If not for them, I wouldn't have done the time that I did. But I had a rep to build. The more time you do, the bigger your cred. My uncles were down with them. I figured if they were a part of the toughest gang in the 'Peg, I should join, too."

"That's part of the intergenerational trauma of the residential schools. I take it your uncles attended one?"

"Yep." Adam swigged a helping of cola to moisten his dry mouth. "I left the gang before Kyle was born. Was fresh out of treatment. We both were. Me and Angela."

"She's Kyle's mother?"

"Yeah. Dead. OD'd." He squeezed his toes again. "We split up before she died. I left the 'Peg 'cause I made a lot of enemies as an enforcer. Guys also wanted to challenge me. It's about rep. Some figured if they took me down, they'd get major props."

"When you moved back to Winnipeg, after you and Bridget broke up, these old enemies were still after you?"

A man like Darryl wouldn't open his mouth to anyone. He'd been kicked around, just like Adam. "One was after me, big-time. Saw him at The Pike that night. Nabe bar. I jumped him before he jumped me. Figured if I took him down, the others might back off."

He squeezed his toes hard enough to pinch them. "Problem was, I was drunk and shooting pool. If I drink, I get into a shitload of trouble. And a pool stick in my hand . . . yeah, led to a shitstorm."

"You beat him bad enough to land you in prison?" Horror didn't reflect in Darryl's eyes or the judgmental glare everyone tossed Adam's way when hearing what he'd done.

"Yeah. He'll . . . he'll never have full use of his right eye or his left arm again. Did major damage to the nerves and muscles." Adam shifted in the chair and stared at the water blackening under the darkening sky. "Guess he was in rehabilitation for a long time."

At least Darryl hadn't made an excuse to run into the house and holler at Emery to call the police because there was a psychotic, sadistic criminal on their deck.

"I'm not proud of what I did." Adam turned to face an expressionless Darryl. "Can't bring myself to ninth step the guy . . . Not that he'd want to hear me make amends, but it's part of the program, y'know? Like I said, I burned a lot of bridges in that city . . . Not surprised it bit me in the ass when I last went back."

He kept squeezing his toes. "It wasn't easy being out there when I was on day parole. Was lucky they locked me up at night. Who knows what would've happened."

"You returned to jail in the evenings?"

"It was for the best. Thing is, nobody bothered me, not even at the job."

"I guess your message worked. Seems the other gangs weren't going to bother you anymore."

Adam flicked the ash off the cigarette. "No idea if they will or won't. I'm in T. Bay now. It's where my boy is. He prefers it over the 'Peg. At least I think so."

"He came up for a visit last month. I took him swimming." Darryl grinned.

"Bridget told me he enjoys swimming lessons. He's a turtle now. More like a shark. Guess Jude has a swimming pool."

"Kyle never told me he was a turtle." Darryl kept grinning.

"Yeah. Guess he'll be a fish next. Then a dolphin. It's why I'm here. Why I came to the workshop. My kid wasn't happy about it. He really got in my face. But he's cool now. Bridget talked to him."

Darryl's Adam's apple bobbled. "Really? That's very thoughtful of her."

"Yeah. She coulda been a bitch about it, turned my own kid against me. She didn't. She's one in a million. All the other women I knew before her, they woulda turned on me. She never did."

She hadn't turned on him . . . for now.

Adam rode shotgun in the truck, used to being up early because of his job. Emery had left around six on the four-wheeler. Bandit stuck her furry face between them, resting her snout on the console.

"We'll have an opening prayer in the basement." Darryl stared straight ahead at the dirt road, wearing the customary sunglasses everyone seemed to wear around here. "Once Mass's finished, there'll be an official opening prayer by Father Bennie and Basil to kickstart the workshop. Then they'll serve breakfast."

Darryl turned the truck onto Church Road, according to the sign.

Hopefully they'd serve more coffee. After the way Bridget had given herself to Adam last evening, she'd invaded his thoughts all night, keeping him wide awake until around four o'clock.

The truck rumbled down the road, generating a shitload of dust. Adam waved his hat about to keep the dirt from his eyes, kicking himself for not bringing his sunglasses. There were already lots of vehicles parked. About twenty people stood on the main lawn, holding signs.

"Just what I expected." Darryl frowned. "Clayton's family's here."

They had no choice but to park next to the line of small trees where the protesters stood, glaring.

Darryl switched off the engine. "Ignore them. Stare

straight ahead."

Adam got out of the truck. Bandit exited on Darryl's side of the vehicle.

"Who're you?" A man with long hair, wearing a feather in a small side braid, huffed over to them. His features were as angular as The Hawk's. Sharp nose. Sharp chin. Sharp cheekbones. He was tall but on the skinny side.

"Keep walking," Darryl murmured.

Bandit barked at the man.

"Who're you?" the man asked again in a voice full of authority.

Adam bristled. Authority could shove itself up its ass.

The man marched around them and stood in their way, holding his sign. "You're joining this traitor? It's what he is. A traitor to his own kind." He thrust his skinny finger at Darryl.

The familiar heat bubbled under Adam's skin. Even after his anger management course, sharing circles, and twelve steps, the silent rage simmering inside him burned to burst through the surface and choke the skinny, arrogant shithead. Nobody got up in his face. Nobody.

Help me do this, Creator. Within seconds, Adam's skin cooled, and so did his internal furnace. He walked around the man and kept staring at the basement door where Bridget worked down below, readying breakfast for Adam and the other participants.

He'd passed a big test. Damned straight nothing was goading Adam into losing his son or Bridget. Man, if he wasn't on parole, he'd love to let the skeleton-looking fucker taste his knuckles.

Running shoes crunched on gravel. Darryl followed.

"Keep turning your backs on who you truly are," the man said in a voice that resembled the hiss of a snake. "Join those who attempted to assimilate us into white culture. Go on. Be an apple."

Apple? Some asswipe had always been tossing around that insult in the bars. White on the inside and red on the outside. Adam wasn't an apple. He wasn't . . . anything. Just a man who wanted to get his life back in order after fucking up the first thirty-seven years.

He trounced down the stairs that led into the basement. The tables formed what was supposed to resemble a circle but appeared more like a square. This was promising. Sharing happened in a circle.

Bridget stood at a side table, readying the coffee supplies.

Adam's heart kicked into overdrive at the sight of the denim shorts hugging her sexy ass and providing a long look at her gorgeous legs she'd wrapped around him last night. For modesty's sake, her shorts weren't those skimpy cutoffs, but covered her thighs. A blue apron draped her tiny waist. The logo of the Catholic Women's Association was emblazoned on the front.

"Unfortunately, you met Clayton." Darryl sidled up beside Adam.

"Is that who that was?" Adam forced his focus to leave Bridget's beauty and stare at Darryl. "The wind could give him a beatdown."

"Yeah. It could." Darryl snickered. "C'mon, let's find a seat. The other participants are upstairs celebrating Mass."

Adam plopped down beside Darryl at a spot affording him a full view of Bridget coming and going from the kitchen. She wouldn't glance his way. He sat taller in his chair.

"I wonder if she did that web cam, video chat, or whatever it's called with Kyle."

"Probably. We have a laptop. Did you want to use it to video chat?" Darryl asked.

"Nope. The Hawk vetoed my request. It's in violation of the supervised visits."

"That's too bad. The goal of Children and Family Services is to reconnect families. It's what our child care worker does here on the reserve." Darryl motioned at an old man stuffing tobacco into a pipe. "Basil. He's the elder for the Traditionalists Society."

"Traditionalists Society?"

"Yeah. My aunt and a few others started the Society about ten years ago to help the community reconnect with their roots."

"You're a member?"

Darryl nodded. "Okay. I gotta help the old man."

Adam sat back in the chair. He should have brought his hand drum up to the reserve. But he'd been worried about losing his most precious gift from the elder who'd given him the sacred item.

His first goal while here was to stay focused on the workshop—not to stare at Bridget sashaying about in her sexy outfit.

Bridget wiped her hands on a dishcloth. Safely back in the kitchen and behind the closed shutters to give the participants privacy, she could still visualize Adam. He was too big and too masculine for his presence to go unnoticed.

Her job was to serve at the main banquet table. Mom and the other women fried up sausages, bacon, and ham. Another worked on the scrambled eggs. Jenny buttered toast.

Basil's singing carried into the kitchen.

For ten minutes, Bridget gripped and re-gripped the tray. Then the kitchen door opened.

Darryl poked his head inside. "We're done. They're just finishing upstairs, too."

"Okay." Bridget forced a smile for her brother-in-law's sake. "Thank you. We're almost done in here. I'll begin serving."

She set the first stack of food on the tray and carried the goodies out to the banquet table. Earlier, she'd set out the cutlery and condiments.

The people who'd attended Mass filed downstairs.

Bridget snuck a peek and caught Adam's intent stare. He dropped his gaze to his hands. She whipped her attention to the meal she was supposed to serve. He was here to heal. *Focus. Focus.*

She launched into assisting everyone, but her vision kept blurring, hands shaking. When Bridget dropped a sausage from the prongs she held, the scream of frustration threatened to leave her mouth.

"No worries," Roy said with a wink. "A lil bit of dirt didn't hurt me as a kid, and it sure won't now."

"Thanks." Heat crept onto Bridget's cheeks.

"I won't say anything to your Mom or Dad." Roy kept grinning. "You always do a beautiful job."

This time the heat came from bashfulness. "You're the best." And Roy was—a great friend of Mom and Dad's.

Adam stepped up, holding his plate.

Bridget's nervousness drew the gooseflesh beneath her skin to the surface. She forced a welcoming smile.

His nod was slow. "Bacon, ham, and sausage."

He'd always had a healthy appetite, since he had so many muscles to fuel. Bridget tightened her grip on the prongs and gingerly set each request on his plate.

"Looks good." He picked up the sausage and bit into it with the same enthusiasm he'd lavished on her last night. "Yep. Delicious."

"I didn't cook. The other women did." Bridget plastered on her most professional work voice and composure.

"It's still good." Adam's lips tugged at the corners, and he moved along the line.

Darryl grinned a *you-can't-fool-me* smile.

"Here." The bacon Bridget shucked onto her brother-in-law's plate was a splattered mess.

"Uh, I think I'll serve myself," Emery murmured, biting his lip to hide his smile.

"Yes, you should." Bridget kicked herself for snapping, but the two lovebirds could take their knowing looks elsewhere.

Once everyone was served, Bridget searched out Adam, who was seated with Emery and Darryl. The three of them laughed, talking about something. The perennial hard line of Adam's mouth had softened to a big smile, big enough to twinkle his eyes and flush his dark-brown skin. He'd cupped his hands together, leaning in for the conversation.

Maybe last night was meant to be. Maybe a man could change, a man as dangerous as Adam. Perhaps there was a good chance that not only Adam would heal this week, maybe Bridget might, too.

CHAPTER TWENTY-FOUR: ONE TRACK MIND

Holding a cup of coffee, Adam exited the church basement through the back door. His butt was a bit numb from sitting for two hours. The trainers had gone over the agenda and objectives for the workshop.

The part about confronting his parents using an empty chair still left his muscles tense. Yelling at nobody was about the stupidest thing he'd ever heard. Therapists and their dumb-ass ideas. He had the twelve steps. Additional therapy seemed pointless.

He'd lost a day seeing his boy for a useless chair and other half-baked suggestions. Aww, crap. He was being a dick. Open mind. Open mind. If the old-timers from the twelve-step program were here, they'd tell Adam to pull his attitude together.

The graveyard, a few feet away, stretched to the lake's south side and to a ditch on the east. He set his paper coffee cup on the wooden fence and lit a cigarette.

"I knew it was you. Brick, what the hell are you doing here?" a woman with a husky voice called out.

An icicle formed along Adam's spine. Nobody but his old gang and the women crazy enough to associate with them had called him by that name. He slowly turned. Huh? Who the hell was this broad?

"It's me. Raven. Raven Kabatay. I used to live with one of your friends. Sully."

This was Raven? The last time Adam had seen her was during his four-month bender in the 'Peg, and she'd been a hell of a lot skinnier and a hell of a lot older-looking. Smacked out. Wearing last month's clothes and last month's everything. Hidden beneath her former addiction was a sleek, tall woman with cheekbones sharper than a shank, legs to her neck, perfect bronzed skin, and long, black hair.

"Don't use that name anymore."

"Gotcha . . . Adam."

"Guess you're not with Sully anymore, hey?"

"Don't feel bad." Raven's laugh matched her husky tone. "Everyone who sees me never recognizes me. I've been clean for a year now."

"Really?" She'd been a hopeless case, always crashing at flop houses. He'd stepped over Raven too many times when he'd checked the drug pads, one of his jobs for the gang.

"I ditched Sully when I went into rehab." Raven moistened her ultra-red lips and inched in closer. She still had the slinky way of coiling around a man like a boa constrictor, ready to suck the breath from a guy.

Heck, he'd cut her a break. People changed. If Raven worked the twelve steps, she might not be a sly seductress anymore, using sex to con money and drugs from a guy.

"You did? Haven't seen him . . . around." Adam puffed on the cigarette.

"Heard you were out. A friend from the 'Peg told me. How you been?" She rested her slim arm on the fence.

"Good. Guess you're doing good, too, if you're clean." She had to be around thirty now, give or take a year, but could pass for twenty-five.

"Word is you're clean, too. It's really cool. I didn't think I'd get out alive. I didn't think any of us would. You're attending this?" Raven pointed at the church.

"Yep."

"My brother's leading the protest against it." She smiled a sincere smile, not her familiar something-in-the-works smile. "You hitting meetings while you're here?"

"Didn't know there were any." Which was why Adam had brought along his books related to the twelve-step program.

"We have three meetings a week. I'm hoping to get more going. Some who're recently recovered need to go every night. If you need a ride, I can get you." There was nothing in Raven's shining black eyes saying she was on the make or after something.

Still, she was part of the protest, and an enemy of the Matawapit family — the woman Adam loved and who cared for his child. "S'okay. I got a ride."

"Are you staying at the Matawapits?"

"Nope."

Raven gave another seductive laugh, the huskiness coating Adam's skin. "Still the same. You were never a man of many words. Like I said, I have no ties to the old gang anymore. I've been living up here since last summer, after I got outta rehab."

Adam nodded.

"I'm guessing you're staying at Emery's and Darryl's then. I heard about you and the deacon's daughter. Word gets around."

He flicked away his cigarette butt. "I'll be at the meeting. Where's it at?"

"The recovery building. Eight o'clock. Where the NNA-DAP worker is based out of."

"The what?"

"Oh yeah, you don't do rez speak." Raven laughed again. "NNADAP stands for the National Native Alcohol and Drug Abuse Program. All reserves have a NNADAP worker. John Morrison's ours. He's been sober longer than Bill W."

They both chuckled, because sober longer than Bill W. meant John had long-term sobriety.

"That long?"

"I'd say about forty years. He's a good guy. He was the one who got me into rehab. Clayton came and got me when I called him while I was in the 'Peg. He brought me to detox. After detox, I came up here, and John did all of the paperwork."

"Clayton's your brother? The guy leading the protest?"

Raven nodded.

"Won't ask. I'm only here for the workshop."

"Got a dart for me? Mom has my purse."

Adam withdrew a smoke and handed the cigarette to Raven. He also withdrew his lighter.

She leaned in to light her cigarette. "Thanks." She puffed a few times. "The workshop's about healing. They figure the Christian and *Anishinaabe* communities should reconcile. They hold these all over Canada on other reserves. Personally, I'm against them. What they did to us is unforgivable."

Adam wouldn't take her inventory, judging someone in the recovery program. If Raven wanted to remain bitter at the church and government, that was her problem. He shrugged.

"You don't agree, do you? The schools are responsible for what's happening right now. If not for those schools, we wouldn't have the gangs or drug problems."

"That's for each person to decide. Not out to save the world. Just my own ass."

"What about the other alcoholics and addicts?" Her sleek eyebrows narrowed.

"If I can help them by sharing my story, I'm there. But I'm not getting involved in that other stuff. Not my fight."

"It's all of our fight." When Raven stood straighter, her prominent collarbones pushed against her skin. "What the government and those schools did to us almost destroyed our people."

"Yeah. Almost. They haven't wiped us out yet. From the way things stand now, we're doing a good job without any help."

"Us?" Raven gasped. "You were an enforcer."

"Hey, who said I excluded myself? I know what I did. Take responsibility for it, too. Is anyone else taking responsibility for what they're doing? Gang-banging? Killing? Fighting? Using? Drinking? Pimping? Whoring?"

"I take responsibility for what I did. Yeah, nobody held a gun to my head, but those schools and the government had a lot to do with what happened to me. My mom attended one. So did my aunts and uncles."

"I get it. I do. Thing is, we can do something about our lives."

"You don't want to understand. I thought you would." Raven's slim shoulders sagged.

Adam had been so intent on their conversation, he finally noticed Bridget beneath the car port. She turned and headed back inside. Great. She'd probably wanted to talk. Thanks to Raven, he'd missed his chance. "I gotta go. I'll be at the meeting tonight."

"Eight. The Recovery Center."

"I'll be there." Adam stalked away. He'd catch Bridget before she disappeared into the kitchen.

Bridget darted inside, pulse still thickly thundering in her throat. Jealousy's bitterness crept into her mouth, its taste tart enough to compel a glass of water to wipe away the overpowering essence strong enough to sour her stomach.

She dashed to the table where a pitcher was kept for the participants. When she swallowed the ice-cold liquid, the rank taste in her mouth vanished, but jealousy's horrendous green flame kept pounding through her veins.

"Saw you outside. Wanted to thank you for the breakfast. It was good." Adam's deep voice invaded Bridget's ears.

She gripped the paper cup. "Everyone is to thank. Lots of women helped."

He frowned and set his hand on the table, leaning in close enough for her to catch a whiff of the waterfall-scented soap he'd used to wash this morning. "What's going on, *kwe*? I know when you're pissed."

"I'm not pissed." She made sure to keep her voice even.

"You are. That broad out there. An old buddy's ol' lady. She recognized me and invited me to attend a twelve-step meeting." His jawline stiffened. "You really think I'd be on the make after what we did last night?"

Bridget stepped back, chin out. "I didn't think anything of your chat with Raven."

"You did, too." Adam's words hissed through his teeth. He inched in closer. "Man, I can't believe you. I told you you're the only *Anishinaabe-kwe* for me. You were the one who went off on a date."

The jealousy evaporated. Just as she was about to apologize, Dad marched over. The doused heat reappeared in Bridget's chest.

"What is it?" she said to him.

Dad motioned at the kitchen. His dark eyes were colder than black stones. "We're about to reconvene. Your mother needs you."

Now Bridget understood how Emery had felt in July when Dad had tried to take charge. For Adam's sake, not Dad's, she'd go to the kitchen.

"You'll do fine." She patted Adam's hand that remained on the table. "Your son's rooting for you. He wants to hear all about the workshop when you get back."

Adam's eyes sparkled. "I'll be sure to tell him." He wandered to his spot at the tables.

Bridget turned and tramped to the back door before Dad dared to lecture. The workshop participants didn't need to witness a fight. It was apparent her parents still disapproved of Adam.

A moment outside to cool down should help. She dashed up the stairs and walked out to a warm autumn breeze. Raven remained beside the graveyard fence. She swiveled on her heel, nodding at Bridget.

Great. Bridget didn't need to engage in a battle of words with a woman who was part of the protest. "Hello."

Raven sauntered over, slim hips rocking and long legs gliding one in front of the other. "Hi. Bridget. Right? We never met. Well, we've met. But you get what I mean. I'm Raven."

"It's nice to meet you." Bridget held out her hand.

Their palms and fingers connected. Cold. Clammy. As icy as they felt about one another.

Bridget wouldn't size Raven up any longer. To do so meant she viewed the other woman as a threat. Still, Raven had been a part of Adam's past. Not as a lover. But Raven probably knew more about him than Bridget did. Bristles stiffer than a brush pricked her skin.

"How's the workshop going?" Raven's red mouth remained in a straight line.

"You're welcome to participate and find out for yourself, if you want to." Bridget used a welcoming voice as she motioned at the door.

"I already told Adam I won't step foot inside a place that attempted to wipe out my people. If your family had any loyalty, you wouldn't either. But maybe you have a reason to be there. You're not a full-blooded *Anishinaabe-kwe*. Only half. Have a nice day." Raven flung back her hair and sauntered off to where the other protesters stood.

If Raven wanted to believe she was a traditional Ojibway, the bitch could keep lying to herself by not honoring respect, one of the Seven Grandfathers teachings.

Bridget trounced back inside. Adam would attend a twelve-step meeting with Raven present. A cunning witch like that had intentions of turning Adam against the workshop — that must be why she'd sought him out.

If Raven dared to interfere, she'd learn Bridget wasn't the kind of woman who backed away. Kyle came first. Her foster child didn't need some hateful witch ruining his dad's chance at healing.

As Adam headed for the trail where he could sit on the rock and enjoy the last of the lunch hour, he was in full view of the protesters. The morning hadn't gone too bad. There'd been a history lesson on the Indian Residential Schools given by a band councilor named Roy Morrison, who'd attended one and also served as chairman for the pastoral council.

"You don't gotta let that family influence you," Clayton called out from where he stood, holding his sign. "You can still join us."

Didn't that loudmouth ever give his lungs a rest? Adam shook his head and tramped down the path.

This morning's lesson had given him a lot to think about. He sure as shit wouldn't let anyone force him to do anything he didn't want to do. Maybe this was why he hated authority. His parents had given the cops attitude, the child care workers attitude, and anyone else who'd tried to interfere in their lives.

After being told who to worship, where to sleep, what language to speak, what to wear, being beaten and molested by powerful people, no wonder his parents had left the school full of rage and rebellion. No wonder they'd drank. No wonder they'd introduced Adam to a life of dysfunction.

The Indian Residential School was trapped in their blood. They'd passed on their hate, defiance, and anger to Adam and his sisters. And his sisters were passing on what they'd learned to their children.

Adam sat on the big rock. No way was his boy going to join a gang, do hard time, or waste his life drinking.

The grass rustled. If the person was Clayton or Raven, they'd get an earful. Adam had come here to sort out his scrambled brain. He lit a cigarette.

His breath jumped at Bridget's graceful scent, dainty painted toes and nails, and long hair pinned into a messy bun on top of her head. He saw lots of women with that style. Yanked up with an elastic and the ends tucked underneath while the rest was left fluffy and cute.

"Well? How'd your morning go?" Bridget sat on the rock. She held out a cup of iced tea and kept the other for herself.

"Lots to digest." Adam took the drink.

"I heard Roy's presentation in the kitchen. We're going to have to stuff cotton in our ears so you can have some privacy."

"It don't matter if you hear us." Adam shrugged. "It's not like the protesters can hear everything."

"Well, the women voted. Mom and I are staying for the afternoon to keep the refreshments going. Once the ladies clean up, they're heading out so you have privacy."

"Thanks." Adam was grateful, although he'd never asked any questions or really participated yet. "We need to talk. There's a meeting tonight. Maybe tomorrow night?"

When Bridget wet her lips, he tried not to groan at her pink tongue he'd savaged last evening.

"Tomorrow's fine. Try to remember . . ." She tapped her nails against her bare knee. "The workshop must come first.

I fully support what you're doing."

A change of heart? Maybe Adam was worried for nothing. She'd come to him again. Last evening did mean as much to her as it did to him.

"*Kwe* . . ." He laced his fingers around her long nails and caressed them.

"The workshop. Stay focused on it." Her fingers stiffened in his palm.

"I will." He kept stroking her nails. "Your ol' man doesn't say much to me. Doesn't even look at me when he speaks, but he looks at everyone else."

"Never mind Dad. He's being . . . Dad." Bridget's nose wrinkled. "There's a lot you can learn from the workshop. And what you learn, Kyle'll benefit from."

"You miss him? I do. I won't see him until next Wednesday."

Bridget sipped the iced tea. "I always miss him. I'll miss him . . ." She glanced to a tree. "I came to speak to you about the Kabatay family."

That was why she'd sought him out? To lecture him about big bad Clayton and his trouble-making sister? "I know all about them. Darryl already told me." The words came out gruff.

"So you know Darryl sided with them at one time?"

"Yeah."

"They try to turn whoever they can against the church." Bridget's voice juddered.

Anger brewed in Adam's chest. "Are we ever gonna talk about what we did last night?"

Bridget fingered the cup she held. "Now's not the time . . ."

"When's it ever gonna be the right time?" Aww, screw this. Ten bucks she was having regrets. "This is about Kyle, isn't it? Thought you could soften me up? Maybe trick me into giving you my kid? Listen good —"

"How dare you!" Bridget yanked her hand free and stood. Rage pounded behind her flashing dark eyes. "How dare you accuse me of selling myself to get a child."

She thrust her finger at him. "What kind of a person do you think I am? If I wanted to manipulate our situation to have Kyle, I could've done that when you told him you'd be here for the week."

She was a car ready to peel out and race off.

Adam rose and snatched her wrist.

"Let. Go. Of. Me."

The tone of her words slapped his face. "Easy . . ."

CHAPTER TWENTY-FIVE: ALL FOR YOU

Bridget's heart continued to thunder. Adam was touching her. Not touching. Gripping. The power in his big hand and the scent of his masculinity was enough to weaken the rage bubbling through her blood.

She turned to meet delicious heat flickering in Adam's eyes. Yes, she'd sought him out to give warning about the Kabatay family, but she'd also come because, well, she couldn't stay away. Not after last evening and what they'd done only a few feet from where they stood now.

Gosh, what a mess. They had too many strikes against them. If Mrs. Dale found out, the cranky social worker would assign Kyle to another foster parent.

When Adam coaxed Bridget into his arms, his strong fingers still draping her wrist, she leaned into his chest. He swathed her in a reassuring embrace scented with his manly aroma and smooth skin.

"What're we going to do?" she muttered into his shirt. The steam of her breath heated her lips, and the warmth of his flesh heated her face.

He petted the back of Bridget's neck. "We'll figure something out. Darryl said the purpose of Children and Family Services is to reunite families."

Bridget shivered. Could she allow them to become a family again?

"I wanna see you tonight . . . after the meeting." Adam's voice was a husky whisper. "Darryl's letting me use his four-wheeler."

Not since Bridget was a teenager, visiting her family for the weekend, had she snuck from the house by tiptoeing out the front door because she'd bunked on the pull-out in the living room.

Excitement shimmered along Bridget's arms and neck. "What time does the meeting end?"

"Nine. They're an hour long."

"Mom and Dad'll still be up." Bridget should feel insulted about having to sneak out to meet Adam, but the excitement kept fluttering in her belly.

"What time do they turn in?"

"Around ten. Dad does his Office of Hours, and Mom prays the Rosary."

"Then we'll meet at ten. I'll be waiting outside the house."

Adam was right. They needed to talk. Already, they'd had one misunderstanding moments earlier. A good talk might clear the air.

Adam sat at the oblong table inside the recovery center. The place had been perfect for having a meeting. Big leather chairs. Oak table with a finished black top. Plenty of refreshments. They'd completed a story and were ready to take a break before moving on to the discussion, where everyone had a chance to speak about what was read. Or anyone was welcome to speak about whatever was on their minds.

He stood to refill his coffee. The other six members also rose to either use the washroom or stretch their legs.

Raven sat at the head of the table, having chaired the meeting. She sashayed to the coffee counter. Adam followed.

"Need a refill?" She held the pot.

"Yeah." He set his mug on the counter. No paper cups here. It'd been a wind-in-his-hair ride to the main section of the reserve everyone referred to as *downtown*. Too bad he couldn't live up here.

"What're you doing after the meeting?" Raven also re-filled her coffee.

"Busy." Adam blew on the steaming liquid and started outside. The squeak of Raven's flip-flops sounded on the floor. She was probably going to have a cigarette, too.

Back in Winnipeg, they'd never been into each other sexually. He'd had a girlfriend, and Raven had been Sully's woman, so she couldn't be hinting around for some action. She was a staunch traditionalist and probably planned to get on his case again about what he owed to the *Anishinaabeg*.

He set his mug on the railing of the small deck and withdrew his cigarettes. "You guys gonna be outside the church tomorrow?"

"Yeppers." Raven leaned in to the lighter. She set the tip of her smoke in the flickering flame and puffed.

"I'm gonna go ahead and ask." Maybe if Adam poked around, she'd finally relent after being able to speak her piece. "You got a problem with the Matawapits?"

"Do you?" Raven's grin was slyer than the bird she was named after. "I can't see the deacon and his wife opening their arms to a man like you."

Boy, she'd hit a home run. "No problem on my end."

"I have nothing against them personally. What I don't care for is the way they promote a place that harmed our people. They think they can erase everything through these workshops by reconciling the traditional and Christian communities."

"You always feel this way? Even in the 'Peg?"

Red dusted Raven's super-high cheekbones. "You know damn well what my priority was at the time."

"Look, we both got our own things going. I wanna get my boy back."

"And what about the rest of our people who're still suffering?"

"Who says I ain't helping? I'm here, aren't I? I'm also helping a buddy back home."

"He getting clean?"

"Yeah. He's a good kid. Having a tough go at sobriety. Got a lot of strikes against him."

"You're his sponsor?" She gasped.

"We're not supposed to talk about who we're sponsoring or who our sponsors are."

"I get it. He's doing okay then? Getting an education and whatnot?"

"Right now he's trying to stay clean. He can think about his education when he's got his head sorted out. What about you?"

"I'm going for my grade twelve. Now that there's a new principal here, I signed up for the adult education classes in the evening."

It figured Raven wouldn't have gone near the school when Deacon Matawapit had been the principal, before Bridget's father had retired.

"I hope your sponsee does well. Do you see what I mean now? I bet the Indian Residential Schools affected him, too."

Adam stiffened. Raven was right. Logan's father was Métis. Cutter's family had also attended the school. Because of what the government and Catholic Church had done, Sheena was dead. And Logan was close to . . . well, he'd better keep his nose clean while Adam was up at the reserve.

"See? I'm making sense. First time I saw you crack your poker face." Raven smirked.

This time Adam schooled his features. He must've shown some kind of reaction to earn that observation from Raven. Shit, he'd been away from gangbanging and the iron house for too long. Being on the outside and living a normal life was making him react . . . normally.

"Hey, I give you props. Won't deny it. Those schools caused a lot of trouble for some."

"Just some?" Raven wrinkled her eyebrows.

"Well, they're some who aren't doing too bad."

"You mean the Matawapits." Raven sneered.

"I'm only stating what I see."

"Remember, their mother never attended one of those schools. Because of her, she was able to keep the family together. How'd you think their kids would've turned out if the deacon's wife was *Anishinaabe-kwe* and had been forced into that school? It was Maria Matawapit's religion that caused all of these problems."

"I won't argue that. The deacon's wife probably had a lot to do with the way their kids turned out."

"Then you understand my point. If both parents attended, what chance did the kids stand?"

"I don't know the reserve well enough to answer. Are you telling me every single one of these families suffered?"

Raven glanced away.

"Well?"

"Jenny and Mark Fiddler."

"They both attended the school?"

"No. But Jenny's parents and grandparents did. Jenny and Mark are members of the church. Sadie and Allen Meekis are Jenny's grandparents. They're traditional."

Huh? Their granddaughter was a hard-core Catholic, but the grandparents were traditional? Adam had never heard of that before. "What about Jenny's parents?"

"Her dad died when she was a baby. He was working in the bush. A widow maker got him. He was dead as soon as the tree fell on him. Jenny's mother raised Jenny and her brother after their dad died. She passed away when Jenny was twelve. Complications from diabetes."

Raven took a drag on the cigarette. "There we go. Another big problem caused by our government and the church. If we would've been allowed to eat traditional food instead of what was forced down our throats, the aboriginal people wouldn't be suffering from diabetes. It's like an epidemic on the reserves. You either have it, or you know someone who has it."

"What's stopping people from eating traditional foods now?" Adam glanced around at nothing but trees and nature.

"You gotta be kidding." Raven sniggered. "Do you really think the puny bit of land the government forced us to use as a reserve provides enough wild game to feed two thousand people? It's why we used to have summer and winter camps. So we didn't over-hunt the area.

"Lots of people still hunt, fish, and trap, but we also have to supplement our food with the white man's meat sold at the Northern Lights Store, which costs an arm and a leg. A lot of people can't afford fresh meat or vegetables. They buy cheap junk to feed their families. Welcome to the north, city boy."

Man, Raven had a sarcastic mouth. "I get it."

"There aren't enough jobs on the reserve to afford high-priced food, either. Even the deacon's precious son doesn't have a job. Darryl supports them."

That was also true. Emery did a lot of volunteer work.

"If you don't work for the band, you get minimum pay jobs from the hotel, the restaurant, the Northern Lights store . . ." Raven scowled. "I'm glad Cookie hired me on as a waitress. He owns Kiss the Cook. It's the only restaurant. Downtown. Where everyone gathers."

Adam flicked his cigarette butt. Talk about having his eyes opened. Seemed urban natives weren't the only ones suffering.

Maybe Raven was right. What could Adam do about the problem? Sure, he was trying his best to help the addicts and alcoholics in the city and had also signed on to the committee to investigate Sheena's death, but maybe he should be doing something more.

Bridget had gone to Emery's old room the same time her parents had turned in. Thirty-six and sneaking out the window. She giggled. Her decision was for the best. If Mom and Dad knew she was meeting Adam, they'd disapprove.

She didn't want to spend her night arguing. She'd rather spend the evening with Adam. When the rumble of the four-wheeler carried into the open window, she winced. What if Mom and Dad thought Darryl or Emery were stopping by? Bridget should have told Adam she'd meet him down the road.

If she waited ten minutes, Mom and Dad might believe someone was passing by. Darryl wasn't the only one who owned a quad.

Bridget sat on the bed and crossed her fingers in hopes Adam wouldn't assume she'd changed her mind.

Once ten minutes had passed, Bridget eased out the window and darted around the side of the house. As she hurried down the driveway and along the road, she kept her hands out, hoping not to crash into or trip over something.

She made out the silhouette of the four-wheeler. The glowing red ember of the cigarette guided her to Adam.

"Wasn't sure if you were gonna be able to get away or not." Adam's voice was the deep, easy essence that always trailed Bridget's skin.

"Sorry. I didn't mean to keep you waiting." She stood at the machine, taking in his fresh scent that matched the aroma of the grass.

"No problem. I would've waited all night." He stuck the cigarette between his lips. "Get on."

"And if I didn't make it?" Heat flickered between Bridget's legs as she slid onto the back of the quad. Her thighs hugged Adam's strong legs, and her stomach pressed against his solid back.

"I woulda come to you. Snuck in your window." He snickered.

She swatted his arm. "My parents would've had a fit."

"Y'know, *kwe*, I take it you've done this before. Should I be jealous?"

"No need for jealousy. He's married now."

"Oh, he is? Who is he?"

"It doesn't matter, you're . . ." Her heart swelled. *You're the man for me.* Oh God, how true. She'd finally admitted the truth to herself.

"I'm what?" Adam fired up the machine.

Thank goodness for the roaring rumble of the engine, but Adam might as well have set off a stick of dynamite with the noise the quad made in the silent of the night.

"Let's go. Fast." She smacked his back.

"You're the boss." Adam revved the throttle, and they took off down the road. "Where to? It's your rez, not mine."

They had to find a quiet place where nobody ventured. Church Road. Just off of the road they were on now. The big old tree overhanging the lake was the perfect spot. "Go to the church."

"The church? Seriously?" he hollered over the roar of the engine.

This time of year was perfect at the reserve. Minimal bugs. The nights warm but not hot. They could stretch out on the grass once they were done talking on the tree.

Bridget laid her head on Adam's shoulder. For such a big, strong man, there was so much warmth coming from his flesh, and his exposed skin was a smooth as silk. She palmed his flat stomach. His abs contracted beneath her touch, so she nuzzled the back of his neck.

"Woman, you'd better be ready to finish what you're starting back there," he said, glancing over his shoulder.

"Hmm . . . keep driving. Like you said, I'm the boss."

Silver light from the full moon lit the lake to deep blue. Water lapped against the rocky shoreline. Frogs and bugs chirped and sang. They provided a great soundtrack to a quiet night alone with the woman Adam loved.

"I can't believe you never officially lived here." If Adam had been born at Ottertail Lake, he wouldn't have left.

"My life was in the city." Bridget's long legs dangled from the massive branch overhanging the lake. "At the time, it was too . . . uh . . . bush for me."

"Bush?"

"Yes. Bush. When Mom and Dad returned here, the rez didn't have hydro. Or a sewage system. They had running water, but nowhere for the water to go. Mom set up a small toilet for Emery to use because he was only eight at the time. For Dad, it was the outhouse."

"Outhouse?" Adam lit his cigarette. Was his home reserve the same way?

"They bathed in a big gray tub every Sunday and Wednesday night. It was the norm up here."

"When'd they finally get to live like normal people?"

"The sewer lines were installed when Emery started high school . . . I think."

"Yeah, can't see you bathing twice a week or using an outside shitter." Adam snickered. Sure enough, his comment earned his arm a cuff.

"I don't mind camping, but I prefer a place with showers

and bathrooms."

"Like Sleeping Giant Park?" Adam's insides warmed. It'd been a great camping trip, the three of them snuggled in a tent together.

"You didn't do too shabby for a city boy. I wasn't sure if you'd know how to start a fire."

"Common sense." Adam shrugged. "You can't start a log on fire. Need something to get it going first and build it from there."

"I guess that's what kept you alive on the streets, hmm?" Bridget's hand rested on the thick branch.

"You know this kept me alive." He curled his fingers into a fist.

"You don't anymore." Her voice dropped an octave to the same tone when, in a non-judgmental way, she'd coaxed Adam to speak about his feelings. "How'd the meeting go?"

"Like any other meeting." Adam couldn't disclose who'd been present. Anonymity was imperative. "At the end of each month, they have an open meeting."

"They do?" Bridget fidgeted. "I'm in."

"You wanna go this time?" She'd never gone before, opting to stay with Kyle. Adam's breathing hitched. She did want this as bad as he did.

"Yes." She pressed her lips together. "I should've gone before. I think it's time I got to know the program better and the people who attend. Are there open meetings in the city? I doubt we'll be here at the end of the month."

"Yep." Adam's breath kept jumping. She was committing to him. To them. "You'll need to get a sitter."

"A sitter's fine. I'll ask Ginny."

"*Kwe* . . ." Adam leaned in. She did love him. She must. His heart begged for her to say those three words. Would she finally tell him tonight?

This time he'd make sure they had a place to be together.

Bridget didn't deserve the outside, although she hadn't seemed to mind being on the trail last evening. Still, a bed would be a wonderful place where she could lie in his arms afterwards.

CHAPTER TWENTY-SIX: SEX AND OUTRAGE

To avoid suspicion, Adam had gotten them the room. At least the owner had been awake, having not turned in yet at the small home beside the eight-room, log motel where the old couple lived.

Adam opened the door to a double bed, TV, dresser, and stuffed chair. "*Kwe . . .*" he said, trying to whisper loud enough for her to hear.

From behind a pine tree, Bridget appeared. Glancing around, she darted across the gravel. The light from above cast her in full view. She scooted passed him and into the room.

Adam closed the door.

She gazed around. "I've been coming up here forever, but I've never been inside one of the motel rooms before. It's nice. Cozy. It'd be kind of neat to own this place."

"That makes two of us. Guess I should've bunked here instead of at your brother's."

"Oh, Emery would've insisted you stay at his home. They try to make the workshops as affordable as possible, the reason why they billet participants and trainers."

Adam flicked on a small lamp beside the bed. The shadows from the dim lighting played across Bridget's features that resembled her mother's fine bone structure.

"I'm glad you never did what most women do . . ." He ran his finger along Bridget's dark eyebrow. These slightly thick babies came straight from the deacon.

"Reshape them?" Bridget giggled. "I wax the strays. Nothing more."

He cupped her face. She searched his eyes. "I don't want you to be too tired tomorrow. It's already late."

"I'll be fine." She tilted her head and snuggled his waist.

It was late and time to get down to business. Both had a busy day tomorrow. He tasted her mouth. Bridget's self-assurance, independence, take-it-or-leave-it nonchalant attitude always made him itch to conquer her sexually, and in the past, she'd always let him.

As Adam slipped his tongue between Bridget's lips, hers was already waiting to claim his. He skimmed her jean shorts until he found the button. Her chest heaved, and she groaned into his mouth.

He'd bet Bridget's pussy was already wet and her clit needing a nice rubbing. Damned straight he'd more than give her cunt what it wanted. He undid her shorts, which drew another moan from Bridget. She melted their crotches together.

He worked the shorts lower. The heat from Bridget's exposed skin was hot enough to warm his cock. Nothing drove him crazier than knowing she desired him.

"Oh yeah." Adam grunted. "You want me to play with your clitty, don't you?" He traced Bridget's bare ass, copping a nice feel while she persistently ground her hips, as if trying to fuck his dick with her snatch.

"That's it . . ." He licked her neck. "I'm eating some pussy."

"Oh, Adam . . ." Bridget groaned.

She yanked on his zipper and tugged. His prick sprang from the underwear. Boy, he'd have to make this fast because his hard-on ached to get inside Bridget.

He eased her onto the bed. She laid back, gazing at him

through the fringe of her lush lashes. He removed her shorts and skimpy panties—his fave kind, silk and barely providing coverage of her pubes. When Bridget spread her slim thighs in offering to him, the tip of his dick throbbed. What an offer she was presenting.

Adam rested on his elbows and ran his hands along her thighs, taking in the musky essence of ripe cunt buried beneath clothing all day.

He kissed the sultry hairs and sucked her fragrance deep into his lungs. "Y'know how bad I wanted you to mail me your underwear when I was in the pen? I would've given anything to smell your panties before I went to sleep each night. Damn, you always smell good."

"Please . . ." Her voice was begging.

Bridget wound her legs around Adam's neck, guiding him to her pussy lips.

He kissed the coarse hairs that carried the scent of musk. Each peck he bestowed on her pussy lips elicited a hunger inside him. Bridget squirmed beneath his light puckers and then raised her hips, silently urging him to feast.

He eased his tongue between the soft flesh, tracing the sensitive folds around her clit. She jerked slightly, panting, and laid her feet on his back. He positioned his palms on her spread thighs, making sure she couldn't squirm along the mattress, because he wasn't going to stop eating until he was good and done.

Her sweet scent assailed his nostrils. He drew in the steamy aroma while moving his tongue in a circular motion around Bridget's tiny, hard flesh. Her wet mess invaded his mouth. He slipped a finger into her snatch and the other finger into Bridget's asshole. Her flesh clenched tight enough that Adam could barely thrust while continuing to bathe her clit with slow licks.

Bridget ground her pussy along his face, silently urging

him to lick faster.

Her excitement was his excitement. The ache in his cock was unbearable. Finger-fucking Bridget's cunt and asshole was taunting the jizz in his balls.

He trailed his tongue to the sexy layer of skin between Bridget's asshole and pussy. After kissing this sensitive spot, he laid his tongue on the crack of her buttocks and washed this area with saliva. Then he trailed her cleft and flicked at her asshole.

"Adam . . . Adam . . ." Bridget panted and gasped.

There was nothing he liked better than watching his beloved *kwe* lose herself to his touch. Bridget's tits bounced, nipples erect for his touch. Her flat stomach muscles strained from the tension her body was experiencing.

"Please," she begged. "Please. Please."

"Mmm . . . you taste good, woman." He kept stealing peeks at her flushed face, gasping mouth, and pleasure making her smile while he drew a spittle path to her pussy.

Her cunt lips were slightly parted. Her clit engorged with excitement. He pecked this spot, and Bridget shuddered. She slapped her palms against the back of his head and seared her cunt against his lips. His tongue was nested between her slit, and he wiggled it. She moaned, and he lapped up her wet mess while she bounced her beautiful ass in rhythm with his licks, holding tight to her

When her squeals invaded the room, she wrapped him in sheer pleasure. His dick ached beyond control. He had to mount her, fuck her good, because her continued groans and pants were enough to drive him insane. He rested his palms on the bedspread for leverage and kicked his jeans to his ankles. Although he always let Bridget have time to savor coming, her silky moans didn't allow Adam that luxury.

With his hands bracing the mattress, he eased into her wet opening. The tip invaded Bridgett's pussy that she clenched, and the heat coating Adam's back thickened to heavy steam strong enough to drench him in a fever that teetered on bursting.

Bridget locked her legs around Adam's hips, trapping him. He yanked her to his chest. His weight crushed her nipples.

He rode Bridget hard and fast, his erection trembling and spasming. Only she could bring him to that special place. Only she could drive him completely wild.

Sheer pleasure swathed Adam. He panted and grunted, still plunging deep inside her. Then the shattering excitement gripped him. He did what he always loved doing—gave Bridget every inch of his heart.

Snuggled under the covers, Bridget rested on Adam's chest. The lullaby of his heartbeat was a song ready to put her to sleep. "I don't want to get up," she murmured. Her breaths dusted his nipple.

"Neither do I, *kwe*." Adam's warm lips brushed the top of her head. "I wanna reload and fuck you all over again."

She giggled and snaked her legs around his strong calves. Her breasts brushed his hard pecs. His body was warm and strong, but also pure satin, an invitation to drape herself in his.

"There's an alarm clock. What time are you usually at the church?"

"Seven. We're making blueberry oatmeal, ham, and toast for breakfast. Jenny already made the muffins for the break." Bridget pecked his cheek.

"What time do your parents get up?"

"Dad's an early bird. Five. He says his Lauds then."

"Lauds?"

"Morning prayers. He prays the Office of Hours. There're

different times of the day he has to pray."

After sex, cuddling was the best. Their words were soft whispers, voices a little scratchy.

"I guess he has no choice but to get up that early."

"Not really. Father Bennie isn't an early bird."

"Your dad would be." Adam grunted. "I guess we can't spend the night here. We'd have to leave at four-thirty. You need your sleep."

"What time is it?"

"Quarter after twelve."

"Let's stay here a wee bit longer. I'm not ready to go home." She remained curled around Adam's muscular body.

Never mind her fears. Emery would tell Bridget to have faith. She needed the Big Guy more than ever. The Exposition of Christ was set out daily for the Catholic participants to utilize during the workshop.

She'd give anything to possess half of her brother's faith. Emery had fought hard for the new life he had now. Where did this leave Bridget? Her life sure didn't mirror Jude's wrapped-in-a-bow Catholic existence.

"*Kwe*, what's crawled up your beautiful ass? You're stiffer than a prison shank." Adam rubbed her arm.

Bridget couldn't confess the truth. She'd hurt him.

His deep breaths eased away the panic settling in her throat. If only they could stay here forever. All they needed was Kyle. Up on the reserve, hidden in a motel room, real life didn't interfere. Real life wasn't present to drive Adam back to drinking.

"*Kwe*, wake up. Wake up. We fell asleep."

Bridget had been dreaming. They'd been on her favorite island, the one with the beach where Randy used to take her. She'd been swimming with Kyle while Adam grilled steaks over a campfire.

"What time is it?" If Mom and Dad noticed she was missing, a fight would ensue.

"Six."

"Six?" Bridget gasped. She scooted off the bed and flung open the curtains, which wasn't a good idea because a man was smoking at one of the picnic tables, under sunlight. Yes, the sun. Dad was awake. So was Mom. Bridget was supposed to be showering before leaving for the church.

Even worse, she'd left her phone in Emery's old bedroom. Not good. Not good. She stamped her feet.

"We gotta go. I don't have my phone. I always have my phone. What if Kyle —"

"Easy. Jude has him. Kyle's fine. If anything happened, I think Emery would've figured out where you were since I didn't go back to his place last night." Adam came up behind Bridget. His strong arms encircled her waist.

"Emery." Bridget smacked her forehead. Just great. He'd also know what had happened. "We'd better go. You still have to shower and dress for the workshop."

When she whipped about, her breasts bounced against Adam's chest. They were naked. They'd slept together all night. As she looked up and into his soft, dark eyes, the scent of their union lingered on his breath and skin.

She buried herself in his hard muscles. Why did he have to have so many demons to fight? Adam was the perfect man, the perfect man for her.

His palm brushed her hair. "*Kwe* . . . maybe we can stay here if everyone knows."

The offer tugged at her insides, but she knew better. "You're here to heal. The workshop is called Healing the Spirit. I need you to do this."

"You need me to?"

"Yes. I need you to." If humanly possible, she'd creep inside Adam, find a safe spot to hide. "I need you to. Kyle needs you to. We need you to do this . . . Please." *Because I love you.*

Bridget slunk up the front steps to the house. From inside, the sound of banging dishes carried from the open window. If Mom was pissed, Dad was probably hiding on the deck.

The first time Bridget had disappointed them, she'd gotten home at two in the morning after partying with Randy and his friends. Mom had told Bridget no more visits for six months. So instead of seeing her parents at the rez, Mom and Dad had traveled to Thunder Bay.

With a big breath, Bridget opened the door. *Please don't let there be fighting. Please.*

First, she'd shower and then sit at the breakfast table to defend herself like a bad teenager who'd done wrong. She padded down the hall to check her phone for messages. Once finished, she darted to the bathroom, undisturbed, but the banging continued in the kitchen.

After Bridget had dressed, she padded to the kitchen. Mom stood in the dining room, readying a quick breakfast before venturing to the church. Dad wasn't present. Great, he'd gone off somewhere to pout.

"Is Dad here?" Bridget sat at the table and poured herself a coffee from the carafe.

"You know why your father isn't here . . ." Mom's lips formed into a straight line. She sat. "Eat. It'll be a long day."

Bridget scooped up a serving of toast and eggs. "You don't have to be angry."

"Then what exactly am I supposed to feel?" Mom readied her own coffee. She stared at the carafe.

"I'm thirty-six. I know what I'm—"

"This isn't only about you." Mom's words came out in small huffs beneath her breath. Her long fingers gripped the coffee mug. "This is about Kyle. He's been through enough already. If you wish to welcome chaos and dysfunction into your life, by all means, go ahead, but I won't let you subject Kyle to *his* behavior."

"His?" Bridget's gut burned. "He has a name. He's also Kyle's father. Adam's working hard to rebuild their relationship. It's the reason why he's here."

"Is he really?" Mom's delicate shoulders sagged. "Or did he follow you here?"

"Mom." Bridget gasped. "How can you say that? Do you really believe I'd associate with a man that shallow? That selfish?"

"Associate?" Mom's face reddened. "I think you did more than associate." She set down the mug. "Why? What about Stephen?"

"We went on one date." Bridget shoved the plate away. "I hardly think one date merits a relationship."

"Sweetie, what am I going to do with you?" Mom pressed her palms to her temples. "Why are you this way? Why do you always give your father and I grief?"

"Grief?" Bridget was simply trying to live her own adult life. Yes — adult.

"Why are you this way?" Mom wilted in the chair. "I've tried so hard to be understanding. I've tried so hard to explain your behavior to your father — "

"What?" Bridget sputtered. "What behavior?"

"How rebellious you've been. Honey, this has been going on since you were a teenager. A child. We tell you to do one thing, and you do another. We wish one life for you, and you find another. All we ever wanted is for you to be happy. You can't tell me Adam makes you happy."

Mom was right. Bridget also wilted in the chair. Was she happy? She was happy when she could disappear with Adam, away from Mrs. Dale, away from Mom and Dad, away from the pressures of life that had sent Adam to drink.

Chapter Twenty-Seven: Living in the Past

Not one word had come from Emery or Darryl when Adam had arrived at the cozy two-bedroom log house. They also hadn't said anything when he'd showered and dressed. And Emery hadn't said anything before leaving for the church.

Now Adam rode shotgun while Darryl drove them to the workshop, who still hadn't said anything. He stared straight ahead at the dirt road, wearing his customary black sunglasses. Bandit stuck her snout between the two seats, resting her paws on the console.

Adam petted the dog's soft fur.

Darryl cleared his throat. "I know it's not any of my business . . ."

Nope, Adam's all-night disappearing act wasn't anyone's business.

"I just don't wanna see you go through what I went through in July."

"The deacon gave you a tough time?"

"Yeah. Sure did." Darryl turned the truck onto Church Road. "Try understand, he's had it tough. Another residential school survivor. He'll share his story this morning. You'll see why he is the way he is when it comes to Em, Jude, and Bridget."

"She's never been the kind of person who listens to her folks."

"You nailed it." Darryl chuckled. "When she'd come up here to visit, she was always getting into trouble."

"She may do things that piss off her parents, but she's a woman devoted to the church. I don't see why this isn't enough for them."

"I wish it was the same way, too." The truck rolled up to the church where Clayton Kabatay and his family continued to protest.

"Talked to Raven at the meeting last night. She made some good points." Adam unbuckled his seat belt, something he'd never done until he'd met Bridget.

"They make a lot of good points," Darryl said. "I used to agree with them. Preserving our culture is extremely important, but we can't disrespect or try discourage another's beliefs, which they're doing."

Darryl spoke the truth. Raven and her family were completely against the church, and completely against the Matawapit family.

"They really hate the deacon, huh?" Adam followed Darryl to the basement door beneath the car port.

"Hate is a kind word to use." Darryl shook his head. "The Kabatays are beyond hate." He opened the door.

They went down the four steps. The kitchen was to their right, the door shut, but the sound of pots clanging and women chattering carried to where they stood.

Adam passed on the coffee for now. Basil sat in the circle of tables before his big drum, ready to begin the morning prayer.

Bridget came in from the other basement door that faced the lake. She stopped. From where Adam stood, he spied red climbing up her cheekbones. At least the deacon wasn't present. He must be upstairs, helping the priest recite Mass for the Catholic participants.

Darryl snickered. "C'mon." He led them to where they'd

sat yesterday.

Adam drew out a chair just as Bridget scooted by, barreling for the kitchen. She'd braided her hair in a tail falling down her back. White cotton shorts showed off the long legs she'd draped around his waist last night. He couldn't forget the perky tits he'd sucked on, or her pussy he'd eaten until he was full. And how she'd thrashed and kicked while he'd held her thighs in place.

"It's a good thing my father-in-law isn't here." Darryl again snickered. "If he saw the look on your face . . ."

Aww, for crying out loud. Adam was doing what he'd done last night—giving away his feelings. "Don't mind me. I'll just pick my tongue up off the table."

Darryl slapped his hand over his mouth, but his body shook from being unable to contain his laughter.

At least someone was having a good time—at Adam's expense.

Bridget vanished into the kitchen. She'd said no to Adam's offer of a motel room. Maybe she was right. The mere sight of her had distracted him from what he should be concentrating on—the workshop and healing.

Time for him to get his act together. He had his son to think about, and a woman whom he'd hurt . . . terribly. A woman who deserved to only smile and laugh when she saw him. A child who could always count on him to be there.

He'd be that man. He'd be that father. He'd be that husband.

Nobody was getting in his way anymore. Not the deacon. Not The Hawk. Not his parole officer. Nobody.

The morning had been the deacon's story of torment, anger, shame, and disillusionment after leaving the Indian Residential School. Adam could understand why the man protected his children—even into adulthood.

Nobody had been there to protect the deacon who'd lost his two best friends—one through neglect by the nuns and priests who'd refused to believe the boy was sick, and the other who'd run away in the dead of winter, preferring to face freezing temperatures over the safety of the little warmth the school had offered.

Adam couldn't begin to imagine what had gone through the deacon's five-year-old mind when he'd spoken about the Indian Agent accompanied by a RCMP officer showing up at the reserve, escorting the children from their homes, boarding them on a plane without an explanation, and taking them far away from the forest and lakes they knew, to be thrust into a cold, dark place full of cold, dark faces expecting complete obedience.

The worst part was, the deacon's parents and grandparents had experienced the same school, the same misery, the same pain, the same terror, the same shame.

No wonder so many had turned to alcohol and drugs to wipe their memories clean of the horrors they'd suffered as children. No wonder they'd left the school at sixteen in utter defeat. They'd not only been stripped of their language and culture, they'd been stripped of love and compassion, and had their dignity stolen from them.

What did they have to offer as parents when they had children of their own? Because of those schools, the adult children had no idea how to speak about their feelings, clueless how to love someone, much less parent their offspring, because they'd never experienced what parenting was.

Generation after generation this had happened, starting when the schools opened in the eighteen-seventies, ordered by the Prime Minister of Canada. Assimilate the heathens.

Even worse, they'd watched the pitiful land allotments they'd been provided by the Crown destroyed, whether through pollution when big businesses dumped waste into their rivers and lakes, flooding to build hydro-electric dams for towns and cities, or being moved to worthless land of bedrocks and swamps because precious gems were discovered on the reserves. The list went on and on, and this bullshit still happened.

A Catholic woman from one of the tourist camps who was participating in the workshop had said if anyone would have tried that with her, she would have called the police. Then she'd lowered her head, face red, realizing the police were enforcing what the government had ordered, so there'd be nobody she could have turned to in order to protect her children.

Adam clutched his coffee cup. He sat in a circle with Darryl and three other men. The group had been broken into smaller groups for sharing.

The deacon was leading Darryl and Adam's group. Bridget's father motioned at the stupid chair Adam had read about on the agenda, where he was supposed to speak to the dumb thing.

Even worse, Adam was first up to talk. What the heck was he supposed to say? Although he'd been sitting, lost in his thoughts, nobody had urged him to address the chair.

If the old-timers from the twelve-step group were present, they'd tell Adam to keep an open mind. Fine, he would. He stood.

The empty chair remained empty.

Before he could think, before he could try to piece together what swarmed through his mind, the words tumbled from his mouth, cold words, icy and stony. "Why'd you have me?"

In the past, Adam hadn't wondered why his parents decided to birth children if they had no clue how to care for them. The deacon's story summed up Mom and Dad's desperation to try live a normal life, but inability to offer love and protection because of their own pain, misery, and shame. Their own hate, resentment, and disgust.

Through the spots in front of Adam's eyes, Kyle appeared in the chair, asking the same question—*Why'd you have me, Daddy?*

Adam swallowed. The saliva wouldn't go down, having turned thick and sticky.

He'd had Kyle for the same reasons Adam's parents had him—someone to love. But they didn't know how to love. Neither did he. He'd tried. Tried so hard. Fear had sent him back to the bottle, running from what he had no idea how to give or receive.

Busting heads and gangbanging had been easier. Easier to hate. Easier to crush people under his boot heel. Easier to keep feeding the misery. Easier to pretend he didn't care.

I want to love, but I don't know how to love.

Adam's body shook. He tried to set down the coffee cup he still held that trembled in his hand.

"Here . . ." Darryl grasped the cup.

The anxiety pounded and thundered at the base of Adam's neck, shivered and quivered up his spine, stretched and cawed, enclosing him like a thick cocoon, wrapping him until he couldn't punch away the horror, couldn't swipe away the distress.

Sweat slithered along Adam's brows, threatening to invade his eyes. More sweat filled his armpits and coated his back.

He had to get out of here, try to shake the cocoon tightening around his skin. He needed a cigarette. Needed . . . something.

He turned and stormed for the back door leading to the lake.

Bridget dashed from her spot at the coffee counter. She should have stayed in the kitchen with Mom. She shouldn't have come out to replenish the refreshment table. Mom had warned this afternoon was a crucial time for the participants. From the previous Healing the Spirit, Bridget knew so, too.

She darted out the back door beneath the car port and scampered by the protesters who had the gall to call her insulting names, from traitor to half-breed. None of what they said mattered. Adam was in pain.

Once Bridget scurried down the path, she emerged from the brush to find him sitting on the big rock, trembling and smoking a cigarette.

Adam kept staring at the water, his eyes glazed over, as if he were somewhere else.

"Adam?" Bridget sank down beside him.

He turned. His dark eyes hardened. "I had no right having my son. This is all my fault."

"What do you mean?"

"Angela . . ." Adam sucked on the cigarette filter. He blew a couple of smoke rings. "She wasn't supposed to get pregnant. Was supposed to be on the pill. I should've kept it wrapped. Should've known the state she was in, she wouldn't remember to take her birth control like she was supposed to."

"But it did happen." Bridget laid her hand over Adam's thigh. His lethal quadriceps stiffened beneath her palm.

"Nope. We had choices. She wasn't sure if she could go through with it 'cause she knew she'd have to stop using."

Bridget's heart froze.

"I told her we'd be fine. A big part of me . . ." The apple in Adam's throat shifted up and down. "A big part of me wanted my boy. Wanted to be a father. I had no right . . ."

"Why?"

"You know why." He scowled. "I'm no good. No better

than my parents. No better than my sisters. Lookit 'em. Always getting their kids taken away. Choosing booze over their rug rats. None of us had any right becoming parents. We're not fit."

No way would Bridget let Adam go on a pity trip. Not after he'd come this far. "The past is the past. This is the present. And you're doing everything you can to change your life for your sake. For Kyle's sake."

"The deacon talked about the biggie—not having any idea how to love someone. How to receive love given to him. Why'd you think I started drinking again?" He tipped the brim of his cowboy hat. "I had no clue how to love you. What to do with the love you gave me. I'm incapable. The schools made sure we'd never figure out how to give a damn about anyone other than ourselves."

"That's not true," Bridget fired back. "You loved me in a way nobody has before. You love Kyle. You're his father."

"It takes more than firing your jizz into a woman to be a father." Hate blazed in his eyes, flashing up like a storm raging over cold, black water. "I was never there for him."

"You are now."

"Am I? I'm not gonna be there tomorrow. I'm here. He was upset about it. Crushed. Again, I let him down. If not for you, he'd hate me."

"Yes, if not for me. Did you ever think . . ." The bottom dropped out from beneath Bridget. *Oh Lord, I'm supposed to show Adam how to love and receive love. Emery's right. God always has a plan. His plan was for me to become a part of Adam's life. To help him heal the way Mom helped Dad heal.*

"Did you ever think all of this was meant to happen?" Bridget's heart churned into overdrive, rattling against her chest. "You left Winnipeg to try to make a better life for you and Kyle. You came to the career fair to see what your options were for post-secondary schooling. We met. We were meant to meet. God willed this."

"Did He really, *kwe?*" Adam stared at her. "I forgot all about a career when I saw you. Forgot about everything. I mean *everything.*"

"I'll never forget how the two of you looked . . ." Adam's shoulders wider than bridges, his *get out of my way* lazy strut as the crowd scampered to give him a wide berth, and his overpowering presence had left Bridget quivering in her seat at the display table. A man with ruthless dark eyes, but a child on his hip, a toddler cuddled around his daddy, held by a big hand on his tiny rump. Adam and Kyle had tugged at Bridget's insides, summoned her from the table, commanded her to approach the man with the street-tough handsomeness and smoldering testosterone.

"It was God," she whispered. "It was God."

"It wasn't God. It was lust." Adam snorted.

"Lust?" Bridget sputtered. "How can you say that?"

"It's true. I took one look at you and thought, *walk it over here, honey.*" Adam shook his head.

Bridget had to remember Adam had been inexperienced at his new life at the time. Naturally, he'd let his crotch goad him. "You were a perfect gentleman."

"*Kwe,* what else was I s'posed to be? You were a lady. Y'know how many ladies I'd known before I met you? None." His words reeked of disgust. "The only women I knew were just like me. I wasn't gonna take you to a bar and get drunk."

"Try to remember you were starting a new life. I didn't expect you to take me to a bar. You took me for coffee."

Adam's lips tugged at the corners.

Bridget breathed a sigh of relief. Maybe she was talking down his anxiety, or whatever was making him fidget. He had the familiar look in his eyes, one she hadn't recognized at the time but understood now. Fear was creeping up his spine, and a man like Adam had no idea how to handle fear, an emotion he wouldn't own up to because of what his parents had put him through, because of what he'd learned to hide on the streets, because of what he'd learned in jail and prison.

Life had taught Adam in order to survive, he had to strike first or be struck down.

"I understand now why you drank." She laid her head on his thigh. When he petted her hair, the apprehension creeping up her back vanished. "You were scared. You told me you didn't know how to give or receive love, so you did what you'd learned to do since you were a child."

He kept petting her hair. "*Kwe*, you deserve a man—"

Bridget sat up, anger erupting in her chest. "Quit feeling sorry for yourself."

Adam swatted at his hat. "Woman, you like telling off men, don't you?"

"No, I don't, but I'm not going to let you talk yourself back to your old life. You're strong—"

"Strong?" Adam faced her. "Why'd you think I call you *kwe*? I told you how our people revered our women. Inside each of you is strength rooted to the earth 'cause you're tied to the earth. Woman is earth. She's strong. She perseveres."

He licked his lips. "She reaches inside a man and shows him . . ." His voice grew softer, soft enough to feather Bridget's warm flesh. "Shows him how to be gentle, be kind, be thoughtful. The earth nurtures us and gives the *Anishinaabeg* life and strength. Woman is earth. She does the same for a man. His strength comes from her. Comes from her . . . love."

Bridget kept stroking his thigh. With the birds singing their songs and the waves lightly lapping at the rocks, where they sat was silkier than a lullaby.

"*Kwe* . . ." Adam's voice shook. "*Kwe* . . ." He cleared his throat. "*Kwe* . . ." His hard thigh muscle contracted under her palm. His jawline quivered. "*Kwe* . . . I'm . . . I'm scared."

CHAPTER TWENTY-EIGHT: CHOKING ON YOUR SCREAMS

Bridget rubbed Adam's leg. For the man she loved to finally acknowledge fear meant he was on the healing path. She moved her hand in a circular motion. "Everyone gets scared. You don't think I'm scared?"

"I don't wanna stay at your brother's." Adam's thigh remained hard beneath her touch. "I wanna stay at the motel."

"Then we'll stay there." Bridget pecked the back of his trembling hand. "We'll pack our stuff after the workshop and get Emery or Darryl to give us a ride to the motel."

"Y'know this'll piss off your ol' man and ol' lady." Adam clasped his hands together. His knuckles remained white.

"They're already pissed." She rubbed his shaking knee, keeping her movements lazy circles, the same kind she used whenever Kyle woke terrified from a nightmare, because her big strong Adam was terrified, and he needed her strength just as she needed his. "We'll talk some more after the workshop. I think Dad and the group are waiting for you."

Adam licked at his lips, slow, lingering. "Yeah, they are." His voice was quiet.

"You can do this." Bridget shifted to her knees and cuddled his waist, gazing up at the fear quaking in his eyes. "I'll be in the kitchen. Only a few feet away." Her words were as gentle as the light laps of water brushing the rocks.

"Yeah. Got it." Adam's jawline twitched. "Lemme have one more cigarette. Who woulda thought I learned all this from a man who's in the iron house for killing another man."

Bridget kissed his cheek, which produced a trembling smile from him.

She wouldn't judge this Cutter person anymore or think of him with disgust and fear. Cutter was a human being, another *Anishinaabe* suffering from what the government had done to her people. What the church she loved had done to her people.

There wasn't a chance she'd let Adam fail. He'd survive, as he always had, for this strong, tall man was a survivor, not a victim.

One of the participants, a man named Vernon, sat, having finished yelling at nothing just as Adam rejoined his group with a fresh cup of coffee in the church basement.

The deacon spared Adam a quick glance before nodding at Darryl, who stood.

Adam made sure to sit straight and lean forward.

Round face tight, Darryl circled the table, his running meeting the floor force by force. "We were living simple lives. Harming nobody. Was our society perfect? No. We had our enemies. We fought and went to war against one another. However, we had a way to live. Our own way to live that was different.

"You cost me my parents. Cost me my aunt. But you didn't destroy me. I'm still standing. I'll always be standing. I'll always fight for the rights of my people."

He swiveled, his small eyes narrowed, and he thrust his finger at the chair. "You tried to take my husband from me. You failed. He's mine now. I forgive you for what you did. I forgive you for your lies and your harsh treatment of us. I forgive you for everything that you touch, you destroy."

He stopped and set his hands on his hips. "Part of me wants to spit on you, but I won't. I'm healing. I'm learning. I could turn around and say, *If you're sincere, you'd give us back what's rightfully ours,* but I won't. We are all here together now, whether we like it or not. All I'm asking from you is respect. Respect who we are. Respect our way of life. And honor the Treaties you signed with the First Nations of Canada."

Darryl stopped and rubbed one of his braids. "You, the Catholic Church, and you, the Canadian Government, are cunning. Coyote. You confounded many people and situations. If not for you, I wouldn't have met my husband. The man Creator made for me. This is why I must forgive you. I must also forgive you so I don't destroy myself from within. This is what Creator asks from me."

Adam had learned in the twelve-step program that whoever wronged him didn't matter. Resentment was the number one offender for alcoholics and what drove them to drink again. What mattered was whether he allowed the offense to keep offending and controlling him.

Nobody controlled him. Nobody. Only Bridget and Kyle were allowed the honor of disturbing the serenity he'd fought for.

Darryl continued to rant about his losses, directing his anger at his aunt and parents.

"You blamed everything and everyone but yourself." He smacked his thigh.

Adam shifted in closer. Darryl was speaking about himself.

"Were you looking for excuses? Were you afraid to face the man in the mirror? You were bitter. Angry. Sad. Depressed. You wanted everything to go your way. When it didn't, you became more bitter and pissed off. You tried to twist and mold people into what you wanted them to be.

You were a selfish jerk.

"What're you gonna do about what you did? Are you gonna man up and accept responsibility for how you reacted? Are you gonna use this workshop to let Creator begin your healing process?"

Darryl slumped, his back rounding slightly. "Yeah. I'm gonna. Coming here was the best thing I ever did. How I used to feel won't disappear overnight. Sometimes I find myself acting the way I used to. The worst part is, even though the Catholic religion and Canadian Government hurt me terribly, I turned around and hurt others in the same capacity I'd been hurt, neglected, and abused."

Face flushed from his tirade, Darryl sank in the chair. He placed his hands over his face, chest heaving.

The deacon's solemn gaze landed on Adam. The option to confront the empty chair was in his hands.

Adam stood. The harmless chair made of gray plastic and silver steel with a hole cut in the back to provide better comfort, did nothing.

This was for Kyle and Bridget, and most of all for himself. "You weren't much of a father. Drank. Kicked my ass. Kicked Mom's ass. Kicked everyone's ass. You were an angry son of a bitch. Guess part of me wanted your respect. Something from you. Anything. But you didn't give me nothing. And you never will.

"Gotta accept something hit you hard enough to take you down. You never shared your residential school story. Maybe it hurt too much. Maybe you walked out of that place unable to talk to anyone. Or didn't know how to talk. They beat you into silence. Guess you learned to keep your trap shut so you wouldn't get another strap across your ass, or back, or wherever they hit you.

"Don't know what they did to you. Wish I did. It'd help me understand why you are the way you are. I'm in Ottertail

Lake. You don't even know. Don't care. Probably didn't know I was in the iron house either. Why would you? You never cared enough to ask about me the other times I went down below.

"When I was born, I was another rug rat you'd fathered for someone else to give a shit about, 'cause you couldn't give a shit about yourself.

"I got a son you never saw. Probably don't even know he's a boy. Or maybe you do. The daughters you fathered keep trying to talk to you, track you down, see what you're up to. If you're still alive. They let me know where you're crashing. Vancouver. Downtown East Side. There's no coming back from there. I know you'll die there.

"I'm not going down. I'm going up."

Heart-wrenching pain infiltrated Adam's blood and raced through his veins. Knowing he'd never see his father again rattled his chest and shook his soul.

He dropped in the chair. Grief was an emotion he'd denied. But he had to grieve. Grieve the loss of his father before the bastard died, because there was no turning back. He couldn't save the ol' man. Jean Marc Guimond was beyond saving. Only Creator could touch a man Adam had once called Dad.

I have no father. I never had a father. I'm simply the result of a horny sperm meeting a horny egg. Nothing else.

The fight was accepting what he couldn't change and finding the courage to change what he could.

Adam stood outside with Darryl, smoking a cigarette. They leaned against the fence overlooking the graveyard. Bandit trotted around the grass, sniffing here and there. Three-thirty. One more intense session to go. Damn, this had been a tough day. Tough enough to knot every muscle. Adam needed a hot shower afterwards to try to relax.

"You okay?" Darryl sipped what he'd referred to earlier

as Mrs. Matawapit's homemade lemonade.

"Yep. What about you?"

"Hanging in there. Looking forward to going home and staring at the TV."

Many of the graves had clan staffs turned upside down. Others with painted white wooden crosses, and there was the odd gravestone. Not too many people could afford a fancy monument.

"From what Bridget told me, I thought everything was cool for you. Guess I was wrong." Adam took a drag.

"It's something I continue to fight. It's part of the healing journey. I'm not cured of what contaminated me for years. It takes time. Sorta like when someone pollutes the water. Only time can clean up the mess."

Darryl had hit the nail on the head. The old-timers had told Adam the same thing during meetings. He'd drank for most of his life, so his recovery would come slowly. The earth had taken a billion years to have creatures walking about on the land. And the longer something simmered, the stronger it became.

Perhaps this what was he was doing—gathering more strength each time he confronted the past and became more accepting of what Creator had given him. Sure, he didn't have much family. But he'd made one of his own. He had Kyle and Bridget.

Mom stood at the kitchen counter in the church basement. She wiped the same pot she'd already dried three times. "How're you supposed to get here to help? The motel's downtown."

"Emery. He takes the four-wheeler every morning to church."

"Your father's not going to like this." Mom shook her

head. She placed the pot in the cupboard to the left of the sink. "What am I supposed to tell him?"

"You don't have to tell him anything. I'll tell him." Bridget didn't need someone else to do her supposed dirty work. Why should telling Dad be a big deal anyway?

"No. No." Mom held up her hands. "You won't tell him anything. This is the week for the participants."

No way would Bridget allow anyone to guilt her into submission. "Adam asked me to be there for him. He needs me.

"Y'know, this doesn't even have to do with Adam. It's Dad, isn't it? What aren't you telling me? Did Grandpa and Grandma McIlroy hate him? Were they upset you didn't marry the perfect Catholic man like Auntie Patti did?" Bridget folded her arms.

Mom's fingers grazed the counter. Her gaze darted along the cupboards. "Honey, I wish you would've taken an interest in Stephen instead. You know the city isn't kind to natives."

"The people at church are, and that's what matters. Kyle enjoys his school. He gets along with his teachers and classmates. You never answered my question about Grandpa and Grandma."

"Does it really matter? Let's let your grandparents rest in peace."

"Were they . . . prejudiced?" Bridget fingered a doily, one of many Mom had made and donated to the parish.

"No. They were wonderful Christian people, but they weren't perfect. They had ideas about my life, and your aunt's life. Understand, times were different then. Yes, our city was built on the fur trade and inter-marriages, but remember as the city grew, so did social standing."

"You mean during the seventies inter-marriage wasn't as prominent?"

"Your dad wasn't the most prestigious person or one of good quality."

"Then if Grandpa and Grandma were against him, why does he act the same way with us? Lookit what he put Emery and Darryl through."

"He never meant to hurt anyone. He simply wants to protect his children from what he endured growing up. I tried to tell him he must let you live your own lives, but you know what your father's like. Until he's ready to listen, he won't listen. I do my best to wait until he's had time to assess his behavior, which usually takes . . . well, you know what happened. Emery and your dad became estranged for over two weeks."

"He didn't mind Jude's choices. Maybe since Jude's just like Dad? They're both principals. They both have their Master of Divinity. They both married . . ." Bridget squirmed. The word *white* sat heavy in her stomach, as it always did. Mom was way more than a color. Too bad most people in the world didn't see things the same way. " . . . non-native women. They both had two children one right after the other, a boy and a girl."

"We may not have planned Emery, but he's a wonderful blessing. I'm overjoyed the Lord gave him to me as a delightful surprise."

"This is why Dad never gives Jude grief, right? Jude listened. I'm surprised he's not a permanent deacon like Dad."

Mom's face reddened.

"Jude considered the diaconate?" What on earth? Jude shared everything with Bridget. Why hadn't he mentioned this to her?

"He chose not to because he won't completely embrace the teachings of the Magisterium. Jude believes the church should welcome everyone since Jesus welcomed all sinners."

"What about you? There's something you're not telling

me."

Mom faced the sink. She reached for an already clean pot and immersed it in the soapy suds. "Alcoholism isn't cured overnight."

"I know. Adam attends his meetings faithfully."

"I wish your father would've done the same thing when we were first married." Mom scrubbed the clean pot.

"Why? I thought the church healed him?"

"Oh, the church helped a lot. Like I said, your dad had a lot to overcome. Don't think marriage is easy. Marriage takes compromise, patience, and understanding. Can you fully accept Adam for who he is? Can you live with the fact he'll battle alcoholism for the rest of his life?"

"Why're you asking me this? He's going to his meetings—"

"But you've had doubts, haven't you? This is why you didn't resume a relationship right away."

Bridget gazed at the silver pot. She could use something to do right about now. "Yes."

"You're too young to remember. So is Jude." Mom kept scrubbing the pot. "Times were different. Nineteen wasn't what it is today. You either were or weren't an adult. People married younger."

When a good twenty seconds passed, the cold ice along Bridget's spine prompted her to say, "And?"

"You know I was eighteen when I met your father at church. Like you, we fell in love right away. I had no intentions of changing him. I loved him for who he was."

If only Mom would turn around, but she rarely spoke about herself. No doubt this was hard for the woman Bridget most admired.

"He resumed drinking when you were one and Jude was two." Mom's slight shoulders stiffened.

Disbelief and horror squeezed Bridget's throat shut, trapping the air in her neck. She gripped the ledge of the counter she leaned against.

"Yes. Drinking. I didn't know what to do. I couldn't leave because I had two kids. Daycare? There was no such thing. I was a housewife, dependent on your father's income." Mom scrubbed so hard, water swished out of the sink.

"I couldn't go home. My pride wouldn't let me. I didn't wish to hear from my parents *I told you so*. I couldn't go to Aunt Patti's. She was leading the perfect life. I was angry, so angry at our Lord." Mom ceased scrubbing the pot. The tension in her shoulders dropped. She rubbed her brow and turned.

Pain buried from long ago reflected at the back of Mom's green eyes. "I also didn't want to take you children from your father." She wiped her hands on the apron. Her gaze shifted from the oven and fridge to the coffee machine and serving cart.

"I went to the one person I thought could help. Although your father was drinking, he continued to attend Mass every Sunday. I spoke to Father Whyte one Sunday. I told him what was going on and how I felt. He was the priest who helped your dad when he first came to church."

The pain in Mom's eyes softened, and her lips tugged at the corners. "He was also the priest who married us and baptized you and Jude. Together, Father Whyte and I sat down with your dad. I left you and Jude at your Aunt Patti's that day. Your dad, thank goodness, listened. He knew he wasn't honoring his marriage vows."

There was hope then.

"Bridget, don't look at me that way." Mom's voice was pleading.

"Look what way?"

"Just because your father never drank again, doesn't mean you're not going to face hardships with Adam. Are you prepared to accept his alcoholism—knowing they're no guarantees he may return to his old ways?"

CHAPTER TWENTY-NINE: ONE SHORT LIFE

Bridget stood at the dresser in the hotel room. She held her panties and bras, squeezing the satin material.

Adam stood by the bed they'd slept in last night, unpacking his duffel bag of meagre possessions, lips tilting downwards, eyes drooping at the corners, square jaw slack. Even his broad shoulders seemed to cave into his chest.

She tossed aside the underwear and inched toward him.

"What's bothering you, *kwe?*" Adam moved from the bed and lumbered to the dresser. He folded his arms, staring down at her, eyes still sagging at the corners.

Bridget snatched the panties and bras. She stuffed them into the drawer. She ran her hands along his biceps, gazing up at him. "I'm fine."

"If we want this to work, partnerships go both ways. If you're upset, you gotta talk to me." Adam clasped Bridget's waist and steered them to the bed. He sat her on his lap. "Talk to me."

She touched his cheek. "You have so much going on. You asked me to stay here because you need me. It'd be selfish—"

"It's not selfish. Like I said, we got a partnership going. What's happening in here?" He tapped his finger against her head.

Adam was right. If they wanted to succeed this time, Bridget must be honest. "Mom and I talked . . ."

"And?"

"She spoke about the rough start her and Dad got off to when they first married. Dad was having a tough time . . . healing, I guess. It makes me wonder what else she's hiding. Mom tends to . . . keep everything inside."

"What'd she say?"

"She talked about Dad. He started drinking again, for about a year, when I was too young to remember." Bridget lowered her head. "His pain was unbearable. He was looking for an escape. Not even . . . having a woman who worshiped him, and two kids who thought of him as a hero, could shake the . . . perhaps you'd call it the nightmares of the school that kept haunting him."

"He's a deacon now. Sounds to me like it worked out."

"Yes, it did." Bridget toyed with a lock of Adam's hair.

"This what's bothering you?" Adam rubbed her arm. "*Kwe* . . ." He licked his lips. "Y'know I can only promise you for today I won't drink."

Bridget's heart tightened into a ball. The hope that had lit her chest after they'd made love for the first time was a flame of a candle snuffed out.

"Is it enough?" His fingers lifted her fallen chin.

"Is . . . is what enough?"

"Y'know what I'm talking about."

"I promise to answer you by the end of the week." Bridget's muscles tensed. "See? This is why I didn't want to say anything. I don't want you—"

"Who says I'm gonna worry?" Adam's gaze searched hers. "You're here with me. For today. With the way I'm feeling right now, that's enough for me. What you did— nobody's ever put their balls on the line for me before. You told your parents you were staying here. I know how they feel about me. You're a true warrior. *Ogichidaa*."

"Is that what warrior means?"

"It means more than that. I told you, Cutter and the elder said our language's hard to translate. Our words are deeper, the meaning richer and fuller than what comes off in English. You've got a brave heart. Courage. Selfless. Help others. Put them before yourself. Sacrifice your own happiness for the good of the elderly, the children, and other women. That is a warrior."

"Will you become a warrior?"

"Dunno. That's up to the elders."

"I believe you're a warrior," she whispered. She meant every word. He wasn't pressing her for answers. Since he'd first shown up in Thunder Bay, he'd patiently waited. "I have to get on the laptop with Kyle after. It's a good thing I brought along an Internet stick. I should be able to catch a signal. The motel's not equipped with free Wi-Fi."

"Nothing's in the twenty-first century up here." Adam's drooping lips shifted to a light smile.

Bridget leaned in and brushed her lips against his. Soft. Silky. She traced the hard muscles of his arms. Adam grunted, and she wound her body around his, still showering delicate licks on his tongue. A pucker here. A pucker there. Light kisses meant to show him how much she cared.

Adam's hands scooted up Bridget's backside, tugging her shirt from the hem of the shorts. Warm air caressed her exposed skin. His finger traced along the bumps of her spine and stopped at her bra. She held her breath, waiting, wanting. When he unfastened the hooks, an ache erupted between her thighs.

With Adam's help, Bridget drew the shirt over her head. As she tossed aside the garment and her bra, Adam's mouth trailed her throat to her breast. His lips fastened around the nipple, heating her bare flesh. He suckled, tender enough to coax a groan from her, and she arched her back. She smothered his hair with kisses, raking each strand.

The drops of pleasure between her legs deepened. She rubbed against his stomach. Adam's cock feathered her lower abdomen, as if searching out her pussy.

"Oh, Adam." She gasped.

He released his mouth from her nipple, lids flickering. His eyes burned with need, raw hunger that shook her insides. He tossed off his t-shirt and shifted, keeping Bridget on his lap while he laid on his back.

"Fuck me, *kwe*. Show me how much you want me."

Bridget scampered off the bed. She tore off her shorts and panties while Adam kicked off his jeans and underwear. His exposed erection was as strong and as massive as him. She eased on top, breath ragged, and leaned in for a kiss.

He draped Bridget in his embrace. His cock brushed the opening to her asshole. He trailed his fingers along her back and rubbed her buttock. Silky sensations erupted between her pussy lips.

Adam smothered her mouth with another kiss. His free hand palmed the back of her neck, urging Bridget to surrender to the kiss, his tongue conquering her mouth with deep licks and fierce strokes. Being dominated while she was on top, having Adam's hot palm stroking her ass, and his cock skimming her hole was a bed of excitement, a hot fever coating her skin.

He broke the kiss, panting. "*Kwe*, if you don't get on me, I'm gonna come all over you."

"You're not the only one." She shifted to her knees, placing soft pecks on his lips and cheeks, unable to tear herself from him.

"Sit up, *kwe*." His voice was deep, husky. "I wanna play with your clit and watch your titties bounce."

Bridget groaned and shifted so he could have a full look at her. Adam bent his knees where she rested her back on his thighs. The look he cast, pure desire, left her clit throbbing.

She settled herself over his cock and slid down his length. His massive girth forced her pussy to accommodate his erection.

"You're so wet . . ." Elation lurked at the back of Adam's eyes. His gaze caressed her breasts, stroked her stomach, and feathered her spread legs.

When his fingers parted Bridget's pussy lips, ripe heat invaded her blood, and lush delight rolled along her spine. Adam toyed with the folds of skin around her clit. Bridget panted and moved in rhythm with his pumping cock. Each thrust coaxed her flesh to submit to his deep invasion. The need to fuck him growled in her chest.

She braced her hands on the mattress and met Adam's cock thrust for thrust.

"Look at me, *kwe*."

Bridget's lids flickered. He'd always asked this of her, and she'd try each time to stare in wonder at his fervent gaze, but a part of her yearned to savor his thick length, lose herself in what he could do to her.

They rocked in the same rhythm, an even pace that quickened the more the ache in Bridget's clit intensified. With Adam's finger fondling her small, hard flesh and his erection thrusting into her, the furious anticipation was close to bursting.

She was enveloped in sticky heat, an electrifying sensation produced by Adam fingering her clit. Gasping and moaning, she rode him hard, draped in the desire he lavished on her.

"Adam. Adam." So good. He always brought her to the most sensual heights.

Adam wrapped his big arm around Bridget's waist, and she met his chest. He pounded his cock deep into her, and she clung to him. His low moans filled the room.

Again, they were one.

Adam rested against the pillow, smoking a cigarette.

Bridget sat swathed in his shirt at the table by the window, doing the web-cam thing with Kyle. Once in a while, she'd smile at Adam. They'd chosen this spot so his boy couldn't see Adam in the background, much to his irritation. They were a family now and should speak as a family.

Maybe not a family after Mrs. Matawapit had scared Bridget into reality with that drunken story about the deacon.

Kyle's voice came through the laptop speakers, chattering about what he'd done at school today.

The more his son's sweet voice caressed Adam's eardrums, the more his heart sagged. He'd done this to himself—unable to speak to his own kid. But never mind his suffering. The person most affected was Kyle, who shouldn't have to pay for Adam's pain.

"I miss Dad." Kyle's longing carried from the laptop.

Adam covered his stomach, his son's sorrow punching him in the gut.

"You'll see him next Wednesday. He misses you, too. He misses you very much." Bridget's tone was soothing.

"Mom?"

"Yes."

"That's Dad's shirt. The one he wore for our last visit."

Bridget's face reddened. Adam squeezed his eyes shut.

"Of course it is. I spilled food on myself at the church today. Your dad gave me his shirt to wear."

Adam shouldn't have panicked. Bridget handled everything with finesse. His chest brightened at his boy remembering what he'd last worn. And Kyle had dressed in a blue t-shirt and white shorts with white running shoes during their precious hour together.

Bridget's cell phone rang. "Mom has to go. I'll talk to you tomorrow. Okay?"

"Please. Just a few more minutes? Please, Mom?"

"I have to answer the phone. It could be important." Bridget picked up the cell and frowned. "I love you, honey. I gotta go. It's Uncle Emery, so it must be important."

Adam sat up.

"Okay. Bye, Mom. I love you. Tell Dad I love him, too."

"I will. I love you, too." Bridget rested the phone against her ear. "Hello."

She listened for a moment. Her dark eyes popped to the shape of eggs. She gaped at Adam and whipped her head to the motel door. "Are you sure?" She nodded. "Okay . . . yes . . . sure . . . I'll let him know. Bye."

Bridget clasped the phone. "The halfway house called."

Adam had given the supervisor Darryl and Emery's number before he'd left Thunder Bay. "What is it?"

"I don't know. They said to call. It's very important." Bridget held out the phone.

Adam took the cell and pressed the numbers on the screen to the halfway house. Three rings.

"Good evening. Joseph Howarth Society."

His throat tightened, but he managed to say, "It's Adam Guimond. I was told to call here."

"Adam. How're you? How's the workshop?" The voice belonged to Ken, the evening supervisor.

"It's cool. 'Sup?"

There was a moment of silence that squeezed Adam's lungs. He butted the cigarette in the ashtray.

"I don't know how to tell you this. I hate to interrupt your workshop, but I know how close you two were."

Were? Why not *are*? "Where's Logan?" Adam gripped the phone.

"That's what I need to talk to you about." Ken sighed. "I

don't know how to say this, so I'll just say it. He's gone."

Adam's heart thundered at the base of his throat. "What'd you mean gone?"

Bridget gasped and sank to her knees at Adam's side.

"He's gone. Dead. I'm sorry. They found him early this morning."

"Found him where?" Adam's skin burned hot and cold, and his head lightened. This couldn't be happening. Not Logan.

"Friendship Gardens."

What? That was where the teenagers drank. They gathered at the mall, pooled their money together, and then headed for the liquor store to find a runner to buy their booze. "What happened?"

"He overdosed." Ken gulped.

This couldn't be true, but it was. Logan was in the morgue. Dead.

"I'm still trying to locate an uncle he listed as next of kin. He's in Manitoba. Brandon."

"His whole family are junkies. His uncle won't give a shit." The fierce words barked from Adam's closing throat. "I'll catch the next flight out." He switched off the phone.

Bridget stared, open-mouthed. "Logan's . . ."

"Dead." Adam tossed the phone on the bed. Dead. The damned kid had gone back out there, after promising not to. They were supposed to unearth, together, what happened to Sheena and the baby.

Dammit, their deaths had been too much for the kid. Logan had nobody. Everything taken from him. What chance had he stood? None. But society, oh, how society loved to blame the kids, the adults, and everyone else suffering, for not sucking it up and moving on with their lives. For not doing better. For not giving in to the pain and loneliness.

Adam curled and uncurled his fingers. Logan would go

down as another using junkie getting what he deserved. People didn't care enough to look into the eyes of a suffering teenager. A suffering adult. A suffering Indian.

"I'm so sorry." Bridget moved off her knees. She reached for him.

He recoiled, suffocation creeping up his spine. "Don't, *kwe*. Don't."

"Why not? You're in pain. You need someone to—"

"I don't need any *I'm sorry* or *cry it out*. I don't need nothing." As for the fucking old-timers, they'd say life happened, whether Adam was sober or drunk. What was he going to do? His head pounded, and he rubbed his temples.

"I don't want you blaming yourself." Bridget's voice was firm.

"Who says I am, woman?" Adam hadn't meant to snarl. Bridget was the last person who deserved his anger.

"See? You're doing it, what you always do. You're denying yourself pain. I understand you're upset. I know how much you cared about Logan. Will you please, for once, let someone in. Let someone hold you. Comfort you."

Adam squeezed his toes. Something kept trying to climb up his throat. A big lump. A fucking lump. He hadn't cried since he was nine, when he'd sworn he wouldn't give the undeserving ol' man anything again. "I-I can't . . ."

For too long he'd held everything inside. Pain. Desperation. Loneliness. Disgust. All he had was hate.

"Don't you see? This is why you hurt others physically. This is why you were an enforcer for the Winnipeg Warriors. You either drink it away or you beat someone to make it go away. You can't keep ignoring what's happening inside of here." Bridget thrust her long nail at his chest.

The lump kept building inside Adam's throat. His chest continued to tighten. His skin prickled. He flopped in the chair.

The damned punk had let life beat him. Nope. Not beat him. Logan had gone to the one place where he was safe, where he could finally smile and laugh. He was in the spirit world with Sheena and the baby.

"Adam . . ." Bridget slid onto his lap. She draped her arms around his shoulders, lips brushing his ear.

The fire in Adam's throat was close to burning his flesh. Close to consuming him. His chest kept expanding and swelling. He held Bridget tight, drew her womanly scent against him. The tears he'd denied himself seeped from his squeezed-shut eyes.

He was alone, in the closet, Dad having beaten him. And he cried.

CHAPTER THIRTY: IN THE NAME OF TRAGEDY

Someone was making horrible noises. Grunts. Groans. Like a pissed-off moose charging an intruder. Through the haze of tears, Adam shuddered. He was the one making noises. He was the one crying. God, he sounded horrible, even comical.

Bridget remained on his lap, fingers tangled in his hair, lips lightly pecking his head that remained nested on her breast. He rubbed her bare thigh.

She didn't tell him to hush. She didn't reassure him it was all better. She didn't say anything, other than rubbing and soothing the pain cutting his chest.

The overpowering desire to reach for a drink and wash away the ugly torture didn't surface. Nor did an overwhelming urge to storm off.

His chest lightened. The suffocating weight of anger, fear, and disgust assaulting his veins, his muscles, his bones, trickled away like the water fading from the rocks down at the special spot at the church.

Healing. This was what the workshop trainers had meant. Many were scared to heal. Frightened of exorcising the negative feelings rooted inside them because they'd carried the horrendous emotions for so long.

Was he ready to shed the skin of negativity that he'd worn since childhood? This was what the old-timers at the twelve-step meetings meant by handing over his defects to a higher power. He was supposed to let Creator take everything. Step seven. Technically, he was on step six, because he was supposed to pray for the desire to undertake step seven.

"*Kwe*, I dunno if I can do it." Adam's voice was muffled since his lips remained against her nipple.

"Do what?" Bridget's voice was softer than silk.

"Let go of everything." Adam continued to speak, his lips brushing her breast. "I've lived like this for thirty-eight years."

"Doesn't your program teach you one day at a time?" she asked in the same silken voice.

"Yeah." The old-timers would tell Adam the same thing.

"What's important is you acknowledged the past and what's bothering you. That's a big step." Her warm lips pecked the top of his head.

"I know." The duffel bag still sat beside the bed. "I gotta go."

"Are you sure?" Bridget shifted, which forced Adam to look at her. She trailed a nail along his cheekbone. "This is a crucial time for you."

"Logan never spoke about this uncle in Brandon. If this uncle gave a shit, he would've taken the kid in, not foster care. Logan needs a funeral. Something."

Bridget's lips flattened. "You know I can't go. I promised to help out here."

"I'm not asking you to go. I'm leaving."

She rose off his lap, hands on hips. "Will they even let you see him? Take care of his funeral?"

"Do you think his uncle's gonna?"

She shook her head. "No. Hardly."

"I'll talk to Ken. See what I can do from my end. The kid's gotta have something, even if it's only me there."

Bridget pivoted. Her features softened. "I understand. I wish I could be there. Is it possible to have it on Saturday?

I'll bring Kyle. I want him to understand we must be there for those in need when family and friends refuse to."

The awful gray color in Adam's heart faded. "Yeah. Saturday. I'll get stuff arranged."

"I'll ask Dad if he can come. Was Logan Catholic?"

"He wasn't anything as far as I know. I'll hold something at the funeral home. Nothing more."

"I'll ask the family to attend. Dad can read some Scriptures. I doubt he can officiate a funeral for a non-Catholic."

"You mean Mass?"

"No. As a deacon, Dad can't recite Mass, hear confession, confirm Catechumens, or anoint the sick. But he can officiate at a funeral that doesn't have Mass if the person is Catholic. I think. I'd have to ask him."

"A few readings sound cool." It'd be the last thing Adam would do for his sponsee. No, not the last thing. He still had to check into Sheena's death.

"I'll talk to Mom and Dad. I know Emery'll come. And Darryl. Jude and Charlene always offer their support to those in need."

All Adam had to do was pack. Hopefully there was a flight out tomorrow. With the reserves owning their own air service, there was a good chance he'd leave.

"We should go. It's what's expected of us as Christians. It's what's expected of us as human beings. I'm just sorry Adam had to leave." Emery sat at the dining room table at their parents' house.

Dad stood out on the deck, smoking a cigarette. Darryl refilled everyone's teacups.

Mom clasped her fingers together. "If Adam was Logan's only friend, we must go. The boy suffered terribly. I'd hate to see him buried without . . . a goodbye of some sort. I wish we could hold a funeral for him, but we can have a nice service at the funeral home. I'll talk to your father about what we can financially contribute."

"We'll be able to make a donation." Darryl set aside the teapot and sat.

"I'm sure Jude and Charlene will wish to contribute." Mom added a sugar cube to her tea. "Adam's considering Saturday?"

"He's going to the morgue tomorrow with a supervisor from the halfway house. When Adam talked to the supervisor before he flew out—the man's name is Ken—Ken mentioned they've done this before, I'm sorry to say. Ken said under Ontario law, a claimant can be anyone. Family. Friends. Colleagues. Neighbors. Churches. Community Groups. The halfway house has claimed bodies in the past." Bridget shuddered at the word. "I guess Logan isn't the first to go unclaimed."

How awful for those who had died—leaving this world without anyone caring about their deaths. Bridget lowered her head.

She'd thought she'd seen everything sitting on the Indigenous Women's Alliance, but until a person stood knee-deep on the streets, they had no idea of the pain people endured, or couldn't endure. Having Adam in her life was a blessing because he came from the streets and had plopped Bridget into the reality of those not as fortunate as her.

"How's Adam doing?" Emery asked.

Bridget glanced up. "He was pretty shaken, but he'll be okay." He'd better be okay. "Are the women fine with cleaning up without us?"

The workshop ended on Friday. Bridget was originally supposed to have stayed and helped clean the basement on Saturday.

"They told me since we've been handling the afternoons

on our own, they want to do the cleanup," Mom said.

"Okay. I just want to make sure." Bridget settled in the chair. The most she could do was wait until she heard from Adam.

Was he strong enough to handle seeing Logan in the morgue? Maybe Adam wouldn't have to. Ken had gone down and identified the body already.

Now that Adam was back in Thunder Bay, he'd called the boss and had gone to work. With his shift done, he sat shotgun in Ken's pickup, on their way to the morgue. At least Adam worked from seven to three and wouldn't need to take time off for Logan's service, if they could get the funeral booked for Saturday, maybe around five that evening.

"You sure you wanna do this?" Ken asked for the third time.

"Yeah. Gotta do this. Gotta see him." A raw rash of pain continued to burn Adam's chest. He'd let the kid down. He shouldn't have gone to Healing the Spirit. Logan hadn't been ready to be left alone, not after the loss he'd suffered.

"Okay." Ken kept guiding them down Oliver Road to the hospital where Logan's body rested. "When did you want to visit the funeral home?"

"It's gotta be after work. Can you get me after three tomorrow at the restaurant?"

"Yessir. Can do." Ken turned onto Keith Jobbitt Drive.

Adam's burning chest constricted at the big hospital, a place he'd never visited before. In about fifteen minutes, he'd see Logan for the last time.

Bridget cleared the dinner dishes. Dad sat at the dining room table, having finally come inside after standing on the deck, smoking.

Bandit pressed her nose against the glass on the sliding doors, barking.

"We should get going. I think she's hungry." Emery stood.

"She's always hungry." Darryl also stood.

Bridget headed into the kitchen and placed the plates on the counter.

Emery followed. "I'll see you tomorrow."

Although he said nothing more, his soothing gaze and warm palm squeezing her shoulder reassured Bridget. He used the hallway off the kitchen to exit the house while Darryl used the living room to leave. At least someone was on her side.

She'd probably get an earful from Mom and Dad pretty quick. While Mom saw Emery and Darryl out, Bridget filled the sink and tackled the dishes. She turned her head to spy Dad staring at his book, since the kitchen gave a clear view of the dining room.

Mom shuffled into the kitchen. She swiped up a tea towel and reached for a plate to dry.

They worked in suffocating silence for fifteen minutes, tension creeping along Bridget's backside. After the last glass and final pot was stored away, Mom motioned at the dining room table where Dad still sat, reading.

"Did you want some lemonade?"

"No. I'm gonna turn in." Bridget planned on calling Adam. He was an hour ahead and should be at the halfway house soon. She glanced at the clock above the stove. A half an hour to wait.

Dad cleared his throat. "Why don't you join us?"

A smidgen of heat appeared in Bridget's stomach. Dad hadn't spoken to her after she'd spent the night with Adam at the motel. Before that, her father's words had been nothing more than rudimentary greetings.

The word *no* invaded Bridget's mouth. "Sure." She hung the tea towel to dry and joined him in the dining room.

Mom filled three fresh drinks.

Dad set aside his reading glasses. "How's my grandson?"

"Good. I told him I'd see him on Saturday and explained we have to attend a service for his dad's friend." Bridget sipped the lemonade. The cold liquid loosened the tension in her throat. *Please don't let me get mad, God. Please don't let him push my buttons.*

Dad rubbed his brow. The gesture meant he had something unpleasant to say and he was searching for the right words. "I've worked with lots of men and women incarcerated at our police building before they're shipped off to the city."

Bridget nodded. Mentioning the jail meant Dad would speak about Adam.

"Understand, I respect what Adam tried to do this week. And I'm sorry he had to leave." Dad's voice remained low, lacking his usual authoritative tone. "I know he hasn't led an easy life. I meet many individuals like Adam who grew up as he did. Our reserve isn't perfect. You're aware many still smuggle alcohol and drugs into the community."

Again, Bridget nodded and gripped the glass of lemonade.

"I know I haven't said much to you this week." Dad let out a heavy breath and sat back in the chair. "I respect the decisions you make. You're a grown woman and did extremely well for yourself. What you did for Kyle was a selfless act and took courage. I'm sure at the time you didn't wish to report Adam to Children and Family Services when he . . . relapsed."

Dad pressed his lips together. "Your mother told you about my own relapse."

"She did."

"Marriage is a sacrament. It's for life. Both must commit themselves to the vows they take. At times, one struggles or both struggle. I was fortunate your mother had the faith to tolerate my weakness.

"I know this isn't my business, but for Kyle's sake, are you sure about allowing Adam another chance? I would gladly officiate at your wedding, as I did at Jude's, if you're one hundred percent sure this is what you desire."

The tightness in Bridget's throat dissipated. Dad was giving his approval? He'd respect whatever decision she made? He wasn't trying to guilt her into being the obedient girl and cutting Adam loose?

"But . . ." Dad raised his finger, something he'd always done over the years to get his point across. "Only if you're one hundred percent sure. If you have any doubts, I highly advise you listen to them.

"I have nothing against Adam. Try to remember, he may spend the rest of his life battling his demons. He was born into a tough environment. Very tough. With his criminal record, his chances for sound employment are highly unlikely. The majority of jobs nowadays require criminal reference checks."

Listening to Dad speak to her like a child prickled Bridget's skin. His voice was a cactus. "I'm aware of everything that you said. Did you wonder if I'm still considering whether I want to pursue a relationship with Adam?"

Dad sputtered. "I presume so since you . . . well, err, stayed out the other night."

"I've already considered everything you told me. I know Adam's chances for a decent job aren't good. He also knows it."

"This hasn't been easy for me. We've never been on the same page, much less the same book." Dad's gaze studied her. "Perhaps because we're too much alike. Neither of us like being told what to do. Don't think I wasn't as rebellious when I was a child. I was in constant trouble with the priests and nuns because of my refusal to listen and obey."

Like Dad? Bridget swallowed her gasp. She was nothing like Dad. Well, she'd better not be.

"We'll stay at Jude's while were in the city." Dad cleared his throat. "You probably want to call Adam and see how he's doing."

At least Bridget had gotten half an approval from Dad. Too bad she'd never get the full approval. "I'm going to turn in. Adam'll be home soon."

She stood and was about to enter the kitchen.

"Bridget . . ." Dad's voice was supple.

She stopped and turned. He rarely used this tone. His pitch-black eyes were as soft as his voice.

"I only want you to be happy. It seems lately my children are forcing me to keep an open mind and take a more tolerant approach, something I've never been successful at. I know my vision's quite tunnel. Don't think I haven't noticed all that you've done through the years."

Dad was giving more than half his approval. He was giving his full approval. Bridget's heart thumped. If she decided to give Adam a second chance, the only hurdle they had to face was Mrs. Dale, who didn't hide her contempt for the man Bridget loved.

CHAPTER THIRTY-ONE: I KNOW WHAT YOU NEED

A dam had left the recovery meeting by himself, had boarded the bus by himself, and had returned to the halfway house by himself. He flicked aside the cigarette butt and trudged into the building. The sound of the TV drifted from the main room. Two guys sat at a table, playing cards. Adam gave them a curt nod and went straight for his room.

Before he closed the door, someone hollered, "Guimond, phone."

The caller must be Bridget. Adam dragged his feet back to the main room and picked up the telephone. His heart didn't patter. Excitement didn't judder down his spine. He was as gray as the shell left of Logan in the morgue.

"Hello." He dropped in the old chair.

"Hi. It's me. I wanted to see how you're doing." Bridget's concern floated through the receiver.

"Okay." His voice couldn't even produce a hint of cheerfulness.

"Please don't do this to me," she begged.

"*Kwe*, there's nothing for me to say." Keeping his voice quiet wasn't difficult with the two card players peeking in Adam's direction. The despondent whisper had easily rolled off his tongue.

"Why not?" This time Bridget's tone shifted to her familiar stubborn mode.

"Little hard to talk with an audience. I'll be okay, *kwe*. I'll see you on Saturday."

Would he be able to see Kyle? The Hawk was strict about the guidelines. Something else to add to Adam's plate of misery. It wasn't his fault Kyle was attending the service. Still, the old crab was going to give Adam never-ending grief. She probably had some rule about a foster parent seeing a biological parent who required supervised visits.

"I went to the funeral home. I have the bill." Jude's voice carried over the phone that Bridget had set on speaker.

The family sat around the dining room table at Mom and Dad's.

Adam had called Bridget last night, letting her know the cost and all the red tape involved if the province covered the expense. He'd been annoyed, but she'd managed to talk down his anger by reassuring him her family would foot the bill. Since Logan was in the process of being cremated, the expense wouldn't run into quadruple digits. Nor was the funeral home hosting the service. Father Arnold had graciously allowed the family to use the basement at Saint Patrick's parish to host the memorial.

"Thank you. Thank you so much, big brother." Bridget's heart fluttered at Jude's generosity. "I'll call Adam and let him know everything's taken care of."

"Dorothy called," Mom piped in. "The women will have sandwiches, dainties, and refreshments after the memorial. Members of the church will also be there."

"Oh my God." Bridget gasped. The Catholic Women's Association was even involved. "I don't know what to say."

"After your years of service to the Association, why are you surprised?" Mom shook her head. "This is the purpose of the CWA."

"I just didn't expect all this." If only Adam was here.

Funny how Bridget's heart had already decided what her brain had mulled over since Adam had first arrived in Thunder Bay.

She belonged to Adam Jean Marc Guimond. There was no need to think any longer. She'd forgiven him some time over the last month and a half. As much as her parents' story had frightened her, Bridget couldn't walk away. Adam was a once-in-a-lifetime man. Yes, he'd messed up, but he was still fighting for a normal life to give himself, to give her, and to give Kyle.

Bridget held the phone against her ear while packing the suitcase laid out on the double bed in the spare bedroom. Adam couldn't be held responsible for being in the presence of his son during a service, but she wanted to notify Mrs. Dale of Saturday's memorial, so their caseworker didn't get the wrong idea. Bridget also had to speak about their relationship and how this impacted her care for Kyle.

"Mrs. Dale."

"Good afternoon. It's Bridget Matawapit calling."

"Ms. Matawapit, what can I do for you?"

"I'm flying out early from a workshop I was volunteering at due to an emergency. Unfortunately, there was a death."

"I'm sorry to hear about this. My condolences." Perfunctory were Mrs. Dale's words, much like the obligatory pat on the back from a well-wisher.

"Thank you." Bridget fiddled with her travel case. "I wanted to inform you that the memorial service Kyle and I are attending Saturday evening will include his father."

"Oh? You do know of the—"

"I'm aware of the policies. I do have the manual you gave me. This is why I'm calling. I can't help that Adam and Kyle will attend the same memorial."

"I will make a note in your file. Kindly limit their communication during—"

No way. "Look . . ." Bridget used her firmest tone. "Kyle is seven years old, and he's been through enough already. I refuse to tell him he can't speak to his father during a memorial at our church. I know the rules. Adam's encounters must be supervised, but there will be many people in attendance."

She clicked her nails against the travel case, waiting on Mrs. Dale, who was no doubt reviewing the policy manual for contingency encounters.

"Ms. Matawapit, I will allow this once. Only once. Next time, however, before committing to—"

"This is a memorial service for a young man who Adam and I both knew. I will commit to such an event again, if, God forbid, we lose another we care about."

This woman and her rules were an itch from a mosquito bite, prickling beneath Bridget's skin. Ottertail Lake's Family Services Worker, along with the chief and band council, wouldn't have hesitated at having Kyle and Adam in the same room during a funeral. They put the welfare of the child first—the child's right to attend a memorial service, and the child's right to be present with his foster mother and his biological father. All Mrs. Dale cared about were her precious rules and policies.

"Are you challenging my authority?" Ice coated Mrs. Dale's question.

"I'm not challenging anything. I'm being realistic. Thank you for granting permission. Enjoy your weekend, and goodbye."

Bridget ended the call and tossed her cell on the bed. Boy, when the cantankerous caseworker found out Adam was back in Bridget's life, the super-stern Mrs. Dale might threaten to put Kyle in another foster home. Bridget squeezed her fist.

If Mrs. Dale wanted to make this tough, she'd met her

match. Nobody had answered about Sheena Keesha's death yet, even when the girl had been in care. As her father, Cutter had a right to demand an investigation.

When Bridget returned to Thunder Bay, first on the agenda, after Logan's memorial service, she'd call a meeting of the committee.

Bridget was up, readying breakfast now that she was home. Kyle sat in front of the TV, watching Saturday morning cartoons. They'd leave soon for Jude's place, where Mom, Dad, Emery, and Darryl had slept.

The memorial was at six this evening, which allowed Adam enough time to get off work and head to the halfway house to shower and change. Now that everything was cleared with Mrs. Dale, Bridget would offer Adam a ride to the church.

Once she dished up the oatmeal and had Kyle eating his breakfast, much to his protests because he always had to dine at the table and not in front of the TV, Bridget called Adam's work place to leave a message.

The sun was out, and she plopped in one of the wicker chairs on the balcony to enjoy the warm breeze and coffee.

"Good morning. Benny's Restaurant. How can I help you?"

"Good morning. This is Bridget Matawapit calling. I need to leave a message for Adam Guimond."

"Sure thing," the girl replied in a voice that matched the cheerful shining sun. "Go ahead."

"Let him know Bridget called. I'll pick him up for the service at five o'clock today."

"Got it. I'll be sure he gets the message."

"Thanks." Bridget hung up, her skim shimmering. She'd done it. They'd ride together like a true family to Logan's memorial service.

She dashed inside to find Kyle in front of the TV, holding his bowl of oatmeal. "You're supposed to eat at the table." She'd wait on telling him the good news.

"Aww, please, Mom?" Kyle asked through a mouthful of food.

Bridget's joy-filled chest wasn't in the mood to lecture. "Okay. This one time. I'm going to shower."

Around eleven, after Bridget had finished dressing and cleaning up the kitchen, the phone rang. She scooped the cordless off the counter, her heart singing because the number was Benny's. "Hello."

"*Kwe?*"

"Are you on your break?"

"Yeah. Got the message." Adam's voice remained solemn. He cleared his throat. "You don't gotta get me. I'll meet you there."

"Why?" She didn't mean to snap, but the wrench in her exciting plan was a knife poking at her stomach.

"Don't be that way." Begging coated Adam's reply. "The Hawk called me yesterday before she left the office. Gave me eight hundred fucking rules to follow for today —"

"Mrs. Dale did what?" The breakfast from earlier curdled in Bridget's stomach. The nerve of that woman.

"You heard me." He'd almost barked his words. No doubt Adam felt the same frustration as Bridget.

"If I can't get you, then I'll get someone to. I won't let you take the bus. This is Logan's memorial service."

"Nothing wrong with the bus. Took 'em all the time."

"Jude and Charlene will take his truck. Mom and Dad always use Charlene's SUV when they're in the city. They'll get you."

"Your folks?" Adam grunted.

"Emery and Darryl normally ride with them. But I'll have to drive them so Mom and Dad can get you."

"*Kwe*, I'm cool taking the bus."

"If you're going to be stubborn about this, I'll get you then." Screw Mrs. Dale and her rules, and enough of people dictating Bridget's life. "I'll be there at five—sharp. Bye."

Adam tucked his cigarettes into his shirt pocket. The only decent shirt he had. The same shirt he'd worn when visiting Kyle for the second time. Bridget was too stubborn. If The Hawk found out Adam had hitched a ride, she'd toss her clipboard at him. Maybe even tell his PO about his supposed rule-breaking and then she'd suspend his visitations.

He couldn't afford to screw up. People on the outside didn't understand the restrictions imposed on parolees. Even out of the pen, there were more rules to follow from parole officers, caseworkers, and whoever else wanted to see Adam back behind bars.

He threw open the door. At the sight of Kyle's silhouette in the backseat of the truck, the prickly ball in Adam's stomach vanished. His boy's small hand came up, waving. Adam hustled down the walkway. Fuck The Hawk. It'd been well over a week since he'd last seen Kyle.

When Adam reached the backseat, the window rolled down.

Kyle strained against his seat belt. "Dad! Dad!" His dark eyes lit, and a big smile plastered his shining face.

Adam threw open the door and reached inside the truck. He engulfed Kyle in a hug. His boy was a small cub cuddling up to his daddy. Damn, too long. Bridget had been smart to force Adam to accept a ride. His gray soul, now a shade of yellow, needed this moment for a small reunion. And by the way Kyle kept squealing, so did his boy.

"Mom said your friend went to Heaven, Dad. Are you going to miss him?" Kyle's light breaths warmed Adam's neck.

"Yep. Will miss him." The dull gray shadowing Adam re-appeared. He'd miss Logan a lot.

"It's okay, Dad. I'm here. I'll never go to Heaven. Not when you're still here."

The heartfelt words squeezed Adam's heart. His boy would never leave him, and like a total dirtbag, he'd turned his back on his son. Never again. He'd spent the rest of his life loving Kyle, and loving Bridget. These two had done so much for him. He didn't deserve their loyalty and love.

First step—accepting their loyalty and love. This time around, Adam would.

Bridget pulled into the parking spot between a compact car and SUV. The ladies of the Catholic Women's Association must already be in the basement, preparing the light dinner to follow Logan's memorial. The scent and warmth coming from Adam sitting beside her wrapped Bridget in cotton. She switched off the truck.

"Ready?"

"Ready as I'll ever be." Adam rubbed his brow.

For half the drive, he'd chatted with Kyle, attentively listening to the activities and crafts his son had engaged in during their absence. As they'd come closer to the church, Adam had retreated into silence.

"Let's go then." Bridget got out.

Adam held open Kyle's door. They held hands and joined Bridget.

"Mom." Kyle held out his other hand, grinning.

Something fuzz-like seeped across Bridget's skin. She laced her fingers with Kyle's. He gazed up, a big smile on his face. While they walked, he chattered and skipped along the pavement.

The straight, hard line to Adam's lips softened. His tender

gaze kept traveling from Kyle to Bridget.

"Penny for your thoughts." They strode up the walkway to the four steps that led into the church.

"What's a penny?" Kyle squinted.

Bridget giggled. "They were a coin we used to use to pay for stuff. Like quarters, dimes, and nickels."

"How come we don't have them anymore, Mom?"

Adam held open the door to the church.

"The government decided we didn't need them."

"What's the government?"

"Like Uncle Darryl. He sits at the table that makes the rules for the reserve. Remember? It's what the government does. They make the rules for everyone, not only the reserve."

Adam grinned. "I forgot how kids are full of questions."

"They sure are." Bridget's heart never stopped throbbing. A true family. She couldn't and wouldn't let Mrs. Dale take this from her.

Adam clutched Bridget's hand. The urn sat on a small, round, fancy table with Logan's picture beside it. A burning bubble appeared in Adam's throat. At least the urge to run or drink wasn't present. Probably because his son sat beside him, and Bridget a seat over.

In the past, Adam would've loathed being surrounded by anyone invading his space during an extremely personal moment, but this was Bridget and Kyle. They had every right to see Adam at his worst, and at his best.

Through the good and the bad, sickness and health— wasn't that how the wedding vows worked?

He'd robbed these two of seeing him at his most vulnerable. He had a second chance, but Logan didn't. Damn that kid now sitting in an urn.

Adam used his free hand to rub his brow. Bridget met his gaze. Compassion warmed her dark eyes, but pain also lingered. Always assisting others in need, no doubt his beloved *kwe* wished to rid him of the horrific misery tightening around his ribs.

Ken had managed to scrounge up a picture of Logan, who frowned in the photograph, his dead blue eyes and brooding mouth a reflection of his short, doomed life. Adam squirmed. He'd used to look the same way. No selfies for him. He'd loathed having his picture taken and had pretty much almost punched anyone into next week for trying to take one of him.

Bridget squeezed his hand again.

The deacon stood and ambled to the podium set up in front of the flowers.

As much as Adam appreciated the Matawapits generosity, he wasn't much for religion. The twelve steps and practicing the Seven Grandfathers teachings was his speed. But the old-timers at the meeting always said keep an open mind.

What mattered was that Bridget's family had come through and supported Kyle. Now they were supporting Adam.

Chapter Thirty-two: Victory or Die

Adam stood at the buffet table. He dished up helpings from the assortment of salads. There were also sweet and sour and barbecue meatballs available. Even chicken drummies and wings. He set a dinner roll on his plate. Bridget and Kyle stood on the other side of the line of three tables. She added whatever Kyle pointed at to his plate, while also dishing herself up some grub.

The ladies of the Catholic Women's Association had done a great job of putting together a last-minute funeral supper. If they took this good care of the Matawapit family, this meant they'd also taken great care of Kyle.

Kyle grinned at the different ladies hovering over the banquet table, assisting those who needed help.

The ladies took the time to ask Kyle how he was enjoying grade two, if he was excited about receiving his First Communion, and other school stuff. Kyle, of course, lapped up the attention. Adam's heart glowed with fatherhood pride at the acceptance of his son at the parish.

There were different desserts to choose from. Adam selected a plate of strawberry shortcake. He waited at the end of the table for Bridget and Kyle.

Besides the Matawapit family, about twenty parishioners, Adam assumed them to be, had also attended the memorial service. Earlier, these people had offered condolences to the Matawapits, but when the parishioners had gaped at him, they'd only nodded and scooted away. Not that he cared. People always avoided him.

"Ready?" Bridget wore a short-sleeved black dress that hugged her small waist.

"Sure. Where you wanna sit?" Only a few tables were set up.

"Over there." Bridget led them to a spot next to a display case where numerous mementos and plaques for the Catholic Women's Association were housed.

"Dad, right here." Kyle patted the chair beside him.

Adam had planned on sitting across from them, but his son's insistence of being bookended by his parents tickled Adam's insides. Yes, parents. Bridget was the true mother of his child.

He sat beside Kyle.

The deacon and his wife, who'd already filled their plates, detached themselves from a few people who'd waylaid them. The deacon ambled over to Adam's table, and his wife walked with her delicate shoulders back, gaze pinned on Bridget and Kyle.

So much for eating. Adam set down his fork and knife. The last time he'd formally joined Bridget's parents for chow was after he'd asked their daughter to marry him. They'd taken the Matawapits out for dinner to tell them the good news, and for Adam to officially meet his future in-laws.

Almost four years later, here they were again.

"Grandpa. Grandma. Sit there." Kyle pointed at the chairs across from them.

Emery, Darryl, Jude, and Jude's children sat at another table. Something about Jude's wife, Charlene, being busy was why she wasn't here.

Adam shifted straighter in his chair. He nodded as the deacon and his wife took their seats.

"Err, thanks. Thanks for saying those prayers."

"It was my pleasure. It was all of our pleasure to give your friend a proper goodbye." The deacon spoke in his low, authoritative tone. "What will be done with Logan's ashes?"

"Keep them for now. Was thinking of scattering them at that really nice spot near the church the next time I'm at the rez."

"The trail?" The deacon forked a meatball.

"Yep. Nice there." Adam scooped a helping of potato salad since Bridget's parents were eating.

"Can I go this time?" Kyle's voice was begging.

"We'll see what I can do." Adam wasn't making any promises. He still had The Hawk to handle. As much as he enjoyed having his son here during such a tough day, the old crab had been adamant about keeping his interaction with Kyle to a minimum. If the bitchy woman heard Bridget and Kyle had given Adam a ride, she'd shut down his supervised visits. As for Bridget as a foster mother . . .

Adam muscles clenched. Raw heat seared his gut. If anyone at Children and Family Services dared to take Kyle from Bridget, they'd answer to him. If that meant going back to the iron house, so be it. All that mattered was keeping Kyle safe and happy, and keeping Bridget happy. Nobody would separate the two people Adam loved most. Nobody.

Upstairs in the dark church, Adam plunked two quarters into the tiny brass collection bin. Light from the candles bounced around in the small glass jars of yellow, blue, red, and green, all lined up in rows of five and about fifteen per row. Shadows played across the statue of a man gripping a club on a platform above the brass stand. The inscription read *Saint Jude, Patron Saint of Hope and impossible causes.*

What Adam faced was an impossible cause. Authority hated him. His PO hated him. The Hawk hated him. Society hated him for being a bad father.

He lit one of the candles in the blue jar.

A warm flicker of hope appeared inside him. There was one way he could guarantee Children and Family Services never took Kyle from Bridget—giving up legal care of his son.

His stomach drooped. He'd worked his ass off to be a part of Kyle's life again. What if the boy got the wrong impression and accused Adam of giving up custody because he was an irresponsible asshole who didn't want full care of his own son? Wrong. Damn wrong.

God, losing Kyle for the second time was a shank in Adam's belly, slicing and twisting through his intestines. He clutched his gut and set his hand on the cushioned kneeler in front of him. Saint Jude stared straight ahead, unfazed by Adam's pain, and all the bullshit his life had been. A lump burned at the back of his throat.

He sank on the cushioned kneeler and clasped his hands.

Footsteps on the stairs carried to where he knelt. Bridget's summery scent surrounded Adam.

"Hey. What're you doing?" She spoke softly, a silken caress on the back of his neck.

"Praying. Well, trying to pray." Adam looked up to the motionless statue.

"For Logan?"

Adam shook his head.

"What about?" She rubbed his shoulder.

The kneading from Bridget's palm worked the stiffness from Adam's muscle. "You. Kyle."

"We'll figure something out. I already gave it some thought. I know if Mrs. Dale finds out we reconciled—"

"She'll give some kind of conflict of interest bullshit and put Kyle in another home." Adam's breath froze for a moment at Kyle being ripped from Bridget's arms.

Dread consumed Bridget's tiny breath for air.

Adam had made the right decision. He'd hurt his ex-fiancée and son enough. "It's why I'm gonna give you legal custody before The Hawk finds out about us."

"What?" This time disbelief filled Bridget's gasp. She sank to her haunches, eyes the size of the hubcaps Adam used to steal.

"You heard me." He squeezed his fingers that were still clasped together.

"I ... uh ... Adam ..." Bridget sputtered. "No." Her voice firmed, and she drew back, staring at him. "No, I won't let you do this."

"It's the only way." He rose off the kneeler.

Bridget also stood.

He ran his thumb along her cheek. "The system's been kicking my ass since I was a kid. I'm not gonna let it start kicking my son around."

"What do you mean? You were never in foster care."

"I'm talking about all systems—government, cops ... you name it. If giving up custody will keep Kyle safe, then it's what I'll do."

"You must have faith—"

"*Kwe*, this is also about you. You could lose him, too. Do you wanna?"

The color drained from Bridget's face. Her lips formed into an O. She took Adam's hand. "Of course not."

"Then it's what we gotta do." He massaged her fingers with the pretty long nails. The heaviness in his chest lightened. "Lookit us. We're making a decision like a real couple.

"*Kwe* ..." He drew Bridget against his chest and stroked her long hair. "We gotta protect *our* son."

"I know." She laid her head on his chest. "I know. But for you to give me legal custody of Kyle ..."

"It'll do for now. In time, we can go back to court. You can legally adopt him. You have my consent. And we can fix it so we can both be his legal caregivers. You and me."

"Parents shouldn't have to be forced to take this route," Bridget murmured.

After dropping Adam off at the halfway house before his curfew, and then sending Kyle off to sleep, Bridget finally sank on her own bed. Ten o'clock. Church tomorrow. Then laundry.

How strange that she'd prayed hard not to lose Kyle when Adam had first arrived in Thunder Bay, and this evening the Lord had granted Bridget her biggest wish. But there was no victory in a father left with no choice but giving up his child. Again, the system had kicked around another Indian.

Bridget shivered at Dad's recount of the old days, when passed-out natives were rolled into the water and drowned. Thank goodness nobody had harmed her father, who'd admitted to sleeping on the banks at night, and then stressed the dangers of going near the McIntyre and Kaministiquia rivers when Bridget and Jude had been in grades seven and eight. Naturally, she'd been so shaken up for once that she had listened.

Last year a native woman succumbed to a slow, agonizing death after being hit by a trailer hitch tossed by a man from a truck.

The Indigenous Women's Alliance, along with the Catholic Women's Association worked hard to support diversity in the city. But rallies, marches, and walks didn't seem enough to stop the racism.

Together, she and Adam must take a stand against their caseworker. Being forced to give up legal care of his own son was wrong. Adam had more than proved he was a fit parent.

Bridget pulled up at the halfway house. She'd sweet-talked Emery into staying for a few more days. He was at the condo, watching Kyle for the evening so she could meet Adam for coffee. Curiosity had filled Emery's green eyes, but in his typical style, he'd never asked questions when she'd mentioned where she was going.

Once she got home, she'd clue Emery in on her decision. He had his BSW and could prove helpful once Bridget set up an appointment to meet Mrs. Dale.

First, she needed Adam to agree.

He lumbered down the sidewalk, smoking the last of his cigarette. His tufts of waves curled beneath the brim of his cowboy hat. Bridget's stomach fluttered at the simple white t-shirt and faded blue jeans molded to his hard muscles.

Adam flicked the butt. Before he got in the truck, he removed his hat. The scent of smoke filled the interior. He leaned over, his dark eyes alight. Bridget's heart almost turned to mush, ready to melt all over the leather seat. His lips brushed hers, warm and softer than satin.

"How'd work go?"

"Good." Adam traced his finger along her cheekbone. "What about you and Kyle. Have a good day?"

"We sure did. He loves attending Mass with his grandparents. And he was very excited to have his Uncle Emery there, too. I'd say those two are stuffing their faces full of pizza right now."

"How long's Emery staying for?"

Bridget shifted the gear stick and started down the street while glancing at the clock on the stereo. Perfect. This wasn't the hour when Mrs. Dale lingered over her tea at Reggie's Donuts. The old woman's evening routine was as predictable as a January northwest wind. "Coffee?"

"Sure."

"I hope you don't mind missing a meeting tonight."

"No prob, *kwe*. Anything for you."

"Losing Logan must really hurt, and I'm sure meetings help."

"Going tomorrow night." He placed his big hand on her arm.

The heat from his palm seared Bridget's skin. She shivered.

"That's s'posed to warm you up, not make you cold." The low rumble of his chuckle caressed Bridget's flesh.

She stopped at the light. "It's good to hear you laugh. I forgot how much I enjoyed hearing you laugh."

"Yeah?" He cocked his brow, grinning.

"That too." She set her nail on his smiling lips.

"Important to you?"

"Yes. When we first met, you never smiled. Or laughed. The first time you laughed, I'll never forget how it surprised me. Scary." She giggled.

"I have a scary laugh?" Amusement flecked his eyes.

"Yes, very scary — if someone doesn't know you. But the laugh is you. It wouldn't be you if it wasn't on the scary side." She turned the truck into the parking lot.

"Let's hit the drive-thru."

"Sure." She stopped at the drive-thru board.

Once they ordered their coffees and left Reggie's Donuts, Bridget turned the truck onto Arthur Street. "Any particular place?"

"Yeah, anyplace where a man can get some suction without the whole world watching."

His deadpan tone coaxed laughter up Bridget's throat. "You're awful." She smacked his hand resting on the console.

"I'm serious." He sipped his coffee. "Y'know how long it's been?"

"You'll get your blow job, but first we need to talk." The mountain would be a perfect place. Located on the reserve, just over the Kaministiquia River, they could have privacy to talk.

Since someone or *someones* had set fire to the swing bridge on James Street a few years back, the shortcut to Mountain View First Nation was inaccessible. They'd have to go in through Chippewa Road. It'd be about a fifteen-minute drive. She'd stay on Arthur and then turn on to the highway.

Fifteen minutes later, the truck tires rolled over the gravel parking spot. Bridget switched off the engine. No other vehicles were parked. The attendant had said a couple of hikers had already ventured down the mountain since light was quickly fading. They had to be out by ten, which wasn't a problem because Adam was due home before nine.

They left the truck and meandered to the lookout point. Both leaned on the wooden railing. Barely visible because of the setting sun was the road they'd driven up to reach the parking lot.

"Forgot how nice it is up here." The breeze ruffled tufts of hair sticking out from Adam's hat. "Peaceful."

"It is. It's been awhile when I last brought Kyle up here." There was always an ever-present wind. Good thing Bridget had braided her hair.

Adam kept his elbow on the railing but slipped his free arm around Bridget's waist. She leaned into the warmth his hard body produced. He kissed the top of her head.

"I missed you and the kid today. Can hardly wait till Wednesday and see him again."

Bridget's face brushed his chest. "I wish it didn't have to be this way. I wish we could all be together."

"That'll happen soon enough. What do we gotta do? Meet with a lawyer? Get him to start the process?"

"Yes." She cleared her throat. "What if we choose to fight

it?"

"Fight what?"

"Mrs. Dale. Her supervisor. Children and Family Services."

Adam snorted. "*Kwe,* the system don't work that way. I should know. All it ever did was kick me around."

"But if we don't try . . ."

"There's no use. If we go the fighting route, the red tape'll be longer than a tape worm, and just as bad. Eat us alive."

Funny how Adam had let nobody on the streets intimidate him, and he'd even fought the toughest men from rival gangs, but if any form of authority entered the picture, he turned and walked away.

"The meeting's on Thursday."

"What meeting?"

"The committee. I think we should confront the police and Children and Family Services as a board, though."

"Aren't we supposed to make recommendations and stuff like that? Then present it to the board? From what I remember."

"Yes. But I think the board should involve itself."

"S'okay by me. You're the one with the brains."

"You earned your high school diploma. You have brains, too. And it takes brains to stay alive in the environment you grew up in."

"When can we meet with the lawyer?"

"Let me talk to Emery first. He has his BSW. I'll see what he says."

CHAPTER THIRTY-THREE: JUST 'COS YOU GOT THE POWER

When Bridget arrived home at quarter after nine, Kyle didn't greet her, which meant he was in bed like a good boy, because tomorrow was a school day. Emery sat in the living room, watching a show. He craned his neck while pausing the TV screen.

"Did you have a good evening?" He tossed a handful of popcorn into his mouth.

Bridget set her purse on the small table she always used for her belongings. "Yes. We had a great time." She hung her jacket on the hook. "What about you? What'd you and Kyle do?"

"He watched a movie. Z Men. Not surprising." Emery grinned. "Then he had his bath, I read him a story, and he went to sleep."

"What're you watching?" She removed her favorite beige clogs.

"A program on the Indigenous Peoples Television Network. I was going to originally watch it with Darryl."

"I'm sorry. I shouldn't have asked you to stay. I didn't know you two had something planned."

"Don't worry about it." Emery set the bowl of popcorn on the coffee table. "Have a seat. I know there's a lot on your mind."

A puff of surprise inflated Bridget's chest at Emery prodding someone to speak. He always waited for the person to ask first. She joined him on the sofa.

"What's going on?" Emery reached for a napkin and wiped his mouth and hands. "Did you want a drink?"

"Wine sounds nice."

"Wine it is." Emery rose and ambled to the kitchen.

Bridget grabbed a handful of popcorn. Through a mouthful of food, she muttered, "He wants to give me legal guardianship."

"He does?" Emery stood at the kitchen counter, pouring the wine. His reply didn't indicate surprise, happiness, or disapproval. Typical of her brother.

"Yes."

"You don't agree?" Emery sauntered back to the living room.

Bridget took the offered glass. She sipped on what might as well be ditch water or the purest grapes of the vineyard. "I think we should fight back."

Emery sat. He wore his spectacular poker face. If he went to Vegas, nobody in the family would have to work again.

"You don't agree?"

"It doesn't matter what I think." Emery angled his leg and rested his foot on his knee.

"Now I know why you're a social worker. You must've aced counseling." Bridget set her elbow on the back of the sofa and rested her fist against her cheek.

"I want you to make the best decision for you, Adam, and Kyle."

"You can have an opinion." Bridget raised her chin.

Sighing, Emery sipped his wine. "I don't know who's more stubborn. You, Dad, or Darryl."

The comment should have offended Bridget, but all it did was usher out the glumness and bring forth a much-needed giggle. "Is there already trouble in paradise?"

"Of course not, but the three of you never give in." He

had another drink and gazed at the TV. "Is there a reason why he wants you to have legal guardianship?"

"Mrs. Dale, my caseworker, mentioned something about a conflict of interest. Then, get this, she said Kyle might have to have another foster parent." A knife settled in Bridget's chest. "I don't understand how she can —"

"You two aren't living common-law. You're only dating. If Adam respects his visitation rules, the caseworker has no right to recommend rehoming Kyle. It's that simple," Emery calmly said. "Understand, she can't up and make decisions. She only makes recommendations to her supervisor. And the supervisor must take into consideration Kyle's emotional welfare. He's been fostered by you ever since Adam started drinking."

"I can tell you she has it out for him. I sit beside her during Kyle and Adam's visits. The notes she takes don't jive with what's happening between Kyle and Adam."

"Really?" Emery raised his brow. "Did you mention this to anyone?"

Heat climbed up Bridget's face. "No."

"Why not?"

"At the time I was still pissed at Adam." Her voice shrank to pea-size at Emery's drawn-in cheeks.

"Y'see what I mean by how stubborn you three are? Why do you always take the hard path? Do you like navigating through mud, washouts, and washboard?"

Although Emery's voice remained gentle, irritation pricked Bridget's pride.

"No." She sipped another taste of the ditch-water-pure-luscious-grapes. "You don't understand. You're too much like Mom."

Emery grinned. "You mean I'm not stubborn?"

Bridget stiffened. She wasn't stubborn. More like staunch in her convictions. Yes, that sounded much better. "Are you coming to the meeting or not?"

"Of course. But . . ."

Oh great, here came Emery's faith-driven advice.

"You have to remember, Adam wants you to have legal guardianship of Kyle. You have to consider his wishes."

"I am." Bridget again lifted her chin.

Emery burst out laughing. His green eyes brightened to the color of lush summer grass. "Geez, we all do that, don't we?"

"Do what?"

"Shove our chins at people." Emery kept laughing.

"At least you inherited something from Dad besides his hair," Bridget muttered. Well, just Dad's rich black color, because Emery's hair wasn't poker straight, but wavy, like Mom's.

"As I was saying, you must consider Adam's feelings. Does he want me involved?"

Only Emery would smash Bridget's plan.

"I think you should talk to Adam first."

"I already did. That's why we went out tonight."

"What did he say?"

Bridget made a face. "He believes the system is there to impede, not help. I tried to tell him that's not the purpose of provincial and federal services."

"But for someone like him, that's all he's encountered. He doesn't have faith in anything controlled by the various levels of government. Think about Healing the Spirit. All different levels of government hurt Indigenous people. And it still happens today."

"So you think I should consult a lawyer?"

"I think you already know the best answer for you, Adam, and Kyle. Going through a lawyer will facilitate a faster process. You know the government and its red tape."

Bridget nodded, but knots formed in her shoulders.

"Is this really about what's right? Or are you nervous about everything happening within a month?" Emery's eyes crinkled.

She traced the rim of the glass. "I'm worried how Kyle will feel. This will go to court, and he'll be interviewed to see how comfortable he is with everything. They're just reconnecting. When Adam couldn't attend the last supervised visit, Kyle freaked."

"Does Adam know about this?"

"Yes. He still insists on giving me legal guardianship."

Emery smiled.

"What?"

"In August, you were intent on gaining full custody of Kyle, no matter what."

How true.

"Did you ever think Adam wants you to have legal guardianship so you can start being a real family again?"

"I know Kyle wants to see more of his dad." Bridget peered at the wine in the glass. "One hour a week isn't cutting it."

"Does the caseworker know?"

"I'll talk to her about it." The mistakes she'd made. If Bridget had sincerely considered Kyle's welfare from the start, she would've reported Mrs. Dale's biased reporting sooner.

"Don't go blaming yourself."

Bridget's hand loosely slid into her lap. "What makes you think I'm blaming myself?"

"You're Catholic. We're famous for guilt." Emery chuckled.

"I made a lot of mistakes." She sipped more wine. "I wasn't sincere enough in my care of Kyle. I should have met with Mrs. Dale sooner about him."

"You can't undo the past, but you can do something

about it now."

"That's why I've got to make this work." She sat forward. "If it wasn't for me being pissed at Adam all the time and letting my personal feelings get involved, he wouldn't have been forced to give me guardianship."

"As I said, you can't undo the past, but you can do something now."

"You mean accept the guardianship?"

"What do you think?"

"But what about Mrs. Dale? How many more Indigenous parents do you think she's sabotaging?"

"That's something IWA should address. You do have a platform."

Bridget ushered Kyle down the hall. From school and during the drive to Children and Family Services, he'd babbled nonstop about seeing his dad. Before she could open the door, Kyle pushed forward and stampeded into the cozy room.

"Dad! Dad! Lookit what I made at school!" Kyle scrambled to Adam, who leaned against the windowsill, grinning.

Mrs. Dale sat in her usual chair, taking notes. Bridget joined the bitchy woman.

"What'cha got here?" Adam held up the big piece of paper.

"It's a drawing of us. My family. You. Mom. Me." Kyle giggled.

Bridget froze in her seat. Earlier, she'd asked about the artwork, but Kyle wouldn't let her see the drawing, insisting what he did during class was a surprise.

Mrs. Dale, for once, lowered her clipboard and stopped writing.

"That's us at Logan's special goodbye." Kyle pointed at the picture. "When we rode there in Mom's truck and back like a real family." His dark eyes danced. "It's us . . . we're walking into the church. Cool, huh?"

Mrs. Dale whipped her narrowed gaze to Bridget and then to Adam. "I don't like to interrupt," she began in her frostier-than-a-snowman voice, "but I would like to meet with you two after the visitation."

The pattering of Bridget's heart was loud enough to shake the building. "I have no one to watch Kyle."

"We are Children and Family Services. Someone can watch Kyle in this room while we meet." Mrs. Dale's tone implied there'd be a meeting no matter what.

Adam remained on his haunches, his eyes harder than steel. He nodded. His hand remained on Kyle's waist, fingers tangled in the boy's shirt, challenging, as if he didn't care what Mrs. Dale said, he wouldn't give up his only child.

Bridget sent up a silent prayer. She must keep Adam in check during the meeting. If he lost his temper, they could lose Kyle.

"This is exactly why I asked you to keep your communication to a minimum." Mrs. Dale's wicked-witch-of-the-west glare and pinched lips sliced into Bridget and then Adam. "He referred to you as his family. Currently, Kyle does not have a family, other than a foster mother. Is this understood?"

Adam grunted. He wore the same harder-than-steel expression he'd spewed earlier in the visitation room where Kyle had been left, much to his confusion, with another caseworker.

Bridget dug her nails into the arms of the chair. If she had to listen to this woman state what Kyle could feel, her temper threatened to spill over Mrs. Dale's desk.

"Ms. Matawapit? Do you acknowledge what I said?" Mrs. Dale tapped her pen on a pad of paper.

If Bridget didn't nod, there'd be trouble. If she nodded, she'd forfeit her beliefs and principles. Adam was bound by government services. Of course he'd grunted in acceptance.

"I assumed you'd be pleased that Kyle is happy about his current situation." Bridget uncrossed her legs and sat straighter in the chair. "My brother's a social worker. He has his BSW. In the winter, he'll begin working toward his master's. I was informed if Adam respects his visitation rules—"

"But he did not on Saturday evening. Kyle stated you picked up his father and drove him back to his facilities." Mrs. Dale's smile was smugger than a cat eating sixteen canaries.

"He was without a ride to the church—"

"Ms. Matawapit . . ." Mrs. Dale retrieved a paper from a manila folder. "Your older brother is listed as an emergency contact. I'm sure he could have retrieved Mr. Guimond. Your parents were also present. Could they have not retrieved your *ex-fiancé*?"

"I think what you should consider is that Kyle wishes to see more of his father. One hour a week isn't sufficient." Bridget's heartbeat accelerated to the full throttle of her truck's powerful engine. "The drawing Kyle made during his art class more than proves he desires a closer relationship. Just what do you write in your notes? I assume as a foster mother I'm allowed to review them."

"This is confidential information—"

"That concerns the welfare of a child. You told me when I first began fostering Kyle that you're in charge of the Indigenous children's case files. I assume you're reviewing Sheena Keesha's death."

Mrs. Dale slammed down the folder. "I will not discuss other cases but yours. I see you are also rerouting this discussion. Why did you retrieve Mr. Guimond when I specifically stated during our telephone conversation, which I documented, to keep contact to a minimum since Mr. Guimond has more than proven he cannot associate with Kyle unless the visit is supervised?"

Fierce heat thundered through Bridget's veins. "My foster child wanted to retrieve his father. Adam had missed the previous visitation. They wanted to see one another."

"So, you blatantly defied the rules."

The truthful accusations discharged at Bridget from Mrs. Dale's wicked gun of words slammed her back into the chair.

Adam sat forward. "Save it."

"Excuse me?" Mrs. Dale sputtered.

"I said save it. I'm meeting with a lawyer to give Bridget full guardianship of Kyle."

Mrs. Dale's beak came out far enough to almost poke them. "You cannot authorize anything while your child is currently in care."

"Yes, we can. And we will." Bridget stood. "Everything you're saying is wrong. My brother counseled me on this matter. Our discussion is over. I'm going to retrieve Kyle."

"Understand this, if I view the foster parent as unfit, I can place Kyle in emergency care—this second." Mrs. Dale's voice was vicious enough to bite someone. She also stood.

"Yes . . ." Bridget yanked the folder off the desk and slapped over the paper bearing Jude's name. She banged her finger on the desk. "You're to place Kyle in my brother's care since Children and Family Services must home the child in his or her next of kin, under the Indigenous Children's guidelines. The days of shipping them off to anywhere are long done." She almost snarled the words at the bitch.

Mrs. Dale sniffed. "Consider Kyle placed under the emergency care of Jude Matawapit until further notice. I will call your brother right now." She yanked up the phone. "Dismissed."

A deafening roar exploded in Bridget's ears. She clamped the desk to steady her jittering knees. "I'm going to see my son."

Adam shifted forward, but Bridget laid her hand over his. "Remember, I sit on the board of the Indigenous Women's Alliance." Her voice shook, but something resembling strength hardened her spine. "When the remaining directors hear what's happened, they'll not take kindly to what you're doing. We fought hard to ensure the safety of our own children. Children and Family Services has more than proven they failed because another child died in your care—Sheena Keesha.

"You'll grant me and Adam the right to see Kyle before we leave so he can hear from his mother and father what's happening. And this organization will also answer for Sheena's death—a sixteen-year-old girl."

Bridget stared at Adam. "Let's go see Kyle."

Chapter Thirty-four: Out of the Sun

Bridget yanked on Adam's hand, hauling over two-hundred pounds of solid muscle from the chair.

Mrs. Dale barreled around the desk. "Mr. Guimond, you are allowed one hour of supervised visits per week. Kindly have a seat. You are not allowed to accompany Ms. Matawapit to the family room."

"This isn't about visiting." Just as Bridget set one foot forward, it was her turn to be yanked backward. She gaped at Adam.

"S'okay." His eyes were reassuring, but the tension in his hand over Bridget's said otherwise. "You go talk to our boy. Go on. I'm fine."

Even though Bridget's palm itched to smack Mrs. Dale, she wouldn't. She was *Anishinaabe-kwe*, and she'd conduct herself as one. Chin raised, shoulders back, and stomach drawn in, Bridget forced her shaky legs from the office and wobbled to the end of the hall where Kyle waited behind the closed door.

Adam was right. If they panicked and started shouting and hollering, they'd upset Kyle. Having to tell him he'd be leaving with his Uncle Jude was bad enough. Bridget must make this a peaceful separation full of hope, although her hope dragged the ground with her curled heart.

She placed her shaking hand on the knob and opened the door.

Kyle sat at the small table, coloring. A social worker sat beside him. He rose and dashed over. "Mom! Mom! What's going on?"

A lump burned at the back of Bridget's throat. She forced a swallow, a smile, and a pleasant, "Don't panic. We had to meet with Mrs. Dale. That's all."

"Okay. Can we go now?" Trust filled his big eyes.

Bridget motioned at the chairs by the pop cooler. "We need to talk first."

"Talk?" Kyle peered.

"Yes. Talk." She took his hand and led him to the chair. *Please, God, don't let him react the way he did when Adam told Kyle he was attending Healing the Spirit.*

"Remember those rules we talked about?" Bridget patted his hand.

Kyle nodded. He kept peering at her fingers on his.

Bridget licked her lips. As much as she wanted to blame Mrs. Dale, the nasty witch was only doing her job. And Bridget couldn't teach Kyle to resent or hate someone for following rules laid out by the Ministry of Children, Community, and Social Services, although Mrs. Dale didn't have to do what she did over a harmless drive to and from a church.

"The people at this building want you to stay at Uncle Jude's for the time being—"

"Mom!" Kyle jumped from the chair, panic whitening his dark-brown skin and draining the color from his rose lips.

"Easy . . . easy . . ." She wrapped him in her embrace, petting his prickly hair. "It's only for a short time. There's stuff your dad and I must do, so Mrs. Dale recommended you stay at Uncle Jude's for the time being."

"No." Kyle squirmed. "No, Mom. I'm not going. I'm staying with you. Tell her. Tell Mrs. Dale we gotta be together."

The begging in his little voice was a slashing knife across Bridget's stomach. She touched his face, hot from his fear. "Remember I told you we must do what God wants? And we must trust He'll make things right if we follow His wishes?"

Kyle trembled, big eyes glassy, but he nodded.

"I don't want us to be apart either, and I'll be there to settle you in. I'll be there for breakfast every day. I'll be there after work to hear about how you did at school. Then I'll go see Dad for a bit. We don't want him to get lonely without us. Once I drop Dad off for his meeting, I'll come back and make sure you have your bath and read to you before you go to sleep."

"You'll . . . You'll . . . You'll come to church, too?" Tears slipped from Kyle's watery eyes and ran down his round cheeks.

Something sharp seemed to dig into Bridget's heart. She gripped his fingers. "Yes. We'll go to The Bistro after. I'll be at Uncle Jude's all weekend. For breakfast. For lunch. The only time I won't be there is when I have to work and you're in school."

"And sleep . . ." Kyle's voice shook.

"I'll be sleeping over Saturday night."

"You . . . You will?" The moisture in Kyle's eyes faded.

"Yes. I will. Saturday night is our night. We'll order in pizza. I'll stay in your room."

"M-M-Mom?"

"Yes."

"Why is Mrs. Dale doing this?" Kyle's voice cracked, and his shoulders drooped. "I thought she liked you? I thought she liked me."

Like? The bitchy caseworker now hated Bridget for daring to fight for her rights. Her son's rights. And Adam's rights. "I told you. She has rules to follow. But your dad, Uncle Emery, and I are going to be doing stuff to help others, and this is why you have to stay at Uncle Jude's. We're going to meet tomorrow night. That's the only night I'll be away."

"Uncle Emery?"

"Yes. He's going to help us. That's why he's here."

"And this important thing is tomorrow?"

"Yes. I'll be at IWA." She didn't need to explain the acronym since Kyle was used to hearing about her meetings at IWA or at the church if the CWA met.

"But . . . but I'll see you in the morning, right?"

"Of course. I'll be there in the morning. Then I'll go to work. Then I'll get your dad for the meeting."

"What about Dad? Are they going to take him away from me?" Fear resurfaced on Kyle's face.

"No, honey. You'll still see him every Wednesday for your visits like you always do." She pointed at the table. "Let's go color and wait for Uncle Jude. Mrs. Dale called him from her office."

For a half an hour, Bridget colored with Kyle while she answered his numerous questions in a calm voice. He stayed between her legs, and she hugged his waist, watching him use the various crayons to shade in his favorite heroes.

When the door opened, Kyle melted into Bridget's chest, quivering. His shakes stopped at his uncles filling the room.

"Uncle Jude. Uncle Emery." His little voice rose higher. He ran over to them.

Both kept grinning, having entered smiling.

Relief seeped across Bridget's spine that her brothers had come through for her, refusing to show their animosity or confusion for Kyle's benefit. She closed the coloring books and put away the crayons.

While Emery kept Kyle occupied, Jude sidled over.

"What's going on? Mrs. Dale called." He stared at Emery and Kyle.

"She didn't tell you anything over the phone?" Bridget said under her breath. She steered them toward the pop cooler.

"She explained you lost care of Kyle and that I was listed as emergency care." Jude leaned against the pop cooler. His pitch-black brows hunched over his pitch-black eyes. "What's she up to? Does this have to do with the memorial service?"

Bridget nodded. "Mrs. Dale found out I drove Adam there and back. She knew Kyle was with us. She said I violated the guidelines. So she's putting him with you until we straighten this out."

There wasn't anything to straighten out. Mrs. Dale had made her decision. All Bridget could do was appeal. Hopefully, Emery could provide more answers.

"This isn't the place to talk. Let's get Kyle to my place," Jude said in Dad's take-charge tone. "I just have to sign some paperwork and see Mrs. Dale. Adam's downstairs in the reception area."

"He is? Then let's get moving. Emery can drive Adam home."

Adam sat in one of the uncomfortable gray plastic chairs in the reception area. He'd watched Jude and Emery enter fifteen minutes ago, shocked enough at the sight of him they'd stopped for a moment, and then they'd hurried upstairs.

The elevator dinged. Bridget, Kyle, Jude, and Emery trooped out with Mrs. Dale and the other social worker trailing them.

"Dad! Dad!" Kyle cried out.

Bridget leaned down, saying something into his ear.

Emery made a beeline for Adam.

Jude led Kyle and Bridget to the door.

"You're coming with me." Emery held Bridget's beaded key chain. "I have to finish packing a few of Kyle's belongings. I only packed enough for tonight. Bridget wants to get

Kyle settled at Jude's."

"Sure." Adam stood. As the father and lover, he should've done something for his son and woman to prevent this from happening. Instead, he was stuck sitting in a chair while the government ripped apart his family. This was his fault. His boozing, his fighting, and his incarceration had thrown the two people he loved most into a nightmare.

Adam followed Emery to the parking lot. He lit a cigarette and stole a few quick drags to calm his racing blood. They reached the truck. Adam flicked the smoke aside and got in.

"Mrs. Dale called Jude." Emery started the engine. They drove off. "She explained she had to make use of his emergency care and to come retrieve Kyle."

Adam squeezed his toes. He dug his fingers into the console.

"I wasn't present when Jude and Mrs. Dale met in her office. Confidentiality, she told me. So I stayed in the family room. Bridget told me they took away her care because you were in Kyle's presence without someone from Children and Family Services, and that she knowingly violated the guidelines."

"It's a load of crap," Adam muttered. He stared straight ahead at the traffic in front of them.

"I'm sure Jude'll get the rest from Bridget. He wasn't too happy about this."

Adam stiffened. "What? He doesn't wanna—"

"He has no problem caring for Kyle. He wants to help. I tried to tell him he was assuming the worst when we drove over here." Although Emery's voice was firm, his naturally soft-spoken tone lacked authority, more along the lines of firm enough to remind someone to keep their emotions in check.

"The worst? What'd you mean?" Adam knew what Emery meant. "He thinks I did something to cause this, hey?"

"I told him you wouldn't have." Emery stared straight ahead since they were heading for the condo. "Try remember how close he and Bridget are. When Mom and Dad moved back to the reserve, they only had each other. Mom and Dad wanted them to come to the rez, but their lives are here. They begged to stay at my aunt and uncle's since they were almost finished with high school. They're a year apart. They had the same group of friends. They're like fraternal twins."

"I get it." Adam glanced around at the various houses they passed. "No offense taken. I used to shoot first and ask questions later, too."

"You don't anymore?" Emery glanced at Adam and then back at the road.

"You see me shooting anyone?"

Emery chuckled. Pink flecked his cheeks. "No."

"The program taught me not to. Saved me a lot of grief. Y'know what assuming leads to."

Emery cracked a light smile. "My dad taught me that. Don't assume, because it makes an ass out of you and me."

At least the joke lifted the weight off Adam's chest that had sat on him like a steel building for the last two hours. "He was acting like . . . Jude . . . I guess."

"Jude's Jude. He's fine." Emery turned into the condominium parking lot. "Like I said, Bridget'll explain everything to him. He won't be running around the city, trying to shoot you."

Adam only half snickered, because grief continued to eat at him.

They got out. He followed Emery to the main door.

The intercom was to Adam's left. His knees twitched at the button bearing the first letter of Bridget's given name, followed by her surname spelled out in full. The last time he was here, he'd stood outside, drunk off his ass, pressing the buzzer, begging Bridget for his son, begging for a second chance, begging for understanding, begging for mercy.

Bridget had told him to go away before she called the police and had also threatened to contact Children and Family Services because he hadn't cared for his son properly if he didn't leave immediately. He'd stumbled off into the night, having no ride since he'd taken a cab to get to the condo. His drunken ass had led him to the bus depot where he'd spent the night on the bench. The following morning, he'd left for Winnipeg.

Adam curled his fingers and rested his palm against the button. He squeezed his eyes shut. Fucking stupid. Fucking pathetic. He deserved The Hawk's wrath.

"Are you coming?"

Adam blinked and whipped his gaze to Emery, who held open the main door, having unlocked it already. "Uh, yeah."

"No use blaming yourself. What's done is done." Emery headed for the elevator.

Adam glanced about. The lobby had been repainted to a fresh olive.

They got inside and rode up, Adam squeezing his toes. Too many memories.

"Are you okay?" The door opened. Emery got out.

"Uh ... yeah." Adam swallowed. He clenched and unclenched his fists as he made the walk to Bridget's condo. Almost four years when he'd last been inside her crib.

Emery unlocked the door.

Adam inched inside. She'd bought new furniture. Fancy. Very modern. Some kind of suede material, from where he stood. She even had a new dining set. The contemporary kind with a rich wood table and high-back upholstered chairs for comfortable eating, meant to linger over a meal.

She still preferred carpet over the fancy hardwood floors everyone seemed to install nowadays.

He followed Emery to the small hallway to their left that led into the room where Kyle used to stay when they'd previously spent the night. Adam's heart warmed at the bunk beds, shelves of toys, a small activity desk, and chest of drawers. Everywhere he looked, Z Men covered the walls, the bed spreads, the curtains.

A warm fire built in his chest. He leaned his hand on the doorframe. "I bet he loves this room." One of those fancy rolling suitcases sat in the corner. "That yours?"

"Yes." Emery opened the chest of drawers. "I sleep on the lower bunk. Kyle prefers the upper bunk."

Shit, Kyle was claustrophobic. There was still much for Adam to learn about his boy.

"We'll pack as much clothes as we can, but I think Bridget wants to go through everything later tonight. She said to get enough stuff until Friday."

"Yep. Gotcha." Adam opened the closet where Kyle's small jeans, small jackets, small shoes, small long-sleeved shirts hung. "What about his school stuff?"

"It's in the back of the truck. Bridget brought him for his visit straight from school."

"Oh yeah, she would." Adam fingered the shirt. He drew the garment beneath his nose, sniffing. Very clean. As innocent and as clean as Kyle.

"I know I fucked up bad—"

"Don't do this to yourself," Emery said quietly. He shut the dresser drawer. "Everyone makes mistakes. What matters is you're doing something to change, to . . ."

"Redeem myself?" Adam slumped alongside the wall and folded his arms.

"Yes." Emery nodded, his voice still soft and quiet. "Bridget's forgiven you. Kyle's forgiven you. But what's most important is have you forgiven yourself?"

Adam's throat thickened. Good question. He had a lot to

think about.

Bridget led Kyle to the spare room he used for sleepovers. It was upstairs. The other bedroom Mom and Dad used was downstairs with an en suite. But Kyle preferred to be where Noah and Rebekah bunked.

Jude was in the family room, explaining to his children what was going on.

"Mom . . ." Kyle stopped walking.

"Honey, you stayed over here lots of times. You can do this." Bridget used an urging tone, one with a smile in it. "Show me what a big boy you are."

"Oh . . . okay." Kyle crept forward. "Where's Dad and Uncle Emery?"

"They're at home, getting more stuff for you to last until the weekend. I'll bring over some other stuff on Saturday morning." Bridget opened the door. "You're with family. Remember, Uncle Jude and Aunt Charlene love you very much."

Putting on a brave front was exhausting Bridget, when all she longed to do was nurse her wounded heart and cry. But that wasn't possible right now. She'd have time later to finally let the tears flow.

"Here we go." She patted the bed. "I'll get your things unpacked."

The suitcase that Jude had brought up right away from his truck sat by the dresser. Bridget petted Kyle's prickly hair. Leaving him here was a punch to the face, forceps reaching inside and wrenching out her heart.

Chapter Thirty-five: See Me Burning

A dam sat on the sofa. A shivering and shaking Bridget sat beside him. She'd cried in the back of the truck all the way to the condo while he'd held her and Emery drove. She'd cried all the way up to the condo. And she was still crying, tears running from her eyes.

She blew her nose.

Guilt niggled at the back of Adam's head. Bridget wasn't used to people telling her what she could or couldn't do. This afternoon she'd experienced clipped wings from a merciless hawk.

"*Kwe* . . ."

"Bridget, we must have faith." Emery set down the pot of tea he'd made.

Adam cuddled Bridget's waist. She'd handled the bullshit for too long while he'd scuttled to a corner, feeling sorry for himself. Emery was right. This was a chance for Adam to prove to his child and the woman he loved that they could lean on him during the toughest time they faced as a family.

He looked to Emery. "I offered her legal guardianship of Kyle. The Hawk said I can't." Adam curled and uncurled his toes.

"The who?" Emery's face slackened.

"The caseworker. Something about if Kyle's in care, I can't do anything, even give someone guardianship."

"You're still Kyle's father, but the province found you unfit to parent because you were incarcerated. Many foster parents adopt children through the system when the biological parents agree to give up their children." Emery filled the three cups.

"What happens is Children and Family Services contact the biological parents, present the formal adoption to them, and the biological parents decide if they wish to relinquish their children, while the children are still under the care of the province." He set the pot on the pot holder. "You can pursue giving legal guardianship of Kyle to Bridget. Your caseworker gave you the wrong information."

"Really? That old bitch lied." A snarl invaded Adam's throat. He did stand a chance.

Bridget's knee twitched beneath his palm. She blinked back the tears threatening to spill over.

Thoughtfulness reflected in Emery's eyes. "I'll leave you to discuss which route you want to take." He glanced at the clock. "It's seven-thirty. I still have to call Darryl." He grabbed his tea. "Excuse me."

Adam's hand remained on Bridget's knee while Emery headed for the short hallway to the left of the living room. The sound of the door closing to Kyle's room carried to where Adam remained on the sofa.

"*Kwe*, I'm gonna handle this."

"How? You're on parole. Mrs. Dale's your caseworker." Bridget again sniffled and sipped some tea.

Adam sank into the sofa. She'd reminded him of his failures, but just because he'd gotten a big fat F in the past didn't mean he'd receive another one. *Think. Think. Think.* "Remember that Raven broad who was protesting outside the church?"

Bridget's jawline tensed, but she nodded.

"We talked. Told me I gotta think about others, too. Said giving back was more than helping other alcoholics. It's why

I wanted to help Cutter find out what happened to his daughter. It's why we gotta . . ." To hell with his own apprehensions. Kyle and Bridget came first. "Help the other *Anishinaabeg*. A lot of our people lost their children. Lots are trying to get them back. People like The Hawk are making it hard for them."

He removed his hand from Bridget's knee and retrieved his cigarettes from the coffee table. "It'd be easier if we let a lawyer handle this shit. But we gotta fight. It might take a bit longer to get Kyle back. We can talk to him about it. You're gonna still see him every day. I still get my weekly visitation."

He stood. "C'mon. Need a smoke."

Bridget's reflection followed Adam in the glass doors that led to the balcony. When he stepped outside, the chill of the night clung to his bare arms. Fall was on the way. He reached inside his pocket and withdrew a lighter.

"What do you think?"

"I think it's the right thing to do." Her voice remained shaky. She wrapped her arms around his waist.

He puffed on the cigarette and hugged Bridget's shoulder, drawing her tight to his chest. Traffic hummed down below. He sucked on the filter. It'd been ages since they'd last stood like this at her place.

"It is. I was only thinking about myself, thinking how I hurt you and Kyle. Didn't wanna hurt you two anymore. Thought giving you legal guardianship would make things right." He took a drag.

"The meeting's tomorrow night. At least Kyle understood." Bridget sniffled. "I . . . I feel like we let him down."

"Hey, he's okay." Adam petted her hair. "He's at Jude's. He's with Rebekah and Noah. He knows he's loved there."

"What if we can't live up to our promise?" She tilted her head upward. Fear flashed in her wide eyes.

"We told him this was only for a little bit. He knows we're coming for him." Adam kept petting her hair.

How he wished he could remain at Bridget's place, let her sleep in his arms. But the old-timers at the recovery meetings would tell him *first things first*. Moving out of the halfway house and into Bridget's pad wasn't the right thing to do. Patience. Their priority was Kyle and Sheena.

"I'll see him next Wednesday."

"I'll come and get you."

"For the meeting at IWA?"

Bridget nodded.

Bridget got in the truck. Emery rode shotgun. Although they were on their way to the halfway house to retrieve Adam for tonight's meeting at the Indigenous Women's Alliance, after praying the Rosary last night, she had something else planned as well. Tonight, she'd give her shrinking heart a reason to inflate.

"It's going to work out. Have faith." Emery patted Bridget's hand.

"My faith's a mess." Bridget steered the truck from the parking lot. "Adam's right. The easy route is gaining legal guardianship, but I can't let down the other parents out there. The other children. Those who truly want to reconnect and become a family again. We owe it to them."

She stopped at the light that would take them on the Expressway. "The Indian Residential Schools destroyed many families. I know there are parents who are too caught up in their addictions to recover their children, but I want to help those who do want help."

"It's never easy. Some never reconnect. Darryl's a fine example."

Bridget's chest heaved—her brother-in-law's upbringing

was so sad.

"Some can't ever get past the pain of colonization, while other's can." Emery sighed. "The most we can do is help those who want help. I can't force someone who isn't willing."

"True. The *leading the horse to water* thing." Bridget kept her foot on the pedal as they zoomed along the expressway. Too bad she wasn't stomping her favorite clunky-heeled leather shoe on Mrs. Dale's face. No, she couldn't think that way. Not after spending a long time reflecting with God last night.

Here went nothing. "We should get some Reggie's first."

"Sounds good. It's Jude's loss he's a Coffee Coffee man. He must not be a true Matawapit."

A giggle invaded Bridget's throat. Always, Emery made her laugh and kneaded away the tension in her shoulders. "Isn't Darryl a Coffee Coffee man?"

"I'm working on him. In time he'll convert to Canada's best. I'm not sure how he can drink that tar he calls coffee."

When Bridget glanced at her brother, his face mirrored a guy who'd drank a pile of ditchwater. How hilarious. It wasn't often Emery made fun of another person. "Should I tell Darryl what you said?"

Emery placed his finger over his red lips. "This stays between you and me."

Bridget pulled into the Reggie's Donuts on Arthur Street. Mrs. Dale would be inside—off the clock, and maybe, just maybe, Bridget could get through to the rigid woman. This was the nasty witch's last chance at redemption. If Bridget failed, they'd go to war. But at least her conscience was clear since she'd tried.

"It'll be faster if I go on in. Why don't you take the truck to retrieve Adam? It'll save us time."

She got out and dashed into the restaurant where a handful of people waited in line. Mrs. Dale also waited. Bridget smoothed her shirt and strode up to her former caseworker.

"I see you're a Reggie's fan, too." Bridget kept her tone welcoming.

Mrs. Dale's eyes lacked any warmth. "I like to partake in a tea in the evening while I read my newspaper."

"I guess everyone enjoys a coffee at this hour. I'm getting a few." She'd first offer the old woman a fistful of benevolence—something Bridget had a hunch Mrs. Dale rarely experienced. "I'll get yours, too."

Mrs. Dale held up her hand. "That is not necessary. If you think gifts will manipulate me into reconsidering my—"

"It was an offer I'd make to anyone." Bridget couldn't help the hiss of her tone at the woman daring to say she'd attempted bribery. "I'm sorry you think everyone can't be sincere in their actions. I hope I don't become as bitter."

Mrs. Dale's perennial frozen eyes actually heated. Flames almost danced in her pupils.

"I'll have you know I am not bitter." The old witch's voice was as hot as her fiery gaze. "You don't think I've been bribed, threatened, and deceived in my position? I'm very careful around clients."

"Well, I'm not a client anymore. You saw to that." Bridget stepped aside to let the man who'd been served his coffee walk by.

"Yes, I did. And I have a good hunch who is waiting in your vehicle." Mrs. Dale sniffed.

"You mean my brother?" At Mrs. Dale's raised eyebrow, Bridget continued. "My younger brother. Emery. Remember? I had to give you my life story before I was allowed full care of Kyle. Don't worry. Jude is watching Kyle like a good foster parent."

"I'm not worried. I never worry. Why would I when I have guidelines to follow? And the full support of my supervisor."

"I guess that's all that matters are guidelines." Again, Bridget stepped aside to let another customer who'd been served walk by.

"Am I supposed to consider something else?"

"Maybe one size doesn't fit all. Are each family's unique circumstances taken into consideration?"

"As I said—there are guidelines to follow." Mrs. Dale huffed up to the counter and fired her battle-axe stare at the attendant. "One medium tea. A teaspoon, exactly, of skim milk. One package of artificial sweetener. Please ensure to stir precisely fifty times so the contents are fully blended."

"I'm paying for her order." Bridget set her purse on the counter. "Three large coffees. Two double-doubles, and one with two milk and two sweeteners."

"I already told you, I cannot—"

"You're not at work and you're no longer my casework-er." Bridget handed the attendant a twenty.

"If everything is off the record, then I accept." Mrs. Dale held her nose high.

"Yes, off the record. I fight fair and square. Never dirty. It goes against who I am." Bridget plunked the change into her wallet and zipped the purse closed.

"I see you ordered three coffees when you told me your brother is in the vehicle."

Mrs. Dale was actually inviting a conversation? Bridget almost gasped. "Emery's on his way to get Adam. The three of us are going to a meeting at the Indigenous Women's Alliance."

The attendant handed Mrs. Dale her tea. Then the girl set Bridget's order on the counter in a cardboard tray.

"We have some concerns with Children and Family Services. We intend on discussing them tonight."

"Really?" Mrs. Dale withdrew the paper tucked under her

arm and held it out. "Perhaps you'll discuss this, too."

Bridget grasped the paper. Her throat dried at the article detailing Sheena Keesha's life — her father's incarceration for second-degree murder, his membership in the Winnipeg Warriors, and her mother's death from alcoholism. The personal information came from a neighbor interviewed by the press, whose daughter had known Sheena in school. The article went on about Sheena's confusion and grief, and her numerous half siblings conceived by a convicted murderer callously impregnating many native women and not sticking around to be a proper father.

"I'm not giving anyone a free pass." Bridget's head lightened. She had to force the words out, since her tongue was drier than the Antarctic. "We have choices. But there're those who're broken, not damaged, but broken, and can't make choices."

"There are *always* choices. You had choices, did you not?" Mrs. Dale snatched the paper. She strode to a table, motioning for Bridget to follow.

Bridget sat opposite the cold woman. The coffees remained in the cardboard tray. She opened her blend of milk and sweetener. "Yes, I had choices. But I was raised by two loving parents."

Mrs. Dale set the newspaper on the table, keeping the article on Sheena Keesha faceup. "It does not matter who raised you. Even if you grew up in dire circumstances, you would have succeeded."

"Easy to say, but living in hell's different. I don't know how life would've shaped me if I grew up in a less fortunate home."

"Please, Ms. Matawapit." Mrs. Dale waved her hand in a dismissing manner. "You would have succeeded. You have the spirit to succeed."

"It's not a matter of spirit."

"For you to accomplish what you have so far, it takes drive and determination. You do not use your past as an excuse. Believe me when I say you would have succeeded, no matter the odds."

"My ex-fiancé's determined to succeed this time." Bridget lifted her chin.

The fine lines around Mrs. Dale's eyes formed to wrinkles resembling a crow's feet. Her long thin nose scrunched. "He will not succeed. After thirty-five years as a social worker, I know who will and who won't. Experience has taught me much about people. He uses his past as an excuse."

Squaring her shoulders, Bridget leaned into the table. "Is there anyone you believe in?"

"I believe in the children." Mrs. Dale harrumphed. "I am always about the children. My job is to ensure each child is placed in a decent home where they will be cared for as stated in the guidelines. I inspect each home thoroughly. I interview each potential foster parent thoroughly. I am about the welfare of the children."

"If you believe in your guidelines, you know your position's to reunite families."

"I'm a realist. The majority of families will not be reunited. Parents do not have the ambition to obtain custody of their children. They'd rather use excuses to drink, partake of illegal drugs . . ."

The scowl in Bridget's chest rose. "Not all Indigenous people are —"

"No. They're not. Your family is a fine example. Your brother is a principal for a Catholic school. His wife is a nurse practitioner. They have a fine home in a fine neighborhood. They are active in their church.

"Your father is a deacon. Your mother devoted her life to raising children capable of contributing to society, not burdens. Your younger brother has his Bachelor of Social Work.

He is studying to become a priest to help the less fortunate."

"Emery's married now. He's starting his master's in January."

"Oh . . . well. See what I mean? His MSW to help the less fortunate."

"What happened?" Bridget's shoulders seemed to sink where her purse rested on the floor. There was no getting through to this woman.

"Excuse me?" Mrs. Dale lifted her coffee.

"What happened to make you the way you are today?"

Mrs. Dale's gasped. "My personal life is none of your business."

"Not buying." Bridget shook her head. "Something must've happened to you as to why you're so jaded."

"I'm. Not. Jaded."

"I think you are." Frustration and disgust lingered on Bridget's tongue. "I've never met anyone so cynical in my life. I feel sorry for you."

"Sorry?" Mrs. Dale sputtered. Her narrowed eyes widened. "Don't you dare feel sorry for me. I've done quite well, considering my circumstances. I see treasures when those children come under my care, however, their parents do not. If I had children, they would have been molded into responsible adults."

"Is this why you are the way you are? Because you couldn't have children?"

"I had every opportunity to have children. But when your husband passes on before you can begin planning a family, you cannot have children, can you?"

Mrs. Dale's honesty and sincerity annihilated the negative emotions coursing through Bridget's veins. "Thank you for sharing. I appreciate you taking me into your confidence."

The wrinkles around Mrs. Dale's eyes softened. Warmth saturated the gray of her irises like a cozy, sunless day.

"You're welcome." Her bony chest heaved.

Bridget almost reached for Mrs. Dale's hand, but just as fast she stuffed the gesture of compassion into her coat pocket. The caseworker wasn't a person who accepted sympathy. "I mean it. It helps me understand why you want the best for children in care."

"Then I'm glad you understand why I placed Kyle with your brother. As I said, men like your ex-fiancé never change. Mr. Guimond comes from a dysfunctional home. And I say this from experience, he will pass on the poor parenting skills he acquired from his mother and father to Kyle."

Tension of steel invaded Bridget's muscles.

"I hope for Kyle's sake you will not rekindle a relationship with that man, but I sense you already have, although you refuse to admit as much." Mrs. Dale sipped her tea. "Kyle's drawing spoke volumes."

A *bing* came from Bridget's cell phone. She checked the message. Emery and Adam were in the parking lot. "I have to go. It was nice speaking to you."

Mrs. Dale nodded.

Bridget's hope seemed to drag along the floor. She'd failed, even when God had told her to give the woman one last chance. Now they'd go to war.

Chapter Thirty-Six: Under the Gun

Seven people surrounded the boardroom table at the Indigenous Women's Alliance. Emery was on hand to advise them. He'd also volunteered to take minutes so the committee members could freely speak. Bridget sat at the head of the table, chairing the meeting.

For over an hour everyone had talked, but no ideas stuck. Adam continued to fiddle with the handle on his coffee mug. Maybe he should finally say something.

He cleared his throat. "S'okay if I throw in a dollar?"

The four women and one man nodded. So did Bridget.

"In the pen, the way to get attention and make changes . . . you riot."

Everyone gaped except Bridget.

"I'm not saying have a riot. But when there were riots, people listened. Even the press. Shit changed for the better." He squeezed his toes. "Lookit what those women did with the Motionless No More movement a couple of years ago. It's still going strong. Up at Bridget's reserve, there's a family still protesting about the Indian Residential Schools. Maybe Emery can say more. He was there when shit hit the fan in July."

Emery's face flushed to a hot shade of pink.

Everyone at the table stared at him.

He laid aside his pen. "Yes, the protest." Emery coughed. "At Ottertail Lake, the local parish proposed a request for financial assistance to chief and council for Healing the Spirit, a workshop hosted last week to initiate reconciliation between the Christian communities and band members affected by the Indian Residential Schools."

Everyone glanced around at each other, nodding.

"There were concerns from a few band members. One being my spouse." More pink climbed up Emery's face. If the guy got any more bashful, he'd turn into a tube of *kwe's* favorite lipstick. "Their concerns were valid. They believed the band shouldn't fund a workshop hosted by a religion responsible for assimilating First Nations people into Western society. Those schools destroyed families and destroyed lives. My father was one of those who attended an Indian Residential School."

Emery blinked a few times. "This family, the Kabatays, staged a protest outside of the church for over a week. And yes, as Adam mentioned, the protest got a lot of attention, especially those from the parish. The protesters' concerns were taken seriously. A special meeting was held by chief and council to address their grievances. My spouse was elected to speak on behalf of the protesters, and the parish asked me to speak on behalf of the church."

"Everything was resolved?" an older woman named Maryanne asked.

"The majority were pleased, except for the Kabatays." Emery tapped the pen he held against his mouth.

"Oh? Why's that?"

"They feel Christian and First Nations communities shouldn't reconcile."

"Did they say why?" Maryanne peered at him.

"They believe what was done to First Nations communities is unforgiveable. When Healing the Spirit happened last week, the Kabatay family protested outside of the church."

Pursing her lips, Maryanne glanced at Adam. "It's too bad the conflict with this family wasn't resolved."

"Not everything is." Adam gripped his coffee mug. The

Hawk was more stubborn than the Kabatay family. The committee might be able to make a dent in Sheena Keesha's case, but nobody at Children and Family Services would reconsider his measly one hour a week.

"I think a walk might get everyone's attention. Round up as many people as we can. Even the Kabatays, if they wanna participate." Adam rose to refill his coffee.

"The Kabatays?" Bridget sounded like she'd swallowed a pack of marbles.

"Yep. Them, too. They got protesting down to a science." Adam poured the coffee into his mug at the fancy serving counter.

"Um, yes, they, uh . . . do." Emery started writing again.

"What kind of walk?" The question came from Maryanne.

"One for Sheena. Get some more numbers on the other kids who've gone missing in care." Adam stirred the coffee and meandered back to his chair. "Call the media. Ask that Clayton guy to speak at the end of the walk in front of Children and Family Services. He knows how to get a crowd worked up. He sure knew how to open his big mouth outside the workshop and hand me some major lip."

Now it was time for Bridget to turn her favorite shade of pink lipstick. She eyed a stiff Emery, who mirrored a cardboard cutout.

Adam slurped back a helping of coffee. "What'd you think?"

"I think it's a great idea," Ralph, said. "We should look at what we want to accomplish for the walk. Think up a date for it to happen. Advertising to get people involved. It's a great start."

"Is, uh, is everyone in favor?" Bridget poked her gaze around the table.

"Adam said rioting gets results. Sometimes people have to stir the pot to get results," the older woman, Nadine, added.

Everyone raised their hands to pass the motion.

Bridget's hand also inched up. "Then that's what we'll do. The walk should start here and end at Children and Family Services so we can address why they failed to keep this girl safe, and what they're going to do to ensure this doesn't happen again."

Once shit hit the fan, The Hawk would kick Adam's ass. But Raven Kabatay was right—it was time he got off his butt and started helping others now that he could. And the old-timers at the recovery meetings usual spiel of trusting a higher power was something Adam must cling to.

Bridget pulled up at the halfway house. She'd dropped Emery off at the condo so she could have a moment alone with Adam. His curfew was killing her. They had no quality time together.

Adam wrapped her hand in his. "I gotta get inside pretty quick or the PO'll bust my balls."

"I know." Emery's words of practicing patience rang in Bridget's ears. But patience sucked. Like a whiny little girl, she wanted everything now—Kyle, nights in bed with Adam, answers to Sheena Keesha.

In order to produce an effective protest, a month was required to establish a walk from the Indigenous Women's Alliance to Children and Family Services.

"I understand, *kwe*." Adam ran his other hand along her hair. "I thought about it, too."

Bridget's sagging chest inflated. "Thought about what?"

"What you're thinking. How much easier if I was at your place." Adam grunted. "I'd hear from the old-timers not to rush it. Leave it in my higher power's hands. If we're together again, it has to be for the right reasons. Something we really want. Not because of a curfew."

Bridget's chest deflated. "I know. God tells me the same thing—to trust Him. But I've always been impatient."

"Hey, it's what I love about you."

"Sometimes you're as logical as Emery." Bridget wanted to laugh, but grief swallowed the giggle.

"Not logical. Streetwise. Keeps you from getting shanked in the pen or knifed in the bar." He leaned in. "I just told you it's what I love about you. You ever gonna get around to telling me how you really feel?"

She fingered Adam's jawline. "You mean that I love you?"

"Yeah."

"I love you." The words flowed easily from her heart.

"I love you, too, *kwe*." And the intensity in his eyes said so.

Adam's lips molded against her mouth. Bridget shifted to get closer, nibble at his warm flesh, and delight in his lush breaths. Pleasure quaked between her legs. The maddening spot between her pussy lips felt as if Adam was tracing his finger around her clit.

Adam broke the kiss. "I'm horny, too. Patience."

"Horny?" Bridget smacked his arm.

"What's wrong with admitting you're horny? You got a helluva beautiful cunt, don't you?"

"Yes. Damn straight I do. The finest cunt around." She giggled. "So if I lowered my hand, I'd find something hard?"

"Don't push it, woman." Adam snorted. "I'd better get inside before I bust my curfew and end up wearing another set of silver bracelets."

Again, Bridget's chest deflated. "I know. I'll see you tomorrow after work. I have to drop off Emery at the airport first. He said Darryl needs him at home, and he sure booked his flight fast. I think they miss each other, but they won't admit it. They are newlyweds."

"Good enough for 'em. If we can't do the nasty, nobody should." Adam snickered.

Bridget cringed. "Don't say that. Nobody wants to hear about their brother's sex life. Ugh."

Adam chuckled. "Get me around five-thirty."

"I will."

He got out of the truck and meandered down the walkway. Halfway there, he stopped to light a cigarette.

Bridget smacked the steering wheel, frustrated about going to bed alone for the umpteenth time. She drove off.

CHAPTER THIRTY-SEVEN: WHEN THE EAGLE SCREAMS

Bridget finished painting the last sign in the basement of the Indigenous Women's Alliance. So much had happened over the last month. Between work's demands, rushing to see Kyle in the mornings and evenings, racing to get Adam at the halfway house for time alone at the condo and then dropping him off at his recovery meeting, she was forever sprinting against the clock.

At least Stephen had taken the news well when he'd called and she informed him she couldn't see him anymore. As a matter of fact, he'd sounded preoccupied when they'd spoken during the middle of September.

Thanksgiving had come and gone. That had been a frigid afternoon from the tension between Jude and Charlene. A fight, Jude had muttered while carving the turkey. A fight he wouldn't elaborate on. After they'd eaten, Charlene had left the house. She hadn't returned by the time Bridget had kissed Kyle goodnight, who'd whined about missing his dad on the special day.

Mrs. Dale wasn't giving an inch. She'd vetoed Adam's request to spend the Monday holiday with his son.

Their walk to Children and Family Services today might bear fruit. Bridget had enough of that woman's interference. Yes, Mrs. Dale was only doing her job, but the woman should allow Adam more visitation time based on his transition into society.

He'd stuck to his curfew, which had been moved to ten o'clock, thanks to the recommendation from his parole officer. He faithfully attended his recovery meetings. He never missed a day of work, and even covered shifts when other cooks called in sick.

Adam was across the room, working on another sign. Because of the amount of overtime he'd put in, he'd scheduled the day off.

The basement was packed. Mom, Dad, Emery, Darryl, and Jude were also helping prepare last-minute items. The Kabatay family pitched in, too. Clayton had agreed to speak on behalf of the protesters. Of course the two families kept their respective distances.

The Catholic Women's Association had asked to also participate in the walk. The women were donating sandwiches and dainties to eat after the demonstration. Many were in the kitchen, readying the dishes.

The participants had enough vehicles to bring everyone back to the building once the walk concluded. In two hours, they'd leave Ray Boulevard and head for Oliver Road. Then they'd continue down Balmoral Street. Once they reached Central Avenue, they'd walk along Amber Drive, ending at Jade Crescent.

Friday afternoon was the perfect day. There'd be much traffic during the walk. Children and Family Services didn't close until four-thirty. They'd reach the building before the doors locked for the weekend.

The chief and the people from Mountain View First Nation were present. A reporter from the paper wandered about, speaking to various people. Even the local news station had arrived.

The committee had created social media accounts where people could interact and receive updates about today's big day.

Bridget sat with her calves tucked under her thighs. She leaned back, resting her bottom against the soles of her running shoes she'd worn for the walk. The weather had cooperated, to a point. Although the sun wasn't present, they wouldn't have to walk in the rain.

"You're Adam Guimond, aren't you?" the reporter asked. "The people over there mentioned your child's in care."

Why had Clayton brought Adam's personal life into the walk? Bridget rose and scurried over to him.

The reporter held up his small recorder. "If you don't mind, might I ask you a few questions?"

"That's what he does." Adam pointed at Clayton, surrounded by his sisters and mother.

"I'm aware of that." The reporter bristled. "I told you already, he said I should speak to you. His sister, Raven, mentioned your own child's in care. She added you're having a tough time acquiring him back."

Adam folded his arms. The look he sent the reporter would have sent anyone else scurrying, but the feisty man, probably used to dealing with intimidating people, continued to hold up his recorder.

"I'm Bridget Matawapit. His son's former foster parent." She held out her hand.

"Former?" The reporter quirked his sagging brow. "Mike Nelson. *Thunder Bay Times*. Might I ask why you're the former caregiver?"

"Yes, you may."

Mike grinned. "Well?"

"Because I developed a relationship with the child's father, Children and Family Services revoked my status as a caregiver for Mr. Guimond's child. They felt it was a conflict of interest on my part and could harm the child's emotional well-being."

"Really? How do you feel about their decision?"

"I more than provided adequate care. I also ensured the visitation rules were enforced. However, when I offered to retrieve Mr. Guimond from his current residence to attend the memorial service of a dear friend of his, Children and Family Services accused me of not following their guidelines, because the child accompanied me in my vehicle."

"So the three of you were in the company of others?"

"Yes. The only time we were alone was during the drive to and from the church. How do you explain to a seven-year-old child that he can't speak to his father at a memorial service, surrounded by numerous people who are speaking to his father?"

"Is this child aware of the rules?"

"Of course. I explained to him that he would see his father one hour a week in the visitation room at Children and Family Services."

"How did that go?"

"Considering the child hasn't seen his father in almost four years, by the second visit they were bonding. Mr. Guimond has done everything required of him, and beyond, to prove he is fit to be a father again."

"And they still haven't relented on his visitation time?"

"No." Bridget made sure the reporter caught the tension in her voice. "Up until my care was revoked, I attended each visitation session and witnessed a father and his child developing a loving and trusting relationship." She motioned at Jude. "My brother has current care of the child."

"The agency at least placed the child with people he knows?"

"Yes. I made sure of that. I fought for Kyle's right to be among people who love him. Putting him with strangers would have harmed his emotional and mental well-being."

"Might I interview your brother?"

"Sure." Bridget waved over Jude.

Jude ambled to them.

"Mike Nelson of the *Thunder Bay Times*. I understand you're the current caregiver for Adam Guimond's child."

"Yes, I am." Jude sent a puzzled look to Bridget and Adam.

"Mr. Nelson's interviewing us about the state of Adam's child in care, and what we're currently challenging," Bridget told her brother.

"Oh, yes." Jude nodded.

"How do you feel about this?" Mike held the tape recorder to Jude.

"I feel Children and Family Services made the wrong decision." Jude's eyes narrowed the same as Dad's did when he was distressed. "My sister cared for this child for almost four years before Adam relocated to Thunder Bay."

"There weren't any problems during this time period?" Mike asked.

"No." Bridget shook her head. "The caseworker and I had a good working relationship. It wasn't until Mr. Guimond returned to Thunder Bay, requesting to become a full-time father to his son again, that problems occurred."

"Problems? Would this be the decision made by Children and Family Services when the two of you entered into a relationship?"

"No. This started beforehand. As I said, Adam more than proved his sincerity."

"May I ask why you lost your child to care?" Mike stared at Adam.

Adam's jawline hardened. He glared at Bridget.

"I think the question's a bit personal. We should focus on what the Children and Family Services mandate is. And that's to provide adequate care and to reunite families. Not to impede the process." Bridget kept her tone even.

"You feel it's being impeded?" Mike again quirked his

thick brow.

"Yes. What's happening right now more than proves they are impeding, not assisting. The child's currently in my brother's care. Adam can only see his child one hour a week, after almost two months. To allow the relationship to develop, they need to spend more time together. The progress they've made has exceeded Children and Family Services expectations."

"Then this walk is more than about Sheena Keesha? Is it also about other parents who lost their children to care?"

"Yes." Bridget nodded. "When parents are making efforts — and succeeding — to reclaim their children, the agency should encourage not only the parents, but the child."

"I'll be sure to contact Children and Family Services about your case. I'd like to hear what they have to say," Mike said into his small recorder.

"Please do. I'd love to hear their answers as much as you." Bridget took Adam's stiff arm.

She steered them away from the reporter.

Jude walked beside them. "Kyle wanted to come. It wasn't easy telling him he had to go to school."

Bridget rubbed the back of her aching neck. Naturally, Kyle wanted to be here. He knew what this walk was about. Although having children present could help the cause, they were minors, and because they were in care, should have their privacy respected.

When would this end? When would she have her child back?

After the opening prayer, conducted by the elder who advised the Indigenous Women's Alliance board of directors, and a song by the Mountain View drum group, they were off.

The Kabatay family walked in front, followed by the board of directors for the Indigenous Women's Alliance. Everyone else brought up the rear. The dreary gray clouds continued to hide the sun. From the west, a strong wind blew.

A few local drummers held their hand drums and sang songs. Some people in the passing vehicles tooted and cheered, while others booed and told the Indians to *go home and quit complaining.*

Bridget had expected a split outcome. She glanced over her shoulder. Adam held his sign. He walked beside Darryl and Emery. Behind them, Mom, Dad, and Jude held their signs.

The cold cut through the layers of Bridget's clothing. The nippy wind cast a chill through the afternoon air. Ice seemed to hover everywhere, looking for available skin to claim. Mittens kept her hands warm while holding the sign she'd made—*What Happened to Sheena Keesha?*

Northwestern Ontario News rode in a van, cameras on hand, to capture the walk. The local TV station mingled amongst the protesters, filming and interviewing people.

Clayton's stone expression remained plastered on his skinny face. Every time a reporter approached him, he launched into one of his heartfelt speeches. Having the Kabatay family present still worried Bridget. Yes, they were quite passionate about their causes, but they tended to lean toward a narrow-minded approach, based on how they handled the Healing the Spirit workshop by attempting to stop band council from funding the church's hydro bill.

They rounded the corner from Amber Drive and headed up Jade Crescent. The big building Bridget used to visit waited. At least the parking lot remained full. They had called the executive director of Children and Family Services to inform them of the walk.

After five more minutes of walking, everyone assembled

in front of the big brown building.

Clayton stood on the cement steps. He held up his arms.

Bridget crossed her fingers and sent up a silent prayer he wouldn't say something too outrageous.

"In the past, the *Anishinaabeg* had their own governing system. We also had our own way to teach our children. Watch. Always, children watched what we did. Girls watched their mothers. Boys watched their fathers. If a child was without a parent, they were cared for by someone. Nobody was ever alone," Clayton said in a voice full of conviction.

A cheer erupted from the crowd.

"There were no policies in place to decide who'd take the orphaned child. Why? Because everyone cared about the child. If family wasn't present, and I speak about the *Anishinaabe* way of defining family — grandfather, grandmother, aunts, uncles, cousins, sisters, and brothers — those close to the family would then raise the child.

"If a child was mistreated, that person no longer cared for the child. The babe was handed to a person who'd show the child the same love and care the absent family members would.

"We were known to adopt others. Brothers. Sisters. Uncles. Aunts. Grandfathers. Grandmothers. Mothers. Fathers.

"We didn't have guidelines telling us *section this* or *rule number that* should be adhered to. Our system worked. It worked from the day Creator breathed life into us.

"Our four-legged brothers and sisters taught us how to care for our young. Animals don't tell their babes what to do and how to do it. They show the fledglings through action. Watch and learn. That was our way.

"Now the Canadian government thinks to interfere again, after interfering in our lives ever since they sailed over here.

"When missionaries attempted to persuade us to enter

their mission schools, many of us said no. In order to have this land, they had to do away with the Indian to make way for the wave of new people settling here. If they couldn't kill us off, as they more than tried to do, they'd assimilate us.

"Thus, they created the Indian Residential Schools in the late nineteenth century. *Take those children when they're very young, five or six years old, and put them in the schools before they can learn by watching their family how they should live.*

"What did they learn in these schools? They sure didn't learn about family, how to be a member of the family, or how to raise a family. They learned how to work in the kitchen, fields, and barn. Learned a trade, if they were lucky. Learned skills to clean, cook, and sew. Learned about religion.

"They also learned about sexual abuse, emotional abuse, mental abuse, spiritual abuse, and physical abuse. They learned this from the priests and nuns who taught them.

"What did they have to give to the community when they returned? Tons of baggage. Bags of abuse. Bags of anger. Bags of confusion. Bags of repression. Bags of silence.

"Yes, silence. What happens in silence? It festers inside you. And it grows bigger the more you feed it.

"So what did our great-grandparents pass on? Their baggage. What did our grandparents pass on? Their baggage. What did our parents pass on? Their baggage.

"Now they tell us we are bad parents and not fit to care for our own children."

Clayton used his thin lips to point at Adam. "That man there. He came to our community at the beginning of September, trying to find a way to heal. This man lost his child to Children and Family Services. He's trying to get his child back, but they won't give him his very own son, after he's proven he's capable of caring for his child.

"Instead, Children and Family Services placed his child in another foster home. They took his child from his original foster mother, a woman who cared for the child for almost four years.

"Would this have happened among the *Anishinaabeg*? No!" Clayton raised his fist and shook it. "We would have said, *He's trying. He's proven he's learned from his mistakes. He's more than fit to care for his child again. Let him have his child.* Then we would've watched him to make sure he was honoring what he promised us—to care for the child in the *Anishinaabe* way, so one day the child could pass on his knowledge, his experience, his culture to his own children.

"A girl went missing under Children and Family Services' care. How many more have to go missing before something is done? She was found in the water. The police investigated. They called it a tragic accident. She drowned.

"For kids who grew up north, who swim all summer in our many lakes, they sure do drown a lot, don't they? Isn't it strange how they never *drown* at their home reserves?

"I'm going to speak about the elephant in the room. The so-called savages drunk at the river banks. When they pass out, they're rolled into the water. Or they're forced out into the water to avoid being beaten by racists. That's what happens. I say this, but everyone tells me there's no proof.

"I know this because it happened to my uncles. All three of them. Two survived. One drowned. To this day, his death is still marked on his file as accidental drowning.

"No more!" Clayton raised his hands in the air. "I say no more will I allow this to happen. Stand up, *Anishinaabeg*, stand up and fight for those who can't speak—the dead, the children, the animals, the standing people we call trees, and for the Great Mother. None of them can speak. So we must speak for them!"

Bridget's breath rattled, and her lungs expanded against her ribcage. Enemy of the family or not, the fine speech, Clayton's passionate words, were nails clawing at her chest, demanding she rise and speak for those who couldn't. And she would.

Once the cheering died down and the drumming stopped, Bridget yelled, "I think we should have the right to speak to those in charge at Children and Family Services!"

"Yes, we should!" Clayton shouted. "Where are they? We stand outside of their building, but they're not here." He whipped around on his heel and faced the double doors leading into the building.

"Where are you? Have you heard what we said? Or will you choose to ignore our cries? Just as your first prime minister ignored our cries. Just as the other prime ministers and government officials ignored our cries. Just as the religious institutions ignored our cries. Just as the people of Canada ignored our cries.

"We are only Indians. What do we matter? In the twenty-first century, is a dead Indian still the only good Indian?"

Again, everyone cheered.

The chairman, Priscilla, for the Indigenous Women's Alliance, stepped forward. "I propose we meet with Children and Family Services. I want results. I want answers. I want to know why Sheena Keesha went missing and drowned under the care of the Province of Ontario. I want to know why this man can only see his child one hour a week, after he's more than proven he's fit for unsupervised visits.

"I don't ask for Children and Family Services to break their own guidelines. I ask why he isn't allowed to take his child out for dinner. Bring his child to a movie in the evening. Spend quality time on the weekend with his child." She thrust her finger at Adam.

"And I also want to know why his original caregiver can't continue caring for the child." She pointed at Bridget.

Bridget swallowed. She moved closer to Adam in the crowd and clutched his arm. Tears formed in her eyes. Everyone was present, fighting for her and Adam's rights.

Fighting for Sheena Keesha's rights. Fighting for all those who'd died in care, and those who died simply for being *Anishinaabe*.

Chapter Thirty-eight: All the Aces

A dam sat on the sofa at Bridget's condo. What a long day. But a good day. As for the reporter getting in his face, at least he hadn't plugged the pushy guy. Anger management class and the recovery meetings were paying off. Good thing Bridget had stepped up to address the asshole's questions. And she'd done so in a way that didn't impede too much on their personal lives.

The Indigenous Women's Alliance had secured a meeting with the heads of Children and Family Services to address aboriginal children in care. But the clincher was Adam and Bridget's chance to meet with the executive director to review Kyle's case file. He'd bet his old canteen at the iron house The Hawk would be there, clipboard and all.

They'd skipped the dinner at Jude's house, since Kyle was there. Of all the stupid bullshit. Adam couldn't even attend a celebration for today's successes.

Bridget handed Adam the cola he'd requested. She held a cup of tea.

"Well?" He set the cola on his knee and patted hers.

"Well what?" She snuggled up against him.

The story of their month. Time alone for a couple of hours. Sometimes they'd talk, and other times they'd hit the sheets. Then she'd drop him off for his twelve-step meeting and race to Jude's.

"We made it a month. We didn't think we would." Adam draped his arm around her.

"No, I didn't think so." Bridget rested her head on his

shoulder. "I guess I need a boost of faith. I worried a lot."

"And what'd worrying get you?"

"A wasted month worrying." Bridget giggled. "What about you? You can't tell me you weren't worried."

"I worried. But I attend twelve-step meetings. The members keep me in line." He kissed the top of her head. "One more hurdle, *kwe*."

"I know." Bridget lifted her head and gazed at him. "I think it'll be a positive outcome. We got a lot of press this afternoon. Our social media pages blew up, too."

"Yeah, lots of support." Adam wasn't sure about people getting a glimpse of his personal life, but swallowing his pride had worked. It'd helped him when he'd first tried to sober up, and the helping hand had paid off again.

"Welp . . ." He shifted on the couch. Squeezed his toes. Ran his tongue along the roof of his mouth.

"Spit it out." Bridget playfully smacked his stomach. "Something's on your mind."

"You're the boss." Again, he ran his tongue along the roof of his mouth. "Am I saving up to buy you an engagement ring or what?"

"Is that your way of asking me to marry you? Like last time?" She straightened to a sitting position, staring at him.

Adam weakly chuckled. "I'm not good at that formal stuff. But if you want me to get on one knee . . ."

"No. Skip the bended knee. It's not you. And yes, you can get me an engagement ring for Christmas." She pecked his lips, her eyes glittering.

"Long engagement?" Maybe that was the best route to take. Last time they'd rushed. This time he'd secure his own pad. A simple room at a boarding house.

"I think we can wait a year." Bridget nodded.

"It'll give us time to scope out a house of our own." Adam sipped his cola. "I can't keep living at the halfway house.

I'm overstaying my welcome. Others need a bed there."

Bridget's skin glowed.

"I'm not hinting to move in either. Like I said, we'll do it right this time. Slow and easy. I think once you get Kyle back, we'll stick to this new visitation schedule the executive director will set up for me."

"I'd like that." Her voice was as toasty as her gaze. "And you're right. It'll give me time to find a permanent place. And plan a proper wedding. I know who I want to give me away."

"Isn't that supposed to be your dad?"

"Silly." She pecked his cheek. "My dad's a deacon. He'll marry us at Christ the King. Jude'll walk me down the aisle."

"I like that. A wedding at the rez. Maybe a fall wedding. Same time next year, hmm?"

"Kyle could be our ring bearer . . ."

"Oh, err . . . I guess Emery could stand up for me."

"Next year. Our wedding."

Bridget and Adam were on the top floor of Children and Family Services. The executive director's office overlooked the street. Mrs. Dale sat in the chair to the right. Bridget in the middle, and Adam on the left. Ms. Fletcher would have the final say regarding Kyle.

Ms. Fletcher removed her glasses. She set the tip of the arm in her mouth, glancing at the file in front of her. "I've had a chance to review your file. I'm sorry it's taken two weeks to get back to you. But we've been readying for the meeting with the Indigenous Women's Alliance." A hint of accusation lingered in her tone.

If the executive director meant to produce guilt from Bridget, tough luck. If Children and Family Services had followed their mandate of reuniting families, this meeting wouldn't have happened.

"Yes, work always keeps us busy. I've had many meet-ings myself." Bridget set her purse on the floor. She squared her shoulders and raised her chin.

"I've reviewed Mrs. Dale's notes," Ms. Fletcher continued on flatly. "The supervised visits are proceeding on a positive note. I won't grant Mr. Guimond full-time care . . ."

Heat raced through Bridget's veins, but Adam clutched her hand. He rubbed his thumb along her scorching flesh, as if reassuring her he was okay.

"Please understand it hasn't been long enough to make a true assessment." Ms. Fletcher's gaze was firm. "I'll with-draw supervised visits, though. Mr. Guimond, you may see Kyle outside of your residence, but the caregiver must be present at all times. I recommend you can spend the eve-nings with Kyle after he's done school up until seven-thirty. Kyle needs time to wind down afterward in order to prepare for bed."

Adam's fingers almost crushed Bridget's hand, but he wasn't angry, he was squeezing her from joy by the way his face glowed.

"Ms. Matawapit, I'll return Kyle to your care. You've more than proven his needs come first. I interviewed your brother, and he's informed me you've been present every evening and have dedicated your weekends to him.

"Understand that what you previously did—not adhering to the rules by providing Adam with a ride to and from the memorial—violated the agreement you consented to as a foster parent when you were first approved as a caregiver. Kyle's still under the legal care of Children and Family Ser-vices." A threat-like tone lingered in her voice.

Although it pained Bridget to agree, she nodded.

"If you two decide to cohabitate, this must be reviewed by Children and Family Services." Ms. Fletcher directed her stare at Bridget and then Adam.

"We won't be." Hopefully Bridget didn't sound flippant. "We've decided to wait until we're married."

"I see . . ." Ms. Fletcher tapped the arm tip of her glasses on the folder. "Is there a set date?"

"We're considering next year. October."

"Then there's no need to speak about this further. If Adam proves to be a fit parent during this time period, my recommendation will be to grant him full custody of his child." Ms. Fletcher sat back in her chair, her assessing look matching the authority she bore. "Are there any questions?"

Bridget shook her head. "I'll be sure to call if I have any."

"I will, too," Adam muttered.

"Then our meeting's over. Thank you for taking the time to come here." Ms. Fletcher directed her attention at Mrs. Dale. "I'll send the paperwork to you. You'll use the amended details for supervising both of their files."

The heat in Bridget's veins vanished. They'd done it. She stood. No more supervised visits. Yes, there'd be monthly home inspections, but they were almost free.

School was finished. Adam had completed work for the day. Finally, they'd have their first family dinner. Kyle pranced into the condo. He hadn't stopped cheering ever since they'd picked up Adam at the halfway house.

"Can I, Dad? Can I help you?" Kyle dumped his backpack on the floor.

"Sure can." Adam swaggered into the condo. He'd announced on the drive over he was looking for a rooming house, and Kyle wanted to help his father find a new place.

"I'll be able to go there, right, Dad?"

"You can if I accompany you. But you won't if you don't pick up your backpack and put it in the right spot." Bridget folded her arms.

"Aww, Mom." Kyle kicked at the throw rug in the small foyer. "It's a special day. I can be with Dad all I want."

"Until seven-thirty." Bridget pointed at the clock. "Go get changed. Dad's going to cook, and I'm going to set the table."

"Okay. Okay." Kyle swiped up his backpack and trudged to his bedroom.

The first thing Bridget had done after the meeting yesterday was retrieve Kyle's belongings from Jude's and cart everything back to the condo. She squealed and did a little victory dance.

"When's that meeting again for Sheena?" Adam lumbered into the kitchen, carrying the bag of groceries.

"Next week. Have you spoken to Cutter?" Bridget pranced after him to the kitchen.

"Nope. Can't have contact with other felons." Adam emptied the groceries and set them on the counter. "But he's got his ways of hearing what's happening on the outside. We all do."

He washed his hands. "I think The Hawk and that foster parent are in big trouble. She didn't look too happy yesterday."

"My intention wasn't to cause trouble for Mrs. Dale. I even gave her a chance to make amends when I visited her at Reggie's Donuts last month, but she refused to take it. Sheena was one of her cases. The investigation's already underway. Next week, we'll hear what Children and Family Services will do to ensure this doesn't happen again."

She had no desire to see Mrs. Dale fired. Bridget's intentions were to make sure children were properly supervised so another child didn't get into drugs and alcohol.

"Now what's eating your brain, *kwe*?" Adam stood at the island, cutting uncooked chicken into thin strips.

"We're a family now, but Sheena and Logan will never

be." Bridget meandered around the island and stopped behind Adam. She hugged his waist.

"Who says they're not?" Adam kept slicing the chicken breasts. "Have some faith. I say they're in a better place."

The phone call Bridget had received at work still irked her. Kyle had been assigned a new caseworker. Mrs. Dale had resigned. Bridget vacated the truck at Reggie's Donuts. Sure enough, the witch sat at a table by the window reading her newspaper.

How cowardly to leave and retire on a cushy pension after what the woman had done. Bridget trounced inside the restaurant and barreled straight for the table.

"Searching me out again?" Mrs. Dale sipped her tea.

Bridget plunked in the opposite chair. "You won't be present at the meeting next week? I see you decided to retire."

"I'm sixty-eight. It's time I traveled. I'm also considering becoming a snowbird. My older sister lives in Florida. A beautiful retirement community."

Bridget bristled. "That's it? You don't want to answer to everyone about Sheena Keesha?"

"Now that I'm no longer officially an employee of Children and Family Services, I'm going to speak my mind, young lady." Mrs. Dale set aside her tea. "As you thought to tell me, there are those who are fixable and those who are broken."

"I see, and Sheena was broken?"

"Very much so. When a child comes into care, they must be young or they will fail. From my interviews, I know which ones will withstand the system and go on to become productive members of society, while others will not. Kyle stands a chance. Excuse me, he did, until you decided to push him back into a life I strove to keep him from."

"Excuse me?" Bridget sputtered. "He's doing extremely

well. His grades are excellent. He enjoys school. He's learning about his culture from his dad. He's going to become an altar server once he receives his First Communion. He loves his extracurricular activities. He sleeps well at night."

"For the time being." Mrs. Dale raised her hand, palm facing Bridget. "But once the novelty wears off for Mr. Guimond, I guarantee Kyle will experience the same unstable environment his father did. You've proven to me you are not as strong as I thought you were, by allowing *that* man into your life again, after what he put you and Kyle through. You think nothing of the child's feelings. You Indian women and your vaginas."

Never was Bridget so insulted. The bitch was referring to women who had children with various partners. "Maybe you should consider using your vagina now and then. If you had, you would've found solace in your job by helping families to reunite. Helping children in need."

"Oh, my job provided satisfaction. The same for the children who could be saved. But day after day, Indian after Indian, giving the same excuses . . ." Mrs. Dale's face contorted. "How many times are your people going to use colonization and the residential schools as an excuse for being unfit parents? When are you going to stop blaming the government and move on?"

"What happened was only recent. The last residential school closed in nineteen ninety-six. And consider this. Your government was so intent on Westernizing us that you forgot to take the good with the bad. Yes, many of us are productive members of society. Good little Indians kowtowing to the system, people as yourself like to think. However, you also taught us your bad qualities. Right?" The old crank could chew on that.

"Another excuse." Mrs. Dale sniffed. "A quarter of Canada's prison population is Indigenous. Your fiancé is one of them."

"Was. W.A.S. Past tense."

"Your population is growing faster than any other race in our country. As a former social worker, do you know how many of them are in care? The number is no surprise. Those women have babies they don't have the wherewithal to care for. Mentally, emotionally, physically, and financially. I bet you see more than your fair share at your work place."

"Yes, I do, and what I see are women determined to educate themselves for better jobs and a better life for themselves and their children."

"Oh please." Mrs. Dale flicked her hand. "They receive financial aid to attend school. They also receive daycare aid. It's free money to them."

"Free money?" There was no getting through to this woman. "You know, I feel sorry for you."

"Sorry?" Mrs. Dale's face reddened, and fire flashed in her gray eyes.

"Yes. Sorry. You haven't enjoyed your life since your husband died. Maybe you didn't even enjoy it before he died."

"How dare you." Mrs. Dale blinked rapidly. "You know nothing—"

"I don't need to be privy to your personal life to see what kind of person you are." Bridget stood. "It shows in your face and the way you judge an entire race based on a few bad apples. No, First Nations people aren't perfect. We have our good and bad like any other population, but people like you refuse to see the good. Instead, you lump us into—"

"I told you once before I classed you as a good person. You're a hard worker. Financially successful. A great career. A good heart with the amount of volunteer work you do. It's too bad you let *that* man—"

"You never thought of me as your equal. You saw me as a

good little Indian who conformed. Nothing more." Bridget snatched her purse. "Enjoy the rest of your miserable life."

Bridget marched out the door of the restaurant and straight to the truck. Her heart bloomed. Yes, it'd been awesome to tell off the bitter Mrs. Dale, who'd die a lonely, angry woman.

CHAPTER THIRTY-NINE: KEYS TO THE KINGDOM

A dam opened the truck door to a squirming Kyle, who'd flung off his seat belt. "Let's go, Dad! Let's go! You gotta see it!"

"See it? I helped you decorate the tree." Laughter filled Adam's chest. He threw his arm around Kyle. They meandered up the walkway he'd shoveled the other day.

A three-bedroom bungalow. He still shivered at the brown siding and brick wainscoting, big picture window, front porch where he liked to sit and smoke a cigarette, and flowerbeds covered in snow that Bridget would tend in the spring.

Next October he'd call this crib home, instead of having to leave every evening, much to Kyle's dismay. Each time his son whimpered when Adam headed off to catch the bus to his twelve-step meeting, his heart shrunk.

"Won't be long. You'll be eight. And I'll be an old man of thirty-nine when we all live here."

Bridget trailed behind them. "Gimme a sec." Her keys jangled.

Adam opened the porch door. He'd fixed up the cozy pad to accommodate a table and chairs. "Boots off, kiddo."

"Yeah, yeah." Kyle snickered and removed his heavy winter boots.

Adam also kicked his off. When he entered the house, his breathing rattled at the living room full of the same classy furniture that had been moved from the condo. After the New Year, he'd save some money to buy some of his own furnishings to add his stamp on the home.

The tree they'd decorated Sunday evening stood in front of the picture window. Already, Adam had wrapped Kyle's presents. They were back at the rooming house. The clincher was Bridget's engagement ring. She deserved a Hollywood movie star rock, but he couldn't afford something like that. The savings he'd scrounged up had gone to presents.

He sank in the plush armchair. Part of him wished he could call Cutter. Even though the Indigenous Women's Alliance had met with Children and Family Services, talks still dragged on. Red fucking tape. Maybe in two or three or even five years they'd see some kind of changes, but the province moved at a slow pace. Survey this. Question that. Reports. Committees. On the bright side, the protest walk had gotten the ball rolling.

"I started the kettle. Want some tea?" Bridget curled up on the sofa.

"Nah. I'm good."

"Is Children and Family Services decision still bothering you?"

"I expected it." Adam ran his hand through his hair. "I told you back in September. Going through these kinds of channels takes forever. I should know. I sat on remand for a year and a half before the judge finally got off his ass. Ain't nothing new there.

"C'mere." He patted his lap.

Bridget rose. "Yes, something concrete would've been nice, but it's a start. I've been on this board for a million years and I'm used to waiting. Always waiting."

Her firm buttocks rubbed against his thighs. She laced her arm around his shoulder. "Look at the positive. We get to spend Christmas together as a family. Mom, Dad, Emery, and Darryl are flying in on Boxing Day. We'll get to see them for five days before they go back to the rez. You get to cook the turkey. And your curfew was upped to eleven."

"My curfew." Adam chuckled.

"Pretty quick you'll be curfew free." She traced her finger along his jawline.

"I'll still be on parole. Got two more years to serve."

"That doesn't matter. You're not going to do anything to violate your conditions." She pecked the top of his head.

"Nope. Those days are done." He rubbed the small of her back. "I wish there was a better answer for Cutter."

"That's how it goes. It's why we have to continue to fight. If we don't, they'll keep walking over us and taking away our rights." Bridget sighed. "And that's why I'll always serve on the board."

"You do a lot for everyone, *kwe*. You taught me a lot."

"I'd say it works both ways. I learned lots from you. Lookit Logan. I never would've gotten to know him if it wasn't for you. The sad part is, to the rest of the world, he's another drug addict who overdosed. Through you, I met the man behind the needle. And he was a good kid who had too much stacked against him."

"Yeah." Adam's chest still tightened at losing Logan. They should have gotten their own crib as planned. "They're a lot more Logans out there."

"Mmm-hmm. Mrs. Dale's right in some ways. I'll give her that. Not all can be saved. But we can help as many as we can. It's too bad we can't foster other children."

"We can't?"

"Not with your record." She brushed her hand through his hair.

Again, he'd let her down. "I'm sorry, *kwe*."

"Don't be. You help other alcoholics in the program. You helped Logan."

"Yep. Helped him as best as I could." He stroked her cheekbone. "What about you? You think too much about others. What do you want?"

"I want Kyle. And I want you."

"That's it?"

"What else could I ask for? The two of you complete me. I've never been happier."

"If we can't foster other kids, what about one of our own?"

"We do have one of our own." She grinned.

"Then I guess we'd better let you adopt him, hey?"

"I'd love that."

"We should think about another one. I'm turning thirty-nine in April. I ain't getting any younger."

"Okay. We can. But we'd better wait a few months. I don't want to be sticking out to here when Jude walks me down the aisle." Her hand cupped the air in front of her flat stomach.

"A few months. I guess we'd better keep practicing, then."

"Practice sounds very tempting. But you have a meeting to go to tonight, and our son doesn't go to sleep until after you leave. How about Saturday? He's sleeping over at Jude's. Hmm?" Her black eyes twinkled.

"It's a date."

They rubbed the tips of their noses together. Adam slid his lips over Bridget's warm mouth.

Footsteps padded across the carpet. "I put everything away. What're we gonna do now, Dad?"

Bridget broke the kiss just as Kyle barreled to Adam.

"Easy. Easy. I got enough room for two." Adam patted his thigh.

Bridget wiggled over.

Kyle slid onto Adam's other thigh. "No kissing. That's

gross."

"Gross?" Bridget burst into a fit of giggles.

The booming chuckle gathered in Adam's chest, and he threw his head back, unable to contain the mighty roar of laughter.

His faith had paid off. He'd redeemed himself for the two people sitting on his lap. A man couldn't ask for anything more than being a husband to the woman he loved and a father to the son he'd give his life for.

YOU MAY ALSO ENJOY THE FOLLOWING FROM EXTASY BOOKS INC:

Blessed
Maggie Blackbird

Excerpt

A meeting package bound in black spiral coils landed on the keyboard of Darryl's laptop. Only one person possessed the audacity to toss stuff at him. He looked up.

Clayton stood in front of the desk, irritation hardening his dark eyes and a scowl twisting his thin lips into a grimace. He rapped the meeting package. "Did you read this?"

Darryl flung aside his pen. So much for getting work done. "I only got mine an hour ago. It's ten o'clock. I have a list of stuff to do before I clock out for the weekend."

"Read it now. It's not good."

Did this man live to order people about? "I have one already. Here. Take yours." Darryl seized his copy off the to-do tray. He shucked Clayton's package back at him. "Gimme a second. Why don't you get a coffee or something from the staff room?"

Clayton strutted to the door. "Are there any muffins left?"

"Yeah. Fresh, too. So you'd better hurry before they're all gone." If Darryl didn't do something to push this guy along, he'd have to endure another long-winded speech about the old ways and how they must preserve their culture.

Damn straight protecting the Anishinaabe traditions was important, but listening to Clayton drone on in his know-it-all tone gave Darryl ten headaches. He sank in the chair and flipped through the pages.

When the letter appeared, he sat up.

Dear Chief and Band Council,

Four years ago, Christ the King Parish hosted Healing the Spirit, a workshop developed by the diocese to reconcile First Nations and Christian communities by initiating recovery for the generations traumatized by the Indian Residential Schools the Canadian Government imposed on the Indigenous people throughout the nineteenth and twentieth centuries.

Thirty people from Ottertail Lake attended. Based on the participants' evaluations of the curriculum and facilitators, they deemed the workshop a success and commenced their spiritual healing journey.

Last year, additional members of Ottertail Lake approached the parish and requested another workshop. At the pastoral council meeting held in January, we passed a motion to host a second Healing the Spirit for this forthcoming September.

Although Christ the King Parish and the diocese can cover various expenses, we are seeking a financial contribution to offset costs, since special facilitators trained to deliver the workshop will require airplane fare to travel to our isolated First Nations community.

If Chief and Band Council could assist with a $500.00 gift, we would be most delighted.

Attached is information on the workshop. If you require a presentation, I am more than willing to meet with Ottertail Lake's most esteemed leadership.

Yours in Christ,

Deacon Norman Matawapit, Christ the King Parish
M.Ed., M.T.S.

Darryl's muscles constricted and then quivered. He dropped the meeting package on his desk. The request for money shouldn't shock him. Deacon Matawapit and his precious church did nothing but take from the reserve.

Clayton leaned against the doorway. He held a mug and muffin and wore his usual smug smile. "Say it. I was right, wasn't I? What are we going to do? It's Friday. The meeting's on Monday."

Through gritted teeth, Darryl choked out, "Give me time to review this. We can meet at the diner this evening."

"See ya then." Clayton disappeared from the entryway. The heels of his boots clicked against the floor.

Darryl huffed across the room and kicked the door shut. The noise in the hallway vanished.

Healing the Spirit. He shook his head. This time he wasn't running to Winnipeg to lick his wounds. He'd face the Matawapits head-on after what they'd done to him.

"Gimme one sec." A tray of drinks rested against Raven's flat stomach. She trudged to a back table where a group of teenaged girls huddled. They giggled and pointed at one another's cell phone screens.

Warm fuzz coiling around Darryl's spine cooled the raw fire that had sizzled under his skin all day. Kiss the Cook remained the same hangout for the youth to gather on Friday nights. The girls would stay put until the drum group began. They always sat in the bleachers at the Treaty Grounds and watched Darryl instruct the boys.

The girls waved, and he raised his hand. Although the Traditionalists Society's mission was to preserve and teach the Anishinaabe ways, the reserve's future women needed their own personal group that built character and pride. Starting a new job and concentrating on her addiction recovery left Raven little time for volunteering, but she did her best to engage the young ladies in cultural activities.

The diner door banged open. "How about the shore lunch special, sis? I'm starving." Clayton promenaded to the counter.

"Okay. What about you?" Raven set some dirty glasses on her tray.

"Get me a ham sandwich on brown and the soup." Darryl flipped the menu closed.

The nurses at the health station would sing his praises. Like a good boy, he'd stuck to his diabetic diet.

Clayton stood behind the counter. He grasped the coffee pot. "Want some?"

"Sure." Darryl flipped over his mug.

Once Clayton poured, he sat. "I'm not surprised the deacon's looking for another hand out. I bet he wants to drum up more support for his church. He's scared we'll yank the monthly donation now that you're part of the leadership. He should be scared. The Society's numbers are growing while the church's are shrinking."

Darryl shifted on the stool. He couldn't fault Clayton's frigid words. The guy was twelve years older and had served on band council three times, which meant voters supported him, and so did Auntie. "I assume you have something in mind."

Clayton stared straight ahead at the cluttered shelves behind the back counter. "We have to reject their request at the meeting on Monday and—"

"I agree." The reserve shouldn't keep forking out money to the church. The diocese was responsible for their parishes. Darryl raised his mug and sipped.

"—make a motion to stop funding the monthly hydro bill. Let the bishop and his lapdog deacon figure out what to do about their money pit. If they make the rules, something we don't have a say in, then they can pay for their church."

The coffee stuck somewhere in Darryl's throat. He

coughed. "A motion was passed five years ago, stating chief and council agreed to cover the cost indefinitely. I don't think it's possible to dissolve the motion."

Clayton shook back his hair. The feather he'd woven into a thin side-braid bobbed. "We owe it to our people. The church has no right hosting healing workshops. Not after what it did to the Anishinaabeg." He turned in his seat. "What about you? Look what it did to your family."

Darryl lowered his head and hunched over the counter. Clayton was right. The pain and shame Mom and Dad endured at the residential school had destroyed them. A bottle helped Auntie dull her bitter anger and grief. Her health was precarious now because of the Catholic Church.

Too many people still suffered, thanks to those schools. Not only the people who'd been forced to attend them, but their children and grandchildren who'd grown up in an environment of agony, disgrace, and rage. "Okay, I'm in."

Clayton patted Darryl's shoulder. "I knew I could count on you. People are afraid to stand up for their beliefs, scared they'll be pegged as troublemakers."

After a fifteen-minute break and holding another can of iced tea, Darryl dropped in the chair beside Clayton. They should do something about the heat in the meeting room at the band office. Fat chance of air conditioning happening. Hydro was too expensive in the remote north. As for the two ceiling fans, they only spread the pungent stench of stale leather, cheap perfume, fried bread, and body odor.

So far there'd been no debates. Whether this was a good or bad sign, Darryl didn't know, because Healing the Spirit was next on the agenda.

Seven councilors sat around the rectangle table, with Chief Willie at the head. Each person represented a geographic area of Ottertail Lake.

"I see the church has its donation basket out again." Clayton stationed his hands on the scuffed table and stink-eyed

Roy Morrison.

Darryl stifled his groan. Ruffling feathers wasn't the best way to persuade the others to favor their forthcoming suggestion. They needed the councilors' support, not generating sympathy for Roy, traitor to his own kind. If Darryl didn't speak up, Clayton would turn the meeting into one of his intense debates.

"With all due respect, our mandate is to the members of the reserve, not one group—"

Roy tapped his meeting package. "Keep in mind Norman's a member of Ottertail Lake and a residential school survivor. He does lots of good work as a deacon. And you also keep in mind, lots of people go to church."

"Like you?" Clayton's tone darkened.

Someone muttered. Another coughed.

Roy folded his arms across his big gut. "This isn't about me. We're talking about much-needed healing for residential school syndrome."

"The Traditionalists Society has healing workshops," Darryl said. Hot knives pricked his stomach. Someone on the reserve was always aiding Deacon Matawapit and his precious parish. "We provide sharing circles for our men, women, youth, and elders. I like to think what we're doing—"

"Yah, it's a good thing. Keep in mind not everyone's traditional." Roy reached for a fresh cookie from the plate at the center of the table. "Some band members prefer workshops held by the church."

Darryl kept his voice even. Like hell he'd let on the conversation was pushing his big red anger button. "I was elected by members of the reserve—we all were—to consider each request at our meetings. I won't favor one when someone has to be baptized in the—"

Roy's small eyes popped to the shape of saucers. "The workshop's open to everyone. Lemme tell you something, nobody has to be baptized."

"Darryl brought up a good point," another councilor said,

while uncapping and recapping her pen. "Band members have benefited from workshops sponsored by the Traditionalists Society and the church. One group has sharing circles, the other, a prayer group. Even the recovering addicts and alcoholics have their own special meetings. We're here to assist the people in all their endeavors, aren't we? Therefore, we should provide options to nourish their spirituality."

"Before the whites showed up, our culture and traditions were good enough. They brainwashed a lot of you through the residential schools, and you're passing on your brainwashing to our children, grandchildren, and their children. The Anishinaabeg practice the Anishinaabe way." Clayton's accusing words sizzled and sneered with the right amount of goading to pinch anybody's skin.

Darryl rubbed his brow. So much for keeping the meeting on a level keel. The fireworks should begin any second.

"Lemme ask you something." Roy tossed aside his cookie and scrambled halfway out of his chair. His big gut bumped the table. "What are the Seven Grandfathers Teachings? You sure ain't practicing respect here, are you?"

Chief Willie adjusted his black cowboy hat and puckered his lips at the clock tacked above the coffee buffet. "Say, it's already ten. If we keep going back and forth we won't get done till eleven. I'm already late getting the wife from bingo. We got six more agenda items. The parish doesn't always have its hand out. They do lots of fundraising. Let's vote."

Darryl reached for his iced tea. Leave it to Willie to snuff out the fireworks. The man was a fence-sitter who attended church and practiced the traditional ways to appease everyone so they'd keep voting for him.

Someone hiccupped. Another coughed.

It was time for Darryl to play his last card. They wouldn't be able to weasel out of this one. "What about the deficit incurred by our contribution to the church's hydro bill? Does this concern anyone? Do we have the funds to make a donation to Healing the Spirit?"

Everyone's focus shifted to the band manager, who shuffled his papers. "We do have surpluses in a couple of budgets."

"Budgets are specific to each program." The band manager couldn't fool Darryl. "Are we going to remove five hundred from . . . hmm . . .the youth initiatives program? This means they'll have five hundred dollars less to run their program, which is badly needed, especially for the girls."

"We won't be disrupting other programs." A drop of sweat slithered down the band manager's forehead to his thick, black eyebrow. "They have additional funds left over, which means we can donate the money to the church's workshop and the youth won't be affected."

Affected? Darryl set down his iced tea. "Why do we have a surplus in the budget for the girls, anyway? I think we should discuss the lack of activity for the future women of our reserve—"

"Say, we're getting off topic. We're talking about Healing the Spirit. He's doing what we pay him to do—manage the shooniyaa and staff on our behalf." Willie puckered his lips at the band manager, who was also the chief's brother-in-law. "It's late. Let's vote."

Darryl snuck a peek at a flaming-eyed Clayton. All everyone cared about was getting home to watch TV or picking up their spouses from whatever activities they were engaged in.

"Fine. Go ahead and vote. Just remember you're robbing your children, grandchildren, and their grandchildren of their culture and what it is to be Anishinaabe. Keep following what the Church and Government started over a century ago." Clayton banged the table.

Everyone jumped.

"I'll make the motion." Roy raised his hand, his beady eyes small slits.

Apart from Darryl and Clayton, band council voted favorably for the parish's monetary request, which meant the motion was passed.

Sharper than the lancet Darryl used to prick the tip of his finger when he checked his blood glucose level, a stabbing pain seared his heart. Again, Deacon Matawapit and his precious church had slapped Darryl's face.

ABOUT THE AUTHOR

An author bio: An Ojibway from Northwestern Ontario, Maggie resides in the country with her husband and their fur babies, two beautiful Alaskan Malamutes. When she's not writing, she can be found pulling weeds in the flower beds, mowing the huge lawn, walking the Mals deep in the bush, teeing up a ball at the golf course, fishing in the boat for walleye, or sitting on the deck at her sister's house, making more wonderful memories with the people she loves most.

* 9 7 8 1 4 8 7 4 2 4 5 6 5 *